MAXWELL'S INSPECTION

MAXWELL'S INSPECTION

M. J. Trow

CHIVERS
THORNDIKE

This Large Print book is published by BBC Audiobooks Ltd, Bath, England and by Thorndike Press®, Waterville, Maine, USA.

Published in 2004 in the U.K. by arrangement with Allison & Busby Limited.

Published in 2004 in the U.S. by arrangement with Allison & Busby Limited.

U.K. Hardcover ISBN 1–4056–3027–2 (Chivers Large Print)
U.K. Softcover   ISBN 1–4056–3028–0 (Camden Large Print)
U.S. Softcover   ISBN 0–7862–6729–1 (General)

The text of this Large Print edition is unabridged.
Other aspects of the book may vary from the original edition.

Set in 16 pt. New Times Roman.

Printed in Great Britain on acid-free paper.

British Library Cataloguing in Publication Data available

Library of Congress Control Number: 2004106696

Chapter One

He'd come across scenes of crimes before, those isolated, random places where Fate had been met, where a solution had been found, where a life had been snuffed out. This one was rather more gruesome than some he'd encountered. The head lay at an impossible angle near the fridge door, the eyes still bright, looking up at him. A short distance away, a leg—the left he guessed, sprawled on the flotex. Somewhere between . . . his world-weary eyes took in the distance—yes, there it was. Viscera, purple and shining in the half-light from the kitchen, a little liver, a heart.

He straightened, looking around, narrowing his eyes in the gloom. It was the old pattern, the signature of the serial killer he knew so well. The doormat was ruched, the bowl turned over in the agony of death he could still feel in that ghastly, bloody room. And it wouldn't have been quick, he knew, as he reached for the rubber gloves; if it had, what would have been the point? He looked again at the lacerations on the dismembered corpse at his feet. She was alive when all that was done to her—every carefully aimed slash, every deliberate precise cut.

He slammed the gloves down, spinning on his heel. Confrontation time. He knew where

1

to find him, this early in the morning, before the warming sun had climbed. He knew his hiding places of old, his lair. He had no friends. Oh, the odd female perhaps, to fill a night on the tiles. And that daft old bat next door who persisted in calling him 'such a pet' even when he was wiping the blood from his mouth. Not for nothing was he known by all and sundry as the Sawney Bean of the South Coast; the Hannibal Lecter of Leighford.

He felt the morning breeze kiss his face; heard, as they did all through the even greater slaughter of Ypres and the Somme, the birds still singing. It didn't take him long to find him. No surprises, no attempt to run. There he was, smug as ever, sprawled in the sun's early rays, eyes half-closed, glutted, sated. He'd have spent a long time planning this, like Ted Bundy, John Wayne Gacy, all the other alumni of that mad school of murder. There'd have been the trawling phase, as he searched for a victim. That would be night. He liked the night. More, he loved the dark. Because to him, it was not dark. That killer's instinct he'd never learned to tame shone like a searchlight through it all, finding his target like the cross-hairs of a sniper. Then, when he'd found her, the seduction. Bundy had done it with a spurious bandaged arm, John Wayne Gacy with the offer of a job. This one? Well, this one did it with a tilt of his head, a tilt that said 'Wanna play?' But it was his game. His rules.

2

And he never lost. The next phase in the serial killer's insane calendar was what it was all about—the kill. And as he looked at him now, dozing in the dawn, he still couldn't quite imagine the horror of that. No rational human being could.

'Yours, I think,' Peter Maxwell dropped the she-mouse's tail onto the sloping asphalt of his shed, an inch or two in front of the pink nose of the black and white cat called Metternich. The giant tom stretched out his bull-neck, defying metaphor, and sniffed. He looked up at Maxwell as if to say, 'No thanks. I've just eaten.'

'I thought we had an agreement,' Maxwell was stern. 'I give you milk, those crunched up bits of cardboard that pass for cat food and which add lustre to your cluster, and every Christmas, however bad you've been, I give you a sodding great Cat Nip Thing. In exchange, you do not scratch my furniture, fart in my lounge or commit your sick ritualistic killings in my kitchen.' He leaned in to the animal, nose to nose in the morning. 'We have a contract, Count,' he purred, 'written in my blood, I seem to remember.'

Metternich the cat raised his head, he who never smiled. Would this bow-tied idiot never understand? His forbears, and it wasn't *that* long ago, for Christ's sake, not in cat years, had snarled, sabre-toothed and bristling with attitude, in search of Man himself. There'd been no bits of crushed-up cardboard then, no fridge-chilled milk. Just blood. And the chase. Metternich's shoulders rippled under the gloss of his fur and he gave Maxwell his trump card, a kiss on the nose.

'He's such a pet, isn't he?' Maxwell stood bolt upright at the shrill sound of his neighbour. He couldn't see her. Not at first. 'Down here,' he heard again. He crouched a little, next to the shed, peering through the privet that marks the boundary of many an Englishman's castle.

'Mrs Troubridge?' he squinted.

'He's so affectionate, your Metternich,' she trilled. 'I expect he'll be round later for a lick of my syllabub.'

That, Maxwell thought, went without saying. 'Er . . . where are you, Mrs Troubridge?' he asked.

'Just here,' she chirped in the bird-like way he dreaded most on a drowsy summer's afternoon, just as he started to nod off. 'I was weeding my leptospermum.'

'Oh, good,' he smiled.

'You're up bright and early today, Mr Maxwell.'

'Ah, yes. Thought I'd get into work early this morning, Mrs Troubridge. Have a spot of breakfast.'

'At a transport café?' It was a phrase Mrs Troubridge had heard once. She had no idea what it was.

4

'No, no, at school. We've just started a Breakfast Club. I rather fancy a full English.'

'A Breakfast Club? Ah, yes, that would be like the 'twenties, wouldn't it? A little before my time, of course, but I remember Father saying he used to take food parcels and shoes and things in for the underprivileged children. I expect you have a lot of that, don't you? Underprivilege.'

'Oh, yes,' Maxwell sighed, straightening. 'You'd be amazed. Well, good morning, Mrs Troubridge. Have a nice day, y'hear?' It was pure Jed Clampett out of the Beverley Hillbillies, but since that was long after Mrs Troubridge's time, it was wasted.

'I will.' She waved an invisible trowel at him.

He turned on the gravel of the path, glowering at the cat. 'No more corpses, Count,' he growled. 'Nature may be red in tooth and claw, but keep it out here. Okay?' Even Peter Maxwell lapsed into Americanisms when annoyed.

Metternich lashed his tail, the feline answer to 'whatever'. The daft old sod was talking to the hedge now, for God's sake. He *had* just kissed him on the nose; and he hadn't done that in a long, long time. Well, that was as cosy as it was going to get. From now on, no more Mr Nice Cat.

Metternich watched Maxwell swing open the shed door and haul out that white contraption with wheels. What *was* that all

5

about? He saw him bend down, as he always did, and clip those metal things around his legs. He never saw Mrs Troubridge do that, nor her at Number Forty-Two. In fact, *nobody* but Maxwell did that, not even those who had similar contraptions with wheels. No wonder everybody called him Mad Max.

*   *   *

The road was a ribbon development over the purple moors. Well, actually, the golf course. Peter 'Mad Max' Maxwell had saddled his faithful velocipede charger, White Surrey, and was pedalling through the morning. He noted how Columbine had changed. When he'd moved into Metternich's house at Number Thirty-Eight, there had still been a kiddies' playground at the far end and a small herd of Herefords had chewed the endless cud at the other. Now, it was all double garages and satellite dishes and the clattering crescendo of skateboards rattling on the tarmac. Surely John Loudon MacAdam hadn't sweated blood for this?

He saw the flat-capped golfers, dots on the green of summer, going through their incomprehensible motions away to his right. Who were these buggers, who had the leisure to play a round all day, wondered he of the thirteen weeks holiday. Yes, all right, he conceded as he stood in the stirrups to take the brow of Harry Hill, teachers had the time. They just didn't have the salary to afford the Club fees. Heigh ho for the open road.

The seven thirty-eight from Tottingleigh was lumbering up from Lansdowne Crescent as Maxwell crested the rise. He eased Surrey's brakes and planted his feet on the grass as he wheeled gently off the road. Why did he never tire of this view? He who had seen it a thousand times? The sea stretched out before him, sparkling like diamonds in the July sunshine, its horizons far, its power limitless. Below the headland called the Shingle, the curve of Leighford Bay was white and as yet unsullied by the guilty families who risked imprisonment by taking their children on seaside holidays in term time. The gulls bickered and fought along the roar of the surf, charging like the white horses that Rudyard Kipling had imagined at the water's edge of his endlessly inventive mind. The seven thirty-eight rumbled past, one-man operated, still childless in this precious moment before the school-run began and daffy women, minds elsewhere on hair-dos and lunches and the morning shop, cut him up without signalling at left turns on street corners.

He kicked the right pedal into position and wheeled Surrey onto the road again, hurtling down the hill for the flyover and the road to perdition.

There were balloons fluttering at the corner

of Gracewell Avenue and a badly painted sign proclaiming that Mrs Baker, the Lollipop Lady, was retiring after seventeen years. Seventeen years! Peter Maxwell had been a mere stripling then, only gradually approaching a cantankerous middle age. His hair had been dark, his eye bright, his boyish heart undaunted by years of government initiatives and crap thrown directly at the Chalk Face, off which it had bounced all over him. And Mrs Baker? Well, she looked today as she'd looked all those years ago—suicidal. Except she wasn't there yet. It would be quarter of an hour before her notoriously bunioned feet hobbled around the corner to shepherd the last generation of little psychopaths across the road. Seventeen years. And not a single death. Not even a serious maiming, and you couldn't say that about many council employees.

Surrey's wheels whistled along the tarmac and the lamp-posts hissed by with the rhythm of the road. Then Peter Maxwell was through the school gates and bouncing up the steps he told Year Seven never to try. You had to be brave to do that, to have the experience and the wisdom of ages. More, you had to be certifiably insane. And yet more, you had to be Mad Max.

He hooked Surrey to the hitching rail of the bike sheds. Shaking his head as he often did at the passing of time which had robbed him

8

of his childhood, CCTV cameras stared voyeuristically down on his shapeless tweed cap. Who knew how many generations of Leighford Hyenas had experienced their first teenaged gropes under those corrugated awnings? How many of the next generation had been conceived? Now, with the all-intrusive eye riveted to the wall, it was no longer I'll show you mine, but I'll show the whole world; or at least the ladies who monitored in the Student Services offices. How sad. Although, thought Maxwell as he whipped off his cycle-clips and hauled his saddle bags over his shoulder, it might yet make the day of Duane 'The Flasher' Billings of Nine Zed Eff.

An unplaceable smell greeted him as he snuck in the back way past the Art Block. What was that? Fear? Or the emanations from Hell's kitchen as he rounded the corner. He tipped his hat and beamed at the cross-grained old besom behind the counter in the canteen.

'Morning, Mrs Lovett. Two of your very excellent meat pies, please, while I nip next door for a shave.'

'Mrs Lovett' never knew what Mad Max was talking about, even on the best of days. And today was Monday, never the best of days. She didn't even know why he called her Mrs Lovett, except maybe he was a bit barmy.

'Will that be a coffee, then?' She chased the endless chewing gum around the cavern that

9

she called a mouth.

'Indeed,' smiled Maxwell, waving at the shy little thing in the chequered overalls in the kitchens' recesses. She was Sharon, one of the three thousand of that name he'd taught in his two and a half centuries at the Chalk Face. She'd never said a word to him then, not from Year Seven when she'd joined to Year Eleven when she'd left. Now she was back, turning the full circle as some kids did, unable to go, unable to leave, trapped by the deadly thrall of their schooldays. She blushed and waved back. He wasn't to know that Sharon had a bit of a thing for older men and that she'd kept a picture of Mad Max Maxwell at the back of her wardrobe at home. One day, she screwed up her lip with renewed determination, *one day* she'd say hello to him.

But the Great Man was gone, university scarf dangling with its heraldry, the black cockerels' heads of Jesus College clucking on their white field. He threw the battered hat down onto the formica-topped table.

'Cap!' he roared and six or seven of the underprivileged, who could only just afford brand new trainers, mobiles and skateboards, whipped off their baseball headgear and looked suitably sheepish.

'Never seen so many Babe Ruths in my life,' he muttered to the colleague slumped behind *The Times* across the table from him.

'This is an honour, Max.'

10

'Ben, Ben,' Maxwell reached out and patted the man's hand. 'It's nothing, really. Finished with that spoon?'

Ben Holton was the Head of Science at Leighford High. He was younger than Maxwell, but had less hair and all the bonhomie of the Ayatollah Khomeini, assuming you were old enough to remember him. He passed the piece of plastic to the Head of Sixth Form.

'Spoon,' Maxwell shook his head. 'Remember when these things were metal, Ben? They had a bowl and a stem. You could hang them on your nose to the endless amusement of your first girlfriend.'

'Is that all you could amuse your first girlfriend with?' Holton was still reading his newspaper.

'Not at all,' Maxwell bridled, stirring his coffee briskly. 'My party-piece—at parties, that is—was shoving sticks of celery up my nostrils. The mark of the true sophisticate. She was putty in my hands after that.'

Holton looked at him over the rims of his glasses. Peter Maxwell wasn't a bad sort. Bit mad, of course. But then, he *was* an historian and they were never the same as other people.

'You a regular then, Ben, at Miss Greenhow's Club for Down and Outs?'

'Certainly not,' Holton shook his paper closed as Maxwell winced at the taste of the school coffee. 'But seeing as our Ofsted

11

inspection starts in . . .' he looked at his watch, 'forty-five minutes, I thought I'd get a head start.'

Maxwell became conspiratorial, leaning forward and closing to his man. 'So, tell me, Ben. What's the official approach in your faculty, eh? You going for the bar of soap on the floor? The wire stretched across the stair? Or what we're doing in Humanities, the subtle stash of crisp tenners?'

Holton scraped his chair back, folding his paper with a resigned flourish. 'I'll let you know,' he said.

Maxwell smiled and leaned back. 'Lang may your lum reek, Mr Holton,' he called as the Head of Science made for the double doors, 'and similar Pictish exhortations.' He lolled back in the hard plastic of the chair, catching sight of the damp patches on the ceiling and the words of King Richard whispered in his brain. 'A black day will it be for somebody.' He caught sight of a tall, pretty thing with bubbly blonde hair scurrying around the corner, carrying trays. 'Ha, Norfolk,' he called to her. 'We must have knocks, ha, must we not?'

Shakespeare was lost on Sally Greenhow, the Head of Special Needs. She'd done *The Taming of the Shrew* for GCSE and had seen *The Tempest* at Stratford. She'd rather enjoyed *Shakespeare in Love*, but Maxwell, she knew, had held horses with the Bard outside The Curtain, got pissed with him at The Mermaid

12

and had given him most of his best lines.

'Mr Maxwell,' Sally was the consummate professional in front of the kids, lounging around as they were, chomping toast and playing on the school's computers. 'What are you doing here?' Maxwell raised the imaginary pistol and shot her dead, since in every television crime drama from *Murder She Wrote* to *Midsomer Murders* that line preceded slaughter. She smiled and sat down next to him.

'So this is the Breakfast Club?' he asked her, raising his paper coffee cup in salutation.

'This is it,' she beamed, looking round at her hapless charges. 'You don't approve, do you?'

Maxwell looked at her. Sally was the wrong side of thirty these days. She had a loving husband, but no kids of her own. He'd never known why. There was talk of a problem of some kind—her, not him. This was her family now. A bunch of misfits and oddballs, the exclusively included who should have been in special schools, except that the government had closed those down and dumped their charges onto the saps who were trying to run mainstream education.

'Look over there,' she raised her eyebrows to her right. 'Little Tommy Weatherall. He's got a reading age of seven, a statement that reads like a rap sheet and a lot of problems. He won't do games.'

'Tut, tut,' Maxwell shook his head.

'Know why he won't do games?'

'Can't be arsed?' Maxwell suggested.

Sally shook her head. 'Doesn't want the other kids to see the cigarette burns on his chest and back, the ones Mum's latest boyfriend put there.'

'Ah.' Maxwell knew a slice of humble pie when he was offered it.

'Over there. Gary Spenser.'

'I know Gary.' Maxwell didn't have to turn in his chair.

'Do you, Max? Know where he lives? Last Wednesday it was on the Dam, under a mattress some thoughtful soul, unable to find the Tip, had left. Thursday, it was in a doss on the Barlichway Estate, with his big sister who's on the game. He was probably there on Friday, but I understand the law raided it, so where he was over the weekend, God knows. I expect he'll tell me later today, when he feels a bit safer. You know Leighford High, Max?' She looked into his dark brown eyes. 'That place where you and I work? Well, it's home to the Garys of this world, Max. That's what Breakfast Club's all about.'

Maxwell smiled at her. 'Sally Greenhow,' he said. 'The lady with the lamp. I know what the Breakfast Club's all about,' he said. He glanced across at Gary Spenser as the boy finished his tea and dragged himself across to sit by little Tommy Weatherall. 'It's about you,'

14

he said to her. 'Leighford High? That's just a sixties pile with peeling paint and leaking windows. Leighford High's just the bricks and mortar where people like you make the world okay for people like them.'

Across the cafeteria area, Gary and Tommy got their heads together. 'Break, then?' Gary said. 'Far hedge?'

Tommy nodded. 'You gott'em?'

'I gott'em,' Gary said, with that strange sideways movement of his lips he'd perfected over his twelve devious years. 'John Players. Pack of twenty.'

'Seen 'em yet?' Tommy asked.

A slow smile crept over the boy's face. 'I seen 'em,' he said.

'Well?'

Gary's hand slipped inexorably into the pocket of his non-regulation hooded top and he passed something to his mate. 'You was right,' he said. 'Old Greenhow's wearing red knickers. I seen 'em.'

Tommy accepted the chewing gum with all humility. ' 'Ow'd you know?'

'Showed 'em to me, didn't she?' Gary swaggered as much as he could while whispering inches from his co-conspirator.

'Bollocks!' Tommy hissed.

'All right,' Gary conceded, unable to sustain this one. 'I caught her gettin' out of her car.'

'Told you they'd be red,' Tommy beamed. 'Got a nose for it.'

15

'What about him?' Gary asked, focusing on the Head of Sixth Form.

'Mad Max?' Tommy frowned. 'I don't want to guess what colour his knickers are, thank you very much.'

'Gross!' moaned Gary. 'No, I mean, d'you think 'e's givin' her one?'

'Mad Max?' Tommy repeated. 'Never. He's way past it. Anyway,' he clambered to his trainered feet. 'He's as gay as a wagon load of monkeys. Luke Jefferies told me—you know, in Year Eleven? Maxwell had it off with him in the showers, last term.'

For a moment, Gary looked up at his oppo, then he slid back his chair and followed him into the corridor. 'Bollocks!' Sally and Maxwell heard him shout.

Sally sighed. Maxwell chuckled. 'Nothing wrong with that,' he told her. 'Young Gary has clearly just finished reading the latest Harry Potter. Nothing wrong with that at all.'

*   *   *

The staffroom at Leighford High was like any other mental institution the length and breadth of this great country of ours. Dodgy insurance offers sponsored by the National Union of Teachers fluttered from a notice board marked *Social.* On the *Political* board there was nothing but a solitary photo of Charles Clarke, Secretary of State for

Education onto which someone, blessed with a higher order of satirical wit, had board-marked the inevitable glasses and second beard. Peter Maxwell could not let that stand. He it was who had added the horns. Elsewhere was the detritus you'd find in every staffroom in the land—old copies of the *Times Ed.*, its job pages pinched, its articles unread. West Sussex In-Service glossies lay at rakish angles on filing cabinets offering courses on Crisis Management and the water-heater gurgled reassuringly in the kitchen corner.

Staff briefing had happened every Monday since Socrates had wandered through these sylvan groves spouting brilliance that his eager young students had soaked up in the cradle of civilisation. Education wasn't quite like that today. Today was all buzz and apprehension. The Week of Weeks. The Five Days That Shook The World. You couldn't see them of course, the Inspectors. Like plague bacilli, they were already in the building, oozing through the heating ducts, dispersing in the dusty air. You could smell them.

'Good morning!' A vague rumbling made one or two heads turn. Most people were still chatting, making silly jokes to keep their spirits up, laughing with a brittleness that screamed their fear.

'Good morning!' louder this time, but still not enough. People were sorting their mail, checking their briefcases, handbags,

17

rummaging for the Prozac.

There was a shattering whistle, the sort the lost generation had heard in the slippery trenches of the Somme, when the donkeys led the lions up the rickety wooden ladders and out into the barbed-wired shell-shocked hell that was No Man's Land—a bit like the boys' bogs by Friday afternoon. Peter Maxwell took his two fingers out of his mouth and waved them gaily at his Headmaster, who was still waiting to start the day.

A silence. 'Thank you.' James Diamond, B.A., B.Sc., M.Ed., God knew what initials he had amassed by now, was standing alone before his staff, the wrong side of forty, veteran of a hundred bad decisions. Was that a new suit, Maxwell wondered? Could be. Diamond's salary was vaguely commensurate with the national debt of Ethiopia.

'The Inspection team is in the building,' he told them, clutching a sheaf of papers to give his hands something to do. Maxwell held up his fingers in the sign of the cross. James 'Legs' Diamond looked like shit, Maxwell thought. He'd watched him over the last days descend, as Maxwell had always presumed Hitler had in the Bunker, into an exhausted madness. Any minute now, Diamond would start to rebuild Linz. 'Mr Whiting will be with me for most of this morning. Make sure your lesson plans are on chairs outside your rooms, everyone. Any notices?'

18

'Er . . .'

Diamond caught the movement from the corner. 'Yes, Sylvia.'

'Heaf tests, I'm afraid. Thursday. I tried to change it, what with Ofsted and all. In the Hall. I'll put timings in the registers.'

'Thank you, Sylvia.'

Maxwell winked at her. Sylvia Matthews, School Nurse, the Florence Nightingale of Leighford High, wandering the lonely wards of S Block, ice-packing sprains here, dobbing out morning after pills without the Headmaster's or the parents' knowledge, wiping eyes and wiping bottoms. She wouldn't have it any other way. They went back a long way, Sylvia Matthews and Peter Maxwell. At one time they'd been . . . an item? No, never that. Oh, she'd loved him all right, that was plain to see. Unless, of course, you were Peter Maxwell, who could be all three wise monkeys at times. But that was before she'd found her Guy and he'd found his Jacquie. Now, Sylv and Mad Max were just comfortable together, like a pipe and slippers, cocoa and a hottie.

'Well, then, everybody,' Diamond did his best to smile. 'Have a good day.'

And the hubbub rose again as the Arch Curriculum Manager exited the room.

'Legs Diamond has left the building,' muttered Maxwell, lifting a weekend's worth of crap out of his pigeonhole.

'Max,' Paul Moss, the Head of History, was

19

at his elbow. 'All set?'

The Head of Sixth Form turned to face him. Disappointingly, young Paul had changed his Daffy Duck tie for a plain blue one and his natty George at Asda shirt had been replaced by something altogether more po from Burtons. Oh dear, he'd caved in. And Mad Max had such hopes for the lad who was Head of History. 'As set as I'll ever be,' Maxwell smiled.

'And . . . um . . . your lesson plans?'

Maxwell waved the equivalent of a rainforest in front of the man's nose. The relief on Moss's face was visible. It was all there, he could tell even at a glance—course units, aims, objectives, resources, seating plans. There was a God. 'Thanks, Max,' Moss beamed. He knew perfectly well that Peter Maxwell had not written a lesson plan in thirty years. William Gladstone had been at Number Ten and beer was 1d a pint.

'Of course,' Maxwell waited until his nominal boss had nearly reached the door, 'there's absolutely no guarantee I'll use them.' And he grinned maniacally before blowing the young man a kiss. Poor Paul. He too had had a fear-struck few weeks, finding this evidence, collating that. Mrs Moss and all the little Mosses had got used to his uncontrollable outbursts, his panic attacks, his collapses into sheer, unadulterated terror. Could Ofsted do that to a man? Yes, if Mad Max was on your team.

*   *   *

Peter Maxwell had been teaching for thirty-four years. He told Year Twelve it was forty-eight. He told Year Seven it was ninety-three. Both Year Groups believed him. And in all that time, he had never, until now, had a free period to start the week. This year he had, for the first time in eternity and it gave him a breathing space, a chance to sharpen his pencils, brew his coffee, focus his mind for the coming hour, the coming day, the coming week. And a chance to sort out the problems of his own, his very own, Sixth Form. The anomaly still existed—they were actually, in Tony Blair's New Cool Britannia, Years Twelve and Thirteen, but the phrase 'Sixth Form' had a veneration of its own and it refused to lie down. There would be those who'd been thrown out of home over the weekend, who'd got into a fight in any one of a number of hostelries between the Vine and the Arms. There'd be those whose boyfriend/girlfriend had dumped them, those who were convinced they'd loused up their A2s, their ASs, their GNVQs. And all of them, *all* of them, would be queuing up on the Mezzanine floor where Mad Max lived. His Number Two, alias Helen Maitland, the Fridge, would be there already, battling well, but not, in the end, coping. She would lay her

21

burden on the Lord. And the Lord—he'd lay it all on Peter Maxwell.

That Monday however, there was just one standing by his office door. And it wasn't one of Maxwell's Own. It was a woman, brunette, attractive, pencil-pleat skirted, with a silk scarf and an elegant Celtic brooch to hold it in place. She was . . . what . . . forty, perhaps? Perhaps less. She spun on her heel to face him.

'Mr Maxwell?' Her hand was thrust out. He glanced at it. No dagger. That was a start.

'That's right.' He took her hand. It was slim, but the grip was firm for a woman. Perhaps she worked out, pumping iron in her spare time for WWF.

'I'm Sally Meninger. This week I'll be taking a look at the pastoral provision in the school. I understand you're a history teacher.'

'Right again,' he said. 'Won't you go in?'

He followed her into his office, that Inner Sanctum where he sometimes had the luxury of closing the door.

'Then we'll be seeing rather a lot of each other. I'm Humanities too.'

'Joy,' Maxwell smiled. 'Coffee?' He ushered her to a soft chair.

'Good Lord,' Sally Meninger was taking in Maxwell's walls. His décor, it was true, took some handling. Ahead of her, Rita Hayworth smouldered seductively, assuring the cinematic world that there *never* was a woman like *Gilda*. An ex-president of the United States to her

22

right appeared to be in bed with a chimp called *Bonzo* and to her left a black-trimmed parasol tossed on the air currents somewhere on the Irish coast over the head of *Ryan's Daughter.* Above Maxwell's already bubbling kettle, Butch and the Kid were making a determined run for it, thumb-breakers blazing against half the Bolivian army.

'Did they make it, do you think?' he asked her, nodding in the poster's direction. 'Butch and the Kid. Did they get out?'

'You're the historian,' she smiled, crossing her legs and declining his coffee with a shake of the head.

'And you?' he was stirring after her shake.

'Sociology, originally,' she told him. 'All rather a long time ago, I'm afraid.'

'Tell me about it,' he said.

'So, did they?'

'Hmm?'

'Butch and the Kid. Did they escape?'

Maxwell sat down opposite her, dropping the scarf and hat to one side. 'Butch's sister said they did. They came home from Bolivia one day and lived to a ripe old age. 'Course, she was a few bullets short of a six-gun. Is this your first visit to Leighford, Miss Meninger?'

'Wearing my Ofsted hat, yes. I came here as a child, of course. You still had donkey rides then, I seem to remember.'

'Ah, yes,' Maxwell nodded. 'That was before Women Against Donkey Abuse took over.

23

WADA. How they've enriched our lives.'

He saw her write something on her sheet. He didn't have to see what it was. He knew. It would read something like 'Chauvinist Pig'. Good start.

'How long have you been wearing your Ofsted hat?' he asked her.

'Six years,' she told him.

'Ah, so you were one of Chris Woodhead's Finest, then?'

She smiled. It was like the silver plate on a coffin.

'Good job?' he asked her.

'Depends on the school,' she shrugged. 'Sometimes it's a positive pleasure.'

'And other times?'

She looked into his eyes. 'Sometimes it can be pure bloody murder.'

Chapter Two

'Oy! Sultans of Swing!' Gerry Cosgrove was in no mood to muck about. His missus had kept him up half the night with her snoring and the brewery delivery had been late. He'd caught his thumb between a couple of barrels and his back was playing up. To cap it all, it was Monday night, the place was empty and his Live Music was guilty of offences under the Trades Descriptions Act; he wasn't sure they were actually alive and he was bloody certain they weren't playing music. 'Come on, it's ten past nine. How much of a break do you blokes want?'

'Sorry, squire,' Duggsy was Lead Guitar and Vocals, the spokesman of the group. His top was grunge, his hair retro punk, his jeans Milletts. 'Monday night, ain't it?'

'Yeah, well, there's not a whole lot I can do about that,' the landlord told him. 'Where's your drummer?'

Duggsy checked behind him. 'Having a slash, I shouldn't wonder.'

'Still?' Cosgrove seized the moment to collect a few empties on the beer-wet table nearby.

'Well, he's old, inne?' Duggsy explained. 'You gotta be a bit, y'know, understandin' ain'tcha?'

'No,' Cosgrove bore down on the lad. 'No, that's precisely where you're wrong. Ah,' he glanced up as six people bustled into the bar, 'Don't look now, but rent-a-crowd's arrived. Your audience just doubled.'

'Bit of acoustic then, Wal?' Duggsy turned to Mr Bassman as the landlord hurried off to look genial. Wal was a beige replica of Duggsy, but terminal acne had hit him at sixteen and had never quite gone away.

'Nah, can't be arsed,' Wal muttered. 'Where the fuck's the Iron Man?'

'Probably can't find his way back.' Duggsy

finished his drink. 'Lord Muck over there's getting a bit pissed off. I may have to hack into Postman Pat in a minute. Fuckin' hell!'

'What?' Wal looked up from checking his leads.

'That's only Mad Fucking Max!'

'Never!'

'As I live and breathe. Look, over there. With that lot just come in.'

' 'Ere, that's that tit Mr Holton. I always hated him.'

'I seem to remember he wasn't overly fond of you, Wal, me ol' mucker. Must be Teachers' Nite Out.'

A wiry man with spiked black hair and a pony tail swaggered his way from the furthest corner, the flickering lights from the pinball machines catching the studs on his leathers and the collection of piercings that adorned his otherwise unremarkable face.

'Well, about fuckin' time, Iron,' Duggsy batted him with his guitar-case, mercifully the soft one. 'We were about to begin our overture.'

'Sorry, man,' the drummer muttered. 'Bit of me old trouble.' He took a serious drag on whatever he was smoking and bared his teeth to the flashing lights that suddenly rotated. The barman switched off Chris Tarrant, much to everyone's relief, and the band struck up.

'Mother of God, what's that?' It was Ben Holton who reacted to the sound first. He still

26

remembered the Vine in the old days, when it reinvented itself from a spit and sawdust dive to a mock-Tudor eaterie. Herring-bone covered the walls and a rather plastic-looking breastplate and halberds gleamed over the huge grate.

'That,' shouted Sally Greenhow over the noise, 'is the Yawning Hippos. Two of them are old Leighford Hyenas.' She had long ago adopted Maxwell's terminology for the alumni of the old place.

'Really?' Maxwell screwed up his eyes to make them out. For all the Vine was virtually empty tonight, a thick haze with a sweet smell hung like a pall over the place, soaking into the rich swirls of the carpet and coating the leaded panes. 'Which ones?'

'Lead and bass guitars,' Sally said, fumbling for her change. It was, she insisted, after the day they'd all had, her shout.

'That'd be those things with leads dangling from them,' Maxwell was reassuring himself. 'Good God, yes. You remember William Thing, Ben.'

'Thing?' Holton repeated, letting his lips dip into the froth.

'Well, that's only an approximation of course. Everybody called him Wallie when those books came out because he was so nondescript. Couldn't find him in a crowd and so on.'

'Still is,' Paul Moss chipped in, gathering up

27

two drinks and heading for a table as far from the band as possible. 'That's why he's playing bass.'

'The crooner,' Maxwell was waving a finger at him trying to find the name in the vast vaults of his memory, 'is Matthew Douglas, who once vied with fourteen others for the coveted title of the stupidest boy in Ten Eff Three; Class, if I remember, of '99.'

'Well, haven't they come on?' Holton muttered, stumbling after Moss to the corner and squeezing himself into one of the snuggeries, the alcoves that lined the far wall.

'Oh, I don't know,' Sally sauntered with him. 'The Hippos have quite a following.'

'So I see,' said Holton, looking round at the deserted pub.

'Well, people,' Maxwell raised his Southern Comfort. 'Here's to a bloody war and a sickly season.' Maxwell's toasts were usually incomprehensible, but as The Yawning Hippos ritually murdered the Nine Inch Nails, the others intoned 'Here! Here!'

Peter Maxwell didn't get out much. What with all the marking and the preparation, the endless worry over his three hundred charges in the Sixth Form, well, there just weren't enough hours in the day, were there? At least, that was what he'd told Sally Meninger first thing this morning as they parried and riposted their way around the opening moves of a routine Ofsted inspection. He didn't expect it to work for a moment. If the woman couldn't sense bullshit when she smelt it, she shouldn't have been on the team in the first place.

'So, how was it for you, Miss Greenhow?' he asked her, lolling his head briefly on her shoulder. 'Much earth movement? Or are we talking whimpers rather than bangs?'

'Mine was all right,' she told the group between sips of her lager. 'I think he said his name was Harding.'

'Bald bloke,' Paul Moss clicked his fingers, remembering him from a chance encounter in the corridor. 'No offence, Ben.'

Ben Holton had stopped taking offence years ago. Cheap jibes about the Crucible Theatre and the Benson and Hedges Masters passed him by these days.

'That's right,' Sally said. 'Reminded me of an uncle of mine.'

Maxwell and Moss, the historians in the party, sucked in their teeth simultaneously. 'Ooh,' wailed Maxwell. 'The worst sort. They lull you, you see, Sal. Find out in advance what your uncles look like and then send in a ringer. It's an old Ofsted ploy, isn't it, Paul?'

'One of the oldest, Max,' the Head of History nodded gaily.

'Then, just when you think it's safe to come into the classroom. Wham!' he bounced the flat of his hand on the table and expertly caught the beer mat, 'It's a Scale 5. Retraining. Failing School.'

Sally caught him one with her handbag strap. 'They don't award numbers any more,' she said. 'Too divisive, apparently. Seriously though, I hear Tommo had a hard time.'

'Tommo?' Maxwell looked at her aghast; Stuart Tomkinson was one of the best. 'When was this?'

'This afternoon. Lesson Four, I think.'

'Ah,' said Moss. 'That would have been Ten Gee Three, the dirty thirty.'

'Well, yes,' Sally said. 'Except that Jason's with us all week in the Slammer. Dave Barton's under a two week suspension and rumour has it that Samantha Westerby's gone to live with her granny in Edgbaston.'

'Well, there is a God, then.' As a scientist, Ben Holton had been looking for proof like this all his life. And to think, it had taken an incident in Leighford to confirm it.

'Not like Tommo, though.' Maxwell savoured the amber nectar as it hit his tonsils. 'From what I know of the man, he's pretty good.'

'Maybe she doesn't like Geography teachers,' Moss suggested.

'Got some taste there,' Maxwell conceded. 'Who did he have?'

'It would be Sally Meninger,' Moss reasoned. 'She's Humanities. Max, you had her this morning.'

'Ah,' Maxwell was at his most enigmatic. 'Had in what sense, dear boy? My private life

30

is my private life. A public schoolboy never divulges . . .'

' 'Scuse me,' a young voice made Maxwell look up. A girl stood there, seventeen, eighteen perhaps. 'Are you Mr Maxwell?' Twelve teachers' eyes were on her. Actually, eleven, because Jeff Armstrong had got something in one of his at the weekend and he was still wearing the NHS patch, much to the hilarity of his kids all day.

'Indeed I am, Miss . . . er . . .'

'I'm Tracey.'

'Of course you are,' Maxwell beamed.

'Duggsy says "Hello" and have you got any requests?'

'Duggsy?'

'Matthew Douglas. Over there.'

The lead guitar and vocalist was gesticulating as much as he could while getting his fingers round a riff and his tonsils around *Hey Joe*.

'Well,' Maxwell chuckled, 'that's very kind, but aren't *I* supposed to ask *him*?' He caught the blankness in Tracey's eyes. 'Not the other way round.'

'Oh, yeah,' the blonde girl wobbled her breasts at him, grinning inanely. 'Only he, like, remembers you from school. And just thought it would be, like, nice.'

'Like, it is,' Maxwell smiled. 'Tell him if he can't do *I'm a Pink Toothbrush* by Max Bygraves, what he's doing is just fine. Oh,' he

31

fished a tenner out of his wallet, 'tell the lads to have a drink on me.'

'Oh, thanks, Mr Maxwell,' and she scuttled away, her buttocks nearly as bouncy as her breasts.

'Soliciting again, Max?' Ben Holton muttered out of the corner of his mouth.

'One of the perks of the job. Good God!' The eleven eyes were fixed in the direction of Maxwell's stare. Wobbling a little uncertainly on what Maxwell knew as Fuck-Me shoes, Sally Meninger, the Ofsted inspector, giggled her way to the bar. Hooked on her arm was another of her number, loosening his collar and looking a little unnerved.

'Christ, that's Alan Whiting, the chief inspector,' Sally hissed. It was. Maxwell had not seen Whiting today. Not in fact since his preliminary visit some weeks before. But it was him, all right; sandy hair, glasses, a rather thick-set bloke with pale eyes and the merest hint of an Irish brogue.

'And that's Sally Meninger,' Maxwell mumbled.

Jeff Armstrong was adjusting his patch. 'Is it me or is she pissed?'

'Does the Pope shit in the woods?' Holton asked. He was always of a rather Presbyterian frame of mind, for an atheistic scientist, of course.

'Bloody Hell!' Paul Moss was ever the master of wit and repartee.

'I'm going to start giggling in a minute,' Sally said.

Maxwell moved her lager aside. 'No more of those for you, my girl,' he frowned. 'I'm going to ask mine host for a large black coffee. Is there a Mrs Whiting?' He was asking the company in general.

'Is there a Mr Meninger?' Holton countered.

'Trust me, Ben,' Maxwell was shaking his head. 'She's not your type.'

Holton was watching the way the female Ofsted inspector was perching on her bar stool, rather admiring the cut of her jib. 'Oh, I don't know.'

'Got your mobile, Sal?' Maxwell asked.

'Yes. Why?'

'Just a quick call to Annette Holton and all the Little Holtons. Time she galloped to the rescue, I think.'

'You're right,' said Sally solemnly. 'Shall I ring it for you, Max?'

'Bollocks!' the Head of Science growled. 'All the same, she's coming on a bit strong, isn't she? For a colleague, I mean?'

He glanced around. Sally Greenhow was the only female colleague in the party and whatever was going on in Ben Holton's mid-life-crisis mind, it didn't tally at all with what was in hers.

'Perhaps it's standard practice, d'you think?' Paul Moss suggested. 'After all, they're far from home. Working hard. Perhaps they're playing hard, too.'

'They certainly are,' Armstrong could tell, even with one eye. 'She's practically got his . . . Oh, God, they've seen us.'

Sally Meninger was waving at them. One by one they looked away, except Peter Maxwell. He was public school. Dance, shipwreck, minor incursion, major disaster, slightly embarrassing situation in a pub—it was all one to him. He waved back.

'For Christ's sake, Max,' Sally hissed, suddenly fascinated by the bubbles in her lager glass. 'What are you . . . Oh . . . er . . . hello.'

Sally Meninger was swaying tipsily next to their table, her skirt rucked up a little, her cleavage just so. Public schoolboy that he was, Maxwell stood up.

'Well, isn't this nice?' the Ofsted inspector giggled. 'Is this a regular haunt of yours?'

She was met with a babble of platitudes. It was actually one of the few places far enough away from Leighford High not to be a magnet for half the kids in the school. Unless you included the Band of course.

'Alan and I were just having a quiet little drinky.' She waved in his direction and blew him a kiss. 'Won't you join us?'

More babbles as Maxwell sat down again.

'I'm not sure,' Sally Greenhow looked steadily up at the swaying woman, 'that that's a very good idea.'

For a moment, the ice refroze in Paul

Moss's gin, then Sally Meninger burst out laughing. 'You know—and I can say this, can't I, as one Sally to another—you're absolutely right. Professional. That's the key word. Alan's favourite, in fact. Well, one of them. I can't tell you what the others are—you see, it wouldn't be professional, would it?' And she turned on her Fuck-Me shoes and bounced away every bit as alluringly as Tracey.

In between gulps of Maxwell's round, Duggsy on his dais was attempting to belt out *House of the Rising Sun.* It was a long way from The Animals. Sally Meninger rejoined Whiting at the bar and whispered in his ear, running a manicured hand up his thigh. He looked taken aback, then shook his head. Suddenly, she'd yanked him to his feet and disappeared with him into the bowels of the Vine, clattering along the corridor.

'Christ,' Holton muttered. 'I think I need a drink.'

'I think we all do,' Maxwell agreed. 'My shout. Paul, be a sweetie and give me a hand, will you? I need to go to the Little Teachers' Room. I'd ask Jeff, but with his current problem, the lot could go anywhere.'

'That sounds like an occulist remark to me,' Armstrong bridled.

'So sue me,' Maxwell patted him on both shoulders as he passed.

'That really is bloody amazing.' Moss was collecting the drinks from the bar as Cosgrove poured them. 'I mean, they're like a couple of kids. Whereas they've got to be . . .'

'Past it, Mr Moss?' Maxwell lowered at him. 'Take great care. With ageist remarks like that, I may yet cut you out of my will.'

'I just find it . . . bizarre.'

'As a church,' Maxwell agreed, thrusting a couple of notes into his Head of Department's hand. 'Pay the man, will you, Paul? Old Mr Wee-wee has come a-calling. Much more of this and I'll bladder me tights.'

The Little Teachers' Room was around the bar to the left, then a sharp right by the dart board. The sign said, in Tudor script, 'Gentlemen' and Maxwell hadn't the heart to tell them that, to get it right, it should have said 'Generosi'. It occurred to Maxwell as he got there, that if Jeff Armstrong was taken short later, he'd need help finding it. One false move on the dodgy double step and he might lose his other eye.

There's something about a loo in a pub. Especially the gent's. The tiles were an unlikely Cartland pink and there was that strange mixture that assaulted the nostrils—mimosa with a hint of carbolic and ammonia. All pretence at Tudor had gone here, presumably because Pub Décor 'R' Us had no idea what a Tudor privy looked like. It was just as well. Maxwell's wrists tingled as he answered nature's call; he didn't realize he had been hanging on for so long. He blew outwards gratefully as men do when in extremis, secretly proud of that most masculine of skills—the ability to pee standing up.

It was mercifully quiet here, the strains of Duggsy's *Street Spirit* merely a rumour three and a half rooms away. At least in this one that idiot on the drums wasn't playing—no doubt grateful to get his hands on Maxwell's freebie drink at last. To Maxwell's right, a slightly battered contraceptive machine promised Heaven and French Ticklers, ribbed for extra enjoyment. And sure enough, some wag had scrawled on it that the chewing gum in this machine tasted terrible.

And extra enjoyment seemed to be emanating from the cubicle behind him. A rising crescendo of heavy breathing, exaggerated as though for effect and a rhythmic thumping on the thin partition walls. Maxwell zipped himself up as soon as was humanly possible and poured pink gunk over his trousers in a rushed attempt to wash his hands. He was still trying to get the pansy-embossed paper towels out of the dispenser as the door opened to his right. Instinctively he turned and came face to face with a flushed Sally Meninger, quickly pulling her skirt down her bare thighs. The head that popped itself round the doorframe next was that of Alan Whiting. He saw Maxwell and his jaw dropped. He swayed like a rabbit in the headlights

37

before she took control of the situation. She smiled winningly at Maxwell, who had now abandoned the recalcitrant towel idea and she paused to check her hair in the mirror while the hot air absolutely refused to dry his hands. She swayed provocatively to the door. The tipsiness of moments ago seemed to have vanished and if Maxwell had asked her to walk a straight line, he felt she'd have had no problem at all with that.

At the door, she met Joe Public, who looked less surprised than he might have done, all things considered. She flashed him a basilisk-style smile and hissed 'Brilliant!' before sauntering into the beer-fumed night and the strains of *Don't Fear the Reaper.*

The three of them stood in the Little Teachers' Room; Peter Maxwell, Head of Sixth Form, Leighford High School; Alan Whiting, Chief Inspector, Her Majesty's Inspectorate; Joe Public, who turned to the urinals and unzipped. For a second, it reminded Maxwell of that splendid three-way shootout at the end of *The Good, the Bad and the Ugly,* where the camera flashes from gun-butt to eye-ball to gun-butt—you remember the picture. Except 'Clint Eastwood' had already emptied 'Eli Wallach's' six gun—Joe Public had turned his back on them, whistling to *The Reaper* as he pissed half a day's wages up the wall. Bad old 'Lee Van Cleef' aka Mad Max decided to see it out. He stood, iron-jawed and steely-eyed until Alan Whiting cleared his throat, straightened his tie and followed his co-operative colleague into the inner sanctum of the Vine.

'All right, mate?' Joe Public reached for the holdall he'd put on the floor.

'Top hole,' smiled Maxwell, still digesting the events of the last few moments. 'You?'

'Triffic,' beamed Public in a passable Del Boy and then he too was gone.

Maxwell found himself looking into the mirror again. Maybe, just maybe, he was too old for all this. Life was passing him by. Time to get home, to his cat, his slippers, his cocoa, his incontinence pads.

*   *   *

The lights burned blue. Through his skylight, Peter Maxwell could see the moon in its silver quarter frosting the sea out beyond the Shingle. He lolled back in his swivel chair, the gold-laced pill box cap he always wore in this attic at a jaunty angle over his left eyebrow. How did they keep these things on, those soldiers of yesteryear, riders to hounds and masters of the gallop? Before him on the modelling table under the powerful glare of the lamp and the magnifying glass, his latest acquisition, sat his charger. Horse and man were still grey at the moment, the raw material provided by Messrs Historex, model-makers extraordinary. But under Maxwell's expert hand, patience and the excellent colours of Messrs Humbrol, he would soon—perhaps by week Thursday—be Captain Bob Portal of the 4th Light Dragoons, complete with blue tunic and overalls and black oilskin-cased shako.

'Freefolk House, Count,' Maxwell was talking to his cat again. 'Portal's birthplace. Lovely name, isn't it?'

Metternich was curiously unmoved. Dunmousin was good enough for him.

'He exchanged from the 83rd Foot,' Maxwell was in full flow. 'Must have cost him a bit, that transfer. Makes Rio Ferdinand look like an amateur. He'd been a captain for eight years by the time of the Charge. Oh, don't worry, he survived—the 4th were in the last line, of course, Paget's reserve. Horse got shot, though.'

Metternich was ambivalent about that. The animal rightist in him could empathize, but horses were big buggers and they were so cack, it would be nothing to them to bring one great steel-shod hoof down on an unsuspecting feline. As far as cats could shudder at the thought, Metternich did. Damn! There was that shrill sound again, the one that shot through his eardrum to his spine and sent his tail into spasm. And sure enough, Maxwell did what he always did, reached across for that bit of white plastic.

'War Office,' he spoke into it.

40

'Max. How the Hell have you been?'

'Policewoman Carpenter. It's been . . . hours.'

'Sorry, Max. I've just got in. How did it go, darling?'

'It?'

'Now don't be coy with me, Peter Maxwell,' he heard her say. 'I know you too well. For all your bonhomie, you've been shitting yourself for days over this Ofsted thing. I repeat—how did it go?'

'Rather odd, really,' he told her. Policewoman Carpenter was actually a Detective Sergeant. More than that, she was Jacquie, a flame-haired girl who could *nearly* have been Peter Maxwell's daughter, had he been a true child of the Free-love generation he grudgingly admitted was his. More than that, she was *his* Jacquie and he loved her.

'How?'

'Well, I haven't been grilled yet. Just a gentle ice-breaker, cosy chat thing with the Pastoral Person. Who by the way is also the Humanities Honcho. Who by the way enjoys sex in public places.'

'What?' Jacquie felt she had to check, in case Maxwell's cordless was playing up as usual. 'Say again.'

'I kid you not, Policewoman.' He rested his crossed ankles gingerly on the top of the bookcase, a move he'd had cause to regret on more than one occasion. 'We all went out for a

41

little drinky tonight . . .'

'Well, thanks for asking me,' she whined, mock-hurt.

'I knew it was your night for giving asylum seekers a good smacking down the nick,' he explained. 'Anyway, it was a Teacher Moment. "We who are about to die"—that sort of thing.'

'Hmm,' she snorted. 'I might consider letting you off this time. And?'

'And, there we were in the Vine, when who should walk in but the Pastoral Person and the Chief Inspector.'

'That's Chief Inspector in your sense,' she reassured herself, 'not mine.'

'Indeed. Bloke by the name of Whiting. Anyway, they were all over each other. Smooching at the bar.'

'Really? How old are they?'

'Well, that's just it. Fortysomething, both of them. But it gets odder—or better, depending on whether you write for the *TES* or the *Daily Sport*. They were at it later—in the Vine loo.'

'At it?' he heard her say.

Maxwell sighed. 'Well, you see, my dear, when your mummy and daddy decided to have you, they planted this gooseberry bush . . .'

'God, you mean, actually, at it?'

'With girls in blue like you, my darling, we tax-payers can sleep sound in our beds.'

'But that's bizarre. How do you know?'

'Yes, that's what Paul Moss said and he didn't see the half of it. I happened upon them. Answering nature's call, minding my own business, as it were. Not quite *in flagrante,* in that they mercifully had the decorum to get on with it in a cubicle rather than on the urinal floor. I could have stepped over them, I suppose.'

'Did they know you were there?'

'Oh yes. She came out adjusting her clothing, grinning like a sixteen-year-old.'

'What about him?'

'Hugely embarrassed, I'd say. If it had been me, I'd have wanted the ground to swallow me up.'

'If it had been you?' she growled. 'What number are you in the queue, Mr Maxwell?'

He laughed, quoting, as he often did, from his favourite film, *The Charge of the Light Brigade,* 'They say her pitcher hath been too often to the well.'

'So what are you going to do about it?' she asked.

'Nothing,' he shrugged. 'It's not a criminal offence . . . is it?'

'Lewd behaviour in a public place. Yes,' she told him.

'Well, that's as maybe,' he said, 'but with all due deference to Ms Sally Meninger, I think I'd better let sleeping dogs lie.'

'Who else have you told?' she asked him.

'Just you, dear heart. Oh, and Martin Bashir of course.'

'How can they face you tomorrow?' she

43

wondered aloud.

'Ah,' he chuckled. 'I shall know them by the paper bags over their heads. Darling, I've got to go. Bless you for ringing. Are we still on for Thursday?'

'Absolutely,' she told him. 'Pick you up at seven.'

'I bet you say that to all the Ofstedees. Goodnight Jacquie Carpenter. Love you.'

'Love you, Peter Maxwell.'

And he waited for the click of her receiver, before taking grey Captain Portal across to the centre of the room. He switched on another lamp and the whole diorama came to life. Three hundred and ninety-one officers and men of Lord Cardigan's Light Brigade, saddled and waiting to ride into Hell that cold October lunchtime back in 1854. He carefully placed the unfinished figure to the right of the line of the 4th Lights, slightly behind Lord George Paget, chewing his cigar, missing his wife and waiting for orders after half a day's inaction. He eased Troop Sergeant Major James Kelly back a little to fit the troop commander in place and crouched to get the eye line right.

Maxwell straightened. He'd leave Portal there tonight, let him get used to his plastic comrades, find the ease of his saddle. He'd start the paint job tomorrow. Tomorrow and tomorrow . . .

*   *   *

'Look lively, Ten Aitch Two, I've got an exam to pass.'

Mad Max was in his Heaven, but not all appeared right with the world. Before him in that theatre of nostalgia known prosaically at Leighford High as Aitch Eight sat that notorious bunch of misfits who had opted for History GCSE last year, because last year it seemed the right thing to do. Now, they weren't so sure. And what it had taken them several months to find out, Peter Maxwell had known from Day One.

Beyond the dirty three dozen, squeezed awkwardly into a corner sat Sally Meninger. Gone was the come hitherness of the Vine. The Fuck-Me shoes were replaced by a sensible court variation, the raunchy frock that proclaimed her cleavage to the world swapped for the pencil-chalk suit and yet another silk scarf. She had Maxwell's Lesson Plan on her lap, only the sixth he'd written in thirty-something years, and a deadpan look on her face.

'Matthew Hopkins,' Maxwell tapped the man's name he had written on the whiteboard behind him. He secretly hated it—the glossy surface that stained at the drop of an aitch; the useless markers that dried up as you looked at them, so that in seconds, the purest sable became the most dismal grey and the most

45

verdant green turned an odd kind of puce. 'What do we know about him?'

The silence could have shattered glass.

'Ah.' Maxwell smiled at the assembled multitude. 'How soon they forget. Jade?'

Jade was a bouncy blonde. Sitting next to Timbrel as she was, the sultry brunette, the pair were every Year Ten boy's wet dream. Maxwell had intercepted the notes last term which left him in no doubt about how Dave felt about them and Tom and Jimbo and Fat Josh. Maxwell had doubted whether Fat Josh could really do what he claimed he could, but it gave him a chuckle before he consigned the note to the bin and Fat Josh to his Year Head for a good letting off.

'Um . . . he was a witchfinder,' Jade managed.

'I'm glad you can read Timbrel's book,' Maxwell said to her, 'but I'd rather it was written in yours. Better still, I'd rather it was engraved on your memory. Can you help us, Dave?'

Dave looked barely able to help himself. A martyr to catarrh, the boy's mouth hung open and his eyelids drooped. Life, to Dave, was one perpetual sniff. 'He used to catch witches.'

'Classic, Dave,' Maxwell smiled. 'I like the keen thrust of your mind. When was this, Tom?'

To Tom, it could have been a week last Wednesday. 'Er . . .'

46

'I'm not being too picky here,' Maxwell was reasonable. 'I'll settle for a century.'

'Seventeenth.' Dave was getting into it now.

'Spot on, Davidovitch.' Maxwell clapped his hands. 'So those dates start with . . .'

'Sixteen something,' most of the class intoned. This drill was well-rehearsed.

'All right,' Maxwell moved through the fair—and not so fair. 'We know who, we know what, we even know approximately when. How about where. Jimbo?'

Now if there was one subject which perplexed Jimbo more than History, it was Geography. 'Um . . .'

Jimbo hated being put on the spot. Maxwell knew that, but a little grilling, *mano a mano*, was good for the soul. 'Come on, Jim.' Maxwell stood behind the lad, circumnavigating the room as he was. 'Think East.'

East, West, North, South, they were all one to Jimbo.

'Anybody?' Jimbo's shoulders visibly sagged. He was off the hook. Mad Max was a bastard, but he wasn't a vicious one. The Great Man saw Sally Meninger scribbling away in the corner, no doubt damning him to all eternity.

'East Anglia,' someone called.

'Nice one, Evelyn.' Maxwell knew if he waited long enough, the class swot would open up her big guns. All year he'd been trying to persuade Paul Moss to promote the girl, because she was clearly misplaced, but there were set complications apparently. Social reasons. You couldn't fight City Hall. 'East Anglia,' Maxwell crossed to the map in the far corner to point to it. He knew perfectly well that Ten Aitch Two were highly conversant with Orlando and Lanzarote—in a couple of years they'd be equally at home in Ibiza. But their own land? Oh, that was a foreign country—they did things differently there. 'Witch country.' He tapped the towns in turn. 'Ipswich, Chelmsford, Colchester, Lavenham. In 1646, if you were an elderly lady in any of these places, if you'd ever crossed anybody, looked at anybody funny, then look out. Somebody would make a quick phone call and that was it—send for Matthew Hopkins and it's a quick few hours being dragged around a room until you confessed. What's wrong with what I've just said, Josh?'

Fat Josh was ready for this one. 'It's not right, Mr Maxwell,' Josh said triumphantly.

'Er . . . good,' Maxwell nodded. 'Good. Like it so far. Why isn't it right, though, Josh?'

'Well, it's rubbish, innit?' Josh could have debated with Dr David Starkey. 'Stands to reason nobody's going to confess to nothing just being dragged round a room.'

'No phones then, dickhead.' Evelyn may have been the class swot, but nobody said she was nice.

'How does it go, Evelyn?' Maxwell reined it all in.

48

'Sorry, Mr Maxwell. But he is.'

'Well, that's something we can talk about later, isn't it? Now, compadres, what's it going to be?' He stationed himself between the board and the telly. It could go either way. 'Half an hour's silent reading on the definitive study of East Anglian witchcraft by Professor McFarlane or a few minutes of Mad Vincent Price in *The Witchfinder General?*'

The hubbub gave him the answer he expected, and as a man, Ten Aitch Two slid sideways or clambered on desks for a good view of the screen.

'We watching a video?' How did Peter Maxwell know the question had come from Dave? He flicked all the necessary buttons, since the remote had vanished within minutes of its arrival at Leighford High, along with scart leads and a whole nest of mouse balls. Maxwell clocked Sally Meninger's demeanour out of the corner of his eye. He'd followed his Lesson Plan to the letter so far—Paul Moss would be proud of him. Now, though, he was sticking his neck out. There were copyright issues about movies in schools and this one, grim little piece that it was, had an 18 category. He saw her write something down. He'd face the music later, reading the banner headlines in what passed for his mind, 'Pervert Teacher Depraves Young'. What a load of warlocks.

On the screen, a bunch of murderous seventeenth century villagers were dragging a

49

hapless crone up a bleak windswept hillside while the priest, whose hysteria had caused all this, intoned mumbo-jumbo behind the lynch mob. The camera wobbled and jostled with the crowd as they hanged the woman from the makeshift gibbet and her body slumped, to dangle in the wind, the hempen rope creaking in its housings. The camera swept away and the orchestra crashed into life. Sitting his horse, cloaked in black, sat Mad Vince himself, Matthew Hopkins, the Witchfinder General.

'I've seen this,' Dave said, although actually he was thinking of *Plunkett and Maclean*.

A bell shattered the moment and Ten Aitch Two descended into uproar.

'All right,' Maxwell switched off the set. 'Leave your stuff, everybody. Jimbo. Leave that.'

'It's my football.'

'You're on form today, Jim,' Maxwell told him. 'But even so, it stays here. You go.'

'What if it's burned to death?' Jimbo asked against the repetitious clanging of the bell.

'That's what God invented insurance for. Straight out, everybody,' Maxwell called. 'Double doors at the end. You know the drill.' And he supervised them as they went, closing windows with one hand. At the door, he met Sally Meninger.

'Is this planned?' she asked.

Maxwell shrugged. 'The Fire Master is

50

Bernard Ryan,' he told her. 'Our revered Deputy. I can't believe even he would be imbecilic enough to plan one of these, this week of all weeks. Unprofessional of me to say so, of course.' But he had a feeling 'unprofessional' was Sally Meninger's middle name.

'Where do we go?'

He closed the door behind her. 'Follow me,' he said, and quickly abandoning the old joke, came out with the feed line anyway. 'Walk this way.'

And he led her into the sunlight.

Chapter Three

The bell was still ringing as the hordes assembled on the tennis courts, just far enough away so that flames wouldn't engulf them. All in all, they didn't look unlike Maxwell's Light Brigade, drawn up in his attic—except the uniforms, of course, and the swords—oh, and the horses. The Head of Sixth Form had taken his place ahead of his Year Twelve cohorts, mixing his military metaphors though he was, the Legatus Legionis standing with his arms folded while chaos sorted itself into a kind of order in front of him.

His own Year were neat enough, in approximate lines behind their respective

Form Tutors, answering to the call of their names ringing out on that bright Tuesday morning. Year Seven as always were hysterical with the excitement of it all. Where's the fire, sir? Where are the fire engines? Is anybody burned yet, stuck in one of the bogs? Who started it? What's going to happen to him? It was always the same. Some wag, probably in Year Ten, would have smashed the glass somewhere, probably in the Art Rooms. Motive? Bravado. It was a rite of passage, really. Year Eleven had gone, their GCSEs over, into that glad goodnight that was forever composed of shelf-filling at Asda or Tesco. The main school had no head, no focus for delinquency. That was where Year Ten came in. And of course, this week of all weeks was a heaven-sent opportunity.

Maxwell could pinpoint it with reasonable accuracy. It could be Jason 'The Torch' Piggott of Ten Why Three, egged on by Squirt Tollfree from Sally Greenhow's Remedials. Sanjit Singh, Mr Diamond's nark, would already be standing in the corridor of power, all too anxious to blurt what he knew. You could bet your life on it.

'All clear, Tutors?' Maxwell called and one by one, they waved to him.

'Kelly's gone,' Helen 'The Fridge' at his elbow told him.

'No,' Maxwell shook his head. 'Tell me it isn't so.' He was always staggered when Kelly showed at all. Mistress of the catwalk and the parachute pants, Kelly's ambition was to get up early enough in the morning to hold down a part-time job in HMV. 'Mr Smith.'

The finger of God beckoned Ben Smith across. 'And the purpose of those shorts would be?' Maxwell looked down at the lad's nether wear. 'Shorts' was perhaps a brave choice of word. They actually reached to mid-calf and could have housed most of the kindergarten class at Leighford JMI across the road.

'Summer, sir.' Ben Smith was always deferential, especially when he was about to get a bollocking.

'And your body is a temple, etcetera, etcetera.'

'Sunshine's good for you, sir.'

'So it is,' beamed Maxwell, more than a little ray of the stuff himself. 'To that end, when this little bit of nonsense is over, you will sign yourself out at Reception and enjoy the sunshine on your way home to change. Clear?'

'Yes sir.'

'What'll you miss?'

A cleverer or a braver man would have quipped back, 'You, sir, always.' But Ben Smith was neither clever nor brave and he came clean. 'Physics.'

'Then you will apologize to Mr Saunders and offer to make up the time at his convenience. You'll do that for me, won't you, Ben?'

53

'Yes, sir,' and the lad moved the regulation three paces backwards.

'That's about it, then, Max,' Helen handed in the registers.

He winked at her. 'Thou, good and faithful servant,' he said and ambled with his armful across to the centre of the courts where the knot of Senior Managers darted hither and yon, doing their best to disappear up their own arseholes.

'All clear, Max?' Bernard Ryan asked.

Maxwell could barely disguise his contempt for this man. Not fit to run a jumble sale, Ryan had inexplicably risen to become Deputy Head of a large comprehensive school somewhere on the south coast. That was because he'd learned the jargon, carried Legs Diamond's books and got his knees and his nose equally brown. It brought him forty-four grand a year and an ulcer the size of the Millennium Dome. He hadn't slept since 1998. And it was beginning to show; wrinkles like the Grand Canyon, more bags under his eyes than were carried by the aptly named Ryanair.

'As clear as it'll ever be,' the Head of Sixth Form told him. 'This little walk in the sun your idea, Bernard?'

'Certainly not,' Dierdre Lessing, Leighford's redoubtable Senior Mistress, chipped in.

How could one describe Dierdre? A cross between Beowulf's Grendel and a pit-bull with attitude wouldn't really come close.

'Didn't see your lips move, Bernard.' Maxwell wasn't looking at her at all.

'Somewhere in C Block, apparently,' Ryan told him.

'The Torch?'

'We don't know yet, Max,' Ryan said, clearly sighting the end of his tether.

'Miracles take a little longer,' Dierdre told him.

He faced her for the first time, smiling broadly. 'Indeed they do, Senior Mistress Mine,' he said. 'When you and Mother Theresa here get to the bottom of it all, I trust there'll be a public flogging? School paraded in hollow square, groundsmen laying on with the cat, that sort of thing?'

Bernard Ryan was called away with a query from someone in Year Eight, never normally the most inquisitive Year Group in any school.

'It's difficult to see how you can be so insufferable,' Dierdre snapped at Maxwell.

'It's not easy, Dierdre,' he admitted, stone-faced. 'None of this comes naturally, you know.'

Dierdre Lessing, Maxwell had to admit in his more maudlin moments, had been a handsome woman in her day. In an Arnie Schwarzenegger sort of way. She was tall and elegant but her hair was so backcombed now that she was in danger of becoming a laughing stock. She and Maxwell went back a long way. He'd been a mere Head of History then and

55

she Head of Business Studies. It did gall the Great Man a little that a typist should be promoted over his head, but he'd long ago decided it wasn't worth the op to become Head of Girls' Welfare. Every now and then, when she'd been particularly psychotic, he toyed with shopping her to the Equal Rights Commission. For Miss PC to be a woman in the post she held was akin to being a Nazi in the twenty-first century.

'We don't know who broke the glass,' she said softly, her lips as tight as a gnat's arse. She looked him up and down. The old reprobate had left his tweed jacket behind. And that ludicrous hat. But he still sported that fatuous bow tie and those ghastly suede brothel-creepers that had jarred as a fashion accessory even in 1975. 'It wasn't you, I suppose?'

'I was just wondering,' he ignored her, 'what *they* think of all this.' He nodded in the direction of Her Majesty's Inspectors, standing apart near the Sports Hall wall, watching with interest the comings and goings of the gallopers feeding information from one command post to another. He could see Sally Meninger with her arms folded around *his* lesson notes, *his* academic future in her all-too-welcoming arms. She was staring at the tarmac.

'There's proof, Dierdre my darling,' Maxwell said, 'if ever it were needed. What do you notice about the Ofsted Six?'

Dierdre looked at them. Just a routine bunch of inspectors. She'd met them all in the last day and a bit. Except there weren't six, there were only five.

'One of them's missing,' she frowned.

Maxwell shook his head. 'Uh-huh,' he said, and his face took on a tortured, terrified look. 'No shadow.' His voice was barely audible and his eyes rolled in his head.

Sally Meninger had turned on her heel and was already marching back into what might have been a blazing building before Bernard Ryan began shouting incomprehensively through the megaphone. Maxwell knew the drill. He returned to his Sixth Form lines, walking backwards and bowing before Dierdre as he went. One by one, the tutor groups were dispersed. Back to Matthew Hopkins and Ten Aitch Two. How was he going to keep them down on the farm after this? And would Sally Meninger have mercy on him, the lesson disrupted by idiocy as it had been?

*   *   *

There was one good thing about Leighford High. Only one. And that was that staff could cut through the kitchens on their way to almost anywhere.

'Morning, Sharon,' Maxwell called to the girl wrestling with a huge tray of pizza. 'I'll have the devilled kidneys please, followed by crown roast, bread and butter pudding and an amusing little Chablis from the Loire.' He paused at the door. '*South* side of the vineyard, of course.'

Sharon waved at him, grinning inanely. The only bit of his conversation she'd recognised was bread and butter pudding, but that wasn't on the menu today. It was never on the menu at Leighford High.

The wizened old crone who was her superior scattered an armful of superfries onto a baking tray. 'Bloody mad, that bloke,' she muttered, blowing her chewing gum into a huge balloon.

Maxwell's way took him up the stairs by the side of the hall, with its cups and shields and trophies of a bygone era, when kids believed in their school and the government hadn't told them that competition was the dirtiest word in the English language. It took him past his own office on the mezzanine floor and into that heartland of Culture known as the History Department. All sixty-three clauses of Magna Carta hung from its hallowed walls, along with the famous lines of Martin Neimoller. And a suitably doctored phrase of Henry Ford's. To his original 'History is bunk', Maxwell had added, 'But what do I know? I'm a car salesman.' From here, as he flashed past the grimy, annually cleaned windows of the first floor, he could see the stragglers of Year Nine dawdling on the edge of the tennis courts, driven grudgingly forward by a less-than-temperate Ben Holton, white coat dazzling in the July sun and arms flying in all directions. His sulphuric acid titration would be well past its flocculation point by now.

And to his left loomed the office commandeered by the Ofsted inspectors. Dierdre had been right, though it stuck in Maxwell's craw to admit it. There had only been five of them. And as he looked in, he saw why. Alan Whiting was still sitting there, apparently engrossed in some papers, his head resting against that expensive high-backed swivel Bernard Ryan had treated himself to out of some development money. Maxwell shook his head. What a bastard. Not content to make an idiot of himself in public last night, now Whiting was ignoring a fire-bell, which *could* have been the real thing on this sweltering summer's day, as though the rules of the rest of the world didn't apply to him. Maxwell could already hear the clacking heels of the others behind him. He half-turned to see the frail shadowy figure of the other female in the Ofsted team and smiled at her in an I-don't-really-want-this job-anyway sort of way. He'd just reached the end of the corridor, ready to plunge two steps down to his teaching lair when he heard a scream that rattled the windows.

He doubled back to see Paul Moss's head pop out of his classroom. 'Flanders—is that you?' Moss shouted, head see-sawing from side to side.

'Suspended for three days,' Maxwell called back. 'Harassing that girl in Year Nine.'

'Oh, yes.'

Maxwell peered into each classroom he reached. A handful of kids in each one were jostling in the doorways to see what had happened, the odd member of staff circling round, shooing them back to their seats. At the door to the Ofsted office, the inspectress was still standing there, her fingers gripping the woodwork, her knuckles white. She was staring ahead, the scream still dying in her throat, the glasses that were seconds ago on the bridge of her nose dangling on their chains on what passed for her breasts.

'Are you all right?' Maxwell asked her, not usually so guilty of so redundant a question.

'It's Alan,' she said, trying in her panic to focus on who was talking to her. Instinctively, the old professionalism kicked in. 'It's Mr Whiting. The Chief Inspector's not well.'

Indeed he wasn't. Maxwell should have looked closer a moment ago. Paul Moss was at his elbow, staring as wild-eyed as the inspectress was.

'Paul.' Maxwell's voice made him jump. 'Get her out of here, will you? And keep the kids away. For God's sake, do that.'

The Head of History had never seen a dead man before. But Peter Maxwell had and Moss

60

knew his place. All his professional life at Leighford High, he'd been a rookie to the Great Man, a number two, a sidekick. He was always destined to be Tonto to the Lone Ranger and he knew it. He gently eased the woman's fingers off the doorframe and led her away down the corridor, barking at children to get back into their classrooms. Concerned staff picked up the vibes and one by one, they closed their doors, trying to answer questions and stifle the chorus of 'Sir' and 'Miss'.

So did Peter Maxwell. It was oddly chilly on this side of the building where the sun had not shone since early morning and some at least of the Inspectorate's blinds were drawn. The Head of Sixth Form approached the man in the expensive swivel chair. He wasn't reading any papers. His eyes were fixed somewhere in the middle distance, about halfway to the door. Except they couldn't see anything. Alan Whiting had stopped seeing anything by this stage. And he would never see anything ever again. He was still wearing the same suit he'd had on the previous day and at the Vine the previous night. At first sight, Maxwell thought Whiting was wearing a rather dissolute dark red tie; but then he realized it was a trail of blood, extending from the dead man's throat to run into a small pool in the folds of his lap. Jutting out of his throat, just below the adam's apple, was a barbecue skewer, driven in so far that it had pinned him to the chair and it was this, rather than intense concentration, that held the Chief Inspector so upright.

Maxwell checked the man's pulse. Nothing, but he was still warm. He glanced up to see a small trickle of bloody saliva slide down the man's chin. He reached for the phone, then everything he'd learned from Jacquie clicked in and he used a hanky instead, tapping buttons carefully with his pen tip.

'Matron,' he heard Sylvia Matthews say. He knew she'd be up to her nurse's buckle in Heaf papers and period pains by now, not to mention the malingerers wandering back from fire drill the long way round, already claiming sunstroke.

'Nursie. Aitch One. On the double,' and he was already punching other numbers.

Sylvia Matthews was on her feet in seconds and she'd cleared the walking wounded from her room. She'd known—and loved—Peter Maxwell for years. She knew when there was trouble—the gravel in his voice, the urgency. She knew the signs. Mad Max had pushed the panic button.

'Emma,' Maxwell was onto Reception now. 'Get me an ambulance and call the police. There's been an accident in Aitch One. Put me through to Diamond.'

Emma's fingers were a blur on her switchboard, lights flashing and winking at her in all directions. 'It's Mr Maxwell,' she turned to her oppos in the Front Office. 'He's never got my name right before. He's always called me Thingy. Something's wrong. Very wrong.'

'James Diamond,' Maxwell heard the Head say.

'Headmaster, Maxwell.'

'Yes, Max.'

'You'd better come to Aitch One right away. One of your Inspectors is missing.'

*   *   *

It looked so incongruous, the blue tape fluttering across the top of Aitch corridor with the words 'Do Not Cross'. More incongruous still were the white-suited members of the SOCO team, like something out of *Outbreak* or any infection-disaster movie you've ever seen. They padded on their cushioned feet in and out of Aitch One, the dead man's office. All the classes on that floor had been rerouted so that the SOCO people had a free hand, and harassed staff stood at the bottoms of stairs, answering, explaining, trying to diffuse a nightmare situation.

The whole school buzzed with rumour and counter-rumour. All the Ofsted inspectors had been butchered, their heads cut off and scattered in waste paper baskets all over the building. A lunatic had gone berserk and had machine-gunned them all. One or two of the more erudite of Maxwell's sixth form, brought up on their dads' cult film of *If.* believed the

63

killer was Malcolm McDowell and the school padre would pop out of a desk drawer any minute. The word 'Dunblane' was on the lips of people who had no idea what the word meant. Year Ten were already running a book on who the murderer was. That Mrs Lessing was odds-on favourite by several miles. Had he heard about it, Peter Maxwell would have had a flutter on that and would have bobbed each way with the best of them.

Henry Hall sat opposite the dead man as the men in white coats who were not Ben Holton went about their business. Henry Hall was an Inspector too, a Detective Chief Inspector to be precise. There was talk of an imminent Superintendency, but for the moment, the paperwork and the PR would have to wait. Here he was on this hot, sticky afternoon, still staring into the eyes of a dead man. Hall had been the wrong side of forty for some time now. He was as bland in his way as Legs Diamond and wore a suit of nearly the same colour. Except Henry Hall knew what he was doing and no one could second guess what was going on behind those curiously blank spectacle lenses. DS Jacquie Carpenter stood across the room, resting her bum against a table she knew had already been dusted by SOCO. The cameras still popped in the shaded office and the blinds were fully drawn against prying eyes.

'Only a matter of time, I suppose,' DCI Hall

said, still looking at the corpse.

'Sir?' Jacquie was poised in mid-note, waiting for her chief's words of wisdom.

'Before a murder was committed right under Peter Maxwell's nose.'

Jacquie didn't respond. She'd been here before, between the rock that was Henry Hall and the hard place that was Peter Maxwell. Her career had been on the line more than once, her loyalties divided, her heart and her warrant card both on her sleeve.

'Who found the body?'

She checked the notebook. 'A Miss Paula Freeling, another of the Ofsted team.'

'Time?'

'Shortly after the fire drill. That was at nine forty. Must have been nine fifty-five, fifty-six.'

Hall turned to Jacquie for the first time. 'She any use?'

Jacquie knew Henry Hall. In his three piece suit, with his bland, gold-rimmed specs and with his inability to smile, he came across as a hard, taciturn bastard. But underneath that was a loving family man, even more grateful now, no doubt, that he'd sent his boys to Harperwell down the road. There'd been sneers about the private sector behind his back, but Henry Hall's back was broad. If they'd invented a private police force, he'd have been part of it.

'Still in shock,' Jacquie told him. 'She's in the school nurse's office.'

'Where are the others?'

'In the Head's office. Their number two has taken over—er—Sally Meninger.'

Hall looked askance. 'Surely, they're not going ahead with the inspection?'

Jacquie shrugged. 'I'm not sure they know what to do,' she said. 'I expect Leighford High will go down in the Guinness Book of Records as the first school to kill an inspector.'

Hall looked over the rims of his glasses at her. 'So what have we got? Twelve hundred suspects?' He was hoping against hope it couldn't be that many.

'Year Eleven and Thirteen are in the clear,' she said, straight-faced. 'They're off on study leave or officially left. That only leaves eight hundred.' It was worthy of Peter Maxwell.

'Wonderful,' said Hall, unmoved by levity in any form, given the situation. He dragged himself to his feet, crouching down on an eyelevel with the dead man's desk. 'Barbecue skewer,' he said. 'Seasonal weapon, that. Single thrust through the throat.' He took in the position of the dead man's hands. 'No struggle. Not even a reaction. That means it was a) unexpected and b) fast. Professional. Neat.' He stood up, already looking beyond the dead man. 'Where does that door go?'

'Er . . . next door, I think, guv,' she followed his gaze. 'To another classroom.'

'Whose?'

'Um,' Jacquie was flicking through her

notebook. 'I don't know,' she confessed.

Hall tapped the desk with fidgety fingers, then turned his back on the dead man; he didn't think he'd object, all things considered. 'Right, Jacquie. Finish up here. Tom, you about done?' he asked the photographer.

'Half an hour, Mr Hall,' Tom reckoned.

Hall nodded. 'Half an hour it is.' He checked his watch. 'We'll meet at six thirty, Jacquie. Leighford nick. I don't suppose there'll be anywhere here big enough to set up an Incident Room, without causing even more mayhem than there's probably been already. So we'll do this one from home. I'm going to talk to the Headteacher. You get an up-to-date map of this place and you seal this room good and tight. Got it?'

'Got it, sir.'

'Oh and Jacquie,' he paused in the doorway, looking deep into her cool, grey eyes. 'Peter Maxwell is just one of several people we'll have to talk to here, okay? And if he so much as clears his throat, I want to know about it. All right?'

She stared back into those blank, impenetrable lenses, trying to be just as enigmatic in return. 'Absolutely, sir,' she said.

* * *

The David Bailey of Leighford nick had done his job well, as always. Several Alan Whitings were ranged around the wall of Henry Hall's Incident Room by mid-evening, a one hundred and eighty degree vista of death. His left side was undoubtedly his best and there wasn't a hair out of place. All of them at the nick had seen corpses before and you got to be detached in the end. Never immune exactly, never *quite* able to forget that this was once a living, breathing human being. The men and women in that fan-assisted room with the Leighford sun streaming in through the windows had all had their share of violent ends—the kid hit by the drunk-driver, the lonely old woman who had hanged herself with the extension lead, the wife who had irritated her old man just once too often. But none of them had seen a man killed with a barbecue skewer. And no one had ever seen a dead Ofsted inspector.

'Office for Standards in Education,' Henry Hall stood in the gap in the horseshoe of his team. 'That's who the dead man worked for. Philip, what do we know about him?'

Philip Bathurst hadn't been a DI for long. He was the same age as Jacquie Carpenter, but of the Sex-More-Likely-To-Succeed, with no glass ceiling in the way and was clearly going places. He was an earnest young man with a permanently furrowed forehead, as though life was one long uphill struggle surrounded by problems on the way.

'Alan Whiting,' Bathurst was clearing his

throat, 'forty-five years old, married, no children.'

'Mrs Whiting?' Hall butted in.

'Lives in Matlock, sir,' the DI said, 'local force have been in touch. She's driving down as we speak.'

'Go on.'

'He's been an Inspector for eight years. Started as a Chemistry teacher, became a Science adviser in Derbyshire, then did a stint at County Hall up there.'

'Popular man?'

'Difficult to say, guv,' Bathurst shrugged. 'The Ofsted teams are continually changing. Only one of them, Sally Meninger, had worked with him before. We've not got very far with questioning the others.'

'All right,' Hall nodded. 'That's on hold. Jacquie and I will begin those interviews for real tomorrow, starting with the Meninger woman. Where are they staying?'

'The Cunliffe,' someone told him.

'Anybody on that?' Hall wanted to know.

'A plainclothesman on the main entrance and exit,' the same someone explained.

'Right. Jacquie. Leighford High.'

Jacquie Carpenter emerged from the horseshoe, the smells of ciggie smoke and instant coffee wreathing around her. She flipped back the cover of the appropriately named flip-chart to reveal architect's plans of a building. Like Bathurst, she cleared her throat.

'The school was built in the 'sixties,' she said. 'What you're looking at is the Centre Block, the oldest part. There are three floors here, but we're concerned with the second. They put in a new staircase in 'eighty-three and a mezzanine floor . . . here.'

She was pointing directly at the office of the man she loved, Peter Maxwell M.A., Ph.D. pending. It had been pending for thirty years now, but somehow the time had never been right. She could see, in her mind's eye, his film posters, the wilting, unmemorable plant in the corner that Mrs B., Centre Block's cleaner, somehow never got round to dusting. She could see his piles of essays and exercise books, smell his coffee, hear the clatter of kids as they moved about the building. This one was close to him, horribly, chillingly close.

'This,' she was using a board marker, 'is Aitch One, actually a History classroom which was used by the Ofsted team as a base for the week. There are two doors . . . here . . . and here. The second one leads into an adjoining room via a store cupboard. Beyond that is another classroom.'

'Are all these doors open?' somebody wanted to know.

'Usually, yes. Only staff and sixth form have access to the store cupboard. This week the room itself was off limits to everyone, staff included, unless they'd been specifically invited.'

70

'Anybody specifically invited today?' Hall asked her.

'Not that we know of, guv,' she told him.

'Right. Geoff.' Hall had perched himself on the corner of a desk. 'You've got the dead man's movements. What?'

Geoff Baldock was cutting his teeth on this one. A tall, gangly lad with blonde frizzy hair and rather tombstone teeth, he'd been a DC for a little over a year but he'd never handled an honest-to-God murder before. There was an adrenalin buzz about him that didn't show in the others. They all felt it, of course, but with him, it flashed like a neon light on the top of his head. 'He arrived in a people carrier with the others at eight fifteen.'

'That was direct from the Cunliffe?' Hall checked. He knew the kid was still wet behind the ears and he didn't like ends that dangled.

'Yes sir. The Ofsted people had a briefing in Aitch One for the first fifteen minutes, then Whiting had a meeting with the Head.'

'That's James Diamond.' Hall was dotting i's so that all his team were in the picture.

'Correct.' Baldock was getting into his stride now, enjoying the moment with all eyes on him. 'That lasted for an hour.'

'So it's . . . what, now? Nine thirty?'

'Spot on,' Baldock enthused, totally immune to the relative lethargy and sideways glances of the others. 'He was back in Aitch One by nine thirty-five. He was seen here by one of his

71

team, a Robert Templeton, who was writing up lesson reports. Then there was a fire drill at nine forty.'

'All right.' Hall was rather relieved to switch the spotlight onto somebody else. 'Pat, you were on that.'

Pat Prentiss was a thick set, no-nonsense Detective Constable who'd been here before. He hadn't got long left on the Force and had his eye on a rather cushy number in security in Brighton. He'd never set the world alight with his incisive intuition, but that wasn't what being a copper was all about. He did his bit, an effective, fully-functioning cog in a justice machine; no one, including Henry Hall, could ask for more than that.

'Not planned,' he told the Incident Room. 'The bloke in charge of fire drills is Bernard Ryan, Deputy Headteacher. He normally has them on Thursdays, usually in the morning. This one took them all by surprise.'

'Not an actual fire, I assume?' Hall grimaced as the stale, cold coffee hit his tonsils.

'No, guv.' Prentiss shook his head. 'Leighford hasn't had a real fire since . . .' he checked his notes, 'ninety-eight. Some basket case kid seeing if crêpe paper in the Art Room would burn.'

There were murmurings around the room. Empirical, investigative education was a wonderful thing.

72

'There is one kid known to us as a bit of an arsonist, but he was firmly ensconced in a French lesson at the time and the teacher swears he didn't move. Except when the fire-bell went of course and then he was out of there like a bat out of hell.'

'So who set the alarm off?' Hall asked.

'We don't know, guv,' Prentiss said. 'I talked to the caretaker, bloke called Bert Martin and he narrowed it down to an alarm in Aitch Block.'

'Jacquie,' Hall turned back to the flip chart. 'Where's that in relation to Aitch One?'

She checked the plans. 'Here, guv,' she said. 'Down the corridor and in that direction.'

Hall tapped his teeth with his biro. 'So what are we saying? The killer sets off the alarm, makes his way from the alarm to Aitch One, kills Whiting, who is either deaf or hasn't bothered to obey the implicit instructions of the fire-bell and is obligingly sitting there. Then he walks out of the school through eight hundred witnesses.' He let it all sink in. 'Well, that's straightforward then.'

'Getting out wouldn't be a problem.' Baldock the boy detective gave everybody the benefit of his superior intellect. 'The assembly point was here, right?' he had crossed to the flip chart. 'So everybody's there, everybody's attention's there. Chummy just has to walk out the other side.'

Chummy? thought Hall. The lad had been

73

watching too many re-runs of *Gideon of the Yard* on TCM on his days off. Even so, the little bastard was essentially correct.

'Or,' Philip Bathurst wasn't going to let it go. He knew when a little shite was after his job. 'He didn't walk out at all.'

'Go on Phil.' Hall was all ears.

'If it's one of the Ofsted team, if it's one of the staff, even if, God help us, it's one of the kids, a cool customer would just mingle with the crowd, wouldn't they, muttering about what a bloody waste of time fire drills were.'

Everybody in that room had been thinking that since word of Whiting's death got around. What if it was one of the kids? Could it be? They all knew that kids killed. From Mary Bell to Venables and Thompson, those two twisted little bastards who battered the toddler Jamie Bulger to death, there were psychos out there who just started out on the trail of havoc a little earlier than most. But Whiting, surely, was different. Most murderous children killed children younger than themselves or at least their own age. When they killed adults, it was the result of a mugging, a burglary gone wrong, the eventual ghastly retaliation for years of abuse. This was altogether something else.

Hall waited until the muttering and the murmuring died down. 'Cause of death.' He had changed tack now, knowing how useless, at this stage of a murder enquiry, speculation

74

was. 'That's down to Dr Astley.' And the mutterings and the murmurings began again.

* * *

Dr James Astley wouldn't normally have worked nights. His patients, after all, were not usually in a hurry and they certainly weren't going anywhere. But his bridge tournament had been cancelled and his wife had her sister over and suddenly, that Tuesday night, the mortuary seemed the only place to be.

Astley would never see sixty again. Unless he *really squeezed*, he couldn't often see his own genitals either, but hey, that was what growing old disgracefully was all about. And as for genitals, well, in his line of work, you got to see plenty of other people's. In his line of work too, you talked to yourself. He hadn't bothered to get his long-suffering assistant, Donald, out of his slippers for routine stuff like this, so he went about the business for which he had been trained and which most of us would find too ghastly to contemplate, alone and talking into a mike that was suspended from the ceiling.

'Well-nourished male,' Astley mumbled, knowing that Donald could translate his mutterings into coherent English for the report later. 'Age . . . mid-forties.' He mechanically checked the knees, the shins and the elbows for childhood scars. Nothing.

75

Perhaps Alan Whiting had been a fastidious child. Perhaps Mr and Mrs Whiting had kept their little boy in a glass bubble. The world of a forensic pathologist was littered with the word 'perhaps'.

For a brief moment, Jim Astley and Alan Whiting held hands. The nails were good, clean and trimmed, the fingers strangers to manual work. No scars even here, no signs of slippage with the hedge trimmer, no careless swing with a hammer which chipped the nail and coarsened the skin. Alan Whiting had been a paper pusher all his life. There was a discoloration around the cuticles that Astley recognized, chemical staining. At some point, the dead man had had access to a chemistry set and over a period of time, well, well, well ... join the club; the man was a scientist.

Astley had scraped the dried blood from the man's chest. His shirt, bow tie and other clothing were with Henry Hall's people now, going through the third degree as all objects from a crime scene did. All that remained now to tell the world how he died was a small black hole in the mid line of his body.

'Incision measuring four millimetres through the sterno-cleido mastoid,' he tilted the dead man's head, 'exiting through the trapezium to the right of the mid line. So,' he dropped the head back and straightened up, adjusting the dangling mike as he went, 'my guess at this stage—and we'll do the surgery

76

tomorrow, Mr Hall, if it's all the same to you, is that the murder weapon is a sharp-pointed, dull-sided narrow blade which passed through the sterno-hyoid above or below the third vertebra. Resistance would have been slight if the blow missed the bone and the impact would have carried the head backwards if . . .' he checked the papers alongside him, 'as the notes contend, Mr Whiting was pinned by said weapon to his chair. Fibres on his hair will confirm that.'

Astley switched off the mike and looked down at the placid face of the dead man, his head supported by the pads. 'Neat but not neat enough. Professional, but amateur. You're a mass of contradictions, aren't you, Chief Inspector?'

And in that chill, stainless steel room as another summer's day died around him, even Jim Astley wasn't sure whether he was talking about Alan Whiting or Henry Hall.

Chapter Four

'That's enormously hurtful, you know.' Peter Maxwell was talking to Jacquie Carpenter on her front doorstep in Sandcroft Way as darkness came down over Leighford.

'What is?' She kissed him and took one of the takeaway bags.

'What you just did,' he told her. 'Looking round to see if anyone noticed my arriving. You're ashamed of me, aren't you? Aren't you?' He was screaming now. 'It's because I'm so old, isn't it? So decrepit. That's what all this is about.'

She kissed him again, giggling and pushing him back in the doorway and draping herself over him, grinding her hips against his. Then she pulled back. 'You,' and she batted him on the nose with a prawn cracker, 'are just a dirty old man.'

He winked at her. 'Works every time, doesn't it?'

She led him through into her kitchen, opening cupboards and clattering crockery as she went. The sun gilded her spice rack and her assorted whisks. 'Anyway,' she said. 'Where's your key?'

'Ah.' His face dropped along with the takeaway bags. 'I've been meaning to talk to you about that.'

'You've lost it,' she said, looking at him sharply.

'Not so much lost as mislaid,' he explained. 'Mrs B . . .'

Jacquie held up her hand. She knew Maxwell's cleaning lady whom he held in common both at home and work. She wouldn't hear a word spoken against her. 'I know for a fact that Mrs B. wouldn't move *any* of your personal items. She's left your truss out on the

78

line for the past three months.'

'Some things just have to be properly aired,' he said, 'lest you reap the repercussions. This may be the warm south, but a damp gusset . . .' his eyes crossed at the thought of it. 'Don't go there, Woman Policeman. Well, you can later.'

'Not tonight, Max,' she sighed.

'That's probably the worst Josephine de Beauharnais I've heard,' he told her. 'Soy?'

'Top shelf. Are you feeling brave enough for chopsticks?'

'If it's good enough for Russ Conway,' Maxwell smiled. That was two people in quick succession that Jacquie Carpenter had never heard of. But she loved Peter Maxwell despite his madness.

'So?' he said once they were hunkered down in her lounge and tucking into Numbers 16, 34, 73 and a double portion of 118.

'Scrummy,' she said, wrestling with a king prawn and looking at him cheekily.

'There's none so obtuse,' he said, 'as they who will not cough. If it's not too much of a mixed metaphor over this particular meal, are you going to spill the beans?'

She looked at him, the sad, dark eyes, always alive at moments like these, sensing the razor mind behind the boyish enthusiasm. He wasn't so different from Geoff Baldock really, except for the brain. Oh, and the insanity.

'You know I can't,' they both intoned together.

79

'Yes,' Maxwell continued alone. 'Of course I do, but there's a difference this time.'

'Oh?' She raised an eyebrow. 'Why so?'

'Come on, Jacquie.' He'd diced with other people's deaths before. This conversation between them had become oddly routine. 'A man died on school premises. *My* school, to be exact.'

'*Your* school?' She was playing with him along with her noodles. It was a losing battle really; only the noodles would go to the wall.

'Figuratively, metaphorically, morally, spiritually,' he confirmed. 'As of last December when old Bill Cater finally did the decent thing and shot himself, I am the oldest serving teacher at Leighford High. Legs Diamond was still working his way through the joined-up writing course at Luton Tech for the Maladjusted when I started there. Paul Moss was at kindergarten.'

'Yes, but it's always different, isn't it, Max?' she reminded him. 'One of your sixth form, an old school chum, the old girl on your doorstep. There's always a reason to be involved.'

'That's how it goes,' he shrugged. 'But this one really *is* different. I wonder what the stats are?' Peter Maxwell had never really had any faith in statistics. Along with Disraeli, he'd rather take the lies and the damned lies any day. 'I wonder how many murders are committed in schools?'

'Dunblane?' She'd stopped chewing now.

'Everyday occurrence in the States, I understand.'

He nodded. 'And I *am* involved already,' he didn't have to remind her.

'You are.' She twisted up her face, sighing. 'And that's why I shouldn't be talking to you now. God knows what would happen if . . .'

'If Henry found out?' Maxwell chuckled. He and Jacquie's boss went back a fair way by now. He'd sparred with him before, but usually had his man on the ropes after a couple of rounds. 'Well, let's not tell him, shall we?'

'Maxwell,' she growled, shaking her head. 'At the moment, I'm in the dark.'

He put down his chopsticks with gratitude and resorted to his fingers for the last pork ball. 'Delicious.' He smacked his lips. 'And only two per pig. Right, heart of hearts,' he wiped his fingers on her kitchen roll. 'Let's put on the metaphorical light, shall we? Alan Whiting. What do we know?'

She sighed as she started. He'd done it again, as he always did. Her career flashed before her, as it had so often in the past. She had dreams about this; Henry Hall standing in front of her, shaking his head in abject disappointment. 'Ofsted Chief Inspector,' she told him. 'Ex-chemistry teacher, science adviser, something or other in the corridors of power in Derbyshire LEA.'

'Lots of knives in his back, I shouldn't wonder.'

81

'But that was rather a long time ago,' she put it in perspective. 'No doubt he's made other enemies since then.'

'No doubt he has,' Maxwell nodded. 'Hair of the dog, poppet?' he nodded in the general direction of her drinks cabinet. 'You know I do my best work pissed.'

She poured for them both, a Scotch for her, a Southern Comfort for him.

'Here's to crime,' he raised his glass.

'It pays the bills,' she had to admit.

'Where was his last Ofsted?'

'We don't know.'

'It's on that thing, what do you young people call it? The Net? It's done by school, so it might take a bit of finding. Or of course you can just ring up and ask David Bell.'

'Bell?'

'The Big Cheese who runs Ofsted. He must have a list somewhere, written down on a fag packet or whatever.'

'Where's this going, Max?' she asked.

'Consider the situation. There's a headmaster somewhere—or a headmistress ... after all, we've given you people the vote now, so it's not *too* long a shot—who was heartily pissed off by Whiting. Not a failing school, that's too general. For all that heads carry the can, a failing school is a collective responsibility thing—everybody shares in it. There'd be eighty skewers in Whiting's neck. No, this would be a situation where the head is singled out personally. He or she festers, worrying it, teasing it, bemoaning the unfairness of it. He or she hatches a plot. Revenge—it's been done before.' He was lolling back against the sofa, looking at the ceiling as the scenario formed in his brain. 'You let a little time go by; wait 'till Whiting's done . . . what, two, three more schools? Just to muddy the waters. Then you hit him, when he's somewhere else entirely, somewhere like Leighford High so that suspicion falls on them—us.'

'And it wouldn't have to be a headteacher,' she was reasoning with him.

'No, indeed. Anybody. Anybody who'd been singled out, unfairly, as they saw it, criticised.'

'Do people *really* feel like that?' she asked. 'Teachers, I mean.'

Maxwell smiled. 'There's no job in the world like teaching,' he told her, he who had had no other. 'What was it Lord Randolph Churchill said to young Winston? "It's the best career in the world if you work at it and the worst if you shirk." All right, he was talking about the army, but the idea applies. Except that today you can't shirk. God, when I started, revered Heads of Classics would get their classes working silently on a bit of Virgil while they had their afternoon nap. Exercise books went for whole terms without being marked. The most we ever had to write on school reports was "unsatisfactory". And it really rankled having to add that "un" to denote the misfits, wierdos and layabouts. These days every report I write takes me twenty minutes *and* it has to be done electronically.'

'What?' Jacquie was disbelieving. 'You mean, you write on a computer? You?'

'Actually,' he closed to her confidentially, 'it's a hologram of myself I cunningly set up in the Computer Room, but don't tell the Director of Studies. No, teaching is a solitary occupation, Woman Policeman. Oh, there's a little thing called the National Curriculum and there are syllabi and so on. But they threw team-teaching out with school milk and now, once that classroom door closes, it's just me and a couple of dozen fine young cannibals. And if I want to teach them the moon's a balloon or Adolf Hitler was a nice man, it'll be a hell of a long time before anyone can stop me.'

'So you're saying . . .'

He leaned across and stretched an arm around her as she snuggled around to his side of the left-over Chinese. 'I'm saying that, as a profession, we're solitary people. Team-teaching went out in the eighties. Classroom Assistants? They stir the paint and make the tea. No, we're lords unto ourselves and we don't welcome interference. Most of us accept Ofsted as an occupational hazard. We know it's for the best. But what if there's someone who doesn't? Someone who rather enjoys his

84

or her relative freedom? Someone who doesn't want to be controlled by David Bell or any of his minions? You ladies of the law are assessed constantly, aren't you?'

'Tell me about it,' she moaned.

'Well, we're not. Ofsted comes but once every four years, like an American election—and look how rigged they are.'

'Don't you get internal inspections?'

Maxwell chuckled. 'Indeed we do,' he told her. 'Last year it was Legs Diamond himself for me, the Big Enchilada—only because I'd refused to be assessed by either Bernard Ryan or Dierdre Lessing.'

'And was he impressed?'

'Legs?' Maxwell snorted. 'Let's just say he threw down his rifle and applauded. You'd think he'd be a tougher nut to crack, wouldn't you?'

'How do you mean?' she frowned.

'Well, a man on his salary. What's he on? Fifty, sixty grand? All it cost me was a tenner to get him to go away. No pride, some people!'

'So . . . you think Whiting's death has nothing to do with Leighford?' she checked.

'That's about the size of it.'

She snuggled closer so that her hand was against his shoulder and her long flame hair splayed across his chest. 'What if you're wrong, Max?' she asked. 'What if Whiting's death had *everything* to do with Leighford? What if, tomorrow, when you walk into school, you're walking past a killer?'

*   *   *

'Please accept our condolences, Mrs Whiting.'

It was rather like a message from an I-Speak-Your-Weight machine. Perhaps Henry Hall had done this once too often; perhaps he'd allowed himself to be too detached; perhaps it went with the job. He got the impression that Pamela Whiting was on something, something that calmed, soothed, took away the edge of reality. She was an attractive woman with short-cropped dark hair and eyes that danced and sparkled on a good day. Today was not a good day. Today was the day she had just come from Leighford Council's Mortuary and an odious toad of a man called Astley had asked her to identify her husband's body.

'Thank you,' was all she could think of to say. The policeman in front of her was about her own age. His jaw was strong, his mouth kind and sensitive, but she couldn't see his eyes, because they were hidden behind the lenses of his glasses and those lenses just reflected the frosted panes of the windows of Interview Room Two at Leighford Police Station. Across to her right, she was dimly aware of a woman, plainclothes, with light auburn hair fastened into a plait swept up behind her head. She looked concerned, as if

86

she were trying to understand what Pamela Whiting was going through.

'I have to ask you some questions,' Hall was saying, as though down a long tunnel in her mind. 'Are you all right with that?'

'Of course,' she said. 'That's why I'm here.'

'DS Carpenter will make notes at this stage,' Hall said. 'We don't need tape recorders, do we?'

Pamela Whiting had no idea. Her husband had never been murdered before.

'When did you last see your husband?' Hall asked.

'Er . . . let's see . . . Saturday. He caught the train from Matlock.'

'You saw him to the station?'

'No, he took a cab. I do Keep Fit on Saturday afternoons. I was the other side of town.'

'And he came to Leighford?'

'I believe he had to change in London. I don't do the train thing any more, Chief Inspector. They're so appalling, aren't they?'

'But your husband did?'

'Oh yes. If truth be told, he wasn't much of a driver. Found it too stressful to add that to a week's inspection. I don't think anyone realizes quite how exhausting it is, being an Ofsted inspector.'

'Hmm,' Henry Hall probably had his own views on that score, but he wasn't likely to share it with the world. 'Did you talk to him,

87

on the phone I mean, since then?'

'No,' the widow shook her head. 'I never liked to bother Alan while he was working. Perhaps towards the end of the week, but never at the beginning.'

'Mrs Whiting,' Hall slid a sheet of paper across the desk, 'Do you recognize any of these names?'

She pulled a pair of glasses from her handbag and checked the list, 'This is the Ofsted team, isn't it?'

Hall nodded.

'This one,' she tapped it with her finger. 'Sally Meninger. Alan worked with her before, I believe.'

'Have you met her?'

'Yes,' she told him. 'Yes, I have.'

'But none of the others.'

She looked again. 'No, I don't think so. No, wait—Templeton; Robert Templeton. I know that name from somewhere . . . Sorry, I can't place it.'

Henry Hall leaned back, resisting the urge to look too casual by resting his hands behind his head. 'Mrs Whiting, it's rather a clichéd question in my profession, but is there anyone you can think of who would want to see your husband dead?'

Pamela Whiting managed a smile. 'Ofsted inspectors are a bit like traffic wardens when they first invented them, Chief Inspector. They must be among the most loathed people in the world. But I don't suppose that helps you very much, does it? When may I have my husband back? There are arrangements to make.'

*   *   *

Peter Maxwell had hung his cycle clips on the hook he'd put on the back of his own door. It was one of those things about teaching. He'd been doing it for fifteen years before he had an office. A carpet had followed three years later and an internal phone. Anything else, like a kettle or a hook, he'd had to find out of his own vast pockets. It was Wednesday, the something or other of July and the sun was still shining on a sleepy seaside town less buzzing with tourists year by year.

But today was not an ordinary Wednesday. He'd passed a crowd of paparazzi at the school gates in earnest conversation with Bernard Ryan, sent out by a harassed Legs Diamond to warn them off council property. He wasn't doing very well. He'd passed a uniformed constable on the school steps who nodded in his direction as he staggered up them. Kids moved in knots of twos and threes, whispering, heads down. Was this how it was after Dunblane? At that school where the Headmaster was knifed at his own gates? The bell went for the end of Lesson One. Time for all to be revealed. Time for all to be put right; because Legs Diamond was in his heaven.

89

Maxwell always felt sorry for his pastoral colleagues, the other Year Heads. He had the civilized end of the sausage-machine that was modern education. Only a few of his sixth formers still wore baseball caps and rode skateboards; only a few still, in the grim depths of winter, wore mittens with strings attached by their mummies. Most of them were developing nicely into those unlikely imagos, human beings. Rosie Leaper, the ex-Head of Year Eleven, was the only one with a spring in her step at this dog-end of the year. The head-cases of her Year Group were just a memory now, washed away with Valium and her Threshold Payment. The nice ones would come back in September to be Maxwell's Own, the others, by and large, would go to Leighford Tech or join that happy band, the Giro Collectors' Club. It would be many weeks yet before she had to turn her attentions seriously to the incoming horrors of Year Seven.

As he joined the group in Diamond's office that side of morning break, the others sat as though in therapy. Graham Hollis had Year Ten, already flexing their muscles to take over their role as the eldest in the main school, already sure their GCSEs would lead nowhere, so what was the use of finishing coursework? The misfits of Year Nine were captained by Jo Pearson, a voluminous woman addicted to nicotine and Ferrero Rocher, balanced perfectly to control her weight. Neil Grannum had Year Eight, but only in the vaguest of senses. The same crowd of in-trouble delinquents hung around his door at the end of the day who had been there in the morning. And Janet Valentine was in loco for Year Seven, that quiet interim bunch who only now were following their elders, if not betters, into the bad habits of the future by not wearing uniform whenever they could get away with it.

They all sat in the Head's office, with Diamond, Bernard Ryan and Dierdre Lessing, the unblessed Trinity, presiding over it all. Was anybody still teaching, Maxwell wondered.

'I've just come off the phone to County,' Diamond told them all grimly. 'The CEO recommends we stay open and field the flak as best we can. The Chairman of Governors is of the same mind.'

It came as a surprise to Maxwell that the Chairman of Governors had a mind at all, but he let it pass.

'The police will start their interviews this afternoon. I'm on first, then Bernard, then Dierdre. This is all very difficult, everybody, and I've asked you all together for your advice, really. Max?'

All eyes in the room were on him.

'Why ask me, Headmaster?' the Head of Sixth Form could be bloody obtuse when the mood took him.

'Well, you've . . . how shall I put it, had experience of this sort of thing, Max. Murder,

I mean.'

It was true. He had. Of all of them squeezed into Diamond's office he was the only one with experience like that. 'You've got the paparazzi at the gate. Presumably, Bernard, you've told them to stay off school property.'

'Yes,' said Ryan, ever on the defensive. 'But how do we stop them talking to the kids?'

'We can't,' said Maxwell. 'Can I suggest assemblies this afternoon at which we spell out to our little dears the need for discretion. Don't talk to strangers, that sort of thing?'

'Will that work?' Graham Hollis asked.

'No,' Maxwell admitted. 'But it's our best shot. That's the trouble with a democracy, Graham, every bugger's got the right of free speech.'

'And how's it going to look,' Dierdre Lessing wanted to know, 'if word gets out that we've told the kids to clam up? The teaching profession isn't the most popular in the country without a conspiracy charge being added to our reputation.'

'All the same . . .' Diamond began.

'All the same . . . and with respect, Headmaster . . . we should keep our eyes and ears open. This is a big school and somebody, somewhere will know something. We can help on that score.'

'How?' Jo Pearson asked.

'We'll have to ask our colleagues for total honesty,' Maxwell said.

'In what way?' Diamond wanted to know.

'Alan Whiting was murdered, we can assume, during the fire drill. If we know who rang that bell, we'd have a pretty good handle on who killed him.'

'How are we going to find that out?' Ryan asked.

'We can start by finding out who was out of a classroom at the time,' Maxwell said. 'Which little darling was bursting to go to the loo or desperate to return a library book. Was anybody put outside a classroom for arsing about? Sorry, misbehaving, Ms Lessing.'

Dierdre snorted at him.

'That's why we need honesty.'

'You won't get it,' grunted Neil Grannum.

'Oh, come on,' Diamond leapt in. 'That's a pretty appalling indictment of one's colleagues, Neil.'

There was a hubbub which subsided only when Maxwell intervened.

'Appalling but accurate,' he said. 'How many times in staff briefing, Headmaster, have you told us not to put kids outside doors? How often has Hannah Snooks nevertheless nipped off to continue her sexual lifestory on the wall of the girls' loos? And how many cases of lung cancer have we condoned by letting the lads out early from PE so that they can come back from the fields the long way round, via Benson and Hedges?'

'Surely,' Dierdre bridled, 'you're not

93

suggesting that one of our children . . .'

'Dierdre,' Maxwell sighed. 'Light of my life, we have to face facts.'

'What facts?' Ryan snapped. 'There's no evidence at all that a child did this terrible thing.'

'And,' the Head of Sixth Form reminded them all, 'there's no evidence that they didn't.'

'Good God, Max,' Diamond stared at him. 'You can't be serious.' It wasn't a very impressive John McEnroe, but from Legs Diamond, nobody was expecting it would be.

'All right,' Maxwell said, 'let me put it another way. I don't happen to think, for what it's worth, that any child at Leighford High is involved in this, but what if they saw something? What if Hannah Snooks bumped into the murderer on her way to write chapter three next to the sanitary disposal unit? What if Gary Spenser was just lighting up when Person or Persons Unknown was setting off the fire alarm or worse, going into Aitch One with a sharp object in his hand? Whichever way you hack it, our kids are at risk, people.' And he instantly became the wise old sergeant in *Hill Street Blues*. 'Let's be careful out there.'

*　　　*　　　*

From lunchtime that day, all Hell broke loose. The school switchboard was inundated with irate calls from irate parents wanting to know what was being done. There was, after all, a maniac on the loose and little Jason/Sharon/Fat Josh was likely to be next on his list. To a generation brought up on *Crimewatch* and *Crime on the Streets,* everybody was a serial killer. It was, in a way, no more than Peter Maxwell had said in the Headmaster's office, but screamed down the buzzing phone lines with a string of expletives, it had all the more punch.

By the time the assemblies were called, in hasty and unlikely corners of the school, Year Group numbers had dwindled and Thingy Two, who had just come on to the switchboard to relieve a sobbing and near-hysterical Thingy One, had no clear idea of who was on site and who wasn't. Her first call, oddly enough, was from a mother complaining that her little Tommy had been told to change his trainers by a teacher whose name she did not know and did the school realize the cost of school shoes, even with that Gordon Brown's Children's Trust money, what with Little Tommy's dad being out of work for nearly four months and her on the social? Well, did they? All in all, Thingy Two, with her mind on grimmer things, was stuck for an answer.

*   *   *

At the end of another imperfect day, a little

95

knot of teachers sat in Peter Maxwell's office, awaiting the Great Man's arrival. It didn't take long.

'Max, we do have homes to go to, you know,' Ben Holton's irritation threshold had been passed by half past ten that morning. Were it not for the situation they all found themselves in, he'd have admitted to feeling pretty homicidal by now.

'Indeed, indeed,' Maxwell hurtled in, flicking on the kettle instinctively. 'Coffee, anyone?'

'I'd kill for one,' Sally Greenhow confessed and shrank down a little as she realized her unfortunate choice of words.

'Right,' Maxwell was busy flicking lids and spooning brown granules, 'let's recap, people,' he said.

'What?' Jeff Armstrong's patch had gone now, leaving him with a painful-looking eye, purple and puffy lid over a blood-red iris.

'Think back, Polyphemus,' Maxwell suggested, the classical allusion lost on Armstrong, who had only seen *Jason and the Argonauts* once, 'to the curious incident of the Ofsted inspectors in the night-time.'

'Oh, the courting couple.' Paul Moss was getting a head-start on marking the pile of battered exercise books in front of him on Maxwell's coffee-table.

'And they weren't just whistling Dixie, bub,' Maxwell informed them.

'What do you mean?' Holton wanted to know.

'Well, call me old-fashioned if you like, but I was rather surprised by it all.'

'You don't get out enough, Max.' Holton was the only one in the room with the age and the gravitas to say it. 'They were only having a drink.'

'And sexual intercourse—you'll excuse my French, Sally.' He passed her her coffee.

'What?' It was Armstrong who found his voice first and, single syllable response though it was, it seemed to say it all.

'In the Gentlemen's Rest Room,' Maxwell explained, 'whence I had gone to point Percy at the porcelain.'

'What, you mean they were actually at it?' Paul Moss had suddenly lost interest, if he'd ever had any, in the Elizabethan Poor Law. 'In the bog?'

'Elegantly paraphrased, dear boy,' Maxwell smiled, 'and, in essence, yes.'

'Do the cops know?' Sally asked.

'One of them does.' Maxwell made no bones about his relationship with Jacquie, although there were times when he had to tread warily.

'Why didn't you say anything?' Holton asked him.

'Well, I don't know.' Maxwell winced as the hot coffee burnt his lip. 'Public schoolboy, I suppose. Mixed company. Delicate matter.

Sheer bloody disbelief. That sort of thing.'

'She must be cut up, then,' Sally was thinking aloud.

'Who?' Jeff Armstrong was, after all, a Craft and Design Technology teacher.

'Sally Meninger,' Sally Greenhow said. 'I mean, if they were an item.'

'Max,' Holton sighed, 'I'm very grateful for this hint of salacious tittle-tattle of course, but I still don't see why you asked us all here.'

'Trying to get a handle on it all,' Maxwell said. 'Think about it. There we all were, in the Vine, enjoying a quiet drink when a pair of Ofsted inspectors came in, groping each other like a couple of kids. Is that how we all remember it?'

They looked at each other, nodding and making general agreement noises.

'Well, not exactly.' Paul Moss was frowning, wrestling with it.

'Ah,' beamed Maxwell. 'It takes a Head of History to be so perspicacious.' He knew. He'd been one himself. 'Say on, oh wise one.'

'Well, *she* was all over *him*, I'll grant you. Looked a bit one-sided to me.'

'No, no.' Holton was shaking his head. 'He was loving it. I'm just surprised they were so public. But actually having it away . . . What do you make of that, Max?'

'I'm asking the questions today, Ben,' Maxwell said. 'That's why I got us all together—several heads etcetera. For what it's worth, I can only conclude it was done for effect.'

'What? For our benefit?' Sally asked.

'In a way. Could they have known we'd be there, in the Vine, I mean, at that time?'

'Don't see how,' Holton shrugged. 'Unless they followed us, of course. This is all getting pretty weird, Max.'

The Head of Sixth Form nodded. 'And I suspect it will get weirder still before the whole thing's over.'

The door swung wide and a dishevelled woman stood there, a fag dangling out of her mouth and a length of hoover hose in her hand. 'I didn't know you had a meeting. Surprised you're here at all with a bloody madman about. Still, that's them for you, innit? That Mr Diamond. Needs takin' in, 'e does. I'll do you later. Tra.'

'No need to apologize Mrs B. It was a spur of the moment thing. So am I, if truth be told. Yes, it is. I couldn't agree more. Personally I can't wait. 'Bye.' Maxwell was a past master at swimming in Mrs B's stream of consciousness. He even had a badge for it. She was a good old sort, a good stick, a brick, all those inanimate objects people used to use as metaphors in the days when they knew what a metaphor was. And, like Arnie Schwarzenegger, she'd be back—Maxwell could count on it.

*   *   *

The Vine was noisier at eleven that night than it had been on Monday. Maxwell jostled his way to the bar past the idiot with the air guitar taking up most of the central floor space and bought himself a drink off of the old tart who served him.

'Have one yourself,' he shouted over the combined roar of the Leighford Bikers' Association' Annual Do and the crashing chords of The Yawning Hippos. Only two of the Band were under thirty and only Maxwell knew what soap was.

'Ta,' and she tucked his fiver down her cleavage. He'd never see that again.

'Tell me . . . er . . . Doris, is it?' Maxwell judged the name to be about right. The woman was fifty if she was a day, bottle-blonde, make up by Grimaldi. Wrong side of the tracks.

'Philomena,' she corrected him.

'Right,' Maxwell smiled. 'Tell me, Philomena, were you here on Monday?'

'I'm here every bloody night, ducks.' She put his Southern Comfort down in front of him.

'I was here on Monday, with some friends.'

'Lovely.' She took a drag on her ciggie.

'Do you remember a couple here at the bar? She was dark-haired, attractive, middle-aged.'

'I'm not a dating agency, darlin',' she informed him. 'This is a respectable place, you know. We haven't been closed down in six months.'

The Bikers whooped and clapped as the Hippos got stuck into their finale, grande though it wasn't. Gerry Cosgrove rang the bell, bellowing in Maxwell's ear, 'Time, gentlemen, please.' Maxwell was probably the only gentleman in the building, but he'd never been a snob about these things and let it pass. 'Er . . . last Monday,' he grabbed Cosgrove's attention.

'What about it?'

'There was a man and a woman, here, at the bar. All over each other.'

'Yeah?' Cosgrove was collecting glasses, wiping surfaces. It was nearing the end of another long day. 'Joke, is it?'

'Do you remember them?'

'No.'

'Thank you so much.'

It was like pulling teeth. To be honest, Maxwell hadn't expected much else. Bar staff must have seen it all in their time, all human life, the flotsam and jetsam of a decaying seaside town, spiralling downwards in the social maelstrom of Tony Blair's England. If they were still surprised or shocked by anything they saw, they kept it to themselves. And the more they kept it to themselves, the less surprised or shocked they were.

Maxwell was about to down his drink and stumble to the door when he found himself face to face with a huge, long-haired Biker

101

with attitude and, apparently, no GCSEs.

'What you looking at?' he grunted.

Maxwell took in the leather waistcoat, the gritty, stained vest and the giant cow skull buckle. The tattoos would have looked good on Caratacus and their owner swayed unsteadily, breathing Boddington's over Maxwell. Maxwell shook his head. 'No,' he said, 'I've no idea. Give me a clue.'

'Do you want a fucking kicking?' the Biker roared, his muscles flexing and the veins throbbing in his neck.

'Neither, thanks,' Maxwell smiled and raised his hat.

The Biker darted sideways to block his path. He was altogether nimbler than Maxwell expected. 'You a poof?' the Biker asked.

'No,' Maxwell told him calmly. 'But it's nice of you to think of me.'

He was ready for the right cross and ducked it, but not for the left hook and it sent him reeling backwards against the crowd. The idiot with the air guitar looked up in surprise as the Biker batted him aside and went for Maxwell again. The Head of Sixth Form steadied himself as Gerry Cosgrove hauled up his counter-ledge to step in. Jostling Bikers grouped themselves to watch the proceedings, clapping and whistling.

The Hippos had stopped playing now and the only noise was the roar of the Bikers' thousands and the thump of Maxwell's heart.

In for a penny in for a pounding at this stage, he spun round catching Death a nasty one in the shin and driving two fingers into the man's eyes. The Biker doubled up on the bar, grunting in agony as Gerry Cosgrove slammed his head down on the counter and blew a loud whistle.

'The law are on their way,' he shouted in the sudden silence that followed. 'Now unless you bastards want to spend the night in the slammer, I suggest you bugger off.'

No one moved.

Maxwell didn't quite see what happened next, but a Biker flew less than gracefully through the air, courtesy of Iron Man who never liked his drum solos ruined by unsavoury elements. The Biker lay pole-axed at the feet of air-guitar man, already carefully packing his instrument away.

'Now!' Cosgrove roared.

One by one the Bikers finished their drinks and swaggered to the Vine's doors. A couple of them dragged Death off the bar and helped him out. A couple more picked up Iron Man's victim.

'Great fucking night, Gerry,' they called to the barman who Maxwell noticed was cradling a baseball bat in his arms.

'Yeah, yeah,' Cosgrove waved at them.

'Next year, then, Gez,' somebody else shouted, patting him affectionately on the shoulder.

'Fuckin' right on, fellas!' yet another called to the Band. 'Great fuckin' gig! But you,' his mood suddenly changed as he jabbed a finger at the drummer. 'You better watch your back.'

When the bat-wing doors had stopped swinging and the sound of Harley-Davidsons roared away into the night, Gerry Cosgrove turned to Peter Maxwell. 'You,' he wagged a finger at him. 'You're banned, mate. I don't need troublemakers like you.'

'I'm sure you don't,' Maxwell nodded, quite glad to have his knee caps still. He turned to the fellas, 'Gentlemen,' he said, 'I fear I have to leave this establishment post-haste,' he grinned at Cosgrove, 'and more or less right away. Can we have a word outside?'

'Well,' Duggsy was doing something unbelievable with yards of cable, 'we would, Mr Maxwell, but . . . well, after that little incident, there might be a few people sort of . . . lying in wait for us . . . er . . . you. Perhaps another time, eh? Want a gig up at the school? Something like that?'

The drummer shuffled back to his high hat, throwing his sticks in the air and catching them expertly. 'What are you babies afraid of?' he asked. 'Man just wants a word, don't he?'

Chapter Five

Starry, starry night. The Hippos stood with Maxwell in the car park of the Vine, having carefully negotiated the vomit as they went. The indefinable smell of KFC and chip shops wafted on the night air and in the stillness you could hear the slapping of the lanyards against the masts in the new marina.

'Lads,' Maxwell turned to the Band, Wal still carrying his glass of Grolsch. 'You were playing here on Monday.'

'That's right, Mr Maxwell,' Duggsy assured him. 'Cool of you to come see us again tonight.'

'I'm one of your most loyal fans,' Maxwell beamed. 'On Monday—bit of a quiet night, right?'

'Monday, Monday,' grunted the drummer. 'Hate that day.'

Maxwell looked at him. He was older than the others, a sad old rocker on his way down. He was the only one of the unholy trio to remember the Mamas and the Papas, though he'd cut his own throat rather than admit to having bought any of their records. 'I'm Iron Man, by the way.' He extended a hand. He had drummer's fingers that could crush tarsals and Maxwell got the feeling he was holding back.

'Delighted,' said Maxwell. 'And I want to

thank you most sincerely for your help back there.'

'That's all right,' Iron Man nodded. 'I just don't like blokes who sneak up on blokes from behind.'

Maxwell got back to the point. 'Monday,' he said. 'Any of you remember a couple at the bar, bloke and a woman in their forties?'

'Yeah,' said Duggsy as the only one whose eyes, by definition, were looking straight ahead while performing. 'Cosy, weren't they?'

At last, somebody with a memory. 'They were,' Maxwell nodded. 'Well, one of 'em's dead.'

Wal swallowed hard. 'Never! Which one?'

'The bloke. Name of Alan Whiting. It'll be in the *Advertiser* tomorrow. I believe it was in the nationals today.'

The term 'nationals' was clearly lost on the Hippos so Maxwell let it go.

'What? Snuffed out, you mean?' Duggsy wanted clarification. 'Murdered?'

Maxwell nodded. 'At your old alma mater, Matthew, to be precise Room Aitch One at Leighford High.'

'Fuck me sideways!' Wal nearly dropped his Grolsch.

'It's been a long day, William,' Maxwell said. 'But thanks for the offer. Think back, people,' he became conspiratorial. 'What do you remember about the pair?'

'Well,' said Duggsy. 'We were playing,

106

of course.'

'Well, I was,' said Wal.

'We'd just started our second set,' Duggsy said. 'You'd just come in, Mr Maxwell. And that bastard Mr Holton.'

'Yes, he is, isn't he?' Maxwell agreed. 'Still, we can't always choose our colleagues, William. After they were cosy at the bar, what then?'

'They buggered off for a bit,' Iron Man remembered, Maxwell hoping he wasn't being too literal. 'Could have gone round to the Snug, I guess.'

'Could have gone anywhere,' Maxwell nodded.

'She came back on her own later,' Duggsy remembered. 'Looked a bit pissed off if I read it right.'

'She was pissed, certainly.' It was all flooding back to Wal now. ' 'Ere, Iron, didn't you see her later having an up and a downer with some bloke?'

Iron Man's brow furrowed as he tried to remember. 'That's right,' he said. 'I was out checking the van during one of Duggsy's quiet numbers. Going at it hammer and tongs, they was.'

'Rowing?' Maxwell thought he'd better check that Iron Man's colloquialisms were on a par with his own.

'She was screaming at him,' Iron Man confirmed. 'Slapped him round the head a

107

couple of times.'

'Really? Was this the man she was with?' Maxwell was confused. 'The man at the bar? Alan Whiting?'

'Nah,' Iron Man shook his head. 'Nah, this was a different bloke, bit younger, I'd say.'

'Do you remember anything about him—or what they were talking about?'

'Hey, man,' the drummer moaned. 'It was a long time ago, know what I mean?'

'Oh yes, of course.' Maxwell fumbled in his jacket pocket and produced a battered twenty from his wallet.

'Nah, man,' the drummer smiled. 'I don't want your money. I mean it was a long time ago, right.'

'Forty-eight hours,' grinned Duggsy. 'That's a long time for Iron Man, ain't it, Iron?'

'My head hurts sometimes,' Iron Man said. 'I don't remember like I used to.'

'Come on, Iron,' Maxwell urged. 'Was he tall? Short? Black? White? What?'

Iron Man pulled a tin from his hip pocket and proceeded to roll a joint. 'Man?' he offered the tin to Maxwell, who shook his head. If he was going to solve a murder, it was necessary for at least *one* of them not to be off his face. 'He was white,' Iron Man inhaled deeply. ' 'Bout thirty, thirty-five maybe. Carried a black bag.'

'A bag?' Maxwell looked at him. 'What sort of bag?'

108

'Black,' Iron Man shrugged.

'Was it a leads bag, Iron?' Duggsy prompted him. 'Like ours.'

'Yeah,' Iron Man nodded. 'Pretty much.'

'Hold-all, Mr Maxwell,' Duggsy confirmed.

'Joe Public,' Maxwell said.

'Eh?'

'Never mind. Iron, this is very important. Did you hear her say anything? Or him, the bloke with the bag?'

'Nah,' Iron Man was looking glazed already. 'Oh, wait a minute, yeah. She said he was fucking late and what was the point.'

'Late and what was the point,' Maxwell repeated, trying to make sense of it.

'*Fucking* late and what was the point,' Wal thought he ought to be as correct as possible.

'Thereby confirming,' Duggsy took it up, 'that this Mrs Whatsername is not a very nice person, Mr Maxwell.'

'Yes,' their erstwhile Head of Sixth Form sighed. 'Thank you all, gentlemen. I fear you're absolutely right. Y'all take care, now, y'hear.' And he was gone, swinging into the saddle of White Surrey and pedalling away into the darkness, only the hum of his dynamo for company.

'What did I tell you?' Duggsy asked his oppos before turning back to the pub to collect their gear and their night's money. 'Still as mad as a bloody tree.'

109

The Kelly's Street Directory for 1861 referred to it as Cunliffe's Temperance Hotel. They'd built it in Sea Street, where the Channel breezes threatened to invert parasols and send toupees scampering off down the pavement with lives of their own. But Temperance was no more, as each successive government sought to win votes by extending the licensing hours and even the Bishop of Peterborough, an old piss-head if ever there was one, had stated his preference long ago for 'better England free than England sober.' So generations of Englishmen had happily reeled home around the streets of sunny Leighford, rejoicing in their freedom and inebriated as ever. Thank God the church was on the right track.

The Cunliffe, then, served ales and spirits with the best of them. Now a two-star hotel with a part-time night staff, its car park was only partially full as Peter Maxwell wheeled Surrey across its painted tarmac and hitched the rattling monster to its railings. He noticed the clean cut young man dozing in the corner of the lobby and knew him at once for a Boy in Blue, not so much a subject of the late Mr Gainsborough, but more a colleague of Jacquie Carpenter. This one he'd have to do quietly and timing was of the essence.

'Mr Maxwell!'

Shit. Plan B.

'Ah, George, isn't it?'

'What a memory you've got, Mr Maxwell.' George was incredibly full of bonhomie considering it was nearly midnight. 'You still up at the school?'

'Yes, George, yes. I'll die there, you know that. Been here long?' Maxwell was mumbling, attempting to avert attention from the not quite sleeping policeman by the door. It was just his bad luck that George Wheelton had won, for three years running, the award for the Loudest Boy in the School.

'Ever since I left, Mr Maxwell. Five years now.'

'Good Lord. Well, George, got any vacancies?'

'Vacancies?' the young man looked a little nonplussed. Perhaps, in the hotel trade though he clearly was, this was a new word for him.

'Yes, you know, rooms?'

'But . . . you live here, Mr Maxwell. Don't you?'

'Oh, indeed,' Maxwell still had his back to the door, leaning forward and trying to cushion the sound. 'But a slight disaster has befallen me. Would you believe it, my roof's caved in.'

Now, five years on, Maxwell couldn't remember what George Wheelton would believe. Not that there was any law against a man staying in a hotel in his home town if such

111

was his wish. And after all, he *was* Mad Max and had a certain reputation.

'Well, that's unusual these days, isn't it?'

Great. George wasn't only loud, he had a degree in Stress Engineering.

'My own fault, I suppose.' Maxwell was in too deep now to beat an embarrassed retreat to the door. 'Spot of DIY that went wrong. Serves me right, of course. Now I'll *have* to get a man in.'

'Couldn't you sleep in the lounge?' George was trying to be helpful.

What was the matter with this lunatic? Maxwell wondered. Didn't he *want* to let a room?

'What, and miss the comforts of the Cunliffe?' he beamed. 'Got anything west-facing?'

'Ooh, now you've asked me,' George gurgled. Maxwell had forgotten that along with everything else, George Wheelton could gurgle for England.

'Just a joke,' Maxwell smiled. 'Anything will do. What time's breakfast?'

'Seven thirty to nine,' George told him. 'Could you just sign the book, Mr Maxwell?'

Mr Maxwell could and did.

'Could I have sight of a credit card?' George asked.

'Cash?' Maxwell hadn't brought his credit card. For fear.

'Well, that's unusual these days, too,'

George was gurgling again. 'Would you mind writing your address there, please, Mr M? Thanking you. Got any luggage? Only, it's just me on tonight and I can't really leave the desk.'

'No, that's fine.' Maxwell took the key. 'I'll sort it later. Goodnight.'

'Goodnight, Mr Maxwell.'

The boy's former Head of Sixth Form padded up the hideously carpeted stairs to his right, without so much as a toothbrush to his name, not before, however, he had noticed the Boy Detective making a little entry in his notebook. Bugger and poo.

*   *   *

Maxwell didn't sleep very much that night. The July darkness was oppressive under the duvet and his ribs were giving him gyp where Mr Intellectual had laid one on him earlier. Above all, what the Yawning Hippos had told him preyed on his mind. Why was Joe Public, that random bloke that Maxwell assumed just happened to be in the Gents in the Vine, rowing with Sally Meninger in the pub car park? And what did she mean, he was late? Late for what? All, no doubt, would be revealed come morning.

A couple of miles away, across town, the black and white killing machine that was Metternich the cat crashed through the flap

113

and took the stairs to the kitchen four at a time. Bugger! Nothing in the food tray again! Was the old duffer doing it deliberately? All right then; Plan B it was. He spun on his pads and thudded back down again, driving his bullet head through the Perspex. God help the rodent that looked at him funny tonight.

*   *   *

Ever mindful of the Celtic past of the area and of the tribe that once lived there, Maxwell had rather set his heart on the Full Atrebates for breakfast. He was up with the lark, but alas, later than George, still on duty and still on top of the world, who greeted him heartily as he entered the Mock Tudor dining room. Was *every* hostelry in Leighford designed by some Elizabethan ancestor of Lawrence Llewelyn Bowen?

'Morning, Mr Maxwell. Coffee or tea?'

'Coffee please, George.' Maxwell noted that the sleeping policeman of the night before had been replaced by an altogether more awake one. 'And white toast, before you ask.'

A couple of reps were sitting opposite each other in the far corner, where the sun streamed in through the morning patio, both on their mobiles and slurping coffee. An elderly couple were arguing over their kippers, as they had probably argued over them for the past forty years. Of the Ofsted team, Maxwell's quarry, there was no sign. He helped himself to orange juice, vaguely aware that he'd worn the same shirt now for twenty-four hours, give or take a few. But no one other than George would know that and George, when all was said and done, was wearing the same gear too.

'Ah, Ms Meninger.' Maxwell had not yet returned to his table. 'Fancy meeting you here.' Even Mad Max was allowed the occasional cliché. 'May I?' and the Head of Sixth Form had swept her chair out for her as he had learned to all those centuries ago when the world was young and politeness ruled O.K.

'Mr Maxwell,' she smiled at him. 'This is a . . . surprise. Bob, this is Mr Maxwell, Head of Sixth Form at Leighford.'

'Bob Templeton,' the suit with her shook Maxwell's hand. 'Don't tell me you're the last of the breed that actually lives in a hotel?' He was a lantern-jawed sort of man with a mane of tawny hair. In a bad light people could have mistaken him for Michael Heseltine or almost anybody out of the cast of the *Lion King*.

'Er . . . no. Bit of a DIY crisis last night.' If you're going to tell a whopper, Maxwell always reasoned, stick to it. 'Popped in here as less hassle than disturbing friends and neighbours. Look, I'm most terribly sorry about Alan Whiting.'

'It's outrageous,' Templeton hissed. 'Look at this.'

The *Mail* in his hand had banner headlines

115

for the second day running, this time with *Inspector Murdered—How Safe Are Our Schools?*

'How safe indeed?' Maxwell murmured.

'Apart from the rubbish they've spouted about Alan, what does it do for the cause of education? Where do they get this stuff? God, it's put Ofsted back ten years.'

'Have the papers been on to you?' Maxwell sipped his orange juice, making a mental note to buy a stash of Dailies later.

'We aren't allowed to talk to anyone,' Sally Meninger said pointedly. 'Anyone at all.'

'Well, they've got it from somewhere.' Templeton was tucking in noisily to his cornflakes. 'You'd think these people would have something better to do than turn over rocks.'

'It's what they're paid for, Bob,' Sally reminded him and noticed the ever-jovial George hovering, pen in hand, at her elbow. 'Just coffee, thanks.'

'Sir?'

Templeton wrestled with a mouthful of cereal. 'Full English, please. No hash browns.'

'Are you sitting over here now, Mr Maxwell?'

'If I may?' Maxwell's question had not yet been answered.

'Well . . .' Sally was a little guarded.

'Of course.' Templeton waved for the man to stay put. 'Come on, Sally, we're all in this together, you know. After all, Alan *was* killed

116

in Maxwell's school. Ah, Malcolm. How's it hanging?'

Maxwell had seen *Liar! Liar!*. He knew the correct answer to that one, à la Jim Carrey, was 'small, brown and always to the left' but he somehow sensed that Malcolm wasn't a Jim Carrey fan. He had the appearance of an old walrus, with a ludicrous toothbrush moustache whose bristles he had allowed to run riot over his upper lip and some of his lower. Were it not for the fact that he was bald, he would have put Maxwell in mind of the late and not very great Harold Macmillan, but not so lively.

'Hmm,' was Malcolm's welcome to the day.

'Malcolm, this is Peter Maxwell, Head of Sixth Form at Leighford.' Templeton was doing the honours now. 'Malcolm Harding, Science and Maths.'

What a ghastly combination, Maxwell thought, but he smiled sweetly and took the man's peremptorily-offered hand. 'Morning.'

'Have you seen the *Mail*, Malcolm?' Templeton asked.

'No. I only read *The Times*. And then only the Foreign Section. You can't trust British papers to report their own affairs properly.'

That logic escaped Maxwell, but he had more important topics to debate. 'Have the police talked to you all?' he asked.

'Oh, yes,' Templeton said, sliding his cereal bowl away. 'I had a young Detective Inspector, name of Bathurst, I think. Seemed reasonably

117

efficient. Who did you have, Malcolm?'

'Just mineral water, please.' Harding was talking to the oft-returning George. The man was a martyr to dyspepsia and the sudden death of a colleague didn't help matters. 'I had a woman. Can't remember her name or rank. Auburn hair. Quite feisty.'

Maxwell smiled. Her name was Jacquie Carpenter and she was a Detective Sergeant. He was in love with her.

'Didn't you have the top man?' Templeton asked Sally.

The woman was clearly reluctant to engage in conversation of this type with Maxwell, of all people, sitting there. 'Yes,' she said eventually. 'DCI Hall. I couldn't help him.'

'David.'

The last male member of the Ofsted team had joined them now, the Lay Inspector whose responsibility covered extra-curricular stuff and those odds and sods schools did which didn't fit easily into a classroom. He was tall and rather stooped, with wild, wispy hair that seemed to have a life of its own. His eyes were coal-black and piercing.

'This is David Simmonds,' Templeton said. 'Peter Maxwell . . .'

'Head of Sixth Form. Yes, I know. Your fame precedes you, Mr Maxwell.'

'Does it?' Maxwell groaned. 'Oh God.'

'Does the name Selina Barrington mean anything to you?'

118

'Selina?' Maxwell repeated. 'Indeed. One of the finest historians it's been my privilege to teach. Left us four years ago. Oxford. Trinity, I believe.'

'That's very impressive,' Simmonds had shaken his head and sat down. 'I'll just have some toast, please,' he nodded to George, who was actually itching to get rid of the kipper plates of the old couple. 'But no more than I'd expect. Selina's my niece. Spoke very highly of you.'

'Well, that's nice of her,' Maxwell smiled. 'And what a small world. Tell me, Inspectors, do you get any choice in the schools they send you to?'

'No, no,' Templeton told him. 'We just go where we're sent.'

'Will the Inspection go ahead?' Maxwell asked. It had been two days now since any of the team had been seen in school.

'On hold,' Harding said. 'And in the meantime, we're cooped up here.'

'Apparently, we're to wait until tomorrow,' Simmonds said. 'Orders from Head Office. Personally, I'm in Wiltshire week after next.'

'I've got Basingstoke,' Harding rumbled.

'Oh, bad luck, Malcolm,' Templeton grinned at him. 'Still, you can get cream for that these days.'

'And where are you off to, Ms Meninger?' Maxwell asked her.

'Yorkshire.' She was on her feet. 'The Dales.

Skipton, to be precise. Should be rather pleasant this time of year, don't you think? Look, I'm going to dig Paula out. The police are coming back for a second interview with all of us this morning, Mr Maxwell. Paula's on first,' and she was gone, swaying her way across the dining room in a pale reflection of her performance at the Vine on Monday night, the routine she'd gone through with the late lamented.

'So,' Maxwell waited until she was out of earshot. 'People, tell me about Alan Whiting . . .' and George returned, carrying Maxwell's Full Atrebates on a plate.

*   *   *

Thursday was a relatively civilized day for Peter Maxwell. He had a free third period which meant that he could get down to the dining room ahead of the hordes and get the lovely Sharon to flambé his crêpes to perfection; either that, or he'd be in with a chance on the pizza and chips. Before that, he had a double helping of European History with Year Twelve, discussing the nuances of Napoleon III's waxed moustache and whether therefore there was any consequential link with Nietzsche, David Lloyd George and Adolf Hitler.

But today was no ordinary Thursday. The police tape still closed the Aitch Block

120

corridor; Dierdre Lessing was less than enchanted that Henry Hall had commandeered her office to have a base on site and half of what was formerly Fleet Street had camped out along Wellington Road where they'd built the school back in the sixties. Kids of all ages were being seduced into sound-bites despite the oft-assured integrity of members of the Fourth Estate. Carrying skateboards and wearing their baseball caps backward, they were a credit to their school and their generation. Maxwell of course would have summarily hanged a couple in the quad each morning, to encourage the others. It would be wonderful how, quickly after that, the skateboards and the baseball caps would disappear and there would be an instant return to the Good Old Days. But Peter Maxwell was a dinosaur, you couldn't get a Lottery grant for the erection of gallows and the Good Old Days had gone for ever. Even so, the collective inside knowledge of Years Seven, Eight and Nine could only fill a book of postage stamps, Year Ten were habitual fantasists and Year Twelve, Maxwell's Own, were following their Year Head's directive not to talk to the Press. And the Fourth Estate itself, of course, had to tread warily. They had, astonishingly, a code of conduct, and parents sued these days.

Be all that as it may, Leighford High was experiencing something of a siege mentality. Inside, the foreign legations tried to behave as if nothing was wrong while at the gates of the Forbidden City, hordes of fanatical Boxers screamed and bayed for a story

On his way in, Maxwell had risked being scraped all over the town's one way system by carrying an armful of dailies. The *Mail* said that Alan Whiting was married, with three kids. The *Express* said he was a single gentleman. The *Daily Sport* said he'd had sex with three kids, but it was not clear whether they were his own or somebody else's. The consensus in the less silly papers was that the dead man's wife's name was Pamela and that she was staying at a hotel in the area pending police investigations. The fact that DCI Hall had made only the briefest of banal comments implied he'd made virtually no headway at all.

Someone who may have got somewhere, however, was slamming her window shut as Peter Maxwell popped his head around the door.

'Matron mine,' he smiled. 'Got a moment?'

There was a time when Sylvia Matthews had had endless moments for Peter Maxwell. But time and the hour had torn them apart and now they were comfortable with that. He would go through the shredder for her and she would walk over hot coals for him. She was still a stunningly attractive woman, with a warmth that could heat the Centre Block, but on this particular morning, the room was suspiciously empty.

'I saw you crossing the quad,' she said, putting on the coffee and pre-empting his question. 'So I gave the walking wounded their hobbling orders. I reckon we have about . . . ten minutes before Fat Josh arrives with his Off Games excuse-me pains.'

'Legs cancelled the Heaf tests, then?' Maxwell moved the well-chewed copy of *Seventeen* off the chair and collapsed against the wall.

'Didn't want any strangers on site,' Sylvia said. 'You know what maniacs work for the NHS.'

Maxwell did, but both of them knew in their heart of hearts that this was actually one of Diamond's better decisions. 'I've had no chance to touch base with you, Sylv. What news on the Rialto?'

'Olly Carson saw an unidentified man on the premises minutes before the fire-alarm went off on Monday.'

'Olly Carson?' Maxwell grimaced. 'Isn't he our unofficial Leighford UFO spotter?'

'Well . . . yes,' Sylvia had to concede. 'You should be proud of him, Max. He writes very long, detailed articles on crop circles and animal mutilations. He's shown me a few. They're not at all bad.'

Maxwell sighed, gratefully sipping from the mug she'd passed him that said 'Nurses Do It In Order To Catch A Doctor'. 'Has it never occurred to you, dear Matron, that at dead of night, the weird little alien *making* those crop circles and mutilating said animals is Olly Carson?'

'Oh, now, Max. He's odd, I'll grant you; strange even, but he's not dangerous.'

'All right,' Maxwell knew a straw when he clutched at it. 'What did Olly say he saw?'

'Chap in a boiler suit.'

'Not silver, was it?'

'Max,' Sylvia growled. 'I didn't actually ask him. I just let him go off on one, you know, like he does.'

Maxwell knew. 'Where was this chap of the boiler suit?'

'Well, that's the pertinent thing.' Sylvia gave Maxwell a Chocolate Chip Cookie to dunk. 'Heading for Aitch Block.'

'Was this before or after the alarm went off?'

'Before.'

'How long before?'

'Christ, Max, I don't know,' she said, a little riled by his attitude. 'Nobody expects the Spanish Inquisition, for God's sake.' She'd long been a Python fan.

'They do in my classroom,' he smiled.

'Minutes; I just don't know. You'll have to ask him.'

'Yes,' Maxwell sucked his teeth. 'I was afraid you'd say that. I'm just not sure I have the intellectual stamina.'

She scuttled round to her side of the desk

and did incomprehensible things on the keyboard, checking today's attendance records on the System. 'Your luck's in,' she told him. 'He's not.'

'Ah, one of the Withdrawn, eh? I get the distinct impression we've lost quite a few over the last couple of days.'

'I get that impression too,' she said.

'All right,' he leaned back against her height chart. 'Back to Olly. Did he give you any sort of description of this intruder?' He bit his lip rather than add, four feet high with grey skin, no ears or mouth and large, limpid eyes.

Sylvia was shaking her head. 'Nothing. Just your average Joe.'

'Joe?' Maxwell sat up.

'Just a figure of speech, Max,' she said. 'Olly had no idea what his name was.'

'No, no,' Maxwell was looking into the middle distance. 'There's another anonymous bloke that keeps turning up in this case. Thirty-fivish, dark hair. Wore a black leather jacket when I saw him and carried a hold-all. The question is, is Olly's Joe and mine one and the same?'

'Where did you come across him?'

'In a toilet, Nurse Matthews.' Maxwell finished his coffee just as Fat Josh, punctual as ever, put his less-than-engaging head round the door. 'And my private life is my private life. Love you to bits.'

He glanced down at the reptilian creature

125

whose bulk he squeezed past in the doorway. 'You too, Josh,' he said.

*　　　*　　　*

'Umbrella Man, Count,' Maxwell was tying his tie in front of his bedroom mirror. The cat was sprawled on his dressing table, casually licking the talcum powder off his paws. 'Badge Man, Black Dog Man, the Baboushka Lady. What do they all have in common, I hear you ask. Or do I hear you ask your altogether more frequent question,' he turned to face his silent inquisitor. 'Has the old buffer finally flipped his lid?' He turned back to the matter in hand. 'Well, possibly by feline standards,' he said. 'No, all the above were bystanders/co-conspirators/assassins in or around Dealey Plaza on November 21st 1963 when one or more of them put several bullets into the body and head of the late JFK. Then there was the mysterious lady in the polka dot dress involved in the shooting of his kid brother, Bobby. There was Mr Kipper who murdered Suzy Lamplugh, and a vast range of oddballs standing sweating in dark suits in Gowan Avenue the day Jill Dando was killed. Well, we've got one now—Boiler Suit Man. Oh, the sighting isn't impeccable, I'll be the first one to admit. Olly Carson; no, you wouldn't know him. In Year Ten. Bit of a UFO freak. Apparently he saw the boiler-suited gentleman on the premises minutes before Whiting died. You see, whoever set the fire alarm off killed the Inspector and he had to move quickly before Whiting did the obvious and vacated his office. So it was the fire alarm in Aitch Block or my name is not Ozymandias.'

The bow round his neck was perfect and Maxwell was pleased with himself. 'Look on my works, ye mighty, and despair. Oh bugger!'

There was that shattering ring and Metternich waited for the inevitable. Yep. There he went. Old man Maxwell picking up that plastic thing again.

'Max?'

'Darling?'

'Bad news, I'm afraid.'

'Does this mean you're not coming over?' he wailed in his best Jewish.

'I'm sorry, darling,' she said.

'Do I smell crisis, Woman Policeman Carpenter? That you should go to these lengths to miss Luigi's cannelloni, specially hand-rolled for you all the way from Perugia?'

'God, Max, you booked.'

'Thursday, sweets,' he reminded her. 'You have the world and his wife beating a path to Luigi's of a Thursday—ever since we started the trend, that is.'

'Sorry,' she said again.

'Can you tell me?'

There was a pause. 'Not really.' Then, 'Oh, sod it. Paula Freeling's gone missing.'

127

'Who?' Maxwell sat on the bed while Metternich took his moment to slink across onto the duvet.

'The other woman in the Ofsted team. She's disappeared.'

'God.'

It all came flooding back to Maxwell. It was Paula Freeling who had not joined them at breakfast that morning; Paula Freeling whom Sally Meninger had gone to find. And neither of them had come to the breakfast room before he'd had to leave. 'When was this?'

'When was she last seen, you mean?'

Maxwell sensed the lack of logic in it. 'Something like that,' he said.

'She didn't appear for breakfast at the Cunliffe. More than that, her bed hadn't been slept in.'

'So she was last seen last night?'

'The team took to playing a little gin rummy before retiring,' Jacquie told him. How unlikely was that? Maxwell thought. 'She went up before the others, about ten fifteen, ten thirty. Just said goodnight, as usual. We're checking the obvious places, of course, next of kin, friends.'

'Dragging the rivers?' To Maxwell, as much as to Jacquie, that, too, was an obvious place.

'We haven't got to that yet,' she said.

'I expect,' he said, 'you want to know what *I* was doing at the Cunliffe last night?'

'I *know* what you were doing,' she said. 'But

Henry Hall doesn't. And he would like a word.'

'Ah.'

'Max. Darling. You will be careful with this one, won't you?'

'Careful is my middle name, heart of hearts. Along with McGanderpoke.'

'All the same, I worry.'

'I know you do,' he laughed at her, ever so gently. 'Is there any need, any special need, I mean? God, I sound like Sally Greenhow.'

'Something . . . I don't know. Indefinable. I can't explain it, Max. Really, I can't. Just . . . well, just watch your back is all.'

'All right,' he said. 'I will.'

'I'll call you.'

'Darn tootin',' he laughed and hung up.

He turned to the mirror and hauled off the immaculately tied bow tie with a sigh. What a waste. 'So, Count. What'll it be? Frozen toad-in-the-hole for me, I think and scrag end of rat for you, eh? I'm not really sure I'm getting the better deal there.'

*   *   *

Bob Portal was coming on. Maxwell had glued his oilskin shako in place, although he knew perfectly well that many officers in Cardigan's Light Brigade wore their forage caps on campaign, not unlike the one now resting on the back of his head.

129

'Shit!'

Metternich had noticed that was often His Lord and Master's response when that ringing sound echoed from downstairs. The Master Modeller hung up his glue, threw down his cap and hurtled down the attic stairs. They'd invented cordless phones, for God's sake; why not cordless doors? He didn't recognize the shape through the distorting twists of his frosted glass front door. The cat of course went by the smell as much as the sight and did a U-turn on the stairs, not altogether happy with this one.

'Mr Maxwell,' the voice said as he opened the door. 'It's late. I shouldn't have come.'

'Not at all, Ms Meninger. Won't you come in?'

She hesitated in the doorway. 'If you make it Sally,' she said.

'Sally it is,' he nodded. 'Most people call me Max.'

That was true enough. Only a brave few also called him Mad.

Chapter Six

'I won't waste time on pleasantries,' she said, looking round for an ashtray. 'Do you mind?' The ciggie was in her hand already.

'Do I mind the lack of pleasantries or do I mind your smoking?'

'Either,' she said. 'Both.'

He slid an ashtray from the drawer of his coffee table. 'Would you like a drink?'

'I don't suppose you have a vodka?'

''Fraid not. I'm a Southern Comfort man myself.'

'That's fine.'

He poured for them both and handed her a cut glass of the amber nectar. 'So . . . Sally,' and he raised his glass to her.

She exhaled sharply. 'Like I said, I shouldn't have come.'

'But you're here now.' He lolled back, giving her time, giving her space.

'I thought about how this would go. Ever since this morning when you joined us for breakfast.' She looked at the ceiling. 'Got your repairs done?'

He caught the look on her face and burst into laughter. 'Pathetic, wasn't it?' he said. 'A little subterfuge that was forced on me by Laughing George, your ever-eager Cunliffe lackey. I'd hoped to sneak in to the hotel anonymously and that would give me all night to dream up a better excuse for being there. But when Decibels George greeted me with such bonhomie and announced to the world who I was, well, I had to think rather more quickly.'

'So why were you really there?' Sally too leaned back, opposite Maxwell, posturally echoing him. 'At the Cunliffe?'

'A man is dead,' he said solemnly.

She sat upright, flicking ash into its receptacle. 'Yes,' she said. 'That's why I'm here. I'm told you have a reputation for . . . getting to the bottom of things like this.'

'What are things like this, Sally?' he asked her. 'I've a feeling you know considerably more than I do.'

She hesitated for a moment then stubbed out her cigarette and fumbled in her handbag. She put a large brown envelope down on the table between them.

'What is it?' he asked. To Peter Maxwell, a buff envelope meant a bill.

'It's for you,' she told him.

'I repeat . . .'

'It's five thousand in cash,' she said quickly, watching his face, gauging his mood. 'There's more where that came from.'

He put his glass down next to it, looking at the envelope as though it were a loaded revolver.

'I know what you earn, Max,' she said. 'You're on a Scale Four. Retirement's . . . what

. . . three, four years away?'

'Five,' he corrected her. 'Assuming the government doesn't have its wicked way and keep us all on until we're ninety. But I'll forgive the ageist slur. How much more?'

'What?'

'You said there was more. How much more?'

'That depends . . .'

'On what?'

'Max,' she paused, wanting to slow down the conversation, steady the moment. 'I don't want you to go all moralistic on me, start spouting Puritan cant and throw me out. There's too much at stake.'

'Au contraire.' Maxwell sat back again, playing it her way. 'As the late, great Sir Robert Walpole once said, "Every man has his price".'

'And what's yours?' she fished out another cigarette and her face flashed fire in Maxwell's lamplight as she lit it.

'That all depends on what this is for.' He tapped the envelope with his foot. 'What does this buy you?'

Sally thought for a moment. 'Discretion,' she said. 'Circumspection. At the very least an open mind.'

'Ah.' Maxwell reached for the bottle to replenish their drinks. 'Those old things.' He could give Sally Meninger a very long list of children he taught whose minds were perfectly open, always. 'You know, Sally, this could be an expensive time for you.'

She looked at him carefully. Had she so easily got his measure? 'Okay, Sir Robert,' she said. 'Name your price.'

'Well, you see,' he told her, 'that's the problem. It's not just *my* price, is it? It's Ben Holton—he's on a Scale Three, by the way. Sally Greenhow likewise. Then there's dear old Paul Moss on a Two. Your cheapest option is Jeff Armstrong, but even so that's quite a tally. What's the government paying people like you these days—fifty, sixty grand?' He shook his head. 'Wouldn't pay for my modelling habit.'

'I don't see . . .'

'We were all there, Sally,' he reminded her. 'Monday night in the Vine. We all saw your little display.'

She was flicking ash again. 'I wasn't talking about that,' she said darkly.

'Oh,' he smiled at her. 'You mean the other.'

'It wasn't what it seemed.'

'No,' Maxwell said. 'It rarely is.' And he picked up the envelope. 'Take this away, Sally,' he said. 'I don't want your money. Whatever you're up to is your business. I want no part of it.'

She hesitated for a moment, gnawing her lip with uncertainty. Then she took it and stuffed it back into her handbag. She was on her feet already. He stood up with her.

'Must you go?' His tone was mocking, chill. He didn't indeed want to sound like a Puritan, but the woman had insulted him, annoyed him. She however was softer. She stubbed out the cigarette and stood close to him.

'I actually came for your help,' she said.

'I know,' he nodded.

'No,' she shook her head. 'I don't mean the money. I told you . . . your reputation.'

'Talk to the police, Sally,' he said. 'I'd only muddy your waters.'

'You don't know that.'

He looked into her large, blue eyes. Was there a softness behind them he hadn't seen before? A vulnerability? Under the pencil skirt and the coiffured hair and the silk scarf was there a little girl lost?

'All right,' he said. 'Let's start this again, shall we?' and he motioned her to sit down.

'Where shall I start?' she asked him.

'Why not,' he smiled, 'at the beginning.'

*   *   *

This time the doorbell rang more persistently. This time, through the twisted glass and under the porch light, Maxwell knew the shape all too well.

'Chief Inspector Hall,' the Head of Sixth Form beamed, looking at his watch. 'On the late shift? I was about to retire.'

135

'Hmm,' Hall looked at him. 'We all have that to look forward to. Do you mind?'

'*Mi casa, su casa,* Chief Inspector,' and Peter Maxwell led the man up the stairs to his lounge. Here, for Maxwell, was a state of relative devastation. Hall took it in with his trained snooper's eye. Two glasses, one half full on the coffee table. Several cigarette ends in the ashtray, in the house of a man Hall knew didn't smoke. 'You'll think my house a common stews,' the Head of Sixth Form said, paraphrasing Kipling, 'and me a careless host. I was going to leave it all 'till the morning, you know how it is.'

Henry Hall didn't. His wife was a stickler for tidying everything away that night. With three boys in the house, it was all too easy and chaotic to leave it all 'till the morning. Hall took a subtle sniff. Had Maxwell changed his aftershave recently?

'Can I offer you a drink, Chief Inspector?' Maxwell asked.

'It's a little late for me,' Hall declined. 'I'll have a seat, though.'

'Sorry,' Maxwell brushed a pile of exercise books aside. 'Please.' When they were sitting comfortably, Hall launched into it. 'Can you tell me what you were doing at the Cunliffe last night?' he asked.

Maxwell wasn't surprised by this. He'd seen the policeman only half dozing in the hotel lobby and Jacquie had tipped him the wink.

Even so, it was a little odd that the DCI himself should come calling, a domiciliary and at this hour. 'Which version would you like?'

Hall looked at him. 'You mean there's more than one?'

'There's the one I told the hotel's desk porter and the Ofsted team and there's the truth.'

'You really are a work of art, Mr Maxwell,' Hall was shaking his head at the sheer effrontery of the man.

'Both, then,' said Maxwell. 'The subterfuge was that my roof had caved in. The truth was I wanted to find out what happened to Alan Whiting.'

'Well, you certainly call a spade a spade.'

'Look, Chief Inspector, we've been here before, you and I. Sudden deaths are the meat and two veg of your life because you're a detective. They happen around me because . . . Well, I wish I knew. It's been like this ever since Jenny Hyde, remember?'

Hall did. Jenny had been a student at Leighford High and she'd been strangled, her body dumped at a decaying old house at the edge of the town. It was then he'd first met Peter Maxwell, as mad as his nickname. 'Jenny Hyde was different surely?'

'One of Maxwell's Own,' the Head of Sixth Form said. 'Yes. That's why I got involved. All right, so I didn't know Alan Whiting from Adam and he wasn't in my sixth form. But he

137

died feet from where I teach, as much on my patch as it is on yours. More. That sort of makes it my business, I'd say.'

'I'm sure you would,' Hall nodded. 'But I'm sure you'll understand when I say you're wrong.'

'Oh, yes,' Maxwell smiled. 'So what is this? The "stay out of it or we'll give you a smacking" speech?'

Henry Hall was never known to smile. 'I'm laughing inside, Mr Maxwell,' he said. 'But in all seriousness, there are two ways this can go. Either you tell me everything you know—and not just your movements on the day in question, but *everything*—or I arrest you for interfering in a police investigation.'

'Well,' Maxwell leaned back. 'That certainly cuts out the middle man.'

'Talking of middle men,' Hall's glasses were as blank as ever, even in the late night dimness of Maxwell's lounge, 'Where is Jacquie in all of this?'

'Ms Carpenter and I . . .'

'. . . are just co-conspirators,' Hall finished the sentence for him. 'Yes, I know.' He stood up abruptly. 'If you care for her at all, Mr Maxwell,' he said, 'you'll leave this one well alone. I'll see myself out.'

*   *   *

The long, good Friday began under a golden sun. The Geography Department might

138

launch the odd government warning about Global Warming, but ordinary people thought it was great. The Saga People were out and about bright and early too as Maxwell's White Surrey whizzed past their coach. He caught the glare of the sun dazzling on their bright new hairdos and their flashing old teeth as he skirted the seafront and made for the hill.

'Good morning,' he swept his hat off to the paparazzi at the school gates. 'I've got some great dirt on the Pope, if you're interested. Catch me later.'

'Who the fuck was that?' the *Mirror* man wanted to know.

'One of the idiots we entrust with our children's education,' the *Mail* man told him. And that little vignette summed up the state of our newspapers today.

He tethered Surrey in the usual place and roared at Gary Spenser, 'I'm sure Mr Diamond wouldn't approve of that, Garrence,' and he swiped the lad's grubby copy of *Men Only*, 'and it'll be at least twenty years before you're eligible to read any of this. Assuming, of course, that you can still see by then.'

'Aw, sir!' Gary whined, but he knew a fair cop when he saw one. No point in taking this one to the Court of Human Rights.

Maxwell tossed the mag into his office bin as he reached the door, only to find Dierdre Lessing standing inside with a face like a smacked arse. 'Senior Mistress,' he bowed.

139

'This is an unlooked-for pleasure.'

Dierdre Lessing had interfered with Maxwell's Sixth Form before—not in any way in which the *News of the World* might be interested, but just enough to make the Great Man see red.

'Your weekend reading, Max?' she nodded at the magazine.

'Tut!' he flung his hat onto the table. 'Fie, for shame that you should even think such a thing. I'm a rubber man myself.'

Dierdre didn't doubt it. She closed the door. This was ominous. Any minute now she'd plunge the room into blackness and slash him with her carefully secreted Bowie knife.

'Can we talk?'

He checked his watch. 'I have a small window in my day,' he said. 'Before I throw my pearl necklace to assorted swine. What's the matter, Dierdre?'

'Max,' she was looking out of the window where the snail schoolboys were dragging themselves into the building, not a satchel between them, but a mobile each. 'We've had our differences over the years, I know.'

Vive la difference, thought Maxwell, but he was too much of a public schoolboy to say so. 'There have been times,' he conceded, 'when I felt we weren't singing from the same hymnbook.'

'Max,' she turned to face him, 'I've got something on my mind, something I shouldn't know, but I do. Oh, dear, this is being so disloyal.'

He crossed to her, risking the Gorgon stare that could have turned a lesser man to stone. 'Has this anything to do with Alan Whiting's death?' he asked her.

She nodded, looking down. Maxwell had never seen Dierdre upset before. Someone had pushed her tenderness button. 'I'm afraid it might,' she said.

He sat her down, taking her shoulders in his grip. 'Come on, old girl. Maybe that hymnbook was the same after all. I was probably just reading mine upside down.'

She looked up at him as he sat on the nasty County-Hall-chosen furniture alongside her. Her eyes were brimming with tears. 'It's James,' she said. 'James Diamond.'

'What is?' he frowned.

She took a breath and launched herself, like many a battleship Maxwell thought she resembled. 'Yesterday, about half two it was, I went to see the Head. It's the old shorts issue again, you know.'

Maxwell did. Every year the shorts issue came up, the brazen hussies of Year Twelve and Ten wearing the skimpiest of netherwear. This year of course the obsession for driving red hot needles into one's navel and showing a Faberge-like cluster of jewels to a gawping world, contrived to make it less and less likely the girls would be wearing anything below the waist come September. Looked at in a positive way, it would save time behind the bike sheds later.

'I should have knocked,' Dierdre was saying, as though to her Father Confessor. 'I should have knocked and I didn't. Oh, Max, it was terribly wrong of me. So is this . . .' She was halfway to her feet when he stopped her.

'Let it go, Dierdre,' he said softly. 'Better we know. Both of us.'

She looked into those dark, flashing eyes. God, how she hated the man. Yet now, he was her dad, her big brother, the husband she'd loved once and lost, her priest. She wanted to tell him, wanted to trust him, just this once . . .

'I opened the door,' she said. 'She was in there.'

'Who?'

'Sally Meninger.'

'And?'

'They were . . . canoodling, Max. There, in his office.'

Maxwell's hands fell away from her shoulders and he sat there, open-mouthed. 'Canoodling?' he had to hear the word again to convince himself he hadn't misconstrued the first time. 'We are talking about Legs Diamond here, Dierdre, the most insipid . . .'

'Max!' she bellowed, on her feet now, dry-eyed, Morgan Le Fay again, chewing on men's bones in her blood-slick lair.

'All right.' He followed her to the window,

142

hands in the air. 'I'm sorry, Dierdre. I shall need details.'

'What?' she spun to face him. 'So you can gloat?'

'She came to see me last night,' he told her. 'Sally Meninger.'

'What? At home?'

He nodded. 'I think we're talking chameleon-woman here, Dierdre. She's involved and she's scared. Now tell me *exactly* what you saw in Diamond's office.'

Dierdre Lessing was taking several deep breaths. This was Mad Max, the man who had solved the murder of Jenny Hyde, the man who had faced lunatics with high-powered rifles. Insufferable old fart he undoubtedly was, but he got results. 'They were the other side of his desk,' she said. Maxwell could picture the scene. 'They had their arms around each other. He was kissing her.'

'Fully clothed?' he checked.

'Of course,' Dierdre snorted. 'Good God, Max. There's a limit.'

'Is there?' he asked her. 'I wonder. Think back, Dierdre—when Whiting came on that preliminary visit, the one before half term, did Sally come with him?'

'No,' Dierdre said. 'He was by himself. Why?'

He brushed past her to consult his desk diary. 'You're privy to the Ofsted timetable. What is it?'

'How do you mean?'

'How many sessions did Sally have with the Headmaster? Before the balloon went up, I mean?'

'None, as far as I know.'

'None?' Maxwell looked at her.

'Why should she? She's Humanities and Pastoral. She may have had a plenary session with him and the others and I daresay she'd be in at the final briefing—that was supposed to be happening this afternoon. But the only one who had one-to-ones with James was Alan Whiting.'

'Not much time to strike up a relationship, then?' Maxwell asked.

'None at all, I shouldn't have thought.'

'Unless Sally is a *very* fast worker.'

'I still can't believe I saw what I did. Poor Margaret.'

'Poor Margaret indeed,' agreed Maxwell. Diamond's wife deserved a medal for marrying the lacklustre git in the first place.

'What did she come to see you about?' Dierdre asked.

'One thing at a time,' Maxwell brought her back to the here, the now. 'What was their reaction when you walked in on them?'

'Well, James was flustered. You know how he blushes in moments of stress?'

Maxwell did, but unlike Dierdre apparently, found it less than cute.

'He straightened his tie, came out with

144

something about a rescheduling of the Inspection and sort of . . . hopped from foot to foot.'

'Par for the course,' Maxwell muttered. 'What about her?'

'Well,' Dierdre was letting her Puritan streak hang out. 'If you ask me, she's no better than she should be. She looked like the cat that's got the cream.'

Some cream, Maxwell thought. Dierdre had already convinced herself that Legs Diamond was the innocent party, that Sally had thrown herself on him, tearing at his clothes and compromising him. 'Was he enjoying it?' he asked her.

'What?'

'The snog, the embrace, the moment of passion, the clacking of tongues; call it what you will.'

'Of course not,' she bridled.

'Dierdre . . .' His tone said it all.

'Oh, all right,' she flustered. 'Yes, if truth be told, he was. He was enjoying it. That's what's so . . . oh, Max. What can we do?'

'We, white man?' It was the old Tonto and Lone Ranger joke, but since Dierdre Lessing would deny ever having heard of the pair, it fell a little flat. He took her by the hand, leading her to his office door. '*You* do nothing. When you see Legs today, smile and nod as though nothing had happened. Leave the rest to me.'

145

He opened the door for her. 'What are you going to do?' she asked him. Outside in the corridor, the Leighford world was already buzzing, kids wondering who'd be left in their classes today and whether the law would be back to arrest anybody. They'd resist, of course and there'd be a fantastic shoot-out in the Sports Hall, all flak jackets and SWAT teams. Instead, for some of them at least, it was Double Physics.

'Me?' he said, watching the merry throng jostling its way down the corridor. 'I'm going to earn my embarrassingly inflated salary and teach some history.'

*　　　*　　　*

'Right.' Henry Hall's ham sandwiches lay like lead on his diaphragm. It was Friday lunchtime and the July sun was at its zenith, burning through the Venetian blinds in the Incident Room at Leighford Nick. 'Let's recap. Philip, Miss Freeling.'

'Paula Freeling,' Bathurst took centre stage in the smoke-filled, coffee-brown room. 'Last seen for certain in the Cunliffe, presumably making her way towards her room at some time during Wednesday evening. We know from the hotel staff that her bed had not been slept in—that was confirmed by Sally Meninger who went to call for her the next morning. Her handbag had gone which

146

presumably contained cash, credit cards and so on, but her suitcase and clothes were still in the room. None of the staff remembered seeing her after Wednesday's dinner.'

'What about surveillance?'

'Ah, well, there's a snag there, guv.'

Henry Hall wasn't surprised by this. Any police operation was only as good as the team. 'Who fouled up?' the DCI wasn't in the mood for papering over the cracks.

Bathurst shifted uneasily. He didn't like his lads exposed like this. Everybody was human. Well, everybody except Henry Hall. 'Roger King does admit to a little ziz, sir,' he said quietly.

Hall scanned the room. If Roger King had been standing in front of him, he'd let him have a totally different definition of being on the carpet. 'King was on the nine 'till six slot?' the DCI asked.

'Yes sir.'

'And this . . . ziz. Is DC King remotely aware of when or for how long he dropped off his twig?'

'He thinks . . . about twelve thirty, but he can't be sure.'

'Time enough for Miss Freeling to leave the building.' Hall was clarifying the situation. 'Or to be helped out by person or persons unknown. The Cunliffe doesn't have anything helpful, I suppose, like a video loop?'

'No, sir. At least, it has, but it's faulty.'

'Do tell,' Hall sighed. Twenty first century technology was wonderful were it not for the gremlins, the ghosts in the machines, the dipsticks to whom maintenance was an empty gesture. 'All right. Tell DC King I shall be seeing him in my office tomorrow morning, nine sharp. Clear?'

'Crystal, guv.' Bathurst could only protect his lads so far.

'Right. Where are we on Miss Freeling? Jacquie?'

'Spinster lady.' Jacquie took over from a grateful Bathurst. 'Fifty-eight years of age. Lives alone in Eastbourne. Local CID there have checked. She hasn't been home since last weekend. According to a neighbour, she left on Sunday afternoon. The Ofsted team seem to think she travelled by train. Southern Trains have yet to confirm this. Their computer was down yesterday and this morning.' She couldn't help an inner smirk. Infuriating though it was to police enquiries, it would have given the technophobic Peter Maxwell yet another chance to say 'I told you so.'

'Next of kin?' Hall asked.

'There's a sister in Colchester; another Miss Freeling who hasn't seen her sister in months. We're still checking on friends, but she seems to have been a bit of a loner.'

'Are we going *Crimewatch* on this one, guv?' somebody asked.

'No, no,' Hall was shaking his head. 'Chins

up, everybody. It's only Day Four. I've arranged a press conference for Monday. I don't want to break our stride as early as this. If we go public at the weekend there'll be questions about our efficiency. And that would never do, would it?' He scanned the room like Robocop. 'Especially for efficient, dedicated officers like DC King.' This wasn't like Henry Hall. Everybody in the room had worked with him before. He had his levels of tolerance, but they were usually higher than this and Jacquie couldn't remember him as waspish. 'She found the body,' Hall reminded the room.

'Allegedly seconds after Mr Peter Maxwell.' Geoff Baldock was a young man in a hurry. Reputations and promotion didn't come to blokes who sat on their arses all day long. One or two in the room, those in the know, risked sideways glances in Jacquie's direction. She ignored them.

'Who interviewed her?'

'I did, guv.' Pat Prentiss was reaching for his notepad. 'This was Tuesday, five thirteen. I've got it all on tape, of course.'

'Just the basics, Pat,' Hall nodded.

'Well, she was pretty shaken up at first, as you'd expect. Obviously, the thrust of my enquiry was Alan Whiting, what she knew about him and so on. She'd never worked with him before, although they did know each other.'

Hall had read all his team's interview transcripts and he'd made a start on listening

149

to the tapes. Even so, it didn't hurt to go over old ground, especially now that the focus had changed. 'In what context?'

'Various conferences, workshops, that sort of thing.'

'But never on an actual inspection?'

'No, guv.'

'Remind us of her movements last Monday,' Hall said.

Prentiss flicked back in the book. 'She was in the Music Department when the fire alarm went off. Seemed a little confused by it, apparently, but followed the crowds to the assembly area.'

'She was back sooner than most,' Hall observed. 'We've depositions from teaching staff that they got back to their rooms ahead of the hordes to get the little darlings back to work. But they know the short cuts and most of them are fit enough to double up. Was she fit, would you say, Pat, Miss Freeling?'

'Not in any sense of the word, sir,' the sergeant said and Henry Hall was content to let the ripples of laughter build around the room. Time, maybe, for a little light relief. But he'd still be seeing DC King in his office next morning, nine sharp.

*　　　*　　　*

'Could a woman have done it, Jim?' Henry Hall didn't like mortuaries. He liked corpses even less, especially now in the height of summer, when the blue-bottles droned, heavy with blood. It made his flesh crawl. Mercifully, he'd caught Dr Astley on the golf course, it being the good doctor's day off and the good doctor was less than pleased about that.

'It *could* have been the fairies, Henry,' he scowled as his ball sailed high through the blue to thump into a thicket. 'Shit!'

'Seriously, though,' Hall followed the cloth-capped pathologist as he rammed home his iron and hauled the bag over his shoulder. Above them was a cloudless sky and the breeze was stiffening from the south-west. Out to sea, a crowd of sails billowed together as the yachts went through their paces, making for the sea-roads of the Solent. Rich men without a care in the world.

'Seriously?' Astley looked at him. 'It's possible. The skewer was pretty sharp, wasn't it? I mean, I don't know much about these things. Contrary to every other family in the land, Marjorie always does our barbecues— excuse for her to nip the meths. Now, where the bugger is that ball?' He'd sloped off beyond the green to rummage in the rough.

'You're saying if the skewer was sharp enough, it could have been used by a woman?'

'Yes. How can you lose something that's brilliant bloody white?' He was hacking about in the undergrowth. 'But you've got the weapon, surely?'

151

'We have. It's your bog standard barbecue skewer. Comes with a spatula and a pair of tongs. Every garden centre and supermarket sells them, from here to John O'Groats. Except this one had been doctored.'

'Oh?' Astley paused in his vicious attack on the undergrowth. 'In what way?'

'The point had been filed.'

'That would make sense,' he nodded. 'The wound definitely tapered. No prints, of course.'

Hall shook his head. 'Chummy wore gloves.'

'Ever known this before?' Astley asked. 'Skewer as a murder weapon, I mean?'

'No,' Hall admitted. 'It's not text book. Still, pretty efficient though. Someone deliberately sets a fire alarm, runs a carefully prepared but otherwise anonymous skewer through a man's throat and disappears like the phantom fiddler.'

'Unless . . . Ah, you little bastard. Got you!' and he stooped to retrieve his ball.

'Unless?' For Hall, it was still Day Five, but high afternoon. It wouldn't be long before Day Five became Day Six. And the Press weren't getting any less impatient and Jim Astley had nothing to do but play a round all day.

'Unless it's an inside job. Why did you ask if it could be a woman? Got someone in the frame?'

Henry Hall didn't usually discuss cases with the pathologist. He and Jim Astley went back more years than either of them cared to

152

remember, but Astley was a difficult, arrogant bastard and his perspective wasn't always the right one. Even so, needs must when the devil drove. 'Possibly,' Hall said as Astley motioned him to stand aside. The breeze slapped the little flag that fluttered in Hole Eight and Astley crouched, shoulders down, lining up the ball and it.

'Say on.' Astley's swing thwacked the ball to bounce on the far side of the green before it rolled obligingly into a bunker. 'Well, for fuck's sake.' He glanced quickly around. He'd already received a threatening letter for using that sort of language in the Clubhouse. True, it was to the wife of the President, but you couldn't be too careful.

'Paula Freeling,' Hall said, trying out the sound in the blaze of a golf course on a sunny summer's afternoon.

'No,' muttered Astley. 'Never heard of her.'

'Oh, I think you will by tomorrow.' Hall sat himself down on the bunker's edge. 'The gentlemen of the Press will have twigged that Miss Freeling is the Ofsted inspector who got away.'

'Done a runner?'

'Perhaps. She was the one who found the body.'

'Bit obvious then, isn't it?'

'Finding the body, no. Actually, it's surprisingly common. Chummy, because he's obsessional or terrified or a smartarse, leads

153

the police to the crime by "coming across" the corpse. He helps said police with their enquiries. You've seen it before, Jim, I know.'

'I have.' Astley swung again, clumps of sand flying upward and, mercifully, a little white ball with them. 'So, what, the woman sets off a fire alarm, drives a skewer through her boss's throat? Why?'

'Indeed.' The DCI was growing more pensive by the minute. 'That is the sixty-four thousand dollar question. I don't know enough about either of them yet.'

'Well,' Astley's ball had clunked at last into the Eighth Hole. 'Got you, you little beauty! When and if, Heaven forfend, you find a woman's body, give me a bell. Until then, I can't be a whole lot of use, can I?'

*   *   *

'It won't take long, Headmaster.' Maxwell was standing along with the man, cheek by jowl as they made for Diamond's office.

'Well, good, Max.' The Head was a little flustered, it being Friday and all and an Ofsted inspector being murdered in his school. 'Because I have a Full Governors' at five.'

The Head of Sixth Form waited until the door had closed before he put a metaphorical toe into James Diamond's murky waters. 'Where did you say you knew Sally Meninger from?'

154

Dierdre Lessing had been right. The Head *did* blush, a rather mottled leprous inflammation spreading up above his tie-knot. 'I don't know what you mean,' he bridled. 'Who said I did?'

'Sally,' Maxwell lied.

'What?'

'What's the matter, Headmaster? Are you all right?'

Diamond rounded on him, his jaw flexing. His fists clenched. 'When did Sally say this? What did she say?'

'When? I really can't remember. As to what, well it was all rather vague, really. A sort of throwaway line. Is there a problem?'

He saw Diamond turn the colours of the rainbow before the man relented and slumped into his chair. Maxwell looked at him, a now colourless man in a colourless room, not a teacher but a manager; a suit held together by conference sound-bites and buzz-words. And the suit was worried and his paranoia was showing.

'Was that it?' Diamond scowled. 'Was that what this was all about? A Peter Maxwell fishing expedition?'

Maxwell clicked open the door. 'Better I reel you in than the law do, Headmaster,' he said. 'Because they've got an altogether bigger line than I have. I've been known to throw tiddlers back; but Mr Plod? Well, he quite often bashes their brains out on a rock. You enjoy your Full Governors', now, y'hear.'

155

Chapter Seven

It must be understood that Peter Maxwell didn't usually go out looking for fifteen-year-old boys on Friday nights. Leave that sort of thing to choirmasters and the Catholic church. No, he saw more than enough of them during the day, those curious denizens of the dark who normally shunned sunlight, who scowled under cowls throughout the winter and wore shorts down to their ankles in the height of summer. But this one was different. This was the anorak Olly Carson, who took his summer holiday in Roswell and whose bedroom door bore the triangular no-go sign 'Area 51'.

The sea was restless below the grass-blown cliffs that edged the Shingle, that spit of land that ran, like Nature's pier, out into the Channel. In the distance, the tankers crawled by in the evening sun, bright in their port colours and the gulls' wings caught the dying embers of its rays.

From the beach below, where the darkening headland had spread its chill, the chatter and laughter of the barbecuers came as snatches of a song, now soft, now loud and the dim, distant racket of the fairground.

Maxwell's brave new world had polarized tourists. Only the very young and the very old came to Leighford now. The bright young things were off to Ibiza or Tenerife; the bright old ones had fallen for John Thaw's old flannel and bought a cheap, crumbling house in Provence. And so the Leighford hotels charged more to keep profits up and so fewer people came and so Leighford spiralled downwards still further. One day it would be a ghost town in some post-apocalyptic world, with tumbleweed blowing along its deserted streets and bloated corpses rolling at the water's edge.

Maxwell's quarry did not concern himself with the micro-economics of an ageing seaside town. His sights were set on altogether higher things as he sat, knees under his chin on the grass of the headland, a bag of sustenance by his side, binoculars on the grass beyond that.

'Hello, Olly.'

'Mr Maxwell.' The lad jumped. Odd enough to be hailed at all, at sunset on a summer's day, but to be hailed by one of your teachers, and a mad one at that . . .

'You're supposed to say "What are you doing here?" and then I kill you.'

'What?' Olly Carson looked perplexed.

'Never mind.' Maxwell sat down beside the boy. 'May I?'

'It's a free country,' Olly shrugged.

'Ah, but is it, Olly?' Maxwell tapped the binoculars. 'I never took you for a twitcher.'

'Not the nervy type,' Olly assured him.

'No, I meant . . . what are the binocs for?'

157

Olly opened his mouth to say something, then changed tack. 'How did you know where to find me?'

Maxwell threw his hat down on the flattened grass, careful to avoid the sheep currants and tucked his knees up under his chin. Nothing like a bit of postural echo to make an oddball feel relaxed. 'What if I said I was just out for a walk and we just bumped into each other?'

Olly leaned a little sideways to look the man fully in the face. 'I'd say that wasn't true,' he said.

'Stout fellow,' Maxwell risked the wrath of Political Correctness and slapped the boy's shoulder. For two years he'd been trying to drum a healthy scepticism into Olly Carson and it seemed to have paid off. 'No, I went to see your dear old mum after school today. She told me where you'd be . . . approximately. Any luck?'

Maxwell noticed Olly's face darken. 'She shouldn't have told you, my mum. Had no right.'

'I expect she thought it was important, Olly—why I wanted to talk to you, I mean.'

'Is it?'

'Oh, yes.' He tapped the binoculars again. 'Any luck?'

Olly took his time, wrestling with himself. When people have spent years of their lives laughing at you—never with, just at—well, you've got to choose carefully. Maxwell was mad, but he wasn't barmy. The boy looked out to sea, feeling the breeze ruffle his hair. 'Too early yet,' he muttered.

'Too early?'

Olly nodded. 'What time is it?' he asked.

Maxwell checked his watch. 'Half eight,' he said.

Olly nodded. 'It'll be about nine, nine fifteen.'

'What happens?'

'Foo fighters.'

'I'm sorry.'

'Well, they're not really Foo fighters, of course. I just call them that.'

'Where do you see them, Olly?' Maxwell was well out on the ledge of no return now. He needed this boy's help, but he needed his trust, too. At the moment he was the old duffer who screamed at him every Thursday because he hadn't finished his GCSE coursework—didn't do much for bonding, that kind of thing.

'Usually low, over the horizon. Bit of a sea-mist building tonight. Might not be lucky.'

'What do you think they are?' Maxwell asked.

Olly shrugged. 'Don't know.' But Olly Carson had been here before. He was used to grown-ups patronizing him with transparently obvious suggestions, so he thought he'd beat Maxwell to it. 'They're not bird formations 'cos they're too fast. They're not clouds, even lenticular ones—I know the difference. They're not aircraft either 'cos the flight path is too erratic.'

'From which you conclude?' Maxwell was almost afraid to ask.

'They are semi-luminous, cigar-shaped objects which routinely invade our air space, travelling, as far as I can calculate, at speeds in excess of eleven thousand miles an hour. That's faster than any aircraft known to exist, Mr Maxwell. I've been observing them now for months.'

Maxwell didn't really know how to follow that. 'Do you come here often?' sounded impossibly clichéd even as it left the Great Man's lips, but Olly Carson was fifteen and, UFO-spotting apart, he didn't get out much.

'Every Friday and Saturday night,' the boy told him.

'But that's party time, isn't it? Down the Front, smashing windows and terrorizing old ladies.'

'I don't do that, Mr Maxwell,' Olly told him straight-faced.

'Tell me, Olly, how long do you stay up here on your own?'

Olly shrugged. 'Depends,' he said. 'Sometimes three hours, four. A couple of times I've stayed up all night.'

'All night?' Maxwell frowned. 'What does your mum say about all this?'

Olly turned away. 'Mum don't say nothing.

160

She's got a new boyfriend.'

Unlovable as Olly Carson was, the father in Peter Maxwell wanted to hug him. He'd been a dad once, long, long ago. And her photo was in his wallet now, on that darkening hillside, under his jacket—a little girl with eyes to drown in. A little girl who was gone. A little girl who was dead. He shook himself free of memories. 'Tell me about the fire drill, Olly,' he said.

'What about it?' This was one leap of logic too many for Olly Carson.

'Nurse Matthews tells me you saw someone; a visitor, not from the school.'

Olly nodded. 'That's right, I did.'

'This could be important, Olly,' Maxwell told him. 'Do you remember what he looked like, this man?'

'Wore a boiler suit,' Olly frowned, trying to reconjure it. 'Blue. Bit grubby. Had a baseball cap on.'

In the twenty-first century, that almost went without saying. 'Where did you see him, Olly?'

'Round the bike sheds, going towards Art. I was late getting down the stairs.'

'The bike sheds,' Maxwell mused. In his mind's eye, he pictured Leighford High's topography. The bike sheds were a stone's throw from the Art Department and the Art Department flowed into the Humanities Block as effluent down a sewer. 'Tell me, this boiler man, did he seem to know where he

161

was going?'

'Don't know,' Olly said. 'He wasn't going to the Assembly area, that's for sure.'

'What about his face, Olly? Height? Colour of hair?'

The boy was shaking his head. 'Sorry, Mr Maxwell,' he said. 'I wasn't really looking at him, you know, in detail.'

'No, of course not, Olly,' Maxwell sighed. 'Why should you? Have you told the police about this?'

'The police?' The boy looked askance. 'No fear. They're in on it.'

It was Maxwell's turn to frown. 'In on what, Olly?'

'The conspiracy,' the boy mumbled, checking from side to side. 'Crop circles, animal mutilations; whatever my Foo fighters are. Stands to reason. That's why no one knows what's causing it all. The cops say they'll investigate and then they do nothing. They're in on it, all right.'

Maxwell smiled at the strange, lonely lad on the hill. 'Well, Olly,' he said, creaking to his feet. 'You may well be right. Hope you get some good sightings tonight.'

'Thanks, Mr Maxwell . . . for not laughing at me, I mean.'

Maxwell winked at the boy. He'd never laugh at Olly Carson again.

*   *   *

162

'Shit!'

'What?'

Peter Maxwell sat up in bed, flinging the covers from him, wiping his face with his hand.

'Can't sleep, pet?' Jacquie was less than understanding in the bed next to him as she tried to focus in the sudden flare of the lamp. It had been a bitch of a day for them all.

'I'm sorry, darling,' he threw himself back on the pillow again. 'It's all whizzing round, you know, like it does.'

She knew. The terrors of the night, when the little things you said and the little things you did blend and blur with the huge things yet to be said and yet to do. It all adds up to the nightmares.

'Tell me,' she said, knowing how just talking brings things into perspective.

'The bike sheds.' Maxwell was now staring at the ceiling. 'If Boiler Man came from the bike sheds, he's not on video. The camera at that side of the building is a dummy.'

'We know that,' she told him. 'Pat Prentiss has been over the CCTV footage with a magnifying glass. Nothing.'

'But don't you see,' he sat up again, wishing at times like these, that he had taken up smoking. 'That proves it's an inside job.'

'What?' Jacquie was sitting up too now, tucking the duvet over her breasts in that pointless way that women have. 'Why?'

'Because he knew that the camera wasn't working. It's the only one of the five that doesn't.'

'Do the kids know that?'

'God knows,' Maxwell shrugged. 'Maybe. I don't know.'

'So what are we saying? One of the kids disguises himself as a Boiler Man by nipping off to the loo to change into a suit, nips back past the non-working camera and stabs an Ofsted inspector just so he can add it to his CV? Come on. Max, that's ridiculous.'

'It all depends,' he was wagging his finger in the half light, 'on how much we can rely on Olly Carson.'

'Well, you know him,' Jacquie said. 'What do you think?'

Maxwell wished she hadn't asked him that. 'This is a lad who watches cigar-shaped objects moving at umpteen times the speed of sound. He wanders the Shingle all night in search of an obsession. For all I know he's barking.'

Jacquie Carpenter knew Peter Maxwell of old. 'But you think?'

He looked at her. 'I think he's telling the truth. I think he saw what he says he saw. Maintenance men, contractors, parents, *anybody*, is supposed to report to Reception, at the *front* of the school where the CCTV picks them up. They have to sign the book and wear a badge. It's not foolproof, but if you're an honest citizen going about your business, it'll

164

do.'

'But if you're a killer bent on murder . . .'

'Then you bypass the system.'

'And you have to know how.'

'Which brings us back to an inside job.'

There was a silence between them. She lay down again. 'How many people know Leighford High?' she asked.

'God,' Maxwell flung himself down beside her. 'Nearly twelve hundred kids, eighty-plus teaching staff, over twenty auxiliaries, cooks, cleaners, groundsmen. And that's before we get to parents, old Hyenas, Governors, people coming for interviews. How many door-to-door have you got?'

He heard her chuckle gaily as she switched off the bedside light. 'Not nearly enough. Now, go to sleep, Peter Maxwell.' And she pulled the covers over her head.

'You mean we aren't going to play around?'

She half turned, reaching behind her, coming out with the old Ronnie Corbett joke. 'Don't tell me you've got a golf club down there?' There was a pause as her hand brushed against something. 'Oh, I see you have.'

And they laughed in the darkness.

*   *   *

'Fuck Saturdays!' The day had not gone well for Brian McGhee. He shouldn't have been here at all, but his fucking boss had rung last

165

night and asked him to fucking do the early morning shift. Well, fuck. Not for Brian the philosophical approach to life. Not for him the joy of helping his fellow man to enjoy a clean and sparkling water supply along the south coast of this great country of ours. He grunted at Mavis, his long-suffering wife who looked less alluring by the day, whichever kid it was, and Brian had more or less stopped counting by now, clamped to one of her breasts. He'd grabbed a cup of tea he'd had to make himself and now he was off to the delights of the Leighford Sewage Plant, Southern Water's show piece west of Brighton.

How fucking come, Brian wondered as he passed the hoarding with its glossy logo and its promise of a brave new water world, that he was actually up to his ankles in other people's shit all day. *And* on a Saturday.

But it was a different kind of other people's shit looking up at him from the bottom of the bore-hole and he'd had to sit down. He looked around. The sky was a cloudless blue, the sun climbing already and bouncing off his bright yellow hard hat. There was his van, where he'd parked it, keys still in the ignition, ready for the off later. There was the portacabin with that frosty bitch who handled the incoming calls on the Complaints Desk. He could hear the rattle and roar of the JCBs being started up on the far side of the site as Patel whatsisface kicked the beast into action. All

166

normal. Everything as usual. Except it wasn't. He got up again, eyes wobbling in the sweat that was running down his forehead and bouncing off his eyebrows. He rubbed his hands on his check shirt and squatted down so that his tools clunked in the leather belt around his waist. He bit his lip, screwed his courage to the sticking place and looked into the bore-hole again.

Down there, in the shadow where the sun had not yet burned, nothing was normal. A hand jutted above the level of the sand, its fingers curled, as though beckoning, saying softly through all the nightmares of his years ahead, 'Come on down.' Nearby a face, old, wrinkled, the mouth pursed, the eyes closed, the skin yellow with dust, protruded from the rubble. Brian McGhee sat back on his monkey wrench, utterly oblivious of the pain that shot through his right buttock.

'Fuck me,' he whispered.

*   *   *

Southern Water were no more enamoured of one of its sites being turned into a murder scene than was Leighford High School. But by lunchtime on that Saturday, that was exactly what had happened. Blue and white tape fluttered everywhere, police cars stood at rakish angles on spoil heaps and an unusually quiet Brian McGhee was helping their occupants with their enquiries, still sitting down, still trying to take it all in.

'What have we got, Phil?' the DCI was in his shirt sleeves, a sure sign of the mounting mayhem as well as the heat.

'Well, at first the site manager thought someone had wandered onto the site and slipped into that bore-hole over there. Now . . .' He was keeping pace with his guv'nor, striding across the yard stacked with every diameter of pipe.

'Now?' Hall wanted one sensible answer at least.

'Now, we know she used to be an Ofsted inspector and there's a deep incision through her throat.'

*   *   *

'It has all the hallmarks, Henry, if you'll excuse the pun.'

Dr Astley's voice sounded echoey, far away at the other end of the phone. That was because he was in Leighford Mortuary at the end of another blistering Saturday. Say one thing for morgues, they were excellent places to be in a heatwave.

'I didn't get you off the golf course?' Hall wasn't about to be Mr Popular and he needed all the friends he could get.

'Not at all. As a matter of fact, you got me out of a wedding. Some ghastly niece I haven't

168

seen for twenty years and her lout of a husband. Chap has earrings and, I understand, tattoos. Is it me or is civilization going backwards?'

'Civilization seems to be a pretty thin veneer in Leighford at the moment,' Hall commented. Even with the fan whirring in his office, his collar felt like a yard of tripe.

'Indeed. "I am down on Ofsted inspectors and I shan't quit skewering them 'till I do get buckled"—I'm paraphrasing, of course.'

'Of course.' Every senior copper in the county knew the famous Ripper letters, those hoaxes sent in by a sick prankster to muddy the Met's waters long, long years ago, when policemen had to be five feet nine, of good character and vaguely male. Even so, Hall was impressed that Astley knew it too. 'Nothing sexual?'

'Nothing yet,' Astley was peering intently at the pale naked corpse on his stainless steel. Hall knew that and was heartily glad they hadn't got video-phones yet. 'The old girl was fully clothed in the sand-pit thingy, wasn't she? As you know, Donald did the honours of stripping her while I was driving back from the wedding of the century. Christ alone knows what she was wearing.'

'The deceased?'

'No, my niece. It was some sort of black creation. She's a Goth, apparently. I always thought they'd sacked Rome or somewhere.

169

Strange that. Her mother's C of E.'

'Your man Donald . . .' Hall began.

'Yes, I know. I can only apologize. Given a head wind and about another four decades, he'll make a tolerable mortuary assistant. I shouldn't have sent him, really.'

'I couldn't find another GP in the whole bloody town, would you believe, to issue a death certificate,' Hall explained.

'I would believe that, dear boy. Ah, appendix scar. Ancient,' Astley was going about his grisly business as he cradled the phone in the crook of his neck. 'It is after all a Saturday in the sailing season and my profession, if it's in practice on the coast, owns boats. Otherwise, what's the point?'

'You don't,' Hall pointed out.

'Ah, but I'm not your run of the mill medical practitioner, dear boy. What's this woman's name, Henry?'

'Freeling. Paula Freeling.'

'Well, Ms Freeling—and I say that because I suspect she's still relatively *virgo intacta*—was tied up for a while.'

'Alive or dead?'

'Both.'

'Sorry?'

'Well,' Astley was concentrating on the dead woman's wrists, 'judging by these marks, I'd say she was tied up while still alive, her hands behind her back. Then she was killed. Then she was left, still tied. There seems to be extra

170

drag on the front of her forearms. I'd say she was standing up, tied to a pipe or something and when she died, she fell forward, but the ropes held her up.'

'They *were* ropes?' Hall was scribbling notes.

'Oh yes. Clear weave marks. It'll be a while before I can tell you what type.'

'Cause of death?' Hall had moved on. He'd had two bodies dumped in his lap in five days and he and the world wanted answers.

'Same old, same old,' Astley assured him. Peering again at the woman's throat. 'Neat as you please through the mid-line. I'd say our friend had more time on this one.'

He followed the dark red rivulets down between Paula Freeling's breasts. At the navel, they divided, like some sort of macabre delta and there were runs into her pubic hair and splashes on her thighs. The blouse, skirt, panties and bra that Donald had removed all bore smudges and splashes of the same.

'A skewer?' Hall checked.

'Consistent bastard, isn't he? Except that this time, presumably, there's no weapon,' Astley mused. He'd read the preliminary reports. 'Want my scenario, then, Henry?'

'I could do with somebody's,' the DCI admitted.

'She's been dead for a day, perhaps two.' Astley could hear Hall limbering up for an interruption on his end of the phone. 'Yes, I

171

know. Rectal temperature shemperature. I'd say something sick about the smile on the camel and the sphinx if I weren't a thoroughly well-brought-up medical student. Like civilization, we're going backwards on time of death, Henry. Sometimes I feel betrayed by my own science. I'll be lucky if I get the year right in the future. Maybe I'll take up carbon dating.'

Henry Hall knew that Jim Astley's dating days were over, but now wasn't the moment to say so.

'He did the deed in some sort of garage or warehouse. I've found diesel oil under the poor dear's fingernails. There's also severe bruising—ante mortem, by the way—on the upper arm. I'd say he grabbed her, pulling her with a fair degree of force. And at some point too, her knees were folded up, like a foetus. Lividity's obvious. Now, where all this happened of course, is anybody's guess, but Donald's buggered off already with her clothes, so your lab boys should be on that by now.'

Indeed they were. Hall had checked on that personally.

'She was killed in said garage or warehouse and left to bleed to death. She wouldn't have lasted long—minutes only. And there she stayed, I'd guess, for the best part of . . . ooh, six, seven hours. Then she was wrapped in a plastic bag.'

172

'What?'

'Plastic bag. Bits of it caught in her hair. There's something else, only I don't know what it is.'

'Something else?'

'Yes.' Astley was annoyed with himself when he couldn't cross tees and dot eyes. 'A residue of some kind, again in the hair. It's not sand from the bore-hole. I'll let you know.'

'Sooner rather than later, Jim?' Hall asked.

Had it been anybody else Jim Astley would have bitten the man's head off, miles apart or no miles apart. But he'd worked with Henry Hall now, doctor and policeman, for a long time and he recognized the desperation edging into the man's voice.

'You'll be the first to know, Henry,' Astley said, and, as he was about to hang up, 'Go home, Detective Chief Inspector,' he said. 'Tiredness kills.'

Hall let the phone click and whirr in this hand. 'So,' he said to the ether, 'does a maniac with a skewer.'

*   *   *

Maxwell had said it before. And Maxwell would say it again. Why, why, why did their lordships at the Horse Guards decide on dark blue for the colour of the Light Cavalry? That had been mistake one, some vague indefinable time in the 1750s. Mistake two was that Messrs

173

Humbrol, paint manufacturers to the gentry, excellent colour-meisters though they were, did not make a colour of the self-same hue. So obsessive oddballs like Peter Maxwell had to *mix* the colours themselves—just the right blend of black and blue. And once this was made up, it had to be used quickly before it went solid and unusable.

'Bugger! Bugger! Bugger!' The inevitable had happened. Maxwell had just blended his colours to perfection, to begin work on plastic Bob Portal's jacket and overalls, when the doorbell rang. He checked the clock across the attic from his modelling chair. Half eight. The dying sun was still streaming in through his skylight as he popped the brush back into the white spirit, hung his pill box on its hook and legged it down the stairs.

Who could this be? He knew it wasn't Jacquie. She'd rung him that afternoon with the news of the finding of Paula Freeling's body and the equally unwelcome information that all police leave was cancelled and the Home Office was about to cop a packet in overtime payments. Couldn't be the Kleeneze man. He only ever called on Wednesdays. If it was the little shit from Number Thirty-Two wanting his ball back again, Maxwell would risk the law suit and shove it right up his . . .

'Mr Maxwell?'

An attractive brunette stood in the Great Man's doorway. She clearly had not come for

174

her ball and didn't look as if she knew how to pronounce Kleeneze.

'Yes?' he said.

'I'm Pamela Whiting. May I talk to you?'

*   *   *

Maxwell was not good around widows. A widower himself, he still remembered the empty small-talk his friends made in the days after his wife died. The futility of it all; the attempt to make the time fly, to put a decent distance between death and life; between then and now. He gave the woman a stiff drink and sat in his lounge, waiting.

'I don't know what you must think of me,' Pamela Whiting said. 'Just turning up on your doorstep like this.'

'I don't know,' Maxwell said, 'if there are any words . . .'

She held up her hand, fighting with all the emotions he had all those years ago. He imagined her wrestling with the same old questions—why him/her? Why us? And why, the most guilty question of all, why me? 'I don't want words,' she said, 'I want action.'

'Action?' Maxwell frowned. 'May I ask . . .'

'Your Head, Mr Diamond. He suggested I come and see you.'

'Legs?' Maxwell was amazed. 'I don't know whether to be horrified or just plain old suspicious.'

175

'Suspicious?' She looked quizzical.

'Let's just say, Mrs Whiting, that Diamond and I carry rather a lot of baggage between us. He and I are the British Airways of Leighford High. But why would he . . .'

'I went to see him,' she explained. 'It wasn't a good time. He had a Governors' meeting. I would assume it was a very difficult one.'

'I'm sure the Governors were very supportive,' Maxwell knew a party line when he was toeing one.

'I'm sure they were.' She sat back on his settee for the first time, cradling the cut-glass in both hands. 'But neither he nor they can help me now. I believe you can.'

'Mrs Whiting . . .' Maxwell wriggled in his chair.

Again, her hand was in the air. 'Please, Mr Maxwell. Hear me out. My husband was murdered last Tuesday, in your school. You, I understand, were first on the scene.'

'Second,' Maxwell corrected her, knowing now the fate of the first.

'I also understand you have . . . shall we say, a reputation for this sort of thing?'

' "Behold, a pale horse",' muttered Maxwell. 'Mrs Whiting, I am not a policeman. I am not a private detective . . .'

'But you solve murders,' she ended the sentence for him.

'If you mean, I can work out who dear old John Nettles is looking for in murder-infested

176

Midsomer, well, yes, sometimes.'

'No, Mr Maxwell.' Pamela was sitting up again, staring into the man's face. 'No, I'm talking about reality. Some . . .' and they both heard her voice go, 'some bastard killed my husband. Snuffed out his life.' She clicked her fingers. 'That's not good enough. Not good enough at all.'

She sat in his lamplight, the sun gilding her face and etching her tears.

'The police,' he said.

'Oh, Mr Maxwell.' Pamela shook her head, a humourless smile on her face. 'I lost faith in them a long time ago. They're shackled by political correctness and bureaucratic inefficiency on a monstrous scale. I just don't trust them to get results.'

'They've talked to you?'

'Of course. A DCI Hall.'

Maxwell nodded. 'Henry's a good man.'

'No, Mr Maxwell. My husband was a good man, and now he's dead.'

There was a pause, a stillness. Outside, on the catflap's rim, Metternich the cat sensed the moment, sniffed once and tiptoed away.

'If it's money . . .' she went on.

This was the second time in two days that an attractive woman had sat in this lounge, offering Peter Maxwell money. 'No, it's not that. Mrs Whiting . . .'

'Pamela, please.'

'Pamela.' He fought for the words. 'If I help

177

you, there are two conditions.'

'Name them.'

'You must accept that I cannot guarantee results—not results you'd particularly want, anyway.'

'No one can,' she said.

'Second, you're going to have to be totally honest with me about your husband. You know there's been a second killing?'

'Oh, my God,' Pamela looked as though she'd been poleaxed. 'No, no I didn't. Who?'

'Will you be totally honest with me?' He ignored her question.

'Yes.' She composed herself. 'Yes, I will, Mr Maxwell.'

'Then,' he smiled and held up his glass, 'you'd better call me Max.'

Chapter Eight

Henry Hall had planned to hold his press conference on the Monday. A demure little spinster had changed all that. Leighford CID was looking at two murders now. Leighford High's child population was dwindling by the day and with Paula Freeling found in Southern Water's bore-hole, there was a serious risk of an exodus from the town too. Leighford nick had been bombarded with calls from hoteliers, B & B proprietors, Amusement

178

Arcade impresarios and the Council. Leighford Theatre was seriously considering cancelling Jimmy Tarbuck for the August season and the under-rehearsed dance troupe that no one had heard of. Everybody wanted the same thing—answers. And Henry Hall didn't have any.

* * *

'So, how did it go?' Peter Maxwell had just fought his way back from the Carvery with the expertise of a bachelor who often took his Sunday lunch al fresco.

Jacquie had passed on seconds and was sipping her half-and-half in the shade of the parasol thoughtfully supplied by the Oak. 'Let's just say it went.'

'Fill me in on the late Ms Freeling.' He reached for the salt.

'Now, Max . . .'

He looked pointedly at his watch. 'For the last forty-five minutes, Woman Policeman, you have made every attempt to small talk for England. First, it was where to have lunch; then what to have; then, what astounding views there are over the Downs; then . . .'

'Yes, all right,' she smiled. 'Point taken. It's just that the DCI is pretty tight on this. I had strict instructions after Alan Whiting not to talk to you.'

'Alan Whiting?' Maxwell swigged his Stella.

179

'That was an eternity ago. You're right,' he sat as far back on the trestle seat as his sense of balance would allow. 'The view is breathtaking, isn't it?'

He saw her blink. 'You're changing the subject,' she said.

'Sorry,' he said. 'I thought I had to.'

She looked out across the fields, the trees heavy in the midday heat. The Oak itself was said to have been the haunt of highwaymen once upon a time in the south. On windy nights, they said, the clatter of hoofs could be heard on the cobbles outside the tap and the rattle of a whip on the window-shutters. There again, it could have been the plumbing. True, the flagstones in the cool of the bar were worn, but you could buy them like that these days and the beams that lined the ceiling were just a tad B&Q for Peter Maxwell's liking. All around them and the old building, holiday-makers clinked their glasses and filled their faces and laughed at the antics of their ghastly children scampering around the adventure playground, carved incongruously into a pirate ship on the hillside. Were Jacquie and Maxwell the only ones, she wondered, talking about sudden, violent death?

'I can only tell you what was said at the press conference this morning.'

'That's not much of a deal,' he wheedled, running his fingertips around the rim of his glass.

'Save you . . . what . . . twenty hours wait. And the cost of tomorrow's dailies.' It was the best she could offer.

'Ah,' he raised his glass to her. 'You can always find a way to a man's heart. Time *and* money—although of course they're the same thing. Go on, then.'

'First—and this is the only bit you *won't* find in the papers.' She closed to him. 'The Ofsted team, or what's left of them, is staying on at the Cunliffe until next weekend. They'll be under close surveillance, so stay away, Max.'

'That must disrupt their lives a tad,' he mused. 'Are you sure we're talking about *next* weekend?'

'Let's say they weren't over the parrot when Henry broke the news to them. His argument is that they are all potential targets and we can protect them better if they're in one place.'

'All right,' he nodded. 'Paula Freeling.'

Jacquie leaned back, putting her feet up on the rail under the table and letting her sunglasses drop back onto her nose. 'She was found yesterday morning by a contractor on the water board site in Lysander Road.'

Maxwell knew the place. There seemed to have been a hoarding and piles of gravel there forever. 'Cause of death?'

'Same as Whiting. Stab to the throat.'

He leaned forward. 'What do you make of that? Quite cranky, isn't it?'

'Uh-huh.' She wagged a finger at him.

'That's out of bounds. That wasn't in the press conference.'

'Only,' he demolished the last of the roast beef with a satisfied flourish, 'because the boys of the Fourth Estate don't know what to ask. All I want is your professional opinion, Jacquie, in a hypothetical sort of way.'

'Bollocks!' she snorted.

He looked appalled. There were, after all, women and children present. 'Tsk, tsk,' he whispered. 'That a Woman Policeman should even know how to pronounce that word. How about it?' He leaned across the table and took her free hand.

She screwed up her elfin face. 'You're a transparent bastard, Peter Maxwell,' she said. 'All right. But just this once.' And she knew how hollow that sounded before it had left her lips. 'We're obviously making enquiries elsewhere, with other forces. But before Whiting, I've never come across it. Stabbing is usually gang-related, dark-alleyway-outside-pub stuff. It's a spur of the moment thing.'

'What,' Maxwell chuckled, 'the perp just happens to have a carving knife about his person when he loses his cool?'

'Not exactly,' she explained. 'Oh, he's carrying a knife "for protection",' her fingers were in the air, 'of course—but we're not usually talking malice aforethought here. I've even known it be manslaughter.'

Maxwell shook his head. His old

182

headmaster used to flog people for having their shoelaces undone. Ah, the good old days. 'But this is different?'

'Of course,' Jacquie nodded. 'For a start, Whiting and Freeling aren't exactly your dark-alleyway clients, are they? Second, they're Ofsted inspectors working in the same team at the same school. And third, one of them at least was done in broad daylight, virtually under the noses of a thousand people.'

'From which you conclude?'

Jacquie began to answer him, then clammed up, removing her hand from his. '*I* don't conclude anything,' she said. 'I am a mere cog in a justice machine.'

It was his turn to say bollocks and he did. 'Humour me, heart,' he said.

'Hitman.'

'What?'

'A professional contract.'

'But that's fiction, surely. Like nymphomaniacs . . .' but Maxwell knew as he said it that it was a bad analogy. The aptly-named Danni Grewcock in Eleven Eff Four a few years back sprang to mind. What she hadn't done with half of Year Twelve in the science labs probably wasn't possible. At least, not in science labs.

'It's rare,' Jacquie agreed, 'but it's not fiction, Max. It's all factual.'

Images of John Travolta and Samuel L Jackson sprang to Maxwell's cinematic mind—

large, black-suited men walking into restaurants and blasting away with outsize automatics. But this was Leighford, a quiet sensible town on the quiet south coast. The Oaks up here on the Downs, a family pub which specialized in Dinosaur-shaped chicken nuggets and West Country cider. It was a Sunday, the day for people to wash their cars and mow the lawn. Some people still went to church, for God's sake. There wasn't even a cure for that yet.

'And if I'm right,' she tilted her glasses up so that he could see her sparkling grey eyes, 'that gives us a double whammy. The thing about hitmen is that they don't do it for laffs. They work, like you and me, and somebody pays them. So, whatever the papers tell you tomorrow, Mr Maxwell, we are in fact looking not for one murderer, but two.'

*   *   *

'Jesus!' It happened to be Geoff Baldock who said it, but it could have been anyone in Leighford nick that Sunday afternoon. He was standing behind the desk man's sliding glass partition and he couldn't quite believe what he was seeing.

'Who's in charge?' the woman wanted to know.

'I'm afraid the DCI's not here at the moment, madam.' Baldock tried to keep his composure.

'I am not familiar with your in-house initials, young man. You'll have to translate.'

'Er . . . sorry . . . the Detective Chief Inspector is Mr Hall. He's not in.'

'I presume he has a number two, so to speak? Some sort of second-in-command?'

'DI . . . er . . . Detective Inspector Bathurst, yes.'

'Is he in?'

'Er . . . no. I'm DC . . . Detective Constable Baldock. Can I help?'

'I very much doubt it.' She looked at him with disdain—the eager face, the blonde hair impressed her not one jot. 'I'm Deborah Freeling. I understand that someone has killed my sister.'

*   *   *

'Jesus!' It was Hall's turn to say it.

'That's more or less what I said, guv.' Baldock was looking through the same two-way mirror his boss was. The thing had cost half the capitation for the entire CID division last year but it had its uses.

'They could be twins.'

Deborah Freeling was being interviewed by Philip Bathurst in Interview Room Number One. Essex CID had talked to her already, but that was routine, when Paula Freeling had merely been a missing person. Now that she

185

was a guest of Dr Astley it was an altogether different proposition. Deborah had refused the offer of a police car and the arm of a policewoman. As Phil Bathurst was now discovering, Deborah Freeling was very much her own woman.

'I was hoping for something more than platitudes, Detective Inspector.'

Phil Bathurst had drawn the short straw here. It was curiously unnerving to be looking at the animated, mobile face of a woman he had last seen as a corpse hours before. Peas in a pod, eggs in a basket, didn't come close. It was as though it had all been some ghastly mistake, a bad dream, and that someone was playing some sort of sick joke on Her Majesty's Office of Standards in Education.

'We are at the early stages of our enquiries, Ms Freeling.'

'Miss, please,' Deborah said, looking the man squarely in the face. 'Ms I assume was invented by dysfunctional and probably hysterical women who wanted to convince the world that society is not run by men and that they have no need of their titles. The opposite is plainly true. Which is why I am talking to you and your boss is likewise, I understand, a male.' Her cold grey eyes had already flickered sideways. 'This is a two-way mirror, isn't it?' She got up and walked right up to the glass, nose to chin with the crouching Geoff Baldock.

'Christ, I wish people wouldn't do that,' he hissed.

'Keep still,' Hall muttered. 'If you don't move, she won't see you.'

'Oh, it's like *Jurassic Park*,' Baldock chuckled. Hall was curiously unmoved.

'How did Paula die?' Deborah Freeling wanted to know. She turned back to face her interrogator.

Henry Hall could tell plainly that Phil Bathurst felt uncomfortable. But he wasn't about to crash in and undermine the man's credibility. The man was a DI—in a fleeting analogy of which Peter Maxwell would have been proud, Hall decided to let him win his spurs.

'She was stabbed, Miss Freeling,' the DI said. 'More than that, I cannot say.'

There was no emotion from the woman, no change of expression. She merely sat there, narrow-shouldered, tight-lipped, watchful.

'When did you last see your sister, Miss Freeling?' Bathurst sounded like a take-off of a famous old painting.

'As I told your colleagues in Colchester, not for some months. We were not close, Inspector, for all our similar looks. Paula went her way. I went mine.'

'Her way being . . . ?'

'Into teaching and eventually the Inspectorate.'

'I was thinking about her private life,'

Bathurst said. He usually was. In murder cases, it went with the territory. The odd quirk, the unlikely link, the weird practice—motives all.

'She had a small circle of friends, I believe. I never met any of them.'

'No one in particular?'

Deborah fixed the man with a steely stare. 'If you're hinting at sex, Inspector, I fear you are wasting your time. Paula was engaged, briefly, at university. It didn't last. She was rather a fastidious person, fussy even. I doubt anyone would have spent any extended time with her for that reason. I expect she was rather lonely.'

'You can't tell me much about her friends, Miss Freeling. What about her enemies?'

For the first time, Deborah Freeling laughed. It was brittle, sharp and all the more unexpected in that bleak, chill room discussing her sister's death. 'If you mean, was there an army of disgruntled teachers queuing up to kill her, I very much doubt it. Although . . .'

'Although?'

'The last time we spoke, on the phone, she told me she'd been receiving abusive letters.'

'What sort of abuse?'

'She didn't elaborate. Merely that she found them hurtful.'

'Did she tell the police?'

'That was my question. She said she was thinking about it.'

'Did she keep them, do you know, the

letters?'

Deborah shook her head. 'I really don't know. She seemed genuinely rattled by them, though. Not like Paula. She was, in her way, something of a brick.'

For a moment the pair faced each other. In the adjoining room, beyond the tell-tale glass, Hall motioned to Baldock. 'Geoff, get on to Colchester. I want Paula Freeling's house gone over with a microscope. We're especially interested in threatening letters.'

'We'll need a warrant, guv,' Baldock's grasp of procedure was commendable.

'Correction,' Hall rumbled, 'Essex CID will need a warrant.'

'On it, guv,' and the DC was gone.

'Inspector,' Deborah Freeling broke the silence. 'You have no doubt formed the opinion that I am a heartless, unfeeling sister. Well, let me assure you that isn't quite so. But I feel more anger than grief at the moment. Daddy always taught us to be proud of the Freeling name; he was on the North Atlantic convoys during the war. Grandfather was at Jutland. No one, no one in the world, has the right to take a life. And never, never, never the life of a Freeling. You *will* solve this case, won't you?'

Bathurst just looked at her, for the moment all platituded-out.

*　　　*　　　*

189

Usually, the Monday after an Ofsted inspection would be rather a joyous affair. In every school that had passed, the Headmaster would wheel in several cases of Moet and Chandon, the children would be given a holiday and there would be massive staff bonuses for colleagues who had done such a fine job. And that was fine for the readers of Mr Chips and Enid Blyton. Reality was curiously muted. Neurotics who had underachieved during the Inspection just whinged more loudly about the unfairness of the system, the straitjacket of the National Curriculum and what an unprincipled wanker James Diamond was.

Except that the Monday following Leighford's inspection was anything but usual. For a start, there had been no inspection after halfway through Day Two. No one had been properly inspected. There were no plus points, no minuses, nothing, as yet, needing urgent attention. Everything and everyone was in limbo, like a film frozen. Piles of lesson plans still lay unread, stacked in Aitch One, feet from where a man had died. Piles of exercise books remained unchecked. And Aitch One was a murder scene, the tape gone now in deference to the kids' sensibilities, but locked and still a no-go area nonetheless. So it was all rather muted; all rather odd. Knots of teachers clustered in corridors, hovered in doorways, huddled in whispers for all the world like the men waiting for Julius Caesar at the Capitol on the Ides of March. A cursory head count via the registers that morning revealed that slowly the clientele was returning, their mothers doubtless driven to distraction by having the little shites underfoot; let them take their chances with a serial-killer—what were the odds? How often could lightning strike twice?

Using that magical free first period, Peter Maxwell went in search of Betty Martin. He wasn't really called Betty of course—Mr and Mrs Martin hadn't been *that* unkind. He was Bert and most of the kids knew the ghastly school caretaker as 'Doc' after the boots he'd never actually worn. Medievalist that he was, Peter Maxwell called him Betty after the old proverb 'all my eye of a yarn and Betty Martin', itself a parody of an old Catholic prayer to the saint—'O mihi beati Martini'. There was no point to it, really, just another reminder that this man was Mad Max.

The pair of them were standing on the edge of the school fields, the sun already merciless as white-kitted Ten Eff Four dawdled out onto the green for some vague, American-inspired ball game. Maxwell looked uneasy—what were the PE Department thinking, giving a baseball bat to Eddie Lurch? Weren't two murders enough?

'So this is the blind spot, then, Betty?'

191

Betty would never see fifty-five again. And many was the kid and member of staff who vowed he'd never see retirement either. He had all the compassion of Heinrich Himmler and, despite his job, care was something he very rarely took.

'I told 'em,' the caretaker was the master of self-justification. 'I told 'em 'till I'm blue in the bloody face. What's the point of a CCTV camera that don't bloody work?'

It was a fair question.

'It's always money, ain't it? Saving here, scrimping there. If that was a real one, we'd have got your bloke on footage. Mind you, that's crap too, ain't it?'

'Is it?'

'Ain't yer seen it on the telly? That bloody Crime-watch.' Betty Martin tried to turn himself into Nick Ross—it wasn't very convincing—' "We'd like your help in locating this man." Okay, the bloke's as black as your hat, but you daredn't say so for fear the bugger'll sue you for racial discrimination. And as for a clear picture, it might as well be Wile Bloody E Coyote.'

It was a fair comment.

'Thanks then, Betty.' Maxwell tapped the man's arm. 'Catch you later.'

'You know who I've got my money on, don't yer?' the uncaring caretaker shouted as the Head of Sixth Form made for the buildings. 'That bastard Ryan.'

192

Maxwell chuckled and winked at him, raising his hat. Now there was a possibility devoutly to be wished.

He took the way Boiler Man would have gone. If Martin was right and the fire alarm was smashed in the Art Block, it would have taken him . . . what . . . two minutes to reach it? Maxwell did it now, reconstructing the thing without the aid of a BBC camera crew, checking himself as he did. The six or seven herberts from Ten Eff Four who had excuse notes ranging from Impetigo to Don't Wanna and were lounging on the edge of the field, watched his antics with disbelief. The Head of Sixth Form was walking purposefully from the hedge that fringed the road, looking at his wrist every few seconds, checking sight lines on building corners, glancing backwards over his shoulder. He was Mad all right, they concurred; could anyone seriously doubt it?

Maxwell was up the stairs to the mezzanine floor. The glass would have been smashed by now, he told himself, the bell ringing, the meter running. Children would have been streaming out of buildings, pouring like ants along the corridor-arteries, delighted at being dragged from Maths/French/Whatever. Boiler Man wouldn't have run as some of them did; that would draw too much attention. He'd have walked, ready with a story, a plausible excuse for being there. Perhaps here, on the landing, Olly Carson would have spotted him.

Perhaps it was in the foyer at the bottom of the stairs. But Boiler Man would have had a problem as he pounded the History department's corridor. Once that alarm went off, there'd be kids everywhere and behind them, staff closing windows, slamming doors, shutting down sections of the school. And once that alarm went off, Alan Whiting would surely be out of his seat and joining the throng. Even an Ofsted inspector would recognize a fire alarm. So Boiler Man had to linger long enough to avoid being seen by a nosy member of staff and yet move sharpish enough to stop Whiting even before he left his desk. Split-second timing didn't begin to describe it.

Maxwell got to Aitch One, approaching it from the opposite direction. Had Boiler Man waited until Paul Moss had evacuated his teaching base next door, then gone in to the room through the stock cupboard? All was locked and barred now by order of Henry Hall, but Maxwell knew that Boiler Man could have entered from behind Whiting's chair, like the actor Wilkes Booth in the box at Ford's Theatre that night he shot Lincoln. One of the many crucial differences of course was that Booth had hit the President from behind, whereas Boiler Man had self-evidently struck from the front. Of course! That was why Alan Whiting hadn't moved. Boiler Man would have come in from the door to Aitch One. Maxwell moved to it now, sliding round the corner out of sight to all except a bemused Year Seven kid on a vital errand for Mr Ryan. Boiler Man would have crossed the corridor, gone on with some guff about it being routine and there was no need to leave the room. It was just a drill and the Ofsted people were exempt. No need to leave his chair, in fact. That would have been fine by Whiting, busy as he was. He'd have nodded, muttered something, sat back down and probably wouldn't have even looked up again as Boiler Man went about what the Ofsted inspector thought was his business. And of course, it was—the business of murder. The skewer out of the pocket, the skewer in the hand, the skewer thrust forward, buried deep in the throat and left there, nodding like the brightly coloured *banderillas* in the shoulders of a dying bull. Wham, bam, thank you, Boiler Man.

Maxwell swept down the stairs in the other direction, to the main corridor and the nasty little cubicle called Reception where Thingee One was the Front Line against the hells of the outside, alien world. A publisher's rep, already risking a double hernia and the fitting of a pacemaker by carrying a cargo of books was being given the third degree by a rampant Dierdre Lessing, a fate Peter Maxwell would not even wish on Messrs Hodder and Stoughton themselves. Didn't publishers *read* papers? Had they no idea of security? The Risk Assessment paperwork alone. How could

195

anyone be so insensitive?

'Thingee,' he ducked past the demolition job and into the outer sanctum where the Ladies of the Office sat surrounded by endlessly ringing phones and the flicking monitors of the school's only partially helpful CCTV: 'The Day in Question.'

'Mr Maxwell?' Thingee One was never exactly quick on the uptake, especially on a Monday morning and Peter Maxwell was an old man in a hurry, with a murderer to catch. Anyway, she was trying to earwig Dierdre Lessing's unprovoked attack on the helpless hawker of books.

'The day of the murder,' he enlightened her. 'Last Tuesday. Can you dree your weird and press any key and give me a butchers at the timetable for that morning?'

Thingee duly complied and the screen in front of her went through the motions under her fingertips, a bewildering series of bars and options and menus, things Maxwell had only ever seen in restaurants. He checked the rooms as she scrolled down for him. His encyclopaedic knowledge of the school grounds told him that the only class on the blind side of the building would have been Eight Dee Three when the fire alarm went off. Maxwell knew them well. Even collectively, their IQs barely reached room temperature. If Boiler Man had marched stark naked through their teaching base, they wouldn't have

196

noticed. If pressed, Melanie would have said he was a big black man with dread locks. Bryony would have said he looked like David Beckham and Racquel would have just grinned at him. So, Maxwell patted Thingee on the shoulder and blew her a kiss. Either Boiler Man had the luck of the devil or . . . And the 'or' Maxwell realised as he went back to his office, meant that the killer was on the inside. One, as Maggie Thatcher was prone to say of her old, loyal Conservative cabinet, of us.

*   *   *

Working lunch at Leighford nick that Monday was a particularly unedifying banquet. Besporting itself as a turkey salad baguette, DI Bathurst knew he could get the canteen on the Trades Descriptions Act for either of those falsehoods. The salad was warm and limp, with indescribable purple bits in it and the meat rather more Turk*ish* than turk*ey*. Henry Hall was sticking his finger in a less than Chief Inspectorly way inside his Salt and Vinegar crisp packet to extract the full benefit. Jacquie was on mineral water.

'What have we got, then, Phil?' The DCI was feeling particularly brittle this morning. Most of the dailies had given him a battering over the previous day's press conference. Even the Beeb on the one o'clock news was persisting in using his bad side. Nothing had come down from Upstairs yet, but Henry Hall sensed it couldn't be long. The Chief Constable's reputation for reasonableness was legendary, but there was talk of importing foreign police chiefs; and anyone could be leaned on.

'Well, these are faxes of photocopies obviously, guv,' Bathurst spread the shiny papers on Hall's desk, 'so they're not top quality. Colchester are going over the originals in their labs, but they're not over hopeful. Six letters, the first one posted March of this year, the last one nearly three weeks ago. All word-processed, all with an Ipswich postmark. Second class stamp.'

'Not only a bastard,' Jacquie muttered, 'but a mean one as well.'

'The late Ms Freeling . . . sorry, Miss . . . is addressed formally. Obviously no signature, not even a pen name.'

'What did you expect, Phil?' Hall consigned his crisp packet to the bin. 'Jack the Ripper?'

Bathurst shrugged. 'It would have been something. What's interesting is the spelling. "Their" in place of "there".'

'Didn't use the spell checker,' Jacquie commented.

'Spell checkers can't help in things like that,' Hall mused, reaching for his canteen coffee and vaguely wishing he hadn't, once he'd tasted it. 'Marks him down as a semi-literate, though.'

198

Jacquie Carpenter knew differently. Nattering to Peter Maxwell in the long watches of the night, their conversation occasionally turned to the educational state of the nation—well, neither of them got out much—and she was perfectly aware that such errors were uncommonly common even among the relatively smart. About a third of Maxwell's colleagues couldn't spell—the other three-quarters couldn't do Maths. But she wasn't going to drag Peter Maxwell into any conversation that didn't absolutely demand it. Instead, she played the sex card. 'Him, sir?'

Hall looked at her over the blankness of his glasses. 'See something we don't, Jacquie?'

She looked at them both. Both her superiors, both men. The way of the world. 'It's just that in my experience, it's women who usually write these things, sir. Men can't be bothered.'

Phil Bathurst smiled. Jacquie was right. Blokes didn't get mad, they just went round and punched somebody's lights out. Smiling wasn't likely to happen in the case of Henry Hall. 'What's the tenor of them?' he asked his people.

The DI shrugged. 'Nothing that malicious,' he said, glancing again at each one. 'And nothing that specific either. This phrase for instance—"I know all about you. And soon everyone will". It's pretty schoolboy—er, sorry, Jacquie, schoolgirl. It's as if the writer picked a series of unpleasantries from Every Child's Book of Poison Pen Letters.'

'Jacquie?' Hall wanted a second opinion.

'I agree, sir. On the other hand, there may well be a lot of things we don't know about Paula Freeling . . . yet.'

The men were nodding. Bathurst had conceded defeat on the baguette and thrown it in the bin.

'Which brings me to a proposition,' Hall said. 'Deborah Freeling.'

'Guv?' Already Bathurst didn't like where this was going.

'Can we use her in some way?'

'What? A reconstruction?'

'Not officially,' Hall said.

Bathurst had worked with this particular DCI for less than a year. Hall and Jacquie went way back to when she was a rookie in uniform and he'd taken her under his chill wing. She, quaking in the Red house over the strangled body of a sixteen-year-old girl. He calm, telling her quietly to go outside into the fresh air. They both thought they knew the man. And they knew that just *sometimes*, Henry Hall threw the rule-book away.

'We keep her in the area,' Hall said, watching them both intently. 'Put her up at the Cunliffe—in her sister's room if we can. We get her into Leighford High on some excuse. Get her to visit the Waterworks on the Front. Let her be seen around town a bit.'

200

'Why, guv?' Bathurst found his voice first.

Hall leaned back in his chair, clasping his hands behind his head. 'I want to give our man a bit of a fright,' he said.

'What? You mean he'll think he's seen a ghost?' Jacquie asked.

'Not quite as crude as that,' Hall said. 'But you've got the gist of it.'

'But what if he doesn't see her, sir?' Bathurst asked. 'Or he does and fails to react?'

'Oh, he'll react all right. If you see the living spit of someone you think you've put away with a skewer to the throat, don't you get just a little rattled?'

'What do we do?' the DI wanted to know. 'Put a disclaimer in the Nationals? Sorry, we've got the wrong woman; Paula Freeling is alive and well after all?' Bathurst was chuckling. Hall was not. Neither was Jacquie.

'If I'd seen Deborah Freeling before the press conference,' the DCI said, 'that's exactly what I'd have done. The woman in the bore-hole would have been Jane Doe and then we could really have made some capital. As it is . . . well, it's worth a shot. We get a plainclothes tail on her at all times. Relays round the clock, watching for reaction.'

'Will she go for it?' Jacquie asked.

'I think she will,' Hall nodded. 'I think she wants to help us catch her sister's killer, don't you?'

Duggsy slumped in the corner of the darkened bar, slurping gratefully on his pint. He'd been playing the Vine for two hours and had lost the will to live.

'Kickarse crowd,' mused Iron Man who joined him from one of his many visits to the loo, sliding his sticks into their case and squatting on an upturned beer crate. The domino players near the door had shuffled off into the night for their cocoa and the idiot playing air guitar was still three numbers behind, oblivious to everything but the noises in his head.

'What the fuck was that riff supposed to be?' The ever-beige Wal returned from the not-exactly-groaning bar with three pints of Stella, some of it at least dribbling down his front.

'Yeah, all right,' Duggsy muttered. 'I'm having an off night. Got any weed, Iron?'

The drummer's hand slipped automatically into his jacket pocket. 'That stuff'll kill you, y'know.' He passed it sideways.

'Yeah.' Wal coated his mouth with Stella foam. 'Killed you years ago, didn't it, Iron? Did you know, Duggsy, Iron here was killed in the war?'

'What the fuck do you know?' the drummer growled.

The lads chuckled. When Iron growled, it

was best to leave him alone.

'Who's that?' Wal was pointing to the door. A finger was curling towards them from the door to the Snug, attached to a hand and a tweed sleeve.

'Looks like the grim fuckin' reaper.' Duggsy tried to focus. 'Piss me, it's Mad Max.'

'What's he doing?'

'Well, he's banned, ain't he? That fuckwit over there threw him out last Bikers' Night. And he's a straight-up bloke is Max. If he's banned, he's banned. Toes the line, he does.'

'Looks like he wants another word.' Trust Iron Man to cut to the chase.

'If he wants us to play a gig,' said Duggsy, 'he only has to ask.'

'I don't know any Count Basie numbers,' Wal said.

The three of them reached the door of the Vine and sauntered out into the warm night air, trying to look casual, past the air guitarman who was having trouble finding F. The stars were bright over the rooftops and the chorus of goodnights and the slamming of car doors told the world that another Leighford day was coming to an end. The gulls had gone wherever gulls go at night time and exhausted families slumbered in their nasty little B and Bs that had looked so inviting in the brochures.

'Mr Maxwell . . .' Duggsy bowed, '. . . and Mrs Maxwell?'

Couldn't be, thought Wal. Talk had been at Leighford High that Maxwell was as queer as a row of tents. Then again, looking at the woman with him, this could have been his daughter. 'Course, if this was his daughter, that sort of implied that he couldn't, in fact, be as queer as . . . it was getting late and Wal was already out of his depth.

'Iron,' Maxwell gripped the man's hand and the five of them sat down at the empty table on the pub's gravelled front, carefully raked to hide the vomit. 'When we spoke last you said you'd seen the woman at the bar . . .'

'The pissed one?' Iron Man had seen a lot of women in his time and a lot of them in bars. It was important he got it straight.

'That's right. Mrs Meninger. You said you saw her having a row with a bloke out here, in the car park. The bloke with the black bag.'

'That's right,' Iron Man remembered.

'Did he look like this?' Maxwell held a sheet of paper up to the light above the table. It had a face on it.

' 'Ere,' Duggsy squinted at it. 'That's an e-fit, ain't it? I seen 'em on *Crimewatch*.'

Iron Man was staring at the face.

'Does it look familiar, Iron?' the woman with Maxwell spoke for the first time.

'Maybe,' the drummer was nodding. 'Maybe . . .'

'What's your interest then, darling?' Wal adopted his most casual bass player pose. He

204

was a rock star on the way up. He'd once had a pee alongside Iggy Pop. Not many people could say that. And she wasn't a bad looker, this one. She was clearly wasted on an old geezer like Maxwell; whereas, anyone with taste might fall prey to *his* raffish charms.

'That's DS darling to you, sonny,' Jacquie flashed her warrant card and a smile at the same time. Maxwell enjoyed moments like these.

'Blimey!' Wal took an involuntary lean backwards and almost fell off his chair.

'Iron,' Jacquie focused on the drummer, talking to him softly and slowly. She'd met the type before, an ageing rocker with a brain fuddled by too much booze, too much grass, too much noise and too many late nights. That's okay when you're twenty, but Iron Man was way, way past that. 'I'd like you to help us put together a picture of the man you saw with Mrs Meninger. At the station. Can you do that?'

'No.' Iron Man looked her full in the face. 'No, lady, I can't do that,' and he'd scraped his seat away and was gone into the bowels of the Vine again to de-rig, to collect his money, to go home.

'Er . . . Iron Man don't do police stations, officer,' Duggsy smirked. 'Far too many unpaid parking tickets, know what I mean?'

'What about you two?' Jacquie asked. 'Did you see the man with Ms Meninger?'

205

'No,' said Wal, looking vague. 'No, we didn't. We saw the bloke she was with at the bar. The dead bloke. Iron says it wasn't the same one though.'

'Did he do it, then?' asked Duggsy, suddenly fascinated to be at the centre of a murder enquiry. 'Did he top him?' Pound signs flashed into his eyes at the thought of his exclusive story to the *News of the World.*

'That, Matthew,' Maxwell tapped him on the scrawny chest, 'is exactly what we're trying to find out.'

And the couple took their leave, turning away into the night.

'What about that then?' said Duggsy. 'Old Mad Max helping the police with their enquiries, eh?'

'Yeah,' muttered Wal, feeling brave enough now to take a drag of his friend's roll-up. 'Who'd have thought it. Do you think he's slipping her one, as well?'

'What, in bed with Joe Law?' Duggsy watched their silhouettes disappear around the corner. 'It's possible. We didn't call him Mad Max for nothing, did we?'

*   *   *

Maxwell looked at the e-fit again in the brief glow from Jacquie's courtesy light. He had gone to the station late that afternoon when the DCI had gone home to tease his problems

206

over a gin and tonic on the patio. He knew a friendly Woman Policeman who knew a computer whizzo who knew which buttons to press.

'I can remember when these things were done by an artist,' he said. 'Budding Van Goghs were queuing up for the job.'

'Too many variables.' She closed the door. 'Artistic licence gets in the way. Computers don't have interpretation. Still think it's a good likeness?'

'Of the man I saw in the Little Teachers' Room at yon hostelry only a week since? Yes, I do. Smaller eyes, perhaps. Oh, God, Jacquie, I don't know. How sure can you be? A total stranger in the gents—chaps that piss in the night.'

She snorted in spite of herself. 'Let's get you home, Peter Maxwell, before we both turn into pumpkins.'

'Does this mean you aren't coming across . . . er . . . over?'

She thwacked him with the e-fit before belting up and hitting the ignition. 'Early start tomorrow. We're trying to reconstruct Paula Freeling's known movements.'

'No chance of me talking to the Ofsted team, I suppose?'

She eased off the brake and the Ka purred down the hill towards the sea. 'Absolutely none,' she said. 'I suppose there's no point in me asking you not to show that e-fit to Olly

Carson?'

He shook his head in the darkness. 'Absolutely none,' he said.

Chapter Nine

It rained that Thursday. Had Leighford been in India, people would have been dancing in the streets after weeks of drought, grateful for the life-giving water. As it was, Leighford was in Sussex and people just moaned about the god-awful weather. Some summer, eh? 'Still,' Peter Maxwell heard Mrs Troubridge say as he saddled White Surrey in the morning, 'the gardens need it.' There'd be a hosepipe ban by nightfall.

Henry Hall had taken over the suite of offices on the first floor of his nick as an incident room. Twice the number of deaths, twice the space needed to investigate them. Or so it seemed. It was time to take stock. House-to-house depositions were piling up on wood-work, phones were ringing off their hooks. VDU screens flickered green in the suddenly dull, dark July day.

'Stop me if I go wrong,' he said to his assembled team. For all it was raining outside, large drops bouncing off the foliage that fringed the nick, it was still unremittingly sticky, so that Hall's shirt was clinging to him already. 'Paula Freeling was last seen alive on Wednesday night, after supper at the Cunliffe. She'd seemed in tolerably good spirits, bearing in mind her shock at finding Alan Whiting dead. The Ofsted inspectors had played a few hands of cards, although inevitably the mood was solemn. What's the next step, Jacquie?'

'She was reported missing the next morning, sir,' Jacquie filled in for him. 'When Sally Meninger went to her room. Her bed had not been slept in, from which we conclude she'd left the hotel the previous night.'

'Right.' Hall stepped in again. 'Thoughts on that.'

'Two possibilities.' As the senior man, Bathurst thought he ought to comment. 'Either she left of her own accord. Or she was abducted.'

'Right,' said Hall again, gratefully accepting a fresh cup of coffee from a WPC. 'Go with the first.'

'If she went voluntarily,' Bathurst had been wrestling with this one for the past two days, 'where did she go? We'd asked the team to stay on at the Cunliffe, but they were free to come and go as they pleased. The inspection at the school had been cancelled, so technically she had nothing to do the next day. Now, we've been working on contacts for her. There's a sister, Deborah, who's staying at Dornford Lodge, in the town.'

'Where?' Pat Prentiss wanted to know.

'Hotel along Sea Street,' Bathurst confirmed, perhaps a little too quickly. Only he and Hall and Jacquie Carpenter knew of the plan to move her into the Cunliffe. 'She'd had no word from the dead woman for several weeks and hadn't seen her for months. Friends are few and far between, but we've drawn a blank so far. She certainly wasn't in touch with Ofsted Head Office—they've no record of a call, e-mail or fax.'

'So, if she left of her own accord,' Hall was still worrying it, 'where did she go and why should she leave?'

'More rattled by her experience than anybody realized, guv?' DC Baldock thought it was time to make his mark on the day's proceedings. Never let a briefing go by. 'Temporarily off the rails?'

'It's possible,' Hall nodded, 'but the bottom line is that somewhere along the way she met up with our friend with the skewer. So, let's assume he's proactive in this. He gets into the Cunliffe on the Wednesday night. How?'

There was a pause. 'It's hardly Fort Knox,' Pat Prentiss had worked on the place. 'It doesn't have CCTV and there are three entrances even without the kitchen door. Chummy could have got in easily without passing the front desk.'

'How would he know which room she was in?' Baldock asked. Henry Hall raised an eyebrow. The man with the blonde hair and the baby face wasn't going for Pat Prentiss's job; he was going for his. All eyes turned to Pat.

'O.K.,' the older DC shrugged. Prentiss was unfazed by whippersnappers. 'He went in past the front desk. That's the only place the register is kept. He must have had a shufti.'

'Get onto that one, Pat. Check with the desk man.'

'I did, sir.'

'Check again.' Hall was firm. He didn't like loose ends. And he didn't like chasing will o' the wisps.

'On it, guv.'

'All right,' Hall leaned back on his desk top, cradling his knee. 'He gets to Paula Freeling's room. Why is he there?'

A silence.

'Anybody?'

'He's on a mission,' Bathurst proffered.

'What?' someone asked.

'To wipe out the whole Ofsted team?'

There were murmurings. It didn't sound likely.

'She'd seen him,' Jacquie suggested. 'Either killing Whiting or at least leaving the room at Leighford High. That whole episode called for split-second timing.'

'She'd seen him,' Hall repeated, recognizing the logic in that. 'Why didn't she tell us?'

'You interviewed her, guv,' Bathurst was the only one with the rank and gravitas to bring it

211

up. 'Did she give any hint?'

Hall was jogging his memory, reliving the moment, shaking his head. 'She was upset, of course,' he said. 'She screamed when she saw the body.'

'Peter Maxwell confirmed that, sir,' Jacquie said.

Hall looked at her. It was That Man Again, although the DCI was too young to remember the programme of the same name. 'She certainly didn't say anything about a sighting, no.'

'Which she would have done, surely,' Bathurst said.

'So, it was only his perception, then,' Jacquie followed on, 'that she'd seen him.'

'Ironic,' Hall nodded. 'But the bottom line's the same. Whether she *actually* saw him or he merely thought she did, the solution would be identical. He had to shut her up. So,' Hall crossed to the plan of the Cunliffe on the flip-chart to his left. 'Our man gets to her room, number Thirty-Two here on the first floor. She opens the door. He's in. What then? Does she struggle? Does he kill her there? Forensics?'

'Things don't match, guv,' Prentiss was checking his notes. 'Astley says she died on the Thursday. That wouldn't give us a hotel killing. And, besides, her room was clean. No blood, no signs of a struggle.'

'Right,' Hall stood, still looking at the hotel's layout. 'So, he takes her, still alive and

212

presumably dressed, down the stairs and out . . . how? The rest of the Ofsted team. Where are they?'

'Depends what time the perp arrived,' Prentiss said. 'The front door is self-locking. After midnight, you'd need a pass key to get in. All the other doors are locked by then, but openable, for fire reasons, from the inside.'

'And by that time,' Baldock added, 'as far as we know, all the Ofsted team are in bed.'

'Or at least their rooms,' Hall was thinking aloud.

'Guv?' Jacquie frowned. 'You don't think, one of them . . . ?'

'That's what we're following up today, people,' the DCI told them. 'We're going back to the Cunliffe for some straight-talking. Meantime, we're back to last Wednesday night. The perp is taking Paula Freeling down the stairs, here.' He pointed to it with his ballpoint. 'Which way does he go?'

'Side door would be my bet,' Prentiss said. Everybody knew the DC's experience. He wouldn't be wide of the mark.

'Side door,' Hall was checking the plan again, 'would take them out to the car park.'

'It's self-closing,' Prentiss said. 'There'd be nothing to show anyone had slipped out. Fingerprinting the bar would be pointless. Too many users. Anyway, he almost certainly wore gloves.'

'He has a vehicle waiting.' Hall was talking

them through it.

'He's taking a hell of a risk, isn't he?' Baldock asked, following the kidnapper's flight path on Hall's diagram.

'Back to the Hendon lecture notes, Geoff,' Hall said. 'Risk-taking is one of the prime characteristics of a psychopath. This man's cool as a cucumber. He kills in broad daylight in the centre of a busy school. He's not going to be fazed by a little night shift in a hotel.'

'Especially one with no CCTV,' Prentiss reminded everybody.

'How did he know?' Jacquie asked. All eyes focused on her.

'Jacquie?' Bathurst wasn't following.

'How did he know where the Ofsted people were?'

There was a silence.

Hall nodded. 'That, Detective Sergeant Carpenter, is the most intelligent question I've heard this morning.'

Baldock's face said it all. He made a mental note, not that he must do better, but that Henry Hall was clearly screwing Jacquie Carpenter. Of such are the Kingdom of Heaven. And somehow, he couldn't get round that one without a bizarre image of himself sitting on Henry Hall's knee. He shook it from his mind.

'We'll get back to that,' Hall said. 'So, the perp is in a vehicle, car, van, we don't know. Where does he take her?'

'His risk's less now,' Bathurst was thinking aloud. 'His problem was getting her out of the hotel. Up to reaching her room, he could have come out with some plausible excuse for being there. But once he was with her, what . . . holding her at skewer point . . . that was his dangerous time. Now, he's in the car, he's relatively home and dry.'

'Self-locking doors.' Baldock was back in the discussion again, worrying it, teasing it, always pointing the spotlight on himself. 'She can't get out.'

'She's a frail, not very physical little woman,' Prentiss said. 'Not likely to wrestle with this bloke in the car.'

'Plus,' Jacquie reminded them all of the woman's viewpoint, 'she's very, very scared.'

'He takes her where?' Hall moved the briefing on.

'To a lock-up,' Bathurst was going through the possibilities. 'Garage, workshop. Forensic say there are traces of sump oil on the dead woman's clothes. And microscopic pieces of metal. Astley's coming to the same conclusion.'

'Lathe filings?' Hall suggested.

'Forensic aren't sure. It's an alloy, but that doesn't really help.'

'We know she was trussed up, both before and after death,' Hall said. 'Why keep her?'

'Sir?' Baldock was out of his depth by now.

Hall was striding around the room, trying to get a handle on it all. 'We're assuming the

215

killer thought he'd been seen dispatching Whiting.' He was looking at his team one by one. 'So he has to silence Paula Freeling. He could do it in the Cunliffe. He doesn't. Why? He takes her elsewhere. Why? He keeps her alive for . . . what does Astley reckon . . . eight to nine hours, depending on what time he snatched her from the hotel. Why?'

'He's busy,' Jacquie said suddenly.

Shit, thought Baldock, ready for the DCI to pat his blue-eyed girl on the bum again.

'Doing what?' was all Hall said.

'Day job,' Jacquie threw back at him. 'Important meeting. Somewhere he has to be.'

'So he hasn't got the time to kill her straight away?'

'He does it later,' Jacquie shrugged. 'When he has a minute.' She hadn't meant it to sound so casual, but she'd been around murderers long enough to know that to some of them, that was exactly what it was. Life was nothing more than a commodity, to be bought or sold as the market went or the wind blew—the analogies, in the end, didn't matter.

'When he'd got a minute,' Hall echoed. 'Right. So he uses the same MO as on Whiting.' A pause. 'Comments, people.'

'His calling card,' Prentiss suggested.

'Signature,' Bathurst was more precise, or better clued up on the jargon, at least.

'Why a skewer?' Hall was asking them as he'd asked himself a thousand times already.

'Cheap,' Prentiss suggested.

'Easily obtainable,' somebody else threw in.

'Who's linking with other forces on that?' the DCI wanted to know.

'That'd be me, guv,' Baldock was where he wanted to be again, centre stage, but his answer left a little to be desired. 'Nothing so far. And nothing in West Sussex CID since records began.'

'All right.' Hall was moving them all on still further. 'He moves her from the garage, workshop, whatever it is. And he dumps her. Phil?'

Bathurst crossed to the second flip chart. 'Southern Water's site off the Sea Front, Lysander Road,' he pointed to it with his biro. 'They're carrying out some sewage removal programme or whatever down there, so there's lots of handy holes to dump a body.'

'Bit public, isn't it?' Prentiss asked. 'Or is Chummy having a larf?'

'Our man's a risk-taker, remember?' Hall said.

'The site's been there for nearly two months now,' Bathurst reported, 'so everybody knows about it. Southern Water had some vandalism there a few weeks back. They replaced wire, strengthened boundary fences. Uniform got nowhere with that.'

Chuckles around the room. In that on-going feud between uniform and plainclothes which had been de rigueur ever since they set up the

Detective Department at Scotland Yard when dear old Sir Robert Peel was still alive, every cheap shot was a cause for mirth.

'But at least it made the water board tighten up security.'

'Night patrol?' Hall asked. 'Dogs?'

'No.' Bathurst shrugged. 'Just a few padlocks and razor wire. Seems to have done the trick, though.'

'It stopped ten-year-olds with spray cans, yes, but not our man with his dead body. No camera surveillance, I suppose?'

'Sorry, guv,' Bathurst smiled. Both men knew they were living in an age of hi-tech which was only as good as the tight-fisted bastard prepared to foot the bill for it.

'So how did he get in, carrying an eight stone woman wrapped in a mysterious way?' Hall wanted to know.

'Through the front gate, would be my guess,' the DI ventured. 'This would have been Friday night, or more likely the wee small hours of Saturday morning. A July Friday doesn't start to quieten down until about half one, two. The perp would have to wait until it was quiet.'

'This gate . . .' Prentiss was confused.

'Steel, Pat,' Bathurst knew the way his DC's mind worked. 'He couldn't shin over it with Ms . . . sorry, Miss . . . Freeling over his shoulder, so it's my guess he cut through the wire mesh and retied it on his way out.'

There were murmurs and a whistle.

'I said he was cool, didn't I?' Hall reminded everybody. 'He'd thought this through, come prepared. No Southern Water operative reported a break-in on the Saturday morning, no gaping gate, so he must have refixed the wire.'

'How come he dumped her there, though, sir?' Baldock was man enough to admit when he was stumped.

'This bore-hole, Phil.' Hall pointed to it.

'They were closing it down,' the DI said. 'It was half-filled with sand when the perp put her in there.'

'So he hoped she wouldn't be noticed?' Prentiss asked.

'That'd be my guess,' Hall said. 'The hole would be filled in before anyone noticed. And Miss Freeling would be just another missing person.'

'Has to be an inside job,' Baldock was confident in his assessment. 'Has to be one of the water board. He'd know about the bore-hole—and that way, he wouldn't even have to dig a grave.'

'That makes sense,' Hall nodded as the boy-wonder preened himself. 'Except for two things.' Baldock looked crestfallen. 'Why shit on your own doorstep? Why hide a body in your own workplace—wouldn't that draw a certain amount of attention? Can you be absolutely sure you'll get to it and fill in the hole before anyone else does. What if his timing's off and something goes wrong? And second, whoever killed Miss Freeling killed Alan Whiting. Is that an inside job too? If you can find me a teacher who moonlights for the water board, Geoffrey, I'd say you've got your man.'

There were guffaws all round; clearly nobody knew how little teachers earned. Eventually, Baldock saw the funny side and chuckled along with them. Maybe he wasn't *quite* ready for the DCI's job just yet.

'Dig deeper, people,' Hall ordered, unaware of his feeble pun. 'We're a week into this one and I've a feeling we've only scratched the surface. Jacquie, a word.'

*　　　*　　　*

One of the many skills that teachers have is the ability to pad silently through still halls on sweltering days, wandering up and down like the restless spirits they are, nosing into other people's work and becoming suicidal with boredom. It's called Invigilation and that, along with the marking and the children, was the bane of Peter Maxwell's life.

The sun had got his hat on again by eleven and its rays were streaming in through the gym windows, the room still vaguely whiffy with old rope and PE mats and other people's jock-straps. Over a hundred hopefuls sat in their uncomfortable plastic chairs in the neat rows laid out by Betty Martin and his lads. Most of them were cheerfully wrestling with the complexities of GCSE Double Science. One or two were doodling, when Maxwell's back was turned, on the desk, telling the world what everyone knew already about the Exams officer. Jay Phillips was fast asleep. He'd written his name on the front and then Lethe had overtaken him. Maxwell shook his head— Winston Churchill had got into Harrow for doing as little as that. Surely, this would qualify young Jay for the AS Physics course.

As he reached the front for the umpteenth time, the useless fan blasting the hair of one lucky student only, he saw the rows of mobile phones the Exam Board rubric had insisted were handed in and switched off before the exam started. For a moment, he toyed with dropping them all into a bucket of water. Then, out of the corner of his eye, he saw a movement in the wired glass of the gym door. It was Thingee from the office, waving at him.

He tiptoed in his suede brothel creepers over the plastic covering that protected the gym's floors and tucked his head round the door.

'It's Mrs Whiting,' Thingee hissed, clearly in a flap. 'The Ofsted inspector's wife . . . um . . . widow. She's here and wants to talk to you.'

Maxwell glanced back at Jeff Armstrong, the oppo who was invigilating with him. He held five fingers in the air and pointed out of the door. Armstrong nodded. The old duffer was always being called away from things for one spurious reason or another. Wonder what it was this time? Probably his bladder. No one had yet invented a Teacher's Friend.

'I just had to see it,' Pamela Whiting said as they walked. 'The room where Alan died.'

'I still don't think this is a good idea, Pamela,' he said softly and he walked with her up the stairs to the mezzanine floor.

The pair were now standing on the History corridor outside Aitch One. She automatically tried the handle.

'It's been locked ever since . . . it happened,' Maxwell told her.

'Have you a key, Max?'

'Yes,' he said.

'Then . . .'

'No, Pamela,' and he led her away to his office, down the corridor that Boiler Man must have walked on his way to do a job.

She took in the film posters, the yellowed plant in the corner, the piles of papers and the bookcase full of bumf. 'Can I get you a coffee?' he asked.

'No, thanks,' she said. 'I read in the papers about Paula Freeling.'

'Number Two,' Maxwell nodded, closing his door. He hoped Jeff Armstrong wouldn't mind. He was going to be rather longer than five minutes.

'Look, I'm sorry about this,' she said. 'It was a stupid, spur of the moment thing. I've disrupted your day.'

'Got me out of invigilation,' he smiled. 'I owe you a huge debt of gratitude and probably a large slice of my over-inflated salary. Any news?'

'From the police, you mean? No. Look, do you mind if I smoke?'

'The school has a no-smoking policy,' he said. 'But I'm sure there are exceptions.' He slid open a drawer and handed her an ashtray, the one he kept for particularly neurotic sixth-formers having a bad hair day. He watched as she drew heavily on her cigarette.

'I suppose their enquiries will have shifted to the Freeling woman now,' she said.

'Probably,' Maxwell nodded. 'But the two are clearly linked. Tell me about Alan.'

She looked at him. 'What's to tell?' she asked. 'You think you know somebody . . .'

'But you don't?'

She shook her head. 'I think . . . I think Alan may have been having an affair, Max.'

'Ah. *Cherchez la femme.*' Maxwell watched the woman closely. 'Do we know who?'

Pamela shook her head. 'No. Oh, it's no big deal, I suppose. It happens, does it not, in countless families up and down the land. You fall in love, you fall out of it. You get busier— Alan had his blessed Ofsted, I have a business. I can't say we saw much of each other in the

223

last weeks, but . . . even so, you notice. Phone calls late at night, on his mobile. Extra meetings which hadn't been scheduled, that sort of thing.'

'You've no suspicions?' Maxwell pressed her.

Her face wreathed briefly in a circle of smoke. 'Sally Meninger,' she said.

'Ah.' Maxwell raised an eyebrow.

Suddenly, Pamela was sitting upright, staring at him. 'You know something, don't you?'

'Pamela, I . . .'

'For God's sake, Max. Somebody has killed my husband. Don't I have a right to some answers? If not from the police, then at least from you.'

'Fair enough,' the Head of Sixth Form sighed. 'They were . . . shall we say, rather chummy.'

'How chummy?'

'Having sex chummy.'

'Jesus.'

'Look. Pamela, I don't think I've any right . . .'

'How do you know?' The woman was on a mission now.

Maxwell shook his head. 'Your husband's only been dead a week,' he told her. 'It's not my place to do this.'

'I have to know, Max,' she pleaded with him, leaning forward, her eyes full of tears.

224

'For my sanity's sake.'

So he told her. The bar at the Vine, the loos at the Vine. What he didn't tell her was the existence of Joe Public, whose e-fit lay on his desk nearby. Because he had no idea who Joe Public was or how he meshed into the whole peculiar box of tricks. Nor did he tell her of Sally Meninger's nocturnal visit carrying wads of cash. Those two titbits he needed to keep to himself for the moment. When he'd finished, he waited for a reaction. It came soon enough. She collapsed, sobbing, into his arms as he quickly took the ciggie from her and held her close. He breathed in the scent of her hair and found himself patting her quivering shoulder. She was a girl again, looking for peace, looking for someone to take away the pain.

The door opened and a startled sixth former stood there, having come to check on the last minute details of the Grad Ball. Maxwell just shook his head over Pamela's shoulder and the sixth former beat a hasty retreat, hurtling to the Common Room to tell the world what she had just witnessed. It was all part of the enigma that was Mad Max.

*　　　*　　　*

David Simmonds sat back in the Cunliffe's sun pavilion, a glass in his hand and a chip on his shoulder.

'This really is the limit,' he snapped. 'I told

225

it all to the other officer.'

'It's just routine, sir,' Jacquie Carpenter assured him, notebook poised on her knee. 'You'd be amazed how things come back after a few days.'

Simmonds snorted. He knew the police had a job to do. And truth to tell, he was just a threat rattled by all this. He hadn't joined Ofsted to become the target of some maniac. 'What did I think of Alan Whiting?' he repeated her question. 'Well, he was effective enough, I suppose. Appeared to be doing his job. Of course, he had a bit of a roving eye.'

'Oh?' Jacquie had already proved herself right. Simmonds hadn't mentioned this in his earlier interview.

'Oh, nothing in it, I'm sure, but he was very . . . shall we say . . . attentive to Sally Meninger. Even swarmed around Paula Freeling.'

'Even?' Jacquie wanted to make sure she understood.

'Oh, come on, sergeant. Let's not let death guild any lilies here. Miss Freeling was a frowsty old besom teetering on the edge of extinction. She had all the sexual allure of a crocodile handbag. To see Whiting chatting her up, you'd swear she was Sharon Stone or somebody.'

'So it was just his way, then?'

'Yes. He was no respecter of persons, if truth be told, and age was no barrier either. Waitresses here at the Cunliffe, even that

226

ghastly harridan Dierdre Lessing at Leighford High.' Jacquie couldn't help a smirk—Peter Maxwell would be loving this. 'She of course was preening herself like a pissed schoolgirl at a party. How he had the brass neck I don't know. No oil painting, was he?'

'Good in the sack, maybe?' Jacquie ventured, a little unprofessionally.

'Maybe,' Simmonds nodded. 'Look, you're not taking this seriously, I hope.'

'What, sir?'

'This twenty-four hour protection nonsense. Can there really be a maniac out there killing Ofsted inspectors? It's preposterous.' Perhaps if he heard himself say it, it would all just go away.

'Two out of six ain't bad,' Jacquie reminded him.

'What's the motive?' Simmonds took a hefty swig from his gin and tonic.

'That depends,' Jacquie said.

'In other words, you people haven't got a bloody clue, have you?'

'That depends,' she ignored him, 'on whether any of you knew each other beforehand.'

'Malcolm did.'

'Malcolm?' Another bingo. This wasn't in the first interview notes either.

'Malcolm Harding. He and Whiting went way back—and not always very happily, I understand.'

'Mr Harding told you this?' Jacquie was putting pen to paper.

Simmonds edged a little nearer. 'Look, I hope I'm not talking out of turn. I mean, I don't want to land a colleague in it, but I *do* want my life back. Cooped up here in this dead-and-alive hole is not exactly why I became an Ofsted inspector. Anyway, Malcolm's not the type.'

'Type?' Jacquie frowned.

'To murder anybody.'

'And what is the type, Mr Simmonds?' the DS wanted to know. 'Because expertise like that is worth bottling.'

*   *   *

'Yes, all right.' Malcolm Harding was popping pills on the Cunliffe's terrace. On the beach far below, summer frolickers lay roasting under the noonday sun, their truanting children scampering and shrieking at the water's edge. Out to sea, the jet skis whined and furrowed the ocean, slicing white through the blue water. Already, three hours on, nobody could remember when it had last rained. 'All right, I *did* know Alan Whiting.'

'You didn't mention this at your previous interview, sir.' Pat Prentiss sat like a piece of the furniture opposite the man. Second interviews were like this. The panic had subsided, the gut reaction had gone. There

228

had been time to think, plan, perhaps even conspire. Especially since all the Inspectors had had ample time to cook any books they might have been preparing.

'Didn't I?' Harding looked balder and more pallid in the light on the terrace, his face almost matching his ice-cream-salesman jacket, his silver moustache drooping in the heat. 'Slipped my mind. Alan and I were at the same school in Derbyshire, oh, years ago.'

'You were friends?'

Harding looked at the constable. Probably as thick as he looked. That's why he was still a constable. This shouldn't take long. 'Of course. Why not?'

'You tell me, sir.'

'Oh, very well.' Harding was on his feet now, pacing the patio. 'We *were* friends, yes, but . . . well, if you must know, he cheated me out of a job.'

'How so?'

'I won't bore you with the details. Let's just say he made a few phone calls, called in a few favours. Knew people in high places, did Alan. He got the Ofsted job I should have had. Imagine his chagrin when I finally turned up on his team.'

'Miffed?' Prentiss wanted to be sure he'd correctly understood 'chagrin'.

'Livid,' Harding confirmed. 'But what could he do?'

'More importantly, sir, what could you do?'

'Meaning?'

'Well,' Prentiss took time sipping his orange juice. 'Here you were, with a man you clearly detested. A man you'd reason to . . . what, exact a certain revenge on . . .'

Harding spun round to face him, blotting out the sun with his slovenly bulk. 'Are you suggesting I got my own back on the bastard by sticking him with a skewer? That's not only ludicrous, it's slanderous.'

Prentiss looked up at him. He'd been here before. 'If I'm wrong,' he smiled, 'I will of course withdraw the implication completely.'

*　　　*　　　*

'How long have you been a detective, Mr Baldock?' Sally Meninger had insisted on being interviewed in her room.

'Eighteen months, madam. Now, if we could . . .'

'I think you've got a great future. Are you sure you won't join me?' She waved her Scotch at him.

'Not on duty, thank you, Ms Meninger.'

'Oh,' she cooed, sitting on the chair opposite his with one delectable thigh crossed over the other. 'I think we know each other well enough to dispense with the formalities, don't you? I'm Sally,' and she held out her hand.

'Um . . .'

'What shall I call you?' she asked, her eyes widening.

'Geoffrey,' he said, limply.

'Geoffrey.' She dropped her hand and sat back, allowing her skirt to ride up just a little higher. 'To what do I owe the pleasure?'

'It's a routine second interview . . . Sally. Covering your relationship with Mr Whiting.'

'Relationship?' Sally frowned. 'What does that mean?'

'Well, um . . . You were colleagues, obviously, but how well did you know him?'

'If you mean was I sucking him off every night after a hard day's inspection, why not come out and say it?' she twinkled.

Geoff Baldock wanted the ground to open up and swallow him. He'd begged the DCI for a crack at this woman and the DCI had been reluctant. Frankly, he wasn't sure the lad was ready. Pencilled in the margin of Hall's notes from the first interview were the words 'Watch this one'. And that was precisely what the DC was doing. In fact, he couldn't take his eyes off her.

'I shouldn't tell you this, Geoffrey,' Sally Meninger was suddenly sitting up, her face dark, her eyes uncertain. 'And I should have told the Chief Inspector when we spoke, but . . .'

'Yes?' Baldock's pen was ready.

'Well, I don't know what it is, but I feel I can trust you.' She leaned further forward still. 'It

231

must be me, I don't know.' She looked at his left hand. 'There's no Mrs Baldock?'

'Oh . . . er . . . No,' the DC laughed.

'Girlfriend?'

The DC shook his head, deciding at that very moment that whatever he had with Kirsty Dale was over.

'Good.' He felt her hand caressing his knee, felt her eyes boring into his. 'Alan Whiting was a bastard. He was stalking me.'

'Stalking you?'

She nodded, pulling her hand away abruptly and getting up to stiffen her drink from the bedside cabinet. 'He specifically asked for me for the Leighford assignment. I didn't realize that until after he was dead and I rang Head Office for some sort of clarification.' She took a swig and shut her eyes. 'He must have seen me at some conference or other; been introduced. I don't remember.' She turned to face him, pencil slim and radiating heat. 'He was all over me on that first night, on the Sunday. I had to,' there was a catch in her voice, 'I had to fight him off, physically defend myself.' Baldock was on his feet, uncertain what to do. Sally Meninger shuddered, the Scotch in her glass quivering. 'He was an animal. His poor wife . . .' and she buried her face in her hands, the half empty glass pouring its contents over the rug.

Instinctively, although he knew he shouldn't be doing it, Geoff Baldock held her in his

232

arms. Their lips and tongues met as she lifted her face to his and they swayed there for a moment. When they parted, Sally turned away. 'I'm sorry,' she said.

'Don't be,' and he turned her back, eager to continue where they'd left off.

'No.' She held her fingers to his lips. 'I can't. I promised James.'

'James?' Baldock was even further out of his depth than he knew.

'James Diamond,' she explained. 'The Head at Leighford High. He and I were . . . lovers once.'

'Really?' Baldock knew he should be writing this down, but couldn't remember where he'd put his pocket book.

'Oh, it was a long time ago. I couldn't believe it when I realized it was *that* James Diamond who was the Head. And when that bastard Whiting came on strong, well, naturally, I turned to James for help.'

'You did?' Reality was flooding back into Geoff Baldock's fevered brain. 'You told him?'

'It was weak of me, I know. I should have coped on my own. But,' she turned to him again, her lips closing to his. 'It's like you and the DCI,' she said. 'There are just some people you know, instinctively, you can trust; you're one of those,' and her tongue snaked between his lips and her fingers curled in his hair. She pulled back a little. 'James Diamond is another. He was furious.'

233

'When was this?'

Sally was running her fingers around the boy's face. 'Hmm?'

'When did you tell Diamond?'

'Oh, I don't know,' she said. 'The Tuesday morning, I think. The day . . . oh, my God,' and she spun away from him.

'What?'

She half turned back. 'Well, you don't think . . . oh, no, it's too ghastly. What have I done?'

'Sally,' Baldock took her firmly with both hands, planting a kiss on her forehead. 'It's not what *you've* done, is it? I think we both know what this case is all about.'

He kissed her hard on the lips and left. Unbelievable, he thought, as he bounded down the stairs into the foyer, a woman like Sally Meninger had the hots for him *and* she'd given him the case on a plate. He checked his watch. What do murdering Headteachers do, he wondered, of a Thursday afternoon?

Chapter Ten

'Well, we had this idea, Mr Maxwell.'

The Loup Garoux wasn't the usual haunt of the Yawning Hippos. In fact, they'd got some pretty dirty looks from the maître dee, who really *was* French and not just some bloke from Walthamstow with a talent for mimicry. But Mr Maxwell had vouched for the unlikely trio, so the maitre dee had reluctantly let them in—albeit only to the garden.

'Oh yes?' Peter Maxwell was with the band on the elegant wooden table under the sycamore. After the heat of the day, it was glorious to be up here on the Downs with the breeze lifting from the west and the line of the blue horizon an uncertain haze between sky and sea.

'About that bloke,' Duggsy was, as ever, the spokesman. 'That e-fit.'

'Yes?' Maxwell had got the call from Duggsy at school that afternoon and had cycled all the way up here, much to the chagrin of his back and calf muscles, because the Hippos wanted somewhere private and Wal had never had a drink with a firework in it before. It was Maxwell's decision to use the Loup Garoux, but he thought Wal might be disappointed. But no, the bass player was as happy as Larry with his sparkler, proving how little he got out.

'We could find him for you.'

'How?' Maxwell was all ears.

'Tell him, Wal.'

Wal was still staring at the sparks flying upwards from his curiously pink glass. 'I read a Sherlock Holmes story once,' he said.

It came as a faint surprise to Maxwell that the boy could read at all, but he tried not to let it show.

'He has these kids, don'e?' Wal explained. 'The Baker Street Irregulars.'

'Indeed he does,' nodded Maxwell, quietly impressed.

'Well, we'd sort of be *your* Irregulars, Mr M.,' Duggsy chipped in.

'Why?' Maxwell asked.

'Well,' Duggsy cradled his pint, vaguely ill at ease in his scruffy leathers with all the Guccis loafing around. 'We're all feeling prats, to be honest, Mr Maxwell. I mean, this bloke, this e-fit one, he's involved in the murders, right?'

'I don't know that, Matthew,' Maxwell said. 'But I'd certainly like to find out.'

'Right. Now, if he hangs around pubs and other places of ill repute, well, that's where we hang out too. And we feel, sort of, involved. 'Mean, if he *did* it, we seen him, didn't we?'

'But only Iron Man saw him up close,' Maxwell reminded them. 'How do you feel about all this, Iron?'

The drummer shrugged. 'We'll keep an eye,' he said. 'No promises, though.'

'Guys.' Maxwell leaned back. 'I'm flattered, of course, but there's a problem. Sherlock Holmes used to pay his Irregulars a shilling every time they worked for him. That's five pee to you, but more realistically, using the multiplier effect, the current rate of inflation and a following wind, that means I'd have to cough up eighty pounds to each of you whenever you were on my payroll.'

'Yeah, well, you're a teacher.' Wal was still making neon circles in the twilight with his dying sparkler, trying to roast the hovering gnats. 'You're loaded.'

'Shut the fuck up, Wal,' Duggsy ordered, unaware of a certain bridling from the paying customers at the nearest table. 'This is Mr Maxwell you're talking to. Won't cost you a thing, sir.'

'That's uncommonly decent of you, gentlemen.' Maxwell raised his glass.

'You'll come and watch us in the Leighford Festival, though, eh?'

'Duggsy,' Maxwell gave the man a high five. 'I wouldn't miss it for the world.'

*   *   *

The lights burned blue at 38 Columbine that night. After he'd made his pact with the Hippos, Maxwell had watched them pile into Iron Man's van and had cycled back from Loup Garoux in the embers of the sun. The other customers were audibly delighted when they left and Maxwell had pressed something brown and folded into the maître dee's hand for his understanding. The rays had flashed on his spokes as Surrey swooped along the Downs road where the grass was cropped short by the sheep and the trees lay flat and stunted in their timeless battle with the wind. He'd freewheeled into Tottingleigh as the street lights came on—'twas almost fairy time.

Captain Bob Portal looked nearly finished now as Maxwell carefully painted the yellow double stripes on the rider's overalls, reflecting sadly as he always did that to anyone not of the cavalry persuasion double yellow stripes meant no parking. The Master Modeller's tongue may have been protruding through his teeth as it usually was at moments like these, but his heart wasn't in modelling tonight. He knew there were four Ofsted inspectors idling their time away at the Cunliffe not two miles away from him and he couldn't get at them. They were under constant protection from Henry Hall's boys in blue and with that particular gentleman, Maxwell was decidedly *persona non grata* at the moment. He checked his watch. Half past eleven. Too late for any meaningful contact now even assuming he could somehow sneak past the cordon. They'd be tucked up in their truckle beds—except for Sally Meninger who'd be tucked up in somebody else's. He'd swung that way from Tottingleigh, taking the

238

sharp bend by the flyover in a flurry of gravel and a whirr of gears. He'd almost purred into the Cunliffe's drive, but he'd seen the squad car near the front door and had thought better of it. One of Leighford's finest would still be inside, perhaps more than one, and they would be looking out for Peter Maxwell almost as much as they were looking out for Boiler Man. Hell, some of them probably hoped they were one and the same person.

He rinsed his paint brush in the white spirit and slid his swivel chair backwards. The cat flap crashed ominously three floors below—the Count on one of his visits. Maxwell had found Olly Carson earlier in the day and showed him the e-fit of Joe Public that Jacquie had made up for him. It had been like pulling teeth. It *could* have been him, Olly had said, but there again . . . Boiler Man had worn a baseball cap that partially hid his face. He was . . . what? Thinner? Older? Difficult to say. Olly, with his particular obsession, had learned to be cagey with strangers, people in authority, friends, *everybody* really. Maxwell had thanked the lad, his usual patient, understanding self, when really he wanted to pin the little freak against the wall in the UFO section of the library and shout at him, in Klingon, of course.

'So,' he stood up in his attic and looked out of his open skylight where the night breeze was still warm and the moon lay a frosted silver on the silent ridges of the sea. The pigeon that seemed to live next door had stopped cooing now and was dozing somewhere, its head under its wing, poor thing, praying not to meet the black and white killing machine that was Metternich. 'Paula Freeling,' Maxwell murmured. 'You should never have gone down to the edge of the town without consulting me.' He caught sight of his own reflection in the arch of the window pane, eyes tired and hollow, hair a mess. 'You're talking to yourself again, Peter Maxwell,' he said. 'Time for bed.'

*   *   *

The Head of Sixth Form's eyes locked on those of his Headmaster the next morning. Peter Maxwell was leaning sideways, his left leg firmly on the ground, his right still over Surrey's crossbar and fumbling blindly for the pedal. James Diamond was in the back seat of a police car, its siren blaring, its lights blazing as it screeched out of the school gates. It was difficult to know which of them was the more gobsmacked.

'I don't usually pull rank, Anthony, as you know,' he said to an equally amazed Year Ten kid standing nearby, his backpack on the floor in his astonishment. He tossed him a padlock. 'But park this for me, will you? I feel a crisis coming on.'

Anthony caught first the lock and then the bike as it left Maxwell's grasp. Somehow he

240

snatched up his own baggage and wheeled Surrey away towards the bike sheds, wondering how it was remotely possible that a thing this old could still be on the road. He thought the same about the bike. Maxwell was up the steps, weaving past knots of astonished kids and staff, all of whom had seen the Headmaster's going. He dummied through the Reception Offices, where every lady was on their feet and peering through windows; shimmied through Reprographics, where the technicians had abandoned their photocopying to watch the action, side stepped his way down the deserted Corridor of Power and hurtled into James Diamond's office. Those two fine Machiavellians, Bernard Ryan, the Deputy Head and Dierdre Lessing, the Senior Mistress stood there as though they'd been pole-axed, gazing wistfully at the door.

'Well, well, Acting Headmaster,' Maxwell saluted Ryan with the flat of his hand, army style. He'd known this man, idiot and jerk, ever since he'd arrived at Leighford with pretensions to be able to do the timetable. Now, through natural wastage and the odd nervous breakdown, he was Number Two in the school. And, as of this moment, it seemed, Number One. Dear old Patrick McGoohan would, of course, have retorted that he was not a number, he was a free man. But there was no such thing as a free man. Not even a free lunch.

241

'Don't say anything, Max,' Ryan warned.

'What just happened?' the Head of Sixth Form felt he had a right to know.

'The police arrested James,' Dierdre said, still wide-eyed with the shock of it all. She sat down sharply, as if she wasn't sure her legs would hold her any more, wishing, all over again, that she hadn't given up smoking eight years ago. She was sitting in the Head's chair.

'Er . . . I think that's Bernard's now, Dierdre,' Maxwell said gently. 'When the colonel's dead and the gatling's jammed, it's usually the number two who takes over. That would be Major Ryan here . . .' and the film buff couldn't resist, '. . . recently promoted from Private.'

'For God's sake, Max,' Ryan thundered. 'Have a heart, will you? Didn't you hear what Dierdre just said?'

'With respect, Acting Headmaster,' and those words brought terror to the hearts of any Senior Management Team member who had ever worked with Peter Maxwell. 'I am waiting for some semblance of sanity to emerge from this morning. Who arrested Diamond and for what?'

'I didn't catch his name,' Dierdre said. She was twisting her many rings as she tried to make sense of it all, too.

'Baldock.' Ryan had caught it. 'DC Baldock. Some kid still wet behind the ears.'

Maxwell was secretly impressed. Ryan was

242

starting to sound like the Head of Sixth Form. 'And the cause?'

Ryan glanced at Dierdre. Neither man had seen her so drawn before, so old, so ill. Better leap back into that magic flame, Maxwell thought, or she'd crumble into dust, thousands of years old, the Ayesha of Leighford High.

'Suspicion of murder,' the Acting Headmaster said.

*   *   *

'He's what?' DI Bathurst was incredulous.

'Interview Room Two,' Jacquie said, waving her arms in the same disbelief.

'Who the fuck authorised this?' Bathurst was on the move already.

'Nobody, Phil,' Jacquie told him. 'He just bulldozed his way into Leighford High this morning and brought him in here. He's been closeted away for nearly two hours.'

'You're a bloody detective sergeant!' he yelled at her while grabbing a pile of incident sheets. 'Why didn't you pull him out of there? We've got enough to do without fending off the bleeding Complaints Authority.' And he was gone, his heels clattering along the corridors that led to his quarry.

'Geoff,' he put his head round the door. 'A word?'

Baldock got up, looking at James Diamond sitting opposite like the cat who'd got the cream. The Headteacher looked ghastly, pale and gaunt under the brightness of the neon strips. His tie was loose, his jacket hanging on the back of his chair. Bathurst nodded to him before he closed the door.

'Before you say anything, sir,' the DC had prepared for the onslaught he knew was coming. Baldock may have been green, but he wasn't emerald. 'You'd better read this.'

Bathurst was boiling mad, but the professional policeman in him took over for long enough for him to take in the gist of the sheet of paper Baldock had given him; Diamond's statement. 'These are his words?' he checked, eyes still blinking, teeth grinding in annoyance.

'They are,' Baldock assured him.

'Procedure,' Bathurst snapped, slapping the younger man in the chest with the statement sheet. 'You, as a detective constable, do not, *ever* interview a potential suspect or even a witness, without the express authority of your case officer—in this case, me. And, regardless of where this leads, you may well have compromised our position hopelessly by going out there like a bull in a fucking china shop. Where's his brief? Where's the tape? Have you taken leave of your bloody senses?'

The corridor was still ringing with Bathurst's verbals and various personnel, who felt it necessary to walk in that direction carrying vital pieces of paper, scurried away when faced with the DI's scowl. Where was that nice, reasonable Mr Hall when you needed him? Bathurst's finger was prodding Baldock in the chest. 'You will write all this up, now. You will explain in words of one syllable—because that's probably all you can manage—why you took the action you did.' He closed to his man. 'And if you still have a job by this evening, you obnoxious, cocky little wanker, I'm a one-legged transvestite.'

Bathurst waited until the DC had gone, then he took several deep breaths and went back into the Interview Room. He noted that a tape was still, in fact, recording in the machine to his right. At least Baldock had got *something* right. James Diamond, B.A., B.Sc., M.Ed., was not a happy man.

'How much longer am I to be kept here?' he asked.

'That all depends,' Bathurst slid back the chair opposite. 'DI Bathurst continuing the interview with Mr James Diamond at . . .' he checked the wall clock '. . . eleven twenty-one.'

'On what?' Diamond wanted to know.

'On your answers to some questions.'

'Am I under arrest?'

'No.'

'No?' Diamond looked the man in the face. 'But the other officer said . . .'

'Form of words,' Bathurst attempted to gloss over the faux pas.

'So I'm free to go?'

245

'Not until I've finished, no.'

Diamond slumped into his chair again.

'Now, what precisely is your relationship with Ms Sally Meninger?'

There was a knock at the door.

'Sir?' Jacquie Carpenter's head popped round the door. 'There's a Mr Maxwell here, demanding to see Mr Diamond.'

Bathurst switched off the tape. What was going on this morning? The lunatics appeared to have taken over the asylum. 'Demanding?' he repeated. 'Does Mr Maxwell have power of attorney?'

'No, sir,' Jacquie was acutely embarrassed, toeing that delicate line as she always was. 'He says he is appearing as Teacher's Friend.'

'Teacher's . . .?' Bathurst was even more nonplussed. 'Send him away,' and he turned back to the tape recorder, switching it on in readiness.

'Aren't I allowed a phone call?' Diamond asked.

'I told you,' Bathurst explained patiently. 'You are not under arrest.' Clearly, James Diamond had been watching too many old B-movies.

'But I have the right to have my solicitor present, even in witness questioning?' Diamond was on shaky ground. Like most members of the great British public saddled with an unwritten constitution, he had no idea what his rights were.

'Indeed . . .' Bathurst was forced to concede.

'Then I'd like to have Mr Maxwell present, please.'

'But he's not your solicitor,' Bathurst objected.

'My choice, surely?' Diamond stuck to his guns.

The DI sighed. 'Very well. DS Carpenter, would you show Mr Maxwell in?' Jacquie had waited there, knowing exactly which way this conversation would go. 'Interview temporarily halted at . . . eleven twenty-seven.'

*　　*　　*

They clattered down the corridor side by side, the lovers. Except that she was working, she was a detective sergeant and this was her patch. He was working too, although at that moment, back at Leighford High, a luckless supply teacher was doing his best with Eight Zed Six. The pair did not hold hands or even look at each other—both professionals to the core.

'Max, what the hell are you doing?' she hissed out of the corner of her mouth.

'Riding with the Seventh Cavalry to the rescue, heart,' he hissed back. 'Although I'm buggered if I know if Legs Diamond deserves it.'

'You're in over your head,' she said, a little too loudly perhaps as they rounded the corner

247

by Interview Room One.

'My favourite position!' he turned to her for the first time, winked and they were there.

'DI Bathurst.' Jacquie did the honours. 'Peter Maxwell.'

The DI nodded. This was not a handshaking moment. Maxwell let his hand fall—his back was broad; he'd get over the slight, in time. He knew this interview room of old. He'd sat there opposite Henry Hall on more than one occasion, in the chair himself, under the spotlight. He, who had two degrees, had faced the third.

'Headmaster,' the Head of Sixth Form nodded to Diamond. He wasn't going to shake his hand, either—throat, possibly, but that would come later. 'Has Mr Diamond been charged?' Maxwell asked.

'Well, er . . .'

'Yes or no, Inspector?' Maxwell had been here before. He didn't have time and he didn't take prisoners.

'No.'

'Then he's free to leave. Headmaster?' He gestured towards the door.

'He is still being interviewed, Mr Maxwell.' Bathurst halted the hasty exit. 'Do you have any legal qualifications?'

'I have a smattering of common law, more than a passing acquaintance with Roman. I concede my Ecclesiastical is a little ropey. Will that do?'

'You see,' Bathurst tried it on. 'If you and Mr Diamond leave these premises, I'd be within my rights to do you both with conspiring to pervert the course of justice.'

'Ah, the course of justice.' Maxwell's impersonation of Homer Simpson downing a keg of Duff beer would have brought a smile to anyone's lips—except those of DI Bathurst, DS Carpenter and James Diamond. 'Now, that ol' thing never did run very smooth, did it?' He turned to face his man, head on. 'Let's recap, shall we, Inspector, because I'm a little confused. You see, I was told at first that Mr Diamond was under arrest on suspicion of murder. Admittedly that was the opinion of the Senior Management Team at Leighford High—never the brightest apples in any barrel. Now you tell me that he's not under arrest at all, but is merely helping you with your enquiries. You understand my confusion?' Maxwell was all disarming smiles.

'It's quite simple, really,' Bathurst began, still desperately trying to defuse Baldock's gaffe, but Maxwell wasn't having any.

'Yes, it is,' he interrupted. 'Stop me if you've heard this one, Inspector. Pushy young detective wants to notch up a couple of stripes on his sleeve by arresting prominent citizen—on what grounds, I've no idea. More streetwise, slightly older detective inspector realizes the kid's blown it and tries to backtrack, saving whatever face and thumping

249

great lawsuit for wrongful arrest he can.'

Bathurst's face said it all.

'Yes, I know, it's a hackneyed old plot, isn't it? Police incompetence only matched by police corruption. But you see, Mr Bathurst, we live in a blame culture, don't we? Now, Mr Diamond here is obscenely overpaid in some people's opinion, but not so obscenely he wouldn't mind a cool half a mill for wrongful arrest. Then, there's the whole defamation of character thing. People are *so* distrustful, aren't they?'

'All right!' Bathurst held both hands in the air. 'You've made your point, Maxwell. Take him away. But,' and he jabbed an index finger towards Diamond, 'we'll talk again, sir, don't you worry.'

'Come along, Headmaster,' Maxwell took the man's arm. 'Mr Diamond has been running a comprehensive school for years. Do you seriously think he'd be worried by a little thing like a murder charge?' He beamed at Diamond. 'Fancy a ride on my crossbar?'

*   *   *

James Diamond couldn't face going back to school that day. He and Maxwell took a cab from Leighford nick to somewhere on the Downs and walked and talked. In the brief moments they'd had together, Maxwell had given Jacquie Surrey's padlock and told her to

250

be extra careful—parking it outside a police station was probably asking for trouble; such riffraff were always going in and out. And then, there was the criminal fraternity.

Two middle-aged men, both in shirt-sleeves, both with jackets draped over their shoulders, one with a silly hat and bicycle clips, one not, wandered the high country in the still of a summer's day. Bees droned on the ox-eye daisies, nodding in the softest of breezes. Anyone who had seen the pair would have assumed they were nature lovers, communing with the flora; ramblers establishing their ancient rights of way; in the endless war between town and country; lovers in the easy-going, enlightened twenty-first century enjoying togetherness under the newly-tolerant eye of the Church of England. In fact, one was a desperate headteacher under suspicion of murder, the other was his Head of Sixth Form. More hang-ups there than stockings at Christmas time.

'From the beginning then, Headmaster.' Maxwell could feel his shirt clammy in the small of his back and the long grass catching in his cycle clips as he walked.

Diamond looked at him. For more years than he cared to remember, Peter Maxwell had been a thorn in his side. He was the conscience of Leighford High School, a dinosaur somehow preserved in the amber of the School That Time Forgot. People called him Mad Max and generations of kids, now parents themselves, had loved him for it. The Blue Max, Max Headroom, Max Taste, the nickname might change with the ad man's weather, but the man himself was unchanging. Never bending, never accepting second best. Diamond knew very well that Peter Maxwell should have been sitting in his study and drawing his inflated salary, the last of the Grand Old Men, but not even in his darkest nightmares would James Diamond have admitted that.

'It was all rather a long time ago, Max,' the Head said and eased himself down in the shade of a little broken hedge that followed the dry bed of what was once a stream, before Geographers and scaremongers had invented global warming. 'Sally Meninger and I met on a course. Brighton, I think.'

'You were already married at the time?'

'Yes.' Diamond looked away. For most of the day he'd been thinking how he could break all this to Margaret. She never rang him at school, so he'd had the time to prepare. But how could he? His sins, albeit on a conference, would find him out. All in all, it was a mess. 'All right,' he said. 'What can I say? What sort of contrition are you looking for? It happens all the time.' Defensive bastard. The front fooled no one—least of all Diamond's Head of Sixth Form.

'It does.' Maxwell rested on one elbow,

252

sliding a piece of grass between his lips and chewing the end of it as he had done as a child in leafy Warwickshire, far to the north. 'And I'm not your Father Confessor, Headmaster. What you do in your spare time is up to you. Except,' he pulled the grass out, 'murder doesn't happen all the time, for all they'll tell you differently in the *Daily Mail*. And, as far as I'm aware, it's *never* happened on the premises at Leighford High. So let's start for real, shall we? Did you have an affair with Sally Meninger?'

'Yes,' Diamond said. He was sitting up now, staring out across the broad sunlit fields that sloped down to the sea. 'It lasted on and off for about six months.'

'And Margaret never suspected?'

'No, bless her, I don't believe she did.'

'Did you know Sally Meninger would be on this particular Ofsted team?'

'Not until the week before. Anyway, you can't pick and choose your teams. How would it have looked if I'd written to Ofsted to say "Not Ms Meninger, please. She and I had a fling a few years ago and there's a certain amount of baggage."'

Maxwell took the point. 'So how was she? In the strictly non-sexual sense, that is? When you met, I mean?'

'Polite,' Diamond remembered. 'Frosty. A little arch.'

'You'd dumped her?'

253

'That's an over-simplification, Max. There was never going to be any future in it.'

'But she bore a grudge?'

'That's putting it a little strongly. But, yes, eventually. I instigated the end of the whole thing. It was going nowhere and . . . well, I suppose I felt guilty.'

'Why did the police come to arrest you this morning, Headmaster?' Maxwell was going for the jugular now. 'Not even the greenest rookie does that kind of thing on spec. What do they know that you're not telling me?'

Diamond hung his head for a moment. 'Sally . . . came on to me.' He looked away. It all sounded so puerile. Here he was, a man fast approaching fifty, spilling the nasty little secrets of his life to the last man in the world he wanted to confide in. He felt like a kid with his hand in the cookie jar, caught in the glare of the world's spotlight.

'Headmaster,' Maxwell said softly, looking the man in the face. 'If we're to get to the bottom of this, I shall need chapter and verse.'

For a moment, Diamond hesitated. There was so much between these two, so many times when Maxwell had outgunned Diamond. In staff meetings and briefings and corridor-passes without number, his famous 'With respect, Headmaster . . .' heralded some new disaster, some impediment to Diamond's otherwise meteoric career. The rise and fall of Legs Diamond at the merest whim of Mad

254

Max. But then again, Maxwell had that infuriating habit of usually being right. 'She first came to see me on Monday afternoon,' he said.

'The first day of the Inspection?' Maxwell checked.

The Head nodded. 'We weren't exactly in private of course. You know what school's like, Max. Phones going all the time, people popping in, just wanting a word. We . . . made small talk. I personally felt very awkward.'

'That was it?' Hardly *News of the World* stuff yet.

'Then, yes. On Tuesday, it got rather . . . heavier.'

'You grappled?' Maxwell remembered Dierdre Lessing's unlooked for experience, the one that had turned the Mummy to jelly.

'It wasn't like that, Max. She . . . she was being, well, stalked, I suppose.'

'Stalked?'

'Harassed; sexually, I mean, by Whiting.'

'Was she now?' Maxwell was all ears.

'Apparently, this had been going on for some months. He requested her as part of his team, told his bosses what a marvellous rapport they had. She detested him, called him the Octopus. She turned to me for help, Max—a sort of *cri de coeur.* Oh, I shouldn't have responded, I suppose, but, hell, I owed the woman something.'

'She asked for your help? How?'

'Oh, I don't know. Nothing specific. Just to be there for her.'

'Not to bisect Whiting's windpipe with a barbecue skewer, then? Or was that just your interpretation?'

'For Christ's sake, Maxwell.' Diamond sat bolt upright in the grass. 'Not even that schoolboy detective came on that strong.'

'You do *have* a solicitor, Headmaster?' Maxwell asked.

'Could you, just for once,' Diamond held both hands in the air, 'call me James? Or Mr Diamond, if you must. But this . . . *formality* is ludicrous. Here I am discussing the most intimate details of my private life . . .'

'No, Headmaster,' growled Maxwell. 'What is ludicrous is a married man in your position in charge of a school carrying on with a tart like some overgrown schoolboy. I don't need to mention things like pillar of society, position of trust, *in loco parentis*, do I?'

'I resent that!' Diamond was on his feet, shouting.

Maxwell was with him. 'And no doubt you'll resent it even more when they send you down for fifteen years.'

'That's preposterous!' Diamond turned away.

'Is it?' Maxwell spun his man round to face him. 'Let's just recap, shall we? A courtroom . . . oh, let's call it Winchester, shall we? Pretty building, up on the hill, next to that flinty place

256

with Arthur's Round Table—you know the one. The CPS will have appointed a smartarse lawyer with more tricks up his sleeve than you've been off on pointless conferences. You, of course, charged with murder, are assumed in English law to be innocent. Except that in the eyes of the jury on whom your freedom depends, half of them don't think you are. They're the half who'll be carrying all kinds of secret baggage from their own schooldays. They don't like teachers and they especially don't like headteachers. They'll all have read about the case in the Press and the Press don't like teachers either. We're all supposed to be like Caesar's wife, except the public don't buy that. We're either drip-feeding leftie ideas into their little darlings' empty heads or we are spreadeagling them over their desks as a perk of the job. The clever ones among us are fiddling the dinner money and the school trip budget. Oh, and of course we're all bullying sadists. And I haven't started on the facts of the case yet.'

Diamond's eyes flickered away. 'That's nonsense,' he muttered.

'The smartarse lawyer,' Maxwell hounded him, 'will have to establish means, motive and opportunity.' He stood in front of Diamond, his hands on the lapels of his invisible lawyer's robes. 'Mr Diamond, do you own a barbecue set? Does it have a skewer?'

The Head shook his head.

'Of course you do and of course it does. But then, there was the spare you bought, wasn't there, the one you sharpened to a razor point.'

'No one could prove that.'

'No, because you paid by cash in a big store—Tesco's, Woolies—and you deliberately picked a checkout where the girl was not an old Leighford Hyena. But then, actual *proof* isn't necessary, is it? We all know that. That scintilla of doubt that lawyers prattle on about over their port cuts both ways. Remember, half the jury hates you anyway. They're going to believe that's exactly what you did. And the other half?'

Maxwell let his man wander away through the tall grass. 'Well, they'll be sold on the motive and the opportunity.'

'What are you talking about?' Diamond muttered.

'I'm talking about an old flame of yours— the smartarse lawyer will call her your mistress, with all the delicious prurience that that wonderfully old-fashioned word conjures up. The mistress who came to see you the day before Alan Whiting died, sobbing on your shoulder. "James, darling, Alan Whiting is a beast. He's all over me. Please help me, please."' All in all, it wasn't a bad impression of Sally Meninger and at least, in a way, Maxwell had called his Headmaster by his Christian name. 'So you, twisted, deranged, knight-errant that you are, decide to sort out

258

Whiting once and for all. Oh, perhaps you didn't intend to kill him. Perhaps just threaten him a bit with the skewer. But he gets shirty, tells you to take a running jump. You lose your cool and whammo!'

Diamond was silent now, shaking his head.

'Which brings me to opportunity. And your window was pretty large, wasn't it, Headmaster?' He closed to his man. 'Because I think the smartarse lawyer will find three, perhaps four dozen witnesses who would swear under oath that you were not in the Fire Assembly Area. And I'm afraid, Headmaster, that I'd be one of them.'

'Jesus!' Diamond groaned.

He suddenly looked years older, the bottom gone from his world and dizzying destruction below. 'I was busy,' he muttered. 'Some last minute paperwork, the attendance records. By the time I left my office everybody was moving back in. There seemed no point.'

'There was every point, Headmaster,' Maxwell sensed the man's despair. 'But, ever the optimist, let's consider other possibilities. There *were* other smartarses on the scene. We know there was an intruder on the premises at the time of the fire alarm. We've got to find him, of course, but he's our man.'

'Do the police know this?'

'One of them does. Jacquie Carpenter will decide when to go public with her boss.'

'I'm not sure that helps,' Diamond scowled.

'Really? Why?'

'Max . . . I haven't been totally truthful.'

Maxwell raised a deadly eyebrow.

'You see, I went to the Cunliffe. Sally rang me and I went to visit her.'

'When was this?'

'When?' Diamond was fighting back his fear. 'That was on the night that Paula Freeling disappeared.'

Chapter Eleven

'How much can you tell me?' Maxwell was on the phone in his lounge at Columbine, defiantly staring at that pile of exercise books that had been staring back at him now for over three days. He'd have to get them back to Seven Gee Eight tomorrow because even his excuses were wearing a little thin—'I want you to work on paper today'; 'it's a sort of test'; 'if it's good enough, it'll go up on the wall.'

'If we had vision-phone,' Jacquie said, 'I'd say something like "I'll show you mine" etcetera, etcetera.'

'So, it's a Leighford standoff,' he laughed. 'Ladies first, of course.'

'All right.' She relented or they would have been swapping platitudes all night. 'Geoff Baldock over-reacted this morning. Phil Bathurst went mildly apeshit and it wasn't helped by your grand entrance.'

'Now, Woman Policeman,' he chided gently. 'Somebody has to stand up to you bullying bastards in this great Police State of ours.'

'I should've thought James Diamond could have looked after himself.'

'Legs?' Maxwell sucked in his breath. 'Not a hope. How that man got beyond third in a department, I'll never know. Besides, I don't expect he's been arrested before.'

'We're looking into previous now,' she chuckled.

'Oh, come on, Jacquie. Legs Diamond may be a sorry excuse for a Headmaster, but a murderer? What's Bathurst doing about Baldock?'

'Sent him home with a flea in his ear this morning.'

'Suspended?'

'Not officially. Just told to cool off, consider his future and so on. It's up to Henry Hall ultimately. Now it's your turn . . .'

'Uh-huh,' he shook his head, sipping the huge Southern Comfort he'd poured for himself. 'I haven't gleaned anything like enough information yet. Why was Baldock so over-zealous?'

'Hey, that's two bits of information,' she sulked, curled up as she was on her settee in a dressing gown with a Patricia Cornwell.

'*Au contraire*,' he argued. 'It's only an extension of the first bit. Probably not even buckers for promotion go out to arrest anyone arbitrarily.'

'All right,' she said after a pause. 'But then it's definitely your turn.'

'Cross my heart.' He did it automatically, those long ago mantras of childhood engraved on people, as they are, for ever.

'Sally Meninger,' she said. 'She told Baldock Whiting was giving her a hard time. Sexual harassment. And she told James Diamond the same—on the day before Whiting was killed. Geoff just put two and two together.'

'Aha,' Maxwell nodded. 'And got twenty-two.'

'Your turn,' Jacquie reminded him. 'What did you get out of Diamond this afternoon?'

'Who says I got anything?' he said coyly.

There was a pause. 'Don't give me that crap, Peter Maxwell,' she warned. 'I rang you at school about three. Talked to the switchboard girl.'

'Yes,' Maxwell stretched his tired feet. The Downs had been hot and the ground had been iron. 'Thingee Two.'

'I think you'll find her name is Amy,' Jacquie said.

'Get away!' Maxwell was learning something every day. 'Amy, Emma; you can see why I can't tell 'em apart, can't you?'

'She said you and the Head left a message that you were in conference. So what did the conference throw up?'

'Ah, conferences.' Maxwell saw a smoke-screen shimmering on his horizon. 'Did I ever tell you about the time . . . ?'

'Max!' He pulled the receiver away in time to save his eardrums from a damn good shattering.

'Sorry,' he chuckled. 'I digress. Diamond told me the same essentially that Baldock got from Ms Meninger. He and Sally were an item, albeit illicitly. He had no idea she'd be on the team and she came to him in desperation.'

'Baldock seemed to think she thinks Diamond did it.'

'How are you spelling Baldock?' Maxwell checked. 'B-o-l-l-o-c-k-s?'

'So what's your reading of it?' Jacquie asked.

'Well, from what I saw in the Vine last week—God, is that all it was? Last week? From what I saw, the sexual harassment was going in the other direction. Sally Meninger seemed to have got Alan Whiting like a rabbit in the headlights. She came to me waving a wad of fivers . . .'

'What?'

'I told you.'

'No, you didn't.' Jacquie was sitting up, the Cornwell book flung aside.

'Surely . . .'

'Max.' Her voice was hard. 'I'd have remembered.'

'Sorry,' he said. 'I honestly thought . . .

263

Anyway, she turned up at mine out of the blue, basically offering me a bung to keep my mouth shut. I pointed out to her that I wasn't alone in witnessing the Vine performance and that hush-money could get very expensive.'

'How did she react?'

'Took my point and left.'

'And that was it?'

'At that stage, yes. Dear old Dierdre Lessing more or less confirms Diamond's story concerning him and Sally at Leighford.'

'She does?' Jacquie was wide-eyed. 'Max, you arsehole, you haven't told me any of this.'

'I'm sure . . .'

'Look!' she snapped. 'I'm putting my career on the line—*again*—for you and I'm getting jack shit in return. What did Dierdre say?'

'Just that she caught Legs and Sally *in flagrante* in his office. Not as *in flagrante* as I caught the Whiting and Sally in the Vine loos, mind, but *in flagrante* nonetheless.'

'And when were you going to tell me this?'

'For Christ's sake, Jacquie, it's not my fault if Henry Hall hasn't interviewed the staff at Leighford High. It's the first thing I'd have done. Then I'd have started on the kids. A man died on our premises, for God's sake.'

'I'm not running the bloody case!' she screamed at him. It was simply a reminder and no more than the truth, but it served to provide a full stop.

His ear rang again as she slammed the

phone down. He sat there fuming for a while, then took a hefty swig of his drink. If Jacquie had waited, of course, he could also have told her that there was Pamela Whiting who'd visited him here at the dead of night, enlisting his help. There was Henry Hall, who'd basically called to say 'stay out of it'. All in all, 38 Columbine was a magnet for people like Tom, Dick and Henry. And there was the fascinating piece of news, that Legs Diamond was sniffing round Sally Meninger on the night that Paula Freeling vanished from the Cunliffe.

But Jacquie was right. He'd been remiss. He knew more than the police now and he really ought to have shared that with her. He dialled the number. Engaged. He shook his head. She'd left the phone off the hook. And for the next couple of hours, as he half-heartedly checked Seven Gee Eight's grasp of Cromwell's Interregnum, he kept trying. And each time, the line was dead.

$$* \qquad * \qquad *$$

'Hello, this is the Cunliffe,' a jovial voice crackled over a particularly bad phone line. 'George speaking. How may I help you?'

Why was it, Maxwell wondered, that public relations firms the world o'er taught their operatives such banal telephone procedures?

'George, it's Mr Maxwell, from Leighford High.'

265

'Hello, Mr Maxwell. This *is* a pleasant surprise. What can I do for you?'

'Can you see the front gate from where you are?'

He imagined George leaning far left and standing on one leg. 'Er . . . yes, yes I can Mr Maxwell.'

'Is there a policeman in the foyer, George?'

'Yes, Mr Maxwell.'

'Well, could you do me a small favour, George and stop calling me Mr Maxwell?'

'Of course, Mr . . . Of course.'

'Right. Look at the front gate again. Got it?'

There was a strangled sound as George adjusted his footing. 'Yes,' he managed.

'Now, don't draw attention or wave or anything, but I'm standing in the callbox to the left. See me?'

'Yes.'

Maxwell was impressed. He could see George now and sure enough, he wasn't jumping up and down or doing cartwheels, just a night porter having a rather loud conversation with someone; could be anyone, really.

'Now, George, I want you to help me and I don't want the policeman in the foyer to know you're doing it. Are we on the same wavelength, George?'

'Gotchya, M . . . mate.' George was warming to all this now.

'I need to get into the hotel, George,'

266

Maxwell told him. 'Unobserved, shall we say. How do I do that?'

Maxwell watched as George disappeared behind the bar. A muffled voice came back at him. 'Side door, Mr M.,' the lad mumbled. 'Give me five.' And he was gone. Maxwell saw him fiddling with the optics behind the bar, tapping them and checking them. Good move. Now, he'd need to go and refill. That would mean a trip to the cellar and the way to the cellar would almost certainly be via the kitchen. Why wasn't this guy in MI5?

Meanwhile, Maxwell had problems of his own. He'd left his trademark tweeds at home and slid quietly out of the telephone kiosk in his gardening anorak. The outcrop of rocks loomed dark against the pale sand of Leighford Beach beyond the road and the surf roared and crashed against them to mark the incoming tide. A wind had risen from nowhere and the strings of lights along the Front were dancing and bouncing, throwing weird shadows over pavement and shrubbery. He padded on his brothel creepers to the right, away from the kiosk, away from the Cunliffe's locked front door and towards the clock and the Amusement Arcade. Suddenly, when he judged the coast, literally, to be clear, he ducked sideways in the lee of the Cunliffe's hedge and strode across the carpark. Now was the danger time. Should any nosy copper be looking out of the hotel's windows now,

Maxwell would be a sitting duck. Then, he was lost in the shadows and tapping on the side door.

It swung open. 'Mr M . . .' but even George knew what a hand clapped over his mouth meant and he let Peter Maxwell push him gently back inside. George closed and locked the door. 'More roof problems, Mr Maxwell?' he whispered.

'Something like that,' Maxwell nodded, checking the corridors were empty. 'George, did anyone ever tell you what a thoroughly good chap you are? Which room is Sally Meninger's?'

The lad's mouth popped open. 'Mr Maxwell, I couldn't . . .'

'George.' The Great Man sensed a certain faltering in the boy's loyalty. 'It might literally be a matter of life and death. Now please. Remember Leighford High, eh? Best days of your life and all that?'

'Well, I . . .'

'George,' Maxwell spun the boy round to face a door. 'What does that say?'

'Fire Exit,' George read the sign. This was a test. He'd had them from Maxwell before.

Maxwell spun him back. 'And for that,' he said, slapping the boy's shoulder, 'thank a teacher.'

'But . . .'

'George,' Maxwell used the killer tone that had silenced multitudes. It was a risk, so loud

268

so late, but it had to be done.

'Thirty-One,' George told him.

'Thank you, George.' A lesser man would have had to have used a monkey wrench. 'When I leave, I can just nip out this way, yes? The door's self-locking?'

'Yes,' confirmed George.

'Right.' Maxwell tapped the lad on the chest. 'Back to your desk before you're missed. I shall, of course, remember you in my will.' And he was gone, hot-footing it up the back stairs with the dreadful carpet to the second floor. Here, all was silence. His footfalls made no sound as he padded past the Brannon engravings of Old Leighford when the place boasted one inn and a row of excise-men's cottages. Lord Liverpool was Prime Minister then and a bunch of softies founded the RSPCA. He tapped lightly on the door, glancing left and right. He checked his watch. Christ, it was gone midnight. He'd left the whole thing far too late. Then it opened and Sally Meninger stood there, her long hair, usually neatly folded and pinned, splayed over her dressing-gowned shoulder.

'Max?' she blinked at him.

He gently pushed her backwards, closing the door as quietly as he could. 'Sorry,' he said. 'I don't really want to be seen hovering in your hallway.'

'Well,' she raised an elegant eyebrow. 'To what do I owe the pleasure?'

269

'It's late, Sally and I'm sorry.'

'Don't be silly. Actually, I'm glad to see you. You've no idea how boring it is here. We've all agreed to stay put until Saturday—and *that* seems an eternity away. Drink?'

'Thanks.'

'I haven't any Southern Comfort, I'm afraid,' she said. 'Scotch?'

'Fine.'

'Water?'

'No, thanks.'

'Take off your . . . things.' She raided the mini-bar for them both, emptying the little bottles. With the light behind her, in fact with the light in front of her, Sally Meninger was a beautiful woman. The white bath-robe showed off her figure to perfection. But then, she knew that perfectly well. She handed him his glass. 'Now, let's see,' she said. 'You haven't come to take up my rather clumsy cash offer of the other night, surely?'

'No.' He shook his head. 'No, it's not that.'

'Actually, I'm glad to have this chance to apologize for that.' She offered him a seat in her outsize armchair. 'It was ludicrous, embarrassing and unfair.'

'Consider it a closed book,' he said, making himself comfortable. 'I'm here about James Diamond.'

'James?' She sat on the edge of her still made-up bed. 'Ah.'

'I've got a strange feeling that my revered

270

leader is up to his neck in a spot of bother at the moment. And that you can shed some light on that. Am I right?'

'What do you want to know?' She sipped her Scotch, unlike Maxwell's, on the rocks.

'I'll settle for the truth,' he said.

'All right,' she sighed. 'The truth. James and I met at a conference in Brighton in ninety-eight. He seduced me.'

'*He* seduced *you*?' Maxwell wanted to get this scenario straight in his mind.

'Well, it may have been half a dozen of one, six of another,' she smiled. 'You know what conferences are like.'

Maxwell did—Blind Date meets Get Your Tits Out.

'That was all it was. Just a short fling. Or so I thought.' Her face darkened. 'I was wrong. He began phoning me, writing, texting once texting became the norm.' It wasn't the norm for Peter Maxwell—he was still trying to send telegrams.

'Are you trying to tell me Legs Diamond was stalking you, Sally?' Maxwell frowned. This wasn't the Headmaster he had come to loathe and despise.

'How well do you know him, Max?' She sensed his incredulity. 'Really *know* him, I mean?'

'I know he's an inept shite,' Maxwell told her, believing the time for pussy-footing around to be over. 'Give him a decision and

271

he's hamstrung. Give him an option, he'll jump the wrong way. Not a people person, is our Legs.'

'I'm impressed by your loyalty,' she scoffed.

'Actually, that's why I'm here,' he answered her. 'It's precisely because I *am* loyal, despite my better judgement, that I don't want to see him drowning in somebody else's cesspool.'

'That somebody else being me?' she looked him squarely in the face.

'Something like that,' he said.

'I lost Keith, my husband, as a result of James.'

'Lost in the sense of . . . ?'

'James started coming round to the house . . . we lived in Bournemouth then, pestering me for sex, sending me presents, flowers. Keith and I . . . well, we'd been having our problems. James was the last straw. But I still think, without him, we'd have got it together; patched up our differences, moved on . . . In the event, we divorced last year.'

'What about Margaret?'

'Who?'

'Diamond's wife,' Maxwell reminded her.

Sally shrugged. 'I never met the woman. James always said he felt sorry for her. I got the picture of a mousy little piece in crimplene. I don't want to sound like a banner headline from something by Virago Press, but you fucking men treat us all like shit.'

'Fucking being the operative word,' Maxwell

272

reminded her. 'That "noises off" performance at the Vine . . .'

'Alan,' she nodded darkly. 'Alan was the complication.'

'In what way?'

She looked at him, biting her lower lip. 'Alan and I were in love.'

'Oh, really?'

She stood up sharply. 'Maxwell, I don't care what you think of me. If I don't measure up to your God-given moral standards, then fuck you. It doesn't matter one way or another. Alan and I had been an item for months. He'd ask for me on as many Ofsted teams as he could so that we could be together. Just feeble, fleeting moments like this, in grubby, one-star hotel rooms. But I didn't care—I was with him.'

'And Pamela?'

'Who?'

'His wife.'

'That bitch,' Sally growled. 'I've never met her either, but she made his life hell. Nothing crimplene mouse about her, I understand. He asked her for a divorce and she just laughed at him. Laughed like she wasn't the one who was the bloody joke.'

'Where does Diamond fit in to all this?'

Sally wandered to the window. Through her still open curtains she could see the night stars twinkling far out against the black headland that was the Shingle. 'When we arrived at

273

Leighford I couldn't believe it,' she said. 'There he was, all testosterone and attitude.' *Testosterone and attitude*? Was she even talking about the same man, Maxwell wondered. 'He cornered me on the Monday afternoon, pawing, licking. In his office. It was disgusting. I told him he had no hold over me; never had. I told him . . . and God help me, this was the most terrible thing I've ever done . . . told him about Alan and me. Hoping it would put him off, make him see sense. He went berserk, shouting, screaming. I got out, just left . . . I couldn't take any more of it.'

She turned back to him. 'That's why I was out of my tree that night, the night of the Vine. I'd been hitting the g 'n' t's is here at the hotel ever since the afternoon. I just wanted Alan, to love and to have him love me. It all got a bit out of hand after that and I'm sorry you had to witness it.'

'How about the man with the black bag?' Maxwell asked her.

'I'm sorry?'

'The man you bumped into on your way out of the gents at the Vine. Joe Public. You said something like "Brilliant" at the time.'

'Did I?' She frowned. 'I was pissed. I don't remember. He was probably standing in my way. I already felt pretty awful, what with you witnessing the whole thing. Either love is the most beautiful thing in the world, or it's a cheap sordid sideshow.'

'He was the same man you were seen rowing with in the pub carpark later that night.'

'What are you talking about? Who told you that? Who saw me?'

'Just someone,' Maxwell shrugged.

Sally replenished her Scotch. 'Well, I don't know, Max, who your "someone" is, but they're wrong. I haven't the first clue who the guy was and after leaving the loo, I never saw him again.'

Maxwell nodded. 'Fair enough,' he said. 'Tell me about Diamond last Wednesday night.'

'What?'

'A week ago,' he reminded her. 'He came to visit.'

She blinked. 'What, here at the Cunliffe?'

'This would be late, maybe eleven or half past.'

'Max,' she frowned, sitting forward with a fierce concentration on her face. 'What are you talking about? Given what I've just told you, do you think for a moment I'd allow that weird bastard to be in my presence alone again?'

Maxwell looked at her. 'Given what you've told me, Sally,' he said, 'no, I don't suppose you would.'

*   *   *

He'd seen himself out. At the dead of night,

he'd crept along Sally Meninger's corridor in the dim half light. He needed time to consider this one, to examine the twists and turns of her testimony. She may have got into DC Baldock's trousers and DC Baldock's mind, assuming he had one, but Peter Maxwell had been round the block a few more times than the boy detective.

'Jesus!' Maxwell was standing stock still, staring ahead as the hairs prickled on the back of his neck.

'Can I help you?' a voice called.

'Tell me you're not Paula Freeling,' he said, 'or I'll have to re-examine my concept of faith.'

'Who are you?' the little woman in the nightgown asked him.

'Er . . . Peter Maxwell,' he said. 'I teach at Leighford High School.'

She held out a cold and tentative hand. 'I'm Deborah Freeling,' she said. 'Paula was my sister. Did you know her?'

'We had the briefest of conversations,' Maxwell said. 'Not even that, really.'

'Mr Maxwell,' Deborah looked up into his bright, deep eyes. 'I'm not in the habit of inviting strange men back to my room, but I need to have some answers. The police are telling me nothing. Do you have a moment?'

*   *   *

'So there we have it, Count,' Maxwell blew

276

imaginary smoke rings to the ceiling. It was very late and he was lolling on his sofa, half getting his head round the latest Simon Schama. He'd tried sleeping—no go. He'd tried counting sheep but half of them had the face of Alan Whiting and the others bore a curious resemblance to Paula Freeling—or was it Deborah? 'Let me recap, shall I?'

Metternich didn't give a monkey's really and his yawn said it all—a narrowing of the eyes, an exposure of the tongue and a flashing of the canines. Odd that, for a cat. Why weren't they called felines? Either way, he should have been Elsewhere a long time ago, eviscerating a rodent. That was what he'd been put on earth to do, after all.

'We have that old dilemma, the lying woman. Or do we? Alan Whiting's all over Sally Meninger. Or is he? Legs Diamond's all over Sally Meninger. Or is he? What's the common denominator, I hear you ask. Why, Sally Meninger of course. All right,' he tossed the book aside and folded his arms, determined to wrestle the problem through. 'Let's say she's lying. First scenario. Alan Whiting is not all over Sally Meninger—she's all over him. Now this much I can vouch for, having seen it for myself. Not only is she all over him, she's all over him in public. And not just a peck or a shy little holding of the hand, but the Full Monty. Well, you're very young, Count, so I won't go into the *Daily Sport*

277

details. And especially with you having no nuts to speak of, etcetera—I don't feel it would be appropriate. The question is, why? Why does a professional, middle-aged woman with a position in the world behave like that? Second scenario. Legs Diamond is not all over Sally Meninger, but rather *au contraire*. Vice versa.' His mind was racing. 'Well,' he wagged a finger at the cat. 'You say that, Count, but it's apparently quite common. Bored middle class housewives spicing up their lives by going on the game. After all, it is, after the Church of England, the oldest profession. So, what are we saying? Sally Meninger is a 50K a year hooker? It's possible. So who killed Whiting? She did, because he'd rumbled her night job and was going to the authorities? A. N. Other did to protect Sally's reputation? Did Sally hire a hitman? Well, I know it's bollocks, but Jacquie seems sold on the idea . . .'

He looked again at the phone. He'd rung her countless times already, since she'd hung up on him. Each time the beep. Each time the answerphone message. 'I can't come to the phone just now . . .' And he mentally finished the sentence for her, 'I'm having a hard time with a devious, ungrateful pig who keeps sticking his nose into police business.'

'All rightee,' Maxwell bowed to the inevitable and got up to pour himself another Southern Comfort. 'What Sally would have us believe, Count, is that she and Whiting were

278

love's middle-aged dream and that nasty, twisted old Legs Diamond, in a fit of jealousy, killed the Inspector in a sort of green mist. Well, actually, that's no sillier than the hitman, is it? But there's a problem.' And he got himself outside a large one.

Metternich rolled over and stretched. God knew what time it was and the silly old fart was still burbling on. Time for a bit of bum-licking at least. He got on with it, right there in Maxwell's dimly-lamped living room.

'What of the curious incident of the Headmaster in the night time?' Maxwell was pacing the room. Any minute now he'd lie down on his front with his bum in the air, ready to pounce. Or if he was a cat he would. 'You see, Sally Meninger says Diamond didn't visit. Diamond says he did. Now why should a man deliberately put himself in the frame by claiming to be somewhere he wasn't, knowing perfectly well that a *second* murder victim disappeared from that self-same spot? Confused? I know I am, and with respect, Count, the cubic capacity of your brain wouldn't fill a thimble, so where does that leave you? On the other hand, why would Sally Meninger lie about Diamond's visit? You see, the problem arises because of George. You won't remember George, Count. You were only a little black nothing of fleas and fur when George was at Leighford High. Now he works twenty-four hours a day solid for the Cunliffe.

279

He's a bright enough sort of chap, observant, honest, loyal. After I'd slipped him a bung on my way out of Sally's room, he told me that, sure enough, Legs Diamond had paid a visit. Typical of Legs, of course, he didn't remember George at all—either that, or he's a better actor than I give him credit for. Like me, Legs realized there'd be a copper on the prowl in the foyer so, like me, he rang George and came out with some crap about confidentiality, needed to see the Ofsted inspectors, actually came out with his name and bloody position. God save us from master criminals like James Diamond. The Napoleon of Crime he ain't.'

Maxwell took a swig and winced as the amber nectar hit his tonsils, trailing around the living room, looking for inspiration. 'But you see the problem, Count? George told me Diamond arrived via the back—that's the kitchen door—at ten thirty, near as dammit. Diamond's version is that he crept up the back stairs to Sally's room on the second floor for nookie, an exchange of pleasantries, a séance, who knows? Sally's version is that he never got there. So where was he? George didn't see him leave and the kitchen door is another fire exit. You just push the bar and out you go. No alarm. Paula Freeling went to her room at a little after ten, the others hitting the trail in ones and twos an hour later. Diamond would have had plenty of time to get into the old girl's room, drug her, truss her up or whatever

280

and whisk her away into the Leighford night. Bob's your uncle and Legs Diamond's a serial killer. Shit!' Maxwell thumped down his glass. 'This is all getting too surreal, Count.' He pinged the cut glass with an expert fingernail. 'And this stuff doesn't help.'

He sat back down on the settee. 'Then, there's Deborah Freeling, sister and spitting image of the late lamented Paula. I tell you, I was glad I was wearing the brown trousers when I met her tonight. She's staying at the Cunliffe, in her sister's old room at the suggestion of . . . wait for it . . . Jacquie. Yes, my Jacquie.' His words hung heavy on the stillness of the night air. *Was* she *his* Jacquie any more? He sensed a hot friend cooling and it frightened him. 'According to Miss Freeling—the live one, that is, a police officer named Detective Sergeant Carpenter called on her in her hotel and suggested she move to the Cunliffe. Said it would help enormously with police enquiries, apparently. Now, a) why didn't Jacquie tell me that? And b) how can it possibly help police enquiries? It seems to me, as it must inevitably seem to you, that, on the contrary, it just confuses the issue, thereby *hampering* rather than helping the boys in blue.'

He looked at the room distorted through the amber and the crystal cuts in his glass. The world was starting to look like that all the time to him now. 'She was rather a pathetic figure, actually, Count. Wanted to know exactly what

281

had happened at Leighford High. She seemed more angry than sad. Pretty determined to find out who killed her sister. Well,' he emptied the glass with an air of finality. 'Aren't we all?'

Silently, and with appalling effect, Metternich broke wind.

*　　　*　　　*

James Diamond went back to Leighford Police Station the next morning with his solicitor in tow. He'd told his secretary to clear his diary of engagements and since he never did any teaching, covering classes wouldn't be much of a problem. He'd spent the most ghastly night of his life coming clean with Margaret, his long-suffering wife. She hadn't screamed, hadn't ranted. And somehow, that had made matters worse. Expecting a rolling pin, he got deathly silence. She quietly and methodically moved into the spare room and vowed to get even. He'd rung the chairman of Governors and explained his problem. And after much 'oh dearing', the stupid old bugger had made patronizing noises while metaphorically wheeling in circles prior to disappearing up his own bum. And he'd rung the Chief Education officer to offer his resignation.

'Now, James,' the nauseating pen-pusher had wheedled. 'We don't have to be too hasty, do we?' He was, after all, the man who'd appointed him in the first place. 'Of course, if the police re-arrest you, I'm afraid we may have to consider suspension.' He was, when all was said and done, a public servant and he knew exactly what a fickle lot the public were.

So while Diamond was waiting in Interview Room One, a pompous, overpaid arse of a solicitor sitting by his side; and while Margaret Diamond was packing a few things to go and stay with her mother; and while the nauseating CEO was checking with the County solicitor and beginning the distancing process, Bernard Ryan was trying to run a school and his Head of Sixth Form was holding back the running feet of progress.

'Time off?' Ryan repeated, trying to make sense of the absent Head's diary entries for the day.

'A day,' Maxwell said. 'Two at most. Come on, Bernard, it's the quiet end of the year. You know, that magic time we teachers dream about—Years 13 and 11 have gone, the exam build-up is all over and we have absolutely nothing to do but sharpen our pencils, sit back and count the huge amount of lolly they pay us.'

'Get real, Max,' Ryan grunted. He'd been Acting Head for sixteen hours now and was already feeling suicidal. He looked at the photo of James Diamond with his kids on the desk in front of him and saw him in a new light. 'This isn't some Famous Five bloody adventure. The Head's in serious difficulties.'

'Precisely,' Maxwell nodded, his cycle-clips still round his ankles, his hat still perched on his barbed-wire hair. 'Which is why I'm asking for a couple of days.'

Ryan dithered. 'Permission denied,' he said. It was a cliché he'd heard in war films without number, but it served no purpose.

'Aaargghhh!' Maxwell jacknifed and scrabbled for the dark corner, his face turning the colours of the rainbow as he clutched his left arm.

'Max!' Ryan moved forward to catch him. 'Are you all right?'

'For the moment,' the Head of Sixth Form beamed, straightening smartly. 'But that could have been a heart attack, my old back trouble or even the first tentative symptoms of galloping impetigo. You see the way this is going, Bernard?'

The reluctant deputy straightened too, more slowly, more furious. 'You're telling me you'll take the time anyway, whether I sanction it or not.'

'Acting Headmaster . . .' Maxwell was appalled.

'You're beneath contempt,' Ryan growled.

'Yeah,' Maxwell grinned, pinching the man's scowling cheek. 'But ain't I just adorable with it?' He saw himself out. 'Don't worry, Bernard,' he called back. 'I'll make sure Thingee has my lesson details. Paul Moss can handle the Department and as we both know, Sixth Form-wise, Helen Maitland's a brick.'

*   *   *

'So,' Henry Hall was leaning forward across the desk. 'It is your contention that you visited Ms Meninger in her room at the Cunliffe Hotel last Wednesday night.'

'That's correct,' Diamond told him.

'For what purpose?'

'You don't have to answer that, James,' the pompous arse said.

'Oh, but I do, Gerald,' Diamond said. 'I've told my wife, for God's sake. Telling the police will be a doddle, believe me. I went there to end it, Chief Inspector.'

'End it?' Hall was confused. 'I didn't think there was anything to end.'

'Perhaps yes, perhaps no,' Diamond and Hall could have been clones of each other. Like bookends they sat there in that sunless interview room, the clock ticking, their arms folded in postural echo. 'When someone comes into your life from the past . . . someone as sexual as Sally, well . . . you weigh up the pros and cons. Oh, I admit, I was tempted. She made all the running in my office that day. But I owed it to Margaret and to my children—and I just thank God they're still away at university—not least to Leighford High. I owed it to them all to stop anything before it started.'

285

'And did you?'

Diamond's gaze faltered. 'Not exactly.'

'James . . .' the solicitor warned again.

'It's all right, Gerald, really. This is all supposed to be good for the soul.'

'I'm more concerned with your career at this precise moment in time,' Gerald snapped.

'Spoken like a true brief, sir,' Hall nodded, stone-faced. 'But souls and careers don't hold a candle to murder, I'm afraid.'

'We had sex,' Diamond said, cutting to the chase. 'I'm not proud of it and it wasn't in my game plan. But there it is.'

'And what time did you leave Ms Meninger's room?' Hall wanted to know, the book-end unfolding his arms and leaning back in his chair.

'I don't know. Twelve, half past.'

'Not exactly the demon lover, then?' Hall ventured.

'Chief Inspector . . .' Gerald scowled.

'I withdraw the slur,' Hall waved a hand. 'There's no need to add insult to injury, is there? When you left Ms Meninger's room, at twelve or half past, where did you go?'

'Home. No,' Diamond changed tack abruptly. 'No, I drove around for a bit.'

'Drove around? Where?'

'Oh, I don't know. Along the Front, out on to the Shingle. I was upset, confused. That terrible business with Alan Whiting . . .'

'Did anybody see you?' Hall asked.

'I don't know,' Diamond snapped. 'What a bloody silly question. How do I know whether anybody saw me or not?'

'All right.' Hall was reason itself. 'Let me put it another way. Did you see anybody?'

'What? On foot, you mean? No, nobody. It was late. There was the odd vehicle. Oh, I remember I saw a fox down on the beach.'

'A fox?' Hall frowned, looking at Diamond, then at the brief.

'Yes, odd, wasn't it? I know they're urban and so on, but you don't expect to see them by the sea. He was . . . sort of . . . playing with the surf, chasing the waves and trying not to get his feet wet.'

There was a pause. 'So what time did you get home?' Hall asked.

'I don't know. Two, half past. I don't remember. It was late.'

'Do you have a garage, Mr Diamond?' the Chief Inspector wanted to know.

'Yes, of course. What . . .'

'I'd very much like to see it, if I may.'

'You'll need a warrant, Chief Inspector,' Gerald told him flatly.

'Will I, Mr Diamond?' Hall ignored him. 'Will I really have to go to these lengths with a man who assured me not an hour ago that all he wanted to do was to help?'

'No,' Diamond said quietly, avoiding Hall's blank glasses and the blank eyes that lay behind them. 'No, you won't.'

287

Chapter Twelve

It was a little after lunchtime that they arrived at Leighford High; two women striding purposefully across the car-laden tarmac in the blazing afternoon sun. The taller and younger of them flashed her warrant card at the Reception Desk and Thingee Two went through the motions. The police had been wandering in and out all week, checking on this, verifying that. But still no interviews of the staff, still no interviews of the kids.

Peter Maxwell did a double-take. He was striding the mezzanine floor like a Colossus when he saw her, his Jacquie, wandering back to her Ka. He tried to slide up the window, but it was jammed by years of regulation white gloss paint, so he hammered on the glass. She turned at the sound, along with a trio of sixth formers about to slope off rather than face double Business Studies. Their eyes locked across a crowded school and no one moved. Then she turned and vanished behind the trees. The sixth formers looked suitably sheepish, astonished anew by their Year Head's ability to smell their scam at a couple of hundred yards. How did he do it, the eagle-eyed old madman?

What the eagle had not seen from his sixth form eyrie was the other woman, the little one with the wiry frame and sprightly step. But everyone who passed her did. Deborah Freeling walked the way that Jacquie had shown her, noting the reactions of all she saw, as Jacquie had asked that she should. The odd wandering kid on his way to the loo via lung-cancer paid her no attention, but every teacher looked twice. Dierdre Lessing opened her mouth to challenge her, she who routinely turned publishers' reps away, but she couldn't find the words. It was as if Paula Freeling had come back to the scene of the first crime. And from the look on Dierdre's face, she'd just vanished through a wall.

*   *   *

That was the night of the Grad Ball. They held it that year at the Old Mill in Tottingleigh and the Ball Committee of Year 13 had decided it should be masked. Umpteen Zorros turned up and even one Lone Ranger, but most of the girls, shining in their lovely gowns, simply wore glittering sequinned and feathered creations which caught the starlight in the Mill's grounds. The place had been gentrified years ago and hadn't seen a corn ear ground in anger for aeons. At the bar, the collective rowdies of the Gorilla Club spent most of the evening belching, trying to outdrink each other and guessing which girl was which by the size and inclination of their breasts.

'That's Hannah Willoughby,' insisted one.

'Never!' another bellowed. 'Janet Levington.'

'Come on, you people,' a third piped up. 'Look at the left one—Sam Haygarth.'

'I think you'll find,' said a voice behind the long, slightly uptilted nose, 'that it's Georgina Adams.'

A pause.

'God, he's right.'

'Thank you, Mr Maxwell.' And the impressed Gorillas saluted him with their raised pints as he swept out onto the terrace.

'Lovely night, Senior Mistress Mine,' the Head of Sixth Form said to Dierdre Lessing, looking positively skeletal in a black velvet number.

'Oh, it's you, Max.' She stepped aside. 'I didn't recognize you without the hat. Who are you supposed to be?'

'Cyrano de Bergerac,' he felt it a little superfluous to say, bowing low with a flourish. 'Swordsman, poet, scientist, man of letters, most of them French. Very like my good self, really, without the scientist bit.'

'What news of James?'

'I'd hoped he'd be here,' Maxwell surveyed the mingling crowd looking for the demon Headmaster.

'Would you,' Dierdre asked him, 'given the situation?'

Maxwell nodded. 'Given the situation I

most assuredly would,' he said. 'If he has nothing to hide. Bearing in mind he was whisked away with a great deal of excitement by the boys in blue, I'd have thought it incumbent upon him to show his face, albeit unmasked.'

'Well, you galloped off the other morning to his rescue,' Dierdre retorted. 'What *does* he have to hide?'

'That, Senior Mistress, remains to be seen. Don't they look lovely?'

Maxwell grinned broadly. The Old Mill was aglow with soft mock-candlelight, the coloured bulbs strung across the terrace swaying in the gentle breeze and just beginning to jump a little as the DJ got into full swing, his woofers and tweeters working overtime as the Peaveys kicked in. The cocktail sausages and other finger-food still lay untouched on the long tables as bevies of lovelies rolled up in the constant relays of stretch limos, black and white, that brought them to the door. They giggled together behind their masks, eyeing the Gorilla Club who lined the bar, each of the lads wearing a bandanna over their noses and mouths which they had to lift up each time they wanted a sip of their drinkies. Not much forward planning had gone on there. The more athletic of the girls were whirling round the tiny dance floor where coloured lights flashed in the semi-darkness. In Maxwell's day, they'd have been dancing around their handbags. On the terrace and the lawns that rolled away to the lake, knots of lovers took advantage of the increasing dark.

'I wonder how many pregnancies Leighford High will be responsible for tonight?' Dierdre asked, eternally seeing life's glass as half-empty.

'"After the Ball was over",' sang Maxwell softly, '"Oh we had such fun, putting the girls in the corner and . . ." you should have more faith in the school's sex education programme, Dierdre. Anyway,' he looked her up and down sharply under the mask, 'weren't you young once?'

She scowled at him. Maybe not.

'Mr Maxwell, Mr Maxwell,' a breathless girl bounced against him as he lolled against the parapet.

'Judith.' He caught her in an expert way that avoided a handling charge, and recognized the matronly bosom. 'Having a good time?'

'We're going to get married,' she slurred happily, dragging a captive geek by the hand. 'Aren't we, Tom?'

Tom wasn't sure what the question was and looked decidedly pissed in his hired black tie and his new marital status.

'Congratulations,' said Maxwell.

'And we're going to call our first baby after you,' Judith wobbled, trying to keep the great man in focus.

'Head of Sixth Form Jennings,' Maxwell

smiled, benignly. 'Yes, that has a certain ring to it.' And he barely had time to duck before Judith had planted a slobbery kiss on his cheek and giggled away into the long goodnight.

'Disgusting!' growled Dierdre.

'Lighten up, Senior Mistress. Tomorrow, Judith will have forgotten this conversation ever took place and Tom will be a happier man for it. Look at them.' He raised his glass to them all. 'You and I remember this lot when they were eleven, all bony knees and big eyes. What's that corny song from *Fiddler on the Roof*? "When did she get to be a beauty? When did he grow to be so tall?" Corny, but true.'

'Max, you old bastard!' Ben Holton slapped the man on the back. It was odd to see him without his white coat.

It was Dierdre's cue to slope off. 'Thank God for that,' the Head of Science muttered, watching her go. 'I haven't had half enough of the tincture to cope with that all evening. What news on Diamond?'

'Is that everybody's sole topic of conversation?' Maxwell asked him. 'Look around you, Ben. The crème de la crème of Leighford High—the golden girls and the lovely lads—or is it the other way round? We made them, Ben, you and I—oh, and their parents of course, a gene here, a chromosome there and a lot of environmental tosh, I'm sure.'

'Could you *be* any more maudlin?' Holton wondered aloud, slurping his pint.

'Sorry,' Maxwell chuckled. 'I'm a funny age. Tell you what,' he twisted his long nose from side to side, 'it's a bitch trying to drink in this.'

'That's why I didn't bother,' Holton said, swigging again.

'Aaarghh,' Maxwell staggered sideways. 'You mean, that's not a grotesque mask?'

'Oh, ha,' was Holton's best response. 'Let me get you another.'

'Thanks, Ben.' Maxwell held up his glass. 'Some of whatever that was. I'd better not mix my drinks. It's not the witching hour yet and I'm cycling later.' And the Head of Science disappeared into the bowels of the Mill, blissfully ignorant of the V signs from the Gorilla Club behind his back.

'No Jacquie tonight, Max?' Sally Greenhow was wearing a stunning emerald green creation that clung to her body like a lawyer to his client.

'Er . . . no,' Maxwell bluffed, kissing her on the cheek. 'Something came up.'

'Diamond?' she whipped up her feathery mask to her hairline to look him straight in the eye.

'I really can't say,' Maxwell said. 'Where's your better half?'

'Looking down some girl's cleavage at the bar. They look nice, don't they?'

'Cleavages?'

'The kids,' she tapped him with her stole ends.

'They do,' he nodded. 'I was saying as much to Dierdre and Ben. They can't see it.'

'Well, there's a surprise. You know Margaret's left him, don't you?'

'What?'

Sally nodded. You got a superior kind of tittle-tattle in Special Needs. 'As I live and breathe. This morning, apparently. Gone to her mother's.'

'A little stereotypical, perhaps,' Maxwell shrugged. 'Mother of God, what's that?'

A crash punctuated proceedings followed by a wailing sound. All heads turned in the direction of the ballroom.

'That'll be the Live Music starting,' said Sally. 'Nice of you to book the Hippos—old Leighford Hyenas and all.'

'I didn't,' Maxwell told her. 'Helen,' he growled.

Maxwell's Number Two had not chosen wisely. Already known as the Fridge by generations of sixth formers, her cream creation with the mock pearl motif merely confirmed the sobriquet. 'Hello, Max.' She appeared to have a male stag beetle on her head.

'I thought the Ball Committee had hired Afterbirth,' he pecked her on the cheek and she kissed thin air.

'Lord, no, they're signed, whatever that

means. Luckily, Glenys Turnbull's sister goes out with the lead singer of the Yawning Hippos. So here they are. Stroke of luck, eh?'

'Top hole.' Maxwell's grin froze as Duggsy's tonsils shattered glass, 'I think you'll find however, there is only one singer, so "lead" is a little optimistic.'

'Who the fuck booked them?' groaned a passing sixth former.

'Shrewd question as always, Dean,' Maxwell called. 'But I'd remind you there *are* ladies present.'

'Sorry, Mr Maxwell. Sorry, Mrs Maitland. Sorry, Mrs Greenhow.'

'Such a polite boy,' beamed Helen.

'Mr Maxwell!' a voice made them all turn. 'They're playing our tune.'

'No.' Maxwell retreated, both hands outstretched at the advance of Sylvia Matthews. It was a ritual they'd played out now for years. 'No, really, Sylv.'

The Nurse still turned heads in her red sequinned dress and could cut a swathe with the best of them. 'That's what they always say.' She laughed and grabbed his wrists, whirling him towards the floor and pecking him on the cheek.

'How can we possibly dance to this?' he shouted as the cheer went up as his sixth form recognized him, elegant and black and white as his cat, but topped with an outsize nose.

'It's a sort of foxtrot,' she lied. 'You'll get

the hang of it.'

'Hanged if I will,' he said, pointing his finger skyward in a passable John Travolta, to the roar of his thousands. 'Anyway, I'm that unfortunate generation that falls between two stools—too young for the foxtrot and decidedly too old for whatever these people do nowadays. I'm more your Gay Gordons, but I'll sue the arse off anybody who says so.' And he wheeled her away in something somewhere between the Veleta and the Mashed Potato.

'At last!' Helen Maitland was patrolling the edge of the dancing area as Maxwell came off the bend like Tony Curtis hurtling out of the Triple in *Trapeze*.

'You can say that again,' he wheezed, steadying himself against a pillar. 'Thank you for caring about me, Helen,' and he mimed a kiss.

'Not you, you old layabout. The photographer's here. We got a call to say he'd been held up. I'll just get whatsisface with the microphone to announce it.' And she was gone, all bustle and flurry.

'So who's doing the speeches in the absence of Diamond?' Ben Holton passed a drink to the grateful Head of Sixth Form, as his graduates got down to some serious boogying.

'Me, I suppose,' Maxwell bowed to Sylvia Matthews who beetled off in search of her life, as opposed to her dancing, partner.

'That'll give us a few yucks, then.' Holton

yawned. 'Tell me, Max, what's the school policy on nookie on Grad Ball night?'

Maxwell groaned. 'Judith and Tom in the rhododendrons?'

'Jeff Armstrong and Hayley Skeggs in the car park.'

Maxwell raised the Cyrano mask and one stern eyebrow. 'As in Jeff Armstrong, of the Design and Technology Department, teacher in loco parentis and with a legal position of trust; and Hayley Skeggs, the Lolita of Modern Languages?'

'More or less,' Holton nodded ruefully. 'She's a bit older than twelve, though, isn't she?'

Maxwell was secretly impressed. That a scientist should know the age of Nabokov's heroine was little short of miraculous. 'Twelve is young Jeffrey's IQ,' he sighed. 'Of course, it's an actual crime now.'

'Indeed,' Holton agreed.

'Man could lose his job.'

'Or worse.'

'So what do you recommend?'

'You're sixth form, Max.' Holton knew when it was time to pass a buck. He had a higher degree in it.

'Don't be ownier than thou about this, Ben. And I won't embarrass us both by asking you exactly where his hands were at the time. I'm going in search of a jug of cold water. Hold this for me, will you?'

298

Holton was glad he was only talking about his drink.

* * *

The rush of cold air on his face was welcome as White Surrey crested the rise. A younger man would have left the ground and done wheelies at this point, but Peter Maxwell was not a younger man. Another Grad Ball was over. He'd made his speeches, presented his daft prizes, got his laughs. The World's Worst Driver, the Man Most Likely to Become PM, the Best Hung Sixth Former etcetera, etcetera. It came as no surprise to anyone that Hayley Skeggs had been voted the Girl Most Likely To and this had been amply proved by Jeff Armstrong or it would have been if Peter Maxwell hadn't arrived in the nick of time. He'd coughed loudly to give the pair time to adjust their clothing, told Hayley to go back to the party and gave young Armstrong the fright of his life. He painted a vivid picture of the story as it would appear in the *Daily Sport* and the *Guardian* respectively. For a while the Design Teacher toyed with going home and shooting himself; then he relented and filled in the entry form for the Benedictine Order. Either way, Maxwell had saved him from himself.

The Head of Sixth Form wished them all well, the kids of Maxwell's Own, as they launched themselves into the rest of their lives. 'If you can walk a straight line,' he said to the Gorilla Club, 'thank a teacher.' And they carried him shoulder high around the Old Mill, laughing, whooping and chanting 'Mad Max! Mad Max!' At one point he was vaguely aware of a camera flashing and of Dierdre Lessing hissing her disgust at the proceedings.

That was then. Now, as the sobering breeze of the early morning hit him, reality kicked in. Jacquie had not arrived. He'd bought her ticket, rung her, left messages. He'd waited until the last minute to hear her key in the lock, the bounce of her Ka horn at the kerb. It hadn't happened. So he'd looked out his Full Dress cycle clips and wheeled Surrey into the evening.

'Going somewhere special, Mr Maxwell?' Mrs Troubridge had trilled, as he was on his way out, a watering can in her bony hand.

Maxwell turned to face her in his Cyrano mask. 'Just down the chippie,' he called and he'd vanished into the Leighford night.

The old girl would be asleep now, her teeth beside her in a glass, her hair in curlers and her Dorothy L Sayers half read on her counterpane. That repellent old man, Mr Troubridge, her late husband, would be grinning at her from the silver frame on her dressing table. Maxwell knew all this because he'd often entered her Cartland-pink boudoir in order to change the old besom's lightbulb.

Metternich the cat, gnawing on something indescribable in the privet, watched the wheel-warrior come home, a huge phallic nose on top of his head. There had to *be* a purpose to it all.

But Maxwell wasn't concerned with his ancient neighbour or the serial killer cannibal with whom he shared a house. He was concerned with what met him on the step of Number 38 Columbine as he swung out of Surrey's saddle. It appeared to be a wino at first, huddled in the doorway like something out of cardboard city. Then, recognition dawned. 'Headmaster?'

The less than demon headmaster clambered to his feet, a little shakily at first. 'Max,' he slurred. 'She's gone. I couldn't face the Graduation Ball. I had nowhere else to go.'

Maxwell steadied the man. He'd heard the gossip. He didn't need the details. You could have stayed put, he thought. If your wife's gone, there's plenty of room. You could get three 38 Columbines into Legs Diamond's gaff. 'You'd better come in,' he said and parking Surrey as best he could, eased open the door and let them both in.

'Max,' Diamond looked at the man, in the Head of Sixth Form's oddly swaying entrance hall. 'You're a friend. A true friend. Bernard Ryan. Dierdre Lessing. They're all arseholes. Utter shits. But you, ah . . .' he grinned inanely, 'Oh, we've had our differences . . .'

'And will, no doubt, continue to do so,

Headmaster.' He turned the man round and put his hand on the banister, pointing Diamond up the stairs. 'Come on, it's way past our bedtime. And that's *not* an invitation, by the way, womanless as we both seem to be at the moment.'

Legless Diamond did his best on the risers and treads.

*   *   *

Craig Edwards lay next to the desk in his office. On the walls around him, his own victims smiled down—three kids with lollipop grins and a St Bernard; an old and loving couple; brides and grooms without number. All of them oblivious of the fact, as the Leighford traffic built that Saturday morning, the sun dazzling on windscreens, that the man who had stood before them, posing, arranging, clicking shutters and angling lights, was dead.

'Clean thrust to the throat,' Jim Astley was wiping his glasses and huffing on the lenses as Henry Hall arrived in a clatter of constables.

'Same MO as the other two?' the DCI wanted to be sure.

'Near as dammit. Talk him through it, Jacquie. I've got a suicide on the slab and contrary to public opinion, corpses don't wait for ever.'

The police surgeon-cum-pathologist looked at Hall for a moment. He saw a man who was drowning rather than waving. 'Bit of a facer, this one, Henry. Moonlighting as an Ofsted inspector, was he?' He chuckled and winked. 'Don't worry, I'll see myself out.'

Craig Edwards' office was being transformed into a crime scene. Other arc lights and tripods replaced his own, men in odd white gear were running paintbrushes over door handles and chair backs. Rubber-gloved hands were searching carefully through drawers and filing cabinets. Outside in the street, a growing crowd of ghouls was peering through the front windows, asking obvious questions of the uniforms told to keep them back. Holiday-makers expecting a bit of sun, sea and sand had a bonus—a grisly murder just off the High Street. Postcards would never be the same again—'Weather lovely. Kids a pain. Some bloke got killed today.'

'Craig Edwards,' Jacquie was talking Henry Hall through it in the room behind the drawn blinds, eerily lit by the SOCO arc lights, 'photographer.'

'Are you all right, Jacquie?' Hall asked. His DS looked tired or perhaps it was just the lights.

'I'm fine,' she said firmly, trying the briefest of smiles. 'Just too many of these, that's all.'

It should have been the Grad Ball last night and she hadn't gone. Like Cinders, she'd stayed at home and no fairy godmother had come to her rescue. Turning a pumpkin into a

303

coach and four was a detail in comparison with patching things up with Peter Maxwell.

Hall nodded. He'd seen too many of those too, and you never, ever got used to it; the stillness of the corpse, the silence of the scene. He knelt beside the body, feeling the dead man's hand with the back of his own. Cold, but not stone cold.

'This is recent,' he said, frowning up at Jacquie.

'Couple of hours ago, Astley reckons,' she said.

Hall automatically checked his watch. 'Eight at the latest,' he said. He automatically took in the dead man's appearance too. He was . . . what, thirty-five, forty perhaps, medium build, on the short side, perhaps five seven. Weight? Difficult to tell lying down, but perhaps eleven, twelve stone. He had a carefully cultivated three-day beard growth and brown eyes gazing dully out under half-closed lids, one slightly more open than the other. His mouth was open, as though he'd love to tell Henry Hall something, if only he could. A thin film of saliva still clung to his pale lips. His black leather jacket was thrown open and his shirt was stained with dark splashes and rivulets. There was a black hole between the collar points, slightly to the left of the Adam's apple.

'Astley thinks the attack took place out there,' Jacquie pointed to the area by the front door, partitioned off by a screen. 'Blood droplets on the flotex.'

Hall nodded. SOCO had already secured them and he'd gone round the pretty way. 'What do we know about him?' he asked.

'Small-time photographer. Weddings, christenings, stag nights. Usual things. Had these offices for three years. He was in Bournemouth before that. And originally from Leytonstone.'

Hall straightened. 'Not exactly David Bailey,' he commented. 'Who found the body?'

'A friend,' Jacquie said, checking her notebook. 'Mr John Anderson. He's next door in the developing room. Bit shaken, needless to say.'

Hall nodded. Murder did that to people. 'You've spoken?'

It was Jacquie's turn to nod.

'Right. With me then. Any anomalies, any deviation from what he told you, let me know about it. Jacquie,' he closed to her so that the alien-suited SOCO team couldn't hear it. 'Are you sure you're all right?'

She wanted to scream at him. She wanted to say, 'No, you nosey interfering bastard, I'm not all right. I'm tired of being woken up in the wee small hours with news that some poor sod has had his wind-pipe severed or his skull smashed in or his face blown away. I'm tired of the man I love using me like something out of Ask Jeeves. I'm tired of being taken for granted. Oh, Jacquie's all right. She's tough.

305

She can cope. Anyway, she's got to be a bit weird to hang out with that mad old teacher—whatsisface?

'Really, sir,' was how it came out in the end. 'I'm fine.'

She led him though a deserted studio where the back wall was a matte blue and lights and cables decorated the spaces. Beyond that was a door and a room lit with a single red bulb.

'Mr Anderson?' Hall spoke to the man sitting on a stool inside. 'I'm Detective Chief Inspector Hall, can we talk out here?'

Anderson took Hall's hand and passed from the dulling scarlet light into flesh and blood reality. Even so, he didn't look well. He was a dapper little man with the air of an aging art student about him, a goatee, spiky hair and an earring that caught the SOCO lights.

'I understand from DS Carpenter here that you found the body.'

Anderson nodded.

'I realize this is extremely painful for you, but I need to understand what happened.'

'Yes, I . . .' Anderson cleared his throat. 'I got here about nine, maybe nine fifteen. Craig was already dead. I knew that at once. I didn't touch anything. At least, I don't think so. I rang emergency services.'

'On the phone through there?' Hall pointed to the dead man's desk.

'No, on my mobile. It's sort of . . . instinctive. I've never waited so bloody long in my life.'

'Response time?' Hall asked Jacquie.

She checked her notebook. 'Eight minutes,' she said.

'Well,' Anderson insisted. 'It felt like fucking forever.'

'How well did you know the deceased, sir?' Hall asked.

'Craig? Oh, I don't know. Couple of years, I guess. I occasionally do the odd bit of work for him, you know, bit of lighting, driving. That's what I do; lighting engineer.'

'And this morning . . . ?'

'Oh, Craig crashed at mine last night. He'd had a bit of a skinful and I live in Tottingleigh where he'd had a job, so he called round. I've got a spare room, so he crashed. He'd left his film behind and I reckoned he'd need it, so I brought it in.'

'What time did he start work on Saturdays, Mr Anderson?' Hall wanted to know.

'Any time,' Anderson shrugged. 'He was his own man, pretty well. Look, can I have a ciggie?'

'I'm afraid not,' said Hall. 'Scene of crime. It causes complexities.'

'Right,' Anderson sighed. It had not been a good morning and it showed no signs of improving. 'No, Craig was a law unto himself, really. Most Saturdays he'd be off doing weddings or parties. I tried his place first and when he wasn't there, I tried here.' He glanced across to the desk behind which the feet of Craig Edwards poked out like those of the Wicked Witch of the East under Dorothy's house on her arrival in Oz. 'S'pose I was too late.'

'He must have left your house early,' Hall was thinking aloud.

'Yeah,' Anderson nodded. 'I didn't hear him go. Like that, was Craig. Not much of a breakfast man and talk about quiet.'

Hall nodded. 'Mr Anderson, there's a lot I need to know. Could you go with DS Carpenter to Leighford police station? We need a statement.'

'Er . . . yeah, sure, of course. I just want to get the bastard who did this.'

'Indeed,' Hall nodded. 'We all do.'

He watched them go, his quietly professional DS and the shambling witness who'd stumbled on a murder, and he wandered into the darkroom. That was odd. He slid open drawers, checked cupboard doors, rifled filing cabinets, all with the rubber gloves of his calling. Then he called through to the team going about their business. 'This is not a trick question, gentlemen,' he said. 'But there's a small prize for the one who can tell me what you expect to find in a photographer's studio.'

There was a pause. Had the guv'nor finally lost it? 'Film,' somebody called back.

'Bingo,' said Hall. 'So would I. But because

308

there isn't any, I shan't be giving out the prize after all.'

And Henry Hall never did find out which one of the white-coated SOCO gentlemen muttered, 'No surprises there, then, welching bastard.'

* * *

It must have been nearly eleven when the doorbell rang. The shape beyond the twisted glass was not that familiar, but Maxwell recognized it all the same.

'Mrs Whiting,' he smiled. 'How are you?'

'I was wondering, Mr Maxwell, if you'd made any progress.'

'Precious little, I'm afraid. Er . . . won't you come in?'

Pamela Whiting suited black. Her skin looked like alabaster against it and the severely cropped hair merely accentuated the hard lines of her mouth and jaw.

'You know where the lounge is.' He followed her up the stairs, trying, as all ex-public schoolboys always did, not to stare at her bum.

A dishevelled-looking James Diamond scrambled to his feet. Try as he might, Maxwell couldn't get used to the man without his three-piece. He was scruffily dressed in jeans and polo top and the fact that he had a neck under his shirt caused the Head of Sixth

Form quite a stir.

'Mrs Whiting,' Maxwell thought he'd better do the honours. 'This is my Headmaster, James Diamond.'

The Head didn't notice the fact that Maxwell had called him by name again or that he had endearingly used the personal pronoun. He was simply staring at Pamela Whiting with his mouth open.

'Oh, God,' he managed at last. 'Mrs Whiting. I am really *so* sorry,' he said, grasping her right hand in both of his. 'What can I say?'

'There's nothing to say,' she told him flatly. 'You may be in loco parentis, Mr Diamond, but I can hardly hold you responsible for my husband's death.'

'Unfortunately,' he muttered, 'the police do.'

'What?'

'Shall we all sit down?' Maxwell suggested, swiftly brushing a cloud of Metternich hairs off an armchair. 'Pamela,' he leaned forward. 'Can I get you a drink? Tea? Coffee?'

'No, thank you, Max,' she said. 'It's been quite a morning one way and another.'

'Really?'

'Well, I think there's been another murder.'

Maxwell and Diamond exchanged glances. 'Who?' they chorused.

'I don't know. I was out shopping in the High Street and came upon this large crowd—I don't know the name of the road. There were police cars and an ambulance. It *could* have been an accident, I suppose, or a suicide. But I overheard people saying it was murder.'

'In the street?' Maxwell checked.

'No, in a photographers', I understand. Gentlemen, I have to inform you of the rather striking fact that your town is not safe. What are the odds in seaside suburbia?'

'I'll drink to that,' Maxwell nodded and reached for his Southern Comfort. 'Headmaster?' He held up a spare glass.

'It's a little early for me, Max.' Even under suspicion for murder, Diamond couldn't resist being soberer than thou. Besides, his head was still exploding from his intake of the previous day and every gesture was rather slow and exaggerated, the sharp edges of everything just a little blurred.

'It's a little early for me, too,' Maxwell conceded, but poured a large one anyway.

'Then I saw a ghost.'

'I'm sorry?' Maxwell had only taken the merest sip by this time. Surely, it hadn't clouded his judgement already?

'I saw Paula Freeling.'

'What?' Diamond blinked at her.

'Where was this?' Maxwell asked, less surprised than his Headmaster to hear that news.

'In the High Street,' Pamela told him. 'Turning out of the photographer's road where all the commotion was.'

'Why do you think it was her?' Maxwell pursued it.

'I've got her picture on my bedside table at the hotel, Max,' Pamela said. 'That and the awful one of Alan the press borrowed. I've got all the press cuttings, national and local. Believe me—I'd know that woman in my sleep.'

'You couldn't be mistaken, Mrs Whiting?' Ever the rational scientist, Diamond was famous for his blinding glimpses of the obvious.

'Of course,' she shrugged. 'But I am not an hysterical woman going to pieces over the loss of her husband. Nor do I believe in the supernatural. Something very odd is going on in Leighford, Mr Diamond. Has either of you any idea what?'

Diamond looked utterly bewildered and left Maxwell to speak for them both.

'No,' he shook his head. 'But leave it with me, Pamela. I know a woman who does.'

Chapter Thirteen

'Have I done something to upset you?'

The sound of his voice made her jump as she switched on the light.

'Max. For Christ's sake, I didn't see you there.' Jacquie stood quaking in the doorway, her key still in the lock, her mind a thousand miles away, coping with murder.

He stood up. 'I'm sorry,' he said. 'I let myself in and it sort of got darkish. I was sitting here thinking.'

'You should have called.' She closed the door and tried to sweep past him, but he stopped her, holding her gently with one arm.

'I did,' he said. 'Several times. Your landline, your mobile. Much longer and I'd have had to break the taboo and ring your place of work.'

'Not a good idea.' She carried on into the kitchen, throwing car keys onto a surface, looking for a beer.

'All right.' He stuffed his hands into his pockets. 'What's it all about?'

Jacquie flicked off the bottle top with the gadget and turned to look at him. 'It's not you,' she said. 'It's me. It's this case. It's getting to us all.'

'We were supposed to go to the Grad Ball last night, Cinders,' he reminded her. 'Instead

I got Dierdre Lessing—*both* of the ugly sisters rolled into one.'

'Oh, Max.' She slapped her forehead with her hand. 'I'm sorry,' she lied. 'I forgot. Really, I did. Drink?'

'No, thanks. I'll pass.' Something told him tonight was not going to be a glittering social occasion.

'How did it go?'

'The Ball? Oh, fine, fine. Usual mix of emotions. Lads trying to get laid. Girls trying to be the belle of the ball and then get laid. Longing to take that leap into adulthood and the brave new world of University or whatever. Yet oddly terrified to kiss school and childhood goodbye. Same every year.' He chuckled.

She nodded. She wasn't really listening.

'Tell me about the photographer,' he said.

She looked at him. 'No,' she said, turning away to sort the mail she'd brought in with her.

He looked at her. 'No, in the sense of . . . ?'

'Max, this is over. I can't go on just being your way into police enquiries.' It was one of the hardest sentences she'd ever said.

He crossed the lounge and looked her squarely in the face. 'Is that what you think you are?' he asked.

She nodded, her eyes full of tears.

'Are you asking me to go?' he said.

She nodded again, unable to trust her voice, unable to look him in the face. It had been a long time since Peter Maxwell had known rejection like this. Not since those long ago Granta days, punting down the Cam for strawberries and cream at Rupert Brooke's Grantchester. That had been a different time—the past, that foreign country where they did things differently. He was not the same Peter Maxwell then. And he could barely remember the girl's name, still less her face. And since then he had known the worst rejection of all—that wet, wild Saturday when his darlings, his family, died on a crazy bend on a slippery road in the middle of nowhere. No goodbyes, only fading memories and fading photographs. And years of emptiness in which he became Mad Max, the dinosaur, his heart, forever broken, on his sleeve. He wanted to say . . . so much. And yet he couldn't. His mind raced over the years they had known each other, he and Jacquie, the dear, already dead days. He'd always teased her, called her Woman Policeman, swept the pale auburn hair from her face, kissed away the tears. He'd been there for her as she had for him, the late night calls and the warm silences, tucked up in his bed or hers. He'd loved the glow of the fire on her cheek, the light of the candles in her eyes and the wind in her hair. They'd laughed along the water's edge and rolled in the sand, her bright face and her musical laughter always in his mind, filling his head, warming his heart.

315

He took her house key out of his pocket and put it on the kitchen surface. She had books of his. He had CDs of hers. Presents, tokens, the silly trinkets that litter a relationship. He took her hand and kissed it—the old, romantic gesture that only someone like Mad Max remembered. Jacquie stood there, not knowing quite how her legs were still holding her up. He seemed a long, long way away at the end of a spiralling tunnel of loss and emptiness. And the old, sad lines of Rupert Brooke rang out on the velvet of his voice— 'And I shall find a girl, perhaps, and a better one than you. With eyes as wise, but kindlier, and lips as soft, but true.'

He looked into her eyes as they swam with unshed tears, tears which matched his own.

'And I daresay she will do.' He let her hand fall away and as suddenly as they had met, he was gone.

She didn't hear the click of her front door or the hiss of Surrey's wheels on her gravel. She didn't see his reflector lights wobbling away in the evening. That was because she was sitting on her settee in the still part-lit living room, her knees under her chin, rocking backwards and forwards like a baby. The unshed tears ran now down Jacquie Carpenter's face and she knew they would never stop.

*   *   *

316

Another Saturday night and Peter Maxwell had nobody. He lay in his lounge, on his settee and stared at the ceiling. He toyed with modelling, but Bob Portal was all but finished except for his horse's reins and that was always the worst part of any modelling job—ask Kate Moss. He tried to think, but thinking was difficult because a smiling girl kept filling his mind. 'I love you, Peter Maxwell,' she said over and over again.

He reached for the Southern Comfort, that glass of the warm south. Excellent though it was, it offered him little comfort tonight. The less-than-demon headmaster had gone, getting a cab back to his empty house. Maxwell knew the feeling. Except that unlike the Diamond estancia, Maxwell's house was always empty. Empty that is except for the black and white bastard that oozed around the door, tail erect, shoulders set, wondering which of his master's walls he should demolish tonight.

'There's been another one, Count.' Maxwell didn't have to glance across to know he was not alone. 'A photographer this time. Pass me the *Yellow Pages*, will you?'

Metternich looked at him with disdain. Skivvying was no part of his brief. He had a reputation in the area, for God's sake. Hunter, night-prowler, cat-about-town. He stretched on the rug and found his left forepaw absolutely fascinating. Maxwell rolled off the sofa and got them himself. You couldn't get

317

the staff these days.

'Off the High Street, Pamela Whiting said.' Maxwell was explaining to the cat. 'Just before she saw the ghost of Paula Freeling. So that means either Belvedere Street or Seacrest Road. Aha,' he tapped the page. 'Craig Edwards, photographer. Edwards. Edwards.' He could picture the shop, but not its owner. He slumped back against the furniture, the phone book abandoned, the drink cradled in both hands. 'So . . . stop me if you've heard this one before, Count, but what do two Ofsted inspectors and a photographer have in common?' He mused for a moment. 'Fucked, as Year Ten would say, if I know.'

*   *   *

The lights were still burning in Leighford nick that night and Henry Hall was in conference with Phil Bathurst, both men tired, both men aware of drowning in what was fast becoming a sea of panic.

'Take me through it again, Phil,' the DCI yawned, lolling back in his chair. 'We're missing something.'

'According to Astley,' Bathurst obliged, 'our friend struck as Edwards opened the shop this morning.'

'So did he have an appointment?'

'There's nothing in his diary,' the DI had it with him, resting on the edge of Hall's cluttered desk, ' 'till a wedding at two o'clock. St Andrews, Tottingleigh and a do at the Belmont.'

'All right,' said Hall. 'We'll come back to that. Astley's scenario.'

'Is that the attack began at the front door.'

'Right. So our man rings the doorbell.'

'Edwards opens it. This is before eight o'clock.'

'Skewer to the throat. Blood drops on the carpet. Edwards staggers backwards, ends up collapsing behind his desk.'

'Out of sight of the pavement so passers by would not spot the body.'

'And nobody was due to call in the morning.'

'Except that John Anderson did.' Bathurst was good at Incident Room ping-pong and providing you didn't miss a return shot, it got you Brownie points as well.

'And found Edwards, no doubt still warm.'

'This was nine fifteen at the latest.'

'Which gave Chummy over an hour to ransack the place. Why?'

'Ah,' Bathurst smiled. 'The case of the missing film.' Like everyone in the last sixty years, he'd been brought up on a diet of Perry Mason, the first thirty through the books of Erie Stanley Gardner and the second via the telly version of Raymond Burr.

'Now, tell me, Phil,' Hall reached for the paper cup containing the dregs of his coffee. 'Why would Chummy want to steal film?'

'Something to hide.'

Hall nodded. 'Something caught on film he doesn't want us to see. But what?'

'Pat Prentiss is working on his computer.'

Bathurst flicked through the dead man's desk diary. 'There again, it could be anybody in here,' he said.

'Who was working on that?'

'Jacquie Carpenter. I sent her home at nine. She was losing it by then.'

Hall's eyes narrowed and he tapped his teeth with his pen top. 'Seems strangely distracted at the moment, does Jacquie. Any views on that?'

'Peter Maxwell?' Bathurst ventured. He'd been at Leighford less than a year, but the policewoman's dangerous liaison was always bubbling under the surface of station conversation. If the old bastard just got on with his day job, no problem, but he would insist on being in at the kill, so to speak and that, mixed metaphors notwithstanding, muddied the waters.

Hall was nodding. 'Peter Maxwell,' he sighed. 'I went to see him, you know. Oh, unofficially, of course. Warned him off.'

'And?'

Hall shook his head. 'Might as well have pissed into the wind. What did Jacquie glean from the diary?'

Bathurst flicked through her typed up notes. 'The diary dates from 2001, July. He's had some two hundred and sixty jobs in that time, mostly weddings, birthdays, graduations. Couple of bar mitzvahs. Pat Prentiss had been on the filing cabinet contents, putting names to faces, as it were. Most photographers keep negatives for six months, then ditch—space problem, I suppose. This might be something, though.'

'Oh?' Any straw would be useful to Henry Hall about now. The killing this morning would only increase the media hysteria. The locals from the *Advertiser* were all over him like flies on shit by lunchtime. The nationals, having lost interest in the events at Leighford High and the Southern Water site, would be swarming all over the little photographic studio in Belvedere Street by morning. Simon Heffer and Peter Hitchens would be hoarse, yelling for a return of the rope.

'Well,' Bathurst was trying to fathom it. 'Jacquie's identified eight entries in that diary which just have a venue and a time. No name.'

'Is that particularly odd?' Hall wondered.

'Eight out of two hundred and sixty-eight sort of limits the odds, don't you think?'

'Got a for-instance?' Hall wanted to know.

'Last April. The Dam. Ten p.m.'

Hall frowned. The Dam was open commonland, on the high ground above Tottingleigh, the haunt, in its day, of glue-sniffers, black magicians and lovers of both sexes. They'd found bodies there before now.

'Well and truly dark by then,' the DCI observed, 'in April. So what sort of photographer goes out to do a job after dark?'

'One with good lighting gear and a state of the art camera.'

'Did he have those?'

'Oh, yes,' Bathurst confirmed. 'Nothing like that had been touched. It was all there in the studio. All that's gone is the film.'

'Was he into wildlife? Birds? Bees?'

Bathurst chuckled. 'Maybe,' he said. 'In an odd sort of way. But no, nothing like that in his portfolio. Strictly a people man.'

'Any more?'

'This one might interest you, guv.' Bathurst passed Jacquie's sheet across and pointed it out. 'The Vine. Nine thirty p.m. That was the night before Alan Whiting was killed.'

So it was.

*   *   *

Henry Hall watched them go that Sunday morning. He had a brief word with each of them in the foyer of the Cunliffe as they checked out, paid their bill and prepared to pass it all on to the taxpayer. Peter Maxwell watched them too, fuming at not being able to have a chat for one last time. The clues to the three deaths in Leighford, he knew, lay with those vanishing Ofsted inspectors, allowed at last to return to the real world and to do what they did best, stick their noses into other people's business. Bob Templeton was crisp and efficient-looking in his suit; Malcolm Harding an unmade bed in his. David Simmonds had made good use of his enforced days in the sun by buying an indescribable Hawaiian shirt. Only Sally Meninger looked enigmatic, her hair in a flowered headscarf, her eyes hiding behind shades. With her in particular, Maxwell had wanted a quiet word, accompanied, were he not a public schoolboy, by inserting lighted matches under her fingernails or tying her in a ducking stool. One or more of them was lying, Maxwell was sure of that. But which one? They piled into separate taxis, each one no doubt anxious to put this little episode behind them. Their goodbyes, even a distance away across the Cunliffe's car park, seemed muted and surreal.

Maxwell leaned against the wall across the road, Surrey parked around the back of the Old Library. He saw Hall chatting to his plainclothesman in the car park, saw him get into his car, saw him drive away. No point in tackling loquacious George again. What you saw with the hotel deskman was what you got. The Head of Sixth Form looked up at the fierce sun already burning through the shoulders of his shirt. Phew! Another scorcher. He wondered where Jacquie was this morning, what she was doing and how she felt. 'A bit like shit, I expect,' he muttered as he swung Surrey

323

into action. He knew. He was there himself.

*   *   *

It wasn't the droning that woke him. It had been the droning that had sent him to sleep. It was what summer Sunday afternoons were all about. An Englishman mowing the lawns of his castle, thanks to the ingenuity of Messrs Black and Decker and the twenty percent off of Messrs B and Q. No, what woke Peter Maxwell on that impossibly hot Sunday was the ringing of his phone.

Metternich the cat lay on the Great Man's patio, looking for all the world as though he'd been flattened by a steam-roller, to allow his important little places to be as cool as possible. Nobody who didn't wear a fur coat for a living could possibly understand. There was that irritating noise again and sure enough, yes, there he went. The mad old duffer was clambering off his garden recliner and dashing indoors.

'Jacquie?'

'Er . . . no, it's Duggsy, Mr Maxwell. Matthew Douglas.'

'Matthew.' Maxwell tried to contain his disappointment. 'How the Hell are you?'

'Never better, Mr M. Sorry I couldn't talk the other night—you know, at the Grad Ball.'

'Well, you were obviously busy, Matthew. And I never stay to the end of these bashes, in

324

case I turn into a pumpkin or worse, have to clear up somebody's vomit. Been there; done that.'

'Yeah, quite.' Duggsy gurgled. He wasn't sure what a pumpkin was, but he was at home with vomit. You had to be, in his line of business. 'Well, I just wondered if you'd caught the lunchtime news.'

'No, Matthew, sorry,' his ex-Head of Sixth Form said. 'Leighford High burnt down?' There was always hope. Or was Matthew hoping to enrol in September in the school's new Current Affairs AS level? It was to be run by Dierdre Lessing and the prospect of the Senior Mistress dealing with Affairs was something Peter Maxwell was probably not going to be able to resist.

'No. It's him, Mr Maxwell. Wal wasn't sure. Iron Man was adamant it wasn't, but I know it was.'

'Sorry, Matthew,' the Great Man confessed. 'You've lost me.'

'The photographer at the Ball.'

'Yes?'

'It was him. It was that bloke they found murdered in his studio. Craig Edwards. He was the photographer at the Ball.'

'Are you sure?' Suddenly, Maxwell was wide awake.

'And that's not all. Iron Man said no, but I reckon he's wrong. It's the bloke, Mr Maxwell. That bloke having an up and downer with that

325

Ofsted woman at the Vine. The one in the e-fit. And now, somebody's gone and put his lights out.'

*   *   *

Peter Maxwell was no stranger to the *Leighford Advertiser* nor they to him. At one time half its reporters were Old Leighford Hyenas or else Old Leighford Hyenas had made the front page for various crimes against humanity. He took advantage of his first lesson being 'free' that Monday morning (although he knew, like every teacher, there was no such thing as a free lesson) and cycled to their offices in Handover Street.

Neil Henslow had been one of the Great Man's great white hopes some years ago, but he'd never quite got it together. Oxford aspirations ended in Sheffield Hallam and the dreaming steelworks equipped him, not for Fleet Street's cutting edge after all, but the flower shows and car boots of the *Advertiser.*

'Day off, Mr Maxwell?' the cub reporter asked.

'We never sleep,' Maxwell winked at him, a Pinkerton man at heart. 'What'll you have, Neil?'

A floozy had appeared at their table in the welcome cool of the Jury House coffee shop and patisserie, order pad in hand, gum in cheek.

'Oh, er . . . latté, please.'

'Two of whatever that is,' Maxwell beamed up at her. The floozy scribbled something down, transferred her gum from one side to the other and disappeared into the bowels of the building. 'I appreciate this, Neil.'

'We could have talked across the road, Mr Maxwell,' Henslow said.

'Too open.' Maxwell shook his head. 'I've often wondered why newspaper offices the world o'er are open plan.'

'Nothing secret about the Press, Mr Maxwell,' the lad said earnestly. Maxwell looked at him. What was he? Twenty-five? He'd never get away from the flower shows with an attitude like that. Napoleon Bonaparte had been a general at his age and William Pitt had been running the country for a year.

'Well, that's a pity, Neil, because it's secrets I wanted to talk to you about. You've got the file I mentioned on the phone?'

'The Edwards file. Sure. Not that there's much in it yet.' He hauled a manila folder out of his briefcase.

'You're writing a piece, though?'

'Yes, but,' Henslow's eyes burnt bright above the table cloth and the doilies. 'The editor said it was time I won my spurs.'

'Excellent!' Maxwell beamed, pleased with the historical allusion and trying not to look too eager. 'A sound fellow. May I?' He eased the folder round to his side of the table and opened it.

'This never happened, of course,' Henslow said.

Maxwell looked at him. Perhaps the lad wasn't quite the ingénue he appeared. Maybe there was hope for him after all. 'Of course not,' his old Head of Sixth Form said. 'It would be most improper. Well, well,' he'd flipped open the cover and a face grinned up at him. 'Joe Public.'

'Sorry?'

The floozy arrived with the coffees and passed the bill to Maxwell. He waited until she'd gone. 'Nothing,' he smiled at Henslow. 'Tell me about the murder of Craig Edwards.'

*   *   *

The pieces were beginning to fall into place, Maxwell thought to himself as he pedalled along the High Street in the Monday morning traffic, weaving past the buggies and babies and avoiding the old people at the kerb, who had grown old waiting to cross the road. The man with the black bag at the Vine, the man in the leather coat in the pub's gents, had smiled up at Maxwell from Neil Henslow's file. The man seen by the drummer of the Yawning Hippos having an upper and downer with Sally Meninger in the pub car park. The man Peter Maxwell had christened Joe Public. That man was dead. The police had released no details to the Press as to the cause of death yet, but that was irrelevant. Peter Maxwell knew that it would be a skewer to the throat, delivered, like Kenneth Connor's funeral services in *'Allo! 'Allo!,* swiftly and with style.

And he was the photographer at the Grad Ball. Shit! Why hadn't Maxwell been more observant? He lashed Surrey to the usual rail and pointed at a hapless lad scurrying about the school buildings. Instinctively, the lad tucked in the tails of his shirt and checked that he wasn't wearing trainers.

'Kelly?' the Great Man had swept like a galleon in full sail through the school and was at his desk and on the phone in a twinkling of an eye. 'Peter Maxwell, from Leighford High School.'

Kelly was still in bed, the prerogative of ex-Year 13 students whose exams are over, before the grey, gritty reality of shelf-filling at Tescos kicks in. She sounded dazed, confused. Certainly, she'd never had a phone call from Mad Max before. 'Oh, hello.'

'You were on the Grad Ball committee? Right?' Her already ex-Head of Sixth Form cut to the chase.

'Yes.'

'The photographer, Craig Edwards. Who hired him?'

'Well, I did, I suppose,' the bleary-eyed girl told him, sitting up in bed and trying to focus. 'The first bloke we got pulled out. Mr Edwards had done my mum's wedding. So I knew he was all right. As it turned out, he was late.'

'Yes,' Maxwell nodded. 'That seems to have been a failing of his. Although two days ago he may just have been too early. Who knew you'd hired him?'

'Um . . . only a couple of us on the committee.'

'No staff?' Maxwell checked. 'No adults?'

'No, I don't think so. Oh, Mrs Maitland knew.'

Yes, Maxwell smiled to himself. His Number Two, Helen Maitland. How *did* Assistant Heads of Sixth Form amuse themselves other than by slaughtering people with skewers? Kelly had got it in one. 'Thank you, darling,' he said. 'And for the rest of your life, may God keep you in the hollow of his hand.' And he hung up.

Bugger! Look at the time. Peter Maxwell was hurtling along the corridor past Aitch One, opened again now and a classroom once again, the swivel chair in which Alan Whiting had died only a Leighford memory and under plastic in the regional crime lab. No enterprising Year Ten kid had yet thought to make a few bob by opening the room to the public; but it was early days. In ten minutes, he had to cast pearls before swine again in the unforgiving white heat of history. Time was of the essence.

'Headmaster,' the Head of Sixth Form had

not waited to be asked in to James Diamond's office. He was a middle-aged man in a hurry and he'd long ago stopped looking at the bad artwork and indescribable sculpture that littered the Head's surfaces. His desk, of course, was empty. 'How's it hanging?'

Diamond looked terrible. His usually crisp shirt was unironed, his hair a tangled mess. Maxwell could believe that Margaret had ironed her husband's shirts, but surely, he combed his own hair? 'I'm here, Max,' Diamond said, as if that was an achievement in itself. 'I'm not going to let this thing beat me.' But he didn't sound sure on that score.

'Indeed not, Headmaster,' the Head of Sixth Form patronized. 'And to that end, I need the addresses of the Ofsted team who've just left.'

'Max . . .'

'I know you have them, Headmaster.' Maxwell stood his ground as he had so often before Legs Diamond, his legs astride, his shoulders set, like an ox, as the late Rudyard Kipling described the Saxons, in the furrow. 'All you need do is tell me where. Oh, and give me two days off.'

'Max . . .'

The Head of Sixth Form closed to his man, leaning over his desk, hands spread on his mock-wood surface. 'Let me take the gloves off, Headmaster,' he grated. 'I don't know how the Governors are reacting currently to your being under police suspicion for murder. Or

331

how the gentlemen of the Press will portray you when they finally tie it all together, which, by my reckoning will be about . . .' he checked his watch, 'half past two this afternoon—which is your good side, by the way?'

'Max . . .' the Head was particularly articulate this morning.

'Give me the addresses and two days, James, and I'll give you the murderer's head on a plate.'

James? Maxwell had done it again. Used the Christian name, the 'J' word. If James Diamond didn't think things were serious already, he knew they were now.

'Reception will have them,' he said. 'Ask Emma. Two days, Max? Can you deliver in two days?' Diamond had a look of desperation on his face.

The Head of Sixth Form stood up. 'Does the Pope shit in the woods, Headmaster?' he asked. And neither of them had an answer to that.

*　　　*　　　*

That Monday was a mad house at Leighford nick. Phones rang off the hook, VDUs flickered, faxes poured in and fans blasted sheets of paper all over the place. There was no natural breeze. The trees on the Dam hung heavy and still in the summer heat and the kids at Leighford High were extra-tetchy or extra-listless depending on their natural proclivities.

Henry Hall was sifting through his paperwork. On the Paula Freeling enquiry, house to house had turned up nothing. Of the hundred plus garages and lock-ups in the area, not one of them had so far yielded any links to the dead woman at all. In the Craig Edwards murder, no one had so far admitted to seeing anybody arriving at the photographer's studio on Saturday morning. No milkmen, no paper child, no postman had seen a damned thing. Indeed no one had seen the photographer until the police had carried him out in a body bag. It was part of the culture of the twenty-first century. No one looked out for anybody any more. John Donne was wrong—every man is an island.

'Henry.' It was Jim Astley's voice at the end of the endlessly ringing phone.

'Jim.' The DCI tucked the receiver under his neck as he sorted yet more files, hands full, brain whirling.

'You won't hear me say this often, so I'll come to the point and make it brief.'

'I wish you would.' Hall was a man in a hurry.

'I missed something on the Paula Freeling case.'

'What?' Hall stopped shuffling papers. This was indeed a moment to cherish. When Jim Astley admitted a mistake, you *knew* the writing was on the wall.

'I said . . .'

'No,' Hall interrupted. 'I mean, what did you miss?'

'You know there were microscopic particles of alloy on the skin and clothing?'

'I do,' Hall confirmed.

'And something else too, largely in her hair and on her stockings.'

'Pieces of a black plastic bag, yes?'

'Black plastic, certainly. Bag—no. They're hard; the chemical consistency is totally different. Any help?'

'Hard plastic? I don't know,' Hall frowned. 'Can you fax over the specifics, Jim?'

'Of course. And I'm sorry, Henry. It's not like me, I think you'll agree.'

'I think I will,' Hall nodded and rang off. He leaned over and ringed the date on the calendar. And, careful that no one in the outer office could see, he smiled.

*　　　*　　　*

'Who in their right minds lives in Basingstoke?' It was a question Peter Maxwell had asked before and he was slogging round to Leighford Station that Monday afternoon in order to find an answer all over again. The sound of a horn made him turn. Was it John Peel with his coat so gay? No, it was a white van with three of the Great Unwashed in it and the badly painted Yawning Hippos motif

334

on the side.

'Mr Maxwell,' Duggsy leaned out of the window. 'Getting anywhere with that photographer bloke?'

'I've made a start, Matthew, thanks,' the Head of Sixth Form said.

'Going to the station?'

'To Basingstoke, actually.'

'Well, hop in. We'll give you a lift.'

'What? To Basingstoke?'

'Yeah, we're doing Reading this year. Oh, not playing, you understand. Just crowd-surfing. Although, this time next year . . .' It was pure Del Boy Trotter and just as believable.

'Oh, I couldn't impose.' Maxwell shook his head.

'No imposition, Mr Maxwell, is it lads, eh?'

Iron Man grunted something from behind the wheel and there was a squawk from Wal in the back. Time was when Peter Maxwell wouldn't be seen dead getting into a white van, especially one belonging to a struggling Rock band. But that was before they privatized British Rail and the country's transport system had started going backwards. Now, needs must when Iron Man drove.

'You're on,' Maxwell said and clambered in the back. The thing was roof high in gear; tops, bins, poles, even the odd rod and perch. There were drum cases everywhere and a crate of Stella. The whole van smelt of stale beer, old ciggies and a strange, sweet assortment of illegal substances. If Johnny Law decided to pull this lot over, he'd have a field day.

'Don't mind sitting on the coffin, Mr Maxwell?' Wal asked him.

'Coffin?' Maxwell paused on his way in.

Wal tapped the long black box under him. 'Iron Man's gear. I can guarantee a numb bum by the time we're out of Tottingleigh.'

'I thought you guys weren't playing,' Maxwell said.

'You never know,' Iron Man was looking for a gear—any one would do, 'when you might get lucky.'

'Counting Crows need a support band,' Duggsy enthused. 'I've got a feeling about this summer, Mr Maxwell. I think we're standing on the threshold of a dream.'

Maxwell stared at the back of the lad's head. He appeared neither moody nor blue. Perhaps he was older than he looked.

'Now, as your official Irregulars, Mr Maxwell,' the lead singer half turned to him. 'What can you tell us about that photographer bloke?'

'It's not him,' Iron Man said, crashing through his gears as the van snarled out of the station car park.

'Yes, it fucking is, Iron,' Duggsy insisted. 'You tell him, Wal.'

'Well, I don't know.' Mr Bassman was sitting on the fence as well as the coffin.

'I don't know who you guys did or didn't see in the Vine car park.' Maxwell played the arbiter as usual. 'But he sure as hell is the one I saw in the gents earlier in the evening. And he sure as hell is the photographer found done to death in his own studio. Now, I call that a coincidence, don't you?'

Chapter Fourteen

You couldn't love Basingstoke. At least, Peter Maxwell couldn't. He'd harboured a grudge all these years, because a long, long time ago when marriage was still an institution and BBC newsreaders had been to Public School, young Peter Maxwell had visited Basingstoke and had walked slap into a brick pillar in the town centre. He was delighted to find the brick pillar gone now and muttered 'Nah nah de nah nah' as Iron Man's van screeched around the corner. On the other hand, he was a bit miffed not to find a blue plaque commemorating the occasion.

'Ease up, Iron,' Duggsy warned. 'Last thing we want is the Filth pulling us over with our particular cargo.'

The Romans had come this way, up from Bohunt with the sun on their backs and their leather boots crunching through the heather. They'd extended the old Celtic town to the north and called it grandly Calleva Atrebatum. To the west was the magic-moated castle of Odiham, square and solid and proud above its lily pads. Old Basing House, once the largest in England, was knocked about a bit by Oliver Cromwell and lay to the east of the town. But the centre itself was just like any other— W.H.Smith's, Next, phone shops and HMVs without number. Maxwell felt the old headaches coming back and the sting of the graze on his cheek.

'Better wait here, guys,' he told the Band. 'I don't want to frighten our friend from Ofsted.' So the Irregulars settled down in a car park to a couple of Stellas and some KFC; Maxwell was paying.

Staystill House was a damn sight quainter than the Cunliffe. It boasted its position as the oldest inn in Old Basing and you couldn't get much older than that. Unless of course you were the old bastard casually sauntering through the foyer that sunkissed Monday evening. The bar was already humming with the chatter of a convention. Glasses clinked and the only sound other than forced laughter was the soft thud as long-bladed knives hit the MD squarely in the back. Sunlight streamed in through the leaded window onto the copper and brasses that ornamented the reception counter.

'Hello, may I help you?' a four-year-old girl tried to look grown up and efficient for

Maxwell's benefit.

'I'm looking for Malcolm Harding.' He tipped his hat.

'Is he a guest?'

'In a manner of speaking,' Maxwell said.

'I'm afraid we can't . . .'

He flashed his NUT card inside his wallet, leaning towards her like a Cato Street conspirator. 'It *is* a police matter,' he confided.

'Oh.' The four-year-old looked suitably impressed and thought of the hotel's reputation. 'Room Twenty-One, sir. Up the stairs. Turn left.'

Maxwell did, bounding two at a time. He was conscious that the Hippos had a tent to go to and copious quantities of ganja to get through before cockshut time. More importantly, his home town was littered with dead people and he wanted some answers.

'Mr Harding.' He doffed his hat to the incredulous occupant of Room Twenty-One. 'Remember me? Peter Maxwell, Leighford High. How's the Inspection business?'

'What are you doing here?'

Maxwell sidled past the pompous windbag and into the room. 'Hoping to avoid clichés like that for a start.'

'Mr Maxwell,' Harding followed him into the centre of the room. 'This is very irregular. I'm inspecting another school.'

'I know,' Maxwell nodded, admiring the four poster bed and the incongruous wide-screen TV. 'How're they shaping up? Beacon of our education system or God-awful crap? And by the way, after the death of Alan Whiting, you're talking to me about irregular?' He turned to face the man squarely, scowling at him, cheek by jowl.

'But why are you here?'

'James Diamond was arrested last week.'

'Diamond?' Harding found himself turning away to close the door.

'The Headmaster of Leighford High. Oh, Headmaster is too grandiose a term, I'll grant you—that's why I use it. But he's all we've got, poor bugger and he's as likely a murder suspect as Mother Theresa. It's my job to prove it.'

'*Your* job?' Harding was trying to make sense of all this as Maxwell sprawled on the bed, bouncing to check its springs.

'Not bad,' he nodded, flicking the chintz of the curtains. 'You didn't like Alan Whiting, did you?'

'How did you know that?' Harding snapped. 'I only told the police that in confidence . . .' Not much of a poker player was Malcolm Harding.

'Yes, well,' Maxwell sat on the edge of the tester. 'Nothing's sacred now, is it? Half the Catholic church are off like rats up pipes out of the Confessional to kiss and tell to the Sunday newspapers. The world and his wife can read their confidential references. MI5 advertise in the *Times Ed*—although why they should imagine they can recruit Intelligence among teachers is beyond me. Why didn't you like him?'

'If you must know,' Harding eased himself into the armchair, 'he stole a job I was after.'

Maxwell shrugged. 'All's fair, surely,' he said.

'There was *nothing* fair about Alan Whiting, believe me.'

'Was he a womanizer, would you say?'

'Alan?' Harding thought for a moment. 'He fancied himself, certainly. That was all part of his arrogance. No woman could resist the charms in his trousers and no man the keen thrust of his mind. 'Course, it could have been the other way round.'

'So Whiting and Sally Meninger?'

'An item?' Harding looked at him solemnly. 'It's possible. Certainly, I heard rumours.'

'From whom?' Maxwell may have been up to his elbows in murder, but the syntax must serve. There were, after all, standards.

'Well, Paula Freeling, for one.'

'Paula Freeling told you?' This was a new direction.

'I'm surprised your police colleagues didn't tell you that, Mr Maxwell,' Harding said archly.

'Yes,' Maxwell frowned. 'So am I.' He'd give Jacquie a good talking to when . . . but there wouldn't be any talking any more, would

341

there? Good or otherwise. Just the long silence that was called moving on.

'Pretty observant old bird was Paula,' Harding murmured. 'Now, there *is* a mystery.'

'What is?' Maxwell asked.

'Why anyone would want to kill her,' Harding shrugged.

'You've answered your own question,' Maxwell told him. 'The old bird was *too* observant, I suspect. Look,' he fumbled in his wallet, 'I don't usually carry these things, but,' he handed him a card, 'if anything occurs to you, anything at all, give me a ring, will you?'

And he made for the door.

'Just a minute.' Harding stopped him. 'How did you know where to find me?'

'Basingstoke!' boomed Maxwell in his best *Ruddigore.* 'You told me yourself. I'm off to Basingstoke you said when we had breakfast together at the Cunliffe. They're very helpful at the Bishop Latymer School, aren't they? When I told them I was your flatmate and that you'd left the iron on, they fell over themselves to give me your accommodation address. Lovely name, isn't it, Staystill? Unfortunately,' he beamed, tipping his hat again, 'that's one thing I can't do. Oh, by the way,' in the door he turned, apart from the lack of mac and two good eyes, a dead ringer for Lootenant Columbo, 'there's just one more thing. Sally Meninger.'

'Oh, yes,' Harding's face darkened. 'She's

trouble, that one.'

'Oh? In what way?'

Harding got up and closed to his man. 'A liar, a schemer, a tart, will that do for openers?'

'Come along now, Mr Harding,' Maxwell chuckled. 'Come off the fence. What do you *really* think of Sally Meninger?'

And he was gone.

'But how did you know I was at the Bishop Latymer School?' Harding called after him. Answer came there none.

*   *   *

'Lads.' Maxwell tapped on the van's side window and Duggsy nearly choked mid-puff. 'Thanks for the lift. But you boys have to be elsewhere and so do I.'

'Where's that, Mr Maxwell?' Duggsy wanted to know.

'Wiltshire. Devizes, to be precise.'

'Well, that's it, then,' Duggsy said, nudging Iron Man who kicked over the ignition. 'Should make it by nightfall.'

'Whoa, hang on.' Maxwell stopped the headlong rush to judgement. 'Look, guys, I'm grateful for the lift, but I can't impose . . .'

'We've been talking it over, haven't we Iron? Wal?'

'Yeah,' came a confident voice from the darkening bowels of the van.

343

'We're unanimous, Mr Maxwell,' Duggsy said.

'Yeah, we all are,' chimed in Iron.

'We're your Irregulars, remember?'

Maxwell laughed. 'But that was on home turf, lads, back in Leighford. Now, you did me a good turn the other day by recognizing Craig Edwards, but this is different.'

'Mr Maxwell,' Iron Man leaned across, looking up at the man who was never *his* Head of Sixth Form. 'You're going it alone, right? Looking for the bloke what iced this Whiting bloke and that old broad and now the photographer?'

'That's right,' Maxwell was patience itself. He'd been talking to younger Iron Men all his working life; just talking to, never down.

'Who'd you talk to in there?' the drummer asked.

'Malcolm Harding, one of the Ofsted people.'

'He your bloke, d'you reckon?'

'The killer?' Maxwell shook his head. 'No chance. Malcolm's too full of himself. I'm looking for a loner, somebody who'd blend in a crowd. Mr Opinion in there couldn't keep his mouth shut for long enough.'

'There you are, then,' Iron Man shrugged, his piercings rattling, 'If it ain't him, it's one of the others. You look like you need a bit of protection.'

Both Wal and Duggsy had seen Mad Max in

action, as much a master with a piece of chalk or with a well-aimed door. But Iron Man was older than they were; perhaps he sensed a vulnerability the younger ones didn't.

'All right,' Maxwell agreed. 'But I'm a teacher, men; I can't afford five star for us all.'

'Christ, Mr Maxwell,' Duggsy was appalled. 'We're rock stars, man, living out of guitar cases. Apart from the vans, everything Iron owns is in that coffin, ain't it, Iron?'

'Yeah,' Iron conceded.

'Look, Mr Maxwell,' Duggsy clambered out of the vehicle. 'You'd better ride up front. Wal was on the chilli burgers earlier and it ain't going to be no pot pourri back there; get the picture?'

Maxwell did and belted up next to the drummer as the Hippos and Mad Max drove south west.

*   *   *

They rattled down the dear dead days of the Vale of the White Horse, where iron warriors had long ago rattled in their chariots, praying to Taranis, the thunder god, and wearing their swirling torcs of gold.

'Look at that,' Iron Man pointed to the ghostly silhouette of Silbury Hill. 'Christ, I could tell you some stories about that place. And Henge, of course. If only I could remember them.'

Maxwell could as well, but they would be altogether more historical than Iron Man's fume-fuddled fondnesses. He knew that to their right, on the star-jewelled Wansdyke, the battlefield of Roundhay Down lay in the summer darkness, the clash of its Puritan steel echoing across the years. Behind them, vanished warriors of another time still lay in the rich, brown earth near the ransacked barrows of East and West Kennet and the canal, with its ramshackle warehouses and breweries ran gleaming into sleeping Devizes.

'Have you any idea of the bloody time?' David Simmonds was not best pleased. Peter Maxwell had posed as his brother in the reception area of the Bear Hotel, come with some dreadful family news. It made him sound like something out of Dickens and he'd tried the same story in three other hotels already, but this time, he struck gold.

'It's half past midnight, Mr Simmonds,' the Leighford man told him, checking his watch in the quiet corridor. 'How's the Inspection business?'

'What are you *doing* here?' Simmonds was beside himself and threatening to wake the entire floor. 'This is a fucking outrage.'

'Tsk, tsk,' Maxwell oozed past the quivering inspector into his room. 'Such language from the uncle of Selina Barrington, late of Trinity, Oxford. And that's before we get on to the reputation of the Bear Hotel.'

'My niece may have thought highly of you, Maxwell,' Simmonds snapped. 'But I don't have to. How did you find me?'

'Process of elimination,' Maxwell said. The Bear wasn't as ancient as Staystill House, but its architecture was impressive nonetheless. 'You gave me Wiltshire. A phone call to Ofsted HQ gave me the rest.'

Simmonds blinked in disbelief. He was looking at Peter Maxwell, but he was hearing Malcolm Harding. 'This is surreal.' He shook his head. 'You actually pretended to be Malcolm Harding on the phone to HQ?'

'And you,' Maxwell smiled. 'Not to mention Bob Templeton. Even I baulked at taking off Sally Meninger however—it needs work, I must confess.' He helped himself to a chair. 'And speaking of surreal, so is an Ofsted inspector being skewered to death in a room not a million miles from my teaching base. We have unfinished business, Mr Simmonds, you and I.'

'Look,' the Ofsted man subsided. 'I told the police . . .'

'That Whiting was a sex maniac. Yes, I know.'

'How . . . ?'

'I have my little ways,' Maxwell told him, wondering how his little way was now. She'd be snug in her bed, the bed she'd shared with him. Or bent double over a computer looking for clues to murder on the superhighway.

Perhaps she was looking up at the stars, as he had been on the Plain with Duggsy and Wal snoring softly in the back, a dreadlocked head lolling on a dreadlocked shoulder. 'You implied that Whiting went for anything in a skirt.'

'So he did. Didn't exactly please his wife, I understand.'

'Mrs Whiting?'

'Have you met her?'

'Yes,' Maxwell said. 'Yes, I have as a matter of fact. She seemed the soul of correctness and dignity.'

'Oh, *she* is, yes. It's her sister I've got my doubts about.'

'Her sister?' Maxwell was lost.

Simmonds looked at him. 'Well, surely you know,' he sneered. 'What with your "little ways" and all. Sally Meninger is Pamela Whiting's sister.'

* * *

He stumbled into the bright lights of Leighford nick, his tie gone, his inevitable three piece suit replaced with an anorak and jeans.

'Can I help you, sir?' the desk man peered at him. This was still a working police station and not Fort Apache, the South Coast, complete with push-button answerphone and couples having it away in the ever-dimming

348

glow of the blue lamp.

'Yes,' he said, summoning up the courage to look the man in the face. 'My name is James Diamond. I've come to confess to the killing of Alan Whiting.'

*   *   *

It was Philip Bathurst who drew the short straw. It was two minutes into Tuesday and he should have gone home hours ago. Instead he found himself staring across the desk in Interview Room One, the tape whirring and DS Jacquie Carpenter by his side. The girl looked tired and drawn under the strip light.

'Would you like a cup of tea, Mr Diamond?' she asked, looking for something normal in the situation facing them all.

'Er . . . no, thanks,' Diamond said. 'I just want to get this over with.'

'When we spoke last, Mr Diamond,' the DI began slowly, choosing his words as he cradled his fingers, 'I was apologizing to you for the precipitate behaviour of one of my DCs. Are you telling me Geoff Baldock was right, after all?'

The Head's eyes flickered. He looked a hundred. 'I'm afraid so,' he said.

'All right,' Bathurst leaned back, sliding an ashtray away from him. 'Tell me why. Tell me why you killed Alan Whiting.'

'I didn't mean to,' he said. 'I want that

understood from day one.'

'It's on the record.' Bathurst nodded to the tape recorder.

'He was . . . pestering Sally. Sally Meninger, treating her like a tramp.'

'What was that to you?' Jacquie asked.

'We . . . I knew Sally some time ago. We were lovers.'

'How long ago?' Bathurst asked.

'Three years. No . . . four. We met at a conference.'

'And had an affair?' Jacquie said.

'We fell in love,' Diamond insisted. ' "Had an affair" sounds sordid. Furtive fumblings in cheap hotel rooms. It wasn't like that.'

'What *was* it like?' the DI could think of no finer way to spend his early Tuesday mornings.

'Love,' Diamond repeated.

'And how did your wife take it?' Jacquie asked. Such relationships loomed large in her thinking at the moment.

'Margaret?' Diamond was twisting his plain gold wedding ring round his finger, unaware that he was doing it. 'She never knew.'

'Until DC Baldock arrested you?'

'Yes,' Diamond said. 'Until then.'

'All right.' Bathurst folded his arms, eyeing up his man, taking his time. 'You don't approve of furtive fumblings in cheap hotel rooms; so where did you meet? You and Sally? How did you keep your passionate love going for three . . . no, four years?'

Diamond's jaw was flexing and his lip curling. 'You're making fun of me, aren't you?'

Bathurst leaned forward, his tether well and truly ended. 'No, Mr Diamond. That's more than my job's worth.' He snapped off the tape. 'You and Sally Meninger have a fling, an affair, a knee-trembler, she's the love of your life, *whatever* three or four years ago. You conduct a relationship, presumably by e-mail with the odd Christmas card and then she pops back into your life. Joy unconfined, you might think, but no—there's a complication in the form of Alan Whiting. Mr Octopus. A wolf in wolf's clothing. Sally comes to you distraught and you put a skewer through his throat.'

'You make it all sound so simple,' Diamond said.

'No, Mr Diamond.' Bathurst scraped his chair back. 'That's what you must think we are. Why did you kill Paula Freeling?'

'She saw me,' Diamond snapped back. 'She saw me kill Whiting. I had to shut her up. That's why I went to the Cunliffe, to reach her.'

'And where did you keep her?' Jacquie asked.

'What?'

'We know from our forensics that the woman was kept bound, for perhaps two days before she was killed,' Bathurst obliged. 'Where did you keep her?'

'In my garage,' he said.

'Mrs Diamond feed her, did she?' Jacquie

351

asked. 'Or just moan at you to tidy up after yourself?'

'I can't believe you're taking this attitude,' Diamond said. It was as though he were talking to a recalcitrant Year Ten student.

'Why did you kill Craig Edwards?' Bathurst snapped, leaning over his man, nose to nose.

'Who?'

'The photographer.'

'I . . .'

The DI stood up. 'Get him out of here, Jacquie, before I lose what little cool I've got left. No, wait. Charge him. Charge Mr Diamond here with wasting police time. After all, we've got nothing better to do at the moment.'

*　　　*　　　*

There were a lot of rumours about Lord Cardigan, the last of the Brudenells who led the Charge of the Light Brigade. One was that on the night of Balaclava he left his exhausted, wounded men and slept aboard his yacht after a champagne supper. In fact, he didn't. He wrapped himself up in a horse blanket and held his bugler in his arms as the boy died. Peter Maxwell didn't intend to go that far, but he couldn't see his lads, the Hippos, stretched on the cold, cold ground while he lorded it in hotel-land luxury. So he dossed down with them, on a layby outside Devizes and waited

352

for the dawn. The van was full of noises, mostly from Wal and nobody what you might call, slept.

Wal was a sight to behold in the early light. A stranger to soap since his GCSE days, the bass man took more care of his guitar than himself. He lovingly cleaned the strings as the sun crept over the bottle bank and Iron Man went off in search of a Circle K, via a pee in the hedge. Breakfast was a six pack and assorted tortilla chips paid for by Mr Maxwell, but then nobody said Iron Man was your galloping gourmet. The van played up as Duggsy surfaced from the indefinable grunge of his sleeping bag and Iron Man and Wal soon had their heads buried under its bonnet, clattering spanners and crooning to it.

'Well, why didn't you bring the other bloody one, then?' Wal asked.

' 'Cause it hasn't got Yawning Hippos on the side, man,' the drummer told him.

'Yeah,' Duggsy chimed in. 'Gotta advertise.'

Nobody feared the Reaper when the Hippos were on the road.

They'd rattled past Gloucester on the M5 by mid-morning, stopping only for petrol and pee-breaks. It was just another Band on the run, two musicians, a drummer and an old bloke standing line abreast and widdling up a castle wall in the middle of nowhere.

*   *   *

353

'Is it me or is this bloke crap?' Maxwell muttered out of the corner of his mouth.

Bob Templeton leapt a mile. 'For God's sake, Maxwell. What are you doing here?'

The Head of Sixth Form from another school began to come out with the cliché, and suddenly couldn't be bothered. 'The door was open.' He pointed to one at the side of the classroom. 'Thought I'd just say "Hi".'

He caught the eye of the French teacher clearly struggling at the front of the class and waved at him. The French teacher's heart plummeted still further. He'd been doing pretty badly with one Ofsted inspector in the room; now he had two, and still Seven Eff were hanging from the chandeliers.

'This is unforgivable,' Templeton hissed. 'Outside!'

One or two of Seven Eff were turning to stare at them. The younger bloke looked furious, as though he was about to hit the older bloke. This was great.

'Only if you come with me,' Maxwell minced.

Templeton scowled at the French teacher and strode for the door.

'Maxwell . . .' they were nose to nose on the walkway outside the Modern Languages block.

'How did I find you?' the Head of Sixth Form saved them both time. 'By impersonating David Simmonds and pretending I needed to

354

reach you urgently—which I do. That got me to the gates of Whatever School This Is, Nuneaton, Warwickshire. And I got here because of the very helpful—and rather lax—work experience kid on the front desk.'

'I shall of course be reporting this,' Templeton snapped, all the relaxed bonhomie of the Cunliffe breakfast having vanished.

'Well, not to my Headmaster, please, Mr Templeton, because he's under suspicion of murder at the moment. Which brings me to cases. Did you know that Sally Meninger was Alan Whiting's sister-in-law?'

'No,' Templeton said after a few minutes' reflection. 'Why should I know that?'

Maxwell sighed. He was tired, all travelled out and this detour to the back of beyond had clearly been a waste of time.

'All I *do* know—and God help me, I should have told the police this—is that Paula Freeling was a bloody thief.'

'What?'

'Quite,' Templeton blustered. 'Cuff-links, cash, even a spare tie—the woman was a bloody kleptomaniac. *That's* why she left the Cunliffe in such a hurry, and that *could* be why she was murdered.'

'And you didn't think to mention it to the boys in blue?'

'I couldn't be sure,' Templeton bluffed. 'Actually, I still can't. Things vanished from my room after a visit from her, that's all I know.'

355

'Well,' Maxwell nodded. 'We all know a little bit more now, don't we?' He glanced back into the classroom where Seven Eff appeared to be re-enacting the attack on the Bastille. 'Don't let me keep you from the fun,' he said.

'I shall still be reporting this, Maxwell,' Templeton warned.

But the Head of Sixth Form was striding away. 'Whatever,' he said.

*   *   *

On the road again by tea-time, Iron Man was accelerating past Sheffield, a *very* wise move, and it wasn't until the sun began to dip that they reached their final destination.

'There's a great castle at Skipton,' Maxwell told them. 'Moat, dungeons, the whole nine yards.'

'Fuck the castle, Mr Maxwell, with respect,' said Duggsy from his position bent double in the back. 'Where's the nearest bloody pub?'

They settled for the Goat and Gargoyle off the High Street where the metal frames of the street market stalls littered the tarmac and rubbish still piled high on the pavements. Southerners though they all were, they tucked into their chips with gravy with relish—all except Maxwell, who wasn't fond of relish. The drinks and the grub, like the petrol, were on Maxwell.

'Where are we then, Mr M?' Duggsy got outside his pint of something dark and menacing from Yorkshire.

'Skipton, you twat,' said Wal. 'I know that and I haven't been navigating.'

'I mean, in terms of our enquiries, you stupid shit,' Duggsy countered, with all the wit and repartee at his disposal. It had been a long day for them all.

'Well, the odd thing is, lads,' Maxwell sucked the gravy from his chip, 'that it turns out Sally Meninger and Pamela Whiting are sisters.'

'Well, there's a turn up,' Iron Man was rolling his own.

'It's certainly a step in an odd direction,' Maxwell nodded. 'As is the fact that Paula Freeling was a tea-leaf.' The Hippos knew lots of those and they were strangely unmoved by the news. Maxwell might as well have said she was a Liberal Democrat.

'How you gonna play it with the tart, then, Mr M?' Duggsy had a way of cutting to the chase. 'Me and Wal ain't much on the heavy side, but we'll slap her about if you like.'

'Nice of you to offer, boys,' Maxwell smiled. 'But I think we'll do the softly, softly approach first. Are we lay-bying again tonight, Iron?' He dreaded the answer.

The drummer paused in mid-lick, his tongue stuck to his roll-up. 'It was good enough for Hendrix,' he croaked. A glazed

357

look came into the eyes of the guitarists. Maxwell was out of his league. To him, Jimi Hendrix was just a great jacket. He checked his watch.

'While you boys were getting some in,' he said, 'I cased the joint. Only two likely hotels. My guess is it'll be the Wheatsheaf. That's where I'll start. It's nine now. If I'm not back by last orders, you have my official permission to head south.'

Wal nodded appreciatively. 'Still got time to make Guildford,' he said.

And Maxwell was gone.

*   *   *

Henry Hall sat alone in his conservatory that night. Moths danced around the light and the fan twirling lazily above his head did nothing to move the still, heavy air. From where he sat he could hear the stream ripple at the end of his garden and the soft hum of the traffic on the A259. All day, he'd been closeted with his Murder Team in the Incident Room, checking this, rechecking that. His Press Officer had threatened to resign, hand in her badge because of the barrage of calls she'd received that day alone. Why was there no progress, everybody wanted to know from the Chief Constable to the editor of *Woman's Weekly*. Surely, *someone* had seen *something* in the photographer's? And as for the Alan Whiting

358

killing, that was nearly two weeks old, for God's sake. What were they paying these outrageous police salaries for? And what about the overtime? The last two questions had mostly come from the Chief Constable.

He'd drafted extra bodies in from the north of the county, men and women going door to door in a town they didn't know, on a case they'd only heard about the previous week. Pat Prentiss was on the diary found in Craig Edwards' studio, sending out his boys in blue to check bookings, timings, suss the ground. What was the punters' relationship with the dead man? How had they chosen him for the job? It was all about body language. Ask the questions and watch the reactions. A turn of the head, a flicker of the eye, a sudden, involuntary twitch of the hands, a tightness of the throat. Flash a warrant card, shake a hand and feel the clamminess of the palm. But it was the eyes. Always the eyes that gave the game away. That and the loud, persistent, obtrusive cough.

Geoff Baldock was rightly in DI Bathurst's dog-house for his maverick performance. But the over-zealous little shit knew his computers and the DI had put him on Edwards' hard drive to download the images. Nothing suspicious so far. Nothing sweaty. Nothing under-age. Just more of the same; grinning kids with no teeth; graduating students; smirking newly-weds.

And then, there was Jacquie. If truth were told, Henry Hall worried about Jacquie. He always had. He noticed things about people, about people he reckoned in particular. And something was wrong with Jacquie. In quiet moments, when everybody's head was down in the Incident Room and the air was palpable, he'd seen her soft, downcast gaze. He didn't need to know the reason. The reason was Peter Maxwell.

Hall looked out of his conservatory window, at his own reflection, lolling shirt-sleeved on the cane-backed settee. He looked beyond in the darkness to the far line of twinkling street lights that led to Columbine, Maxwell's home. He'd be there now, cradling his Southern Comfort, playing with those stupid toy soldiers, plotting yet more mayhem and confusion for Wednesday morning.

And then there was James Diamond. What did Maxwell call him? Legs? Anyone less like Ray Danton's fictional gangster, with the fedora, the spats and the machine gun, Hall couldn't imagine. What *was* all that about? A less-than-enchanted Phil Bathurst had told his DCI that morning that the man had come into the station to confess, not to one murder but to three, each with less likelihood and conviction than the last. Few people in the town rated Diamond very highly; Peter Maxwell rated him not at all. Had he finally flipped, as so many teachers had before him?

Driven to dribbling lunacy by the pressure of having an Ofsted inspector killed in his school? Hall shook his head. A greater man would have dined out on that for the rest of his life.

The doorbell made him jump and he focused beyond the glass to recognize the face of Geoff Baldock. He beckoned him in and the lad slid back the door and stood there, like the cat that's got the cream.

'I'm sorry, guv. I know it's late,' he mumbled.

'Just come off duty?' Hall asked.

'Yes, sir.'

'Then you're due one of these,' and he crossed to his drinks cabinet to pour them both a Scotch. 'I assume there's a good reason why you've snuck round the back of private premises and disturbed your superior at this hour.'

'Didn't want to disturb Mrs Hall and the little Halls, guv,' Baldock smiled.

'Thoughtful of you,' Hall nodded, offering the lad a seat. 'But the little Halls are out at some God-awful disco tonight, so don't push it. What've you got?'

'These, guv. From Edward's hard-drive. Took a bit of finding, but they're not your run-of-the-mill Esplanade type stuff.'

Hall looked at the photos the DC had splayed on the coffee table. There were a series of action shots, dim and indistinct in places, but the meaning was clear enough. A naked woman was straddling a man twice her age and by the blur of her body, was bouncing up and down. The room appeared to be a hotel room. It was single-bedded, with a cheap, nasty carpet.

'I particularly like these,' Baldock pointed to the handcuffs that held the man's left wrist to the bedhead.

'It's why you joined the force, no doubt,' Hall nodded. 'Do we have any ID?'

'Not yet, guv. And there's more where this came from. I thought you'd like to see these for starters.'

'Indeed,' Hall nodded. 'Well, Detective Constable, let's see if you can wipe the blot from your escutcheon, shall we? What do you make of them?'

Baldock sat on the edge of his seat opposite his boss, sampling the spirit. 'Taken from an open window,' he said. 'Three weeks ago. Look at the date. Edwards must have been perched on some kind of platform, ladder, something. This has to be on the first floor. Could be any one of a couple of dozen hotels or B & Bs in Leighford.'

'Or the far side of the moon,' Hall offered a helpful alternative.

'Quite,' Baldock conceded. 'But wherever it was taken, Edwards was supplementing his income. Photographer by day. Peeping Tom by night.'

362

'Hardly hardcore though, is it?' Hall mused. 'Couldn't have been hoping to make much on Weirdo Street. So what's his motive?'

'Self-abuse?' the lad suggested.

'No,' Hall was shaking his head. 'No. Try again.'

'Er . . .'

'Look at the faces.'

'Er . . .'

'They're clear, aren't they? The bodies may be blurred, but the features are unmistakeable. Get another print out and take the heads off. We'll go door to door on this in the morning.'

'I'm not sure what they're doing is against the law, guv,' Baldock said. 'Even in a hotel room.'

'I'm sure you're right,' Hall agreed. 'And it's not even against the law if this lady and gentleman aren't married to each other. But it would make very interesting viewing for the actual spouse of one or both of them, wouldn't it?'

'Blackmail?'

Hall shrugged. 'Blackmail. Confirmation of an affair. I think our Mr Edwards was a bit of a private eye on the quiet, at the predictably grubby end of the market, of course.'

'Right.' Reality dawned on Baldock.

'Well, get on with it, lad.' Hall took the DC's Scotch from him. 'Back to the photocopier. I want to know who those two are by lunchtime at the latest.'

'Yes, sir,' a hangdog Baldock was already on his feet.

'Oh, and constable,' Hall stopped him at the door. 'Well done.'

Chapter Fifteen

'I'm afraid I couldn't wait 'till breakfast,' Peter Maxwell stood in the corridor outside Sally Meninger's room at the Wheatsheaf, aching in every limb from another lay-by night.

'Good God,' she said softly, trying to gather her wits.

'No, but close,' Maxwell said. 'Got a minute, Inspector?' and he brushed past her into the room. 'I've seen quite a few insides of hotel rooms in the last few hours. This isn't the best, but I suppose it's home for now.'

'Max, what are you doing here?' She stood, hands on hips, already dressed and ready for the off.

'Can't you guess?' he asked.

'I would have given you a "very good" you know,' she said, 'had the inspection gone ahead at Leighford. Perhaps even an "excellent". You really didn't have to chase me all the way up here.' She smiled at him playfully and closed the door.

'If I'd taken the money and run, you mean?'

She dropped the smile. 'Oh, that. Look, I'm

deeply ashamed of that,' she said. 'It was pointless and childish. Please forget it.'

'Oh, I've tried,' Maxwell said, flinging himself down in her armchair. 'Like all our other lurid conversations, I've tried to wipe them from my memory. But it's no good. You see, I've been taken for a ride and not just by those three down there,' he flicked aside the nets and jerked his head in the direction of the window.

Sally crossed to it and saw a white van in the car park, battered, scruffy with the legend Yawning Hippos painted badly on the side. Three men lolled against it, dragging on suspicious-looking ciggies, swigging from six packs.

'Good God,' she said again.

'You'll remember the lads from the Vine,' he said. 'Oh not exactly chart material, but they can carry a tune in a bucket. Duggsy's the lead vocalist, friendly guy. Got a girlfriend called Tracey, but you can't have everything. Wal's the bass player. IQ of about forty, but he means well. Then there's the drummer, Iron Man . . .'

'Is there a point to all this?' she cut him short. 'Only I'd like a little breakfast before I carry out my inspection today.'

'Oh, I don't think there'll be an inspection, today, Sally,' Maxwell let the nets fall, 'or any other day. You see, the lads down there know all about you. Two of them went to Leighford

High and while they weren't exactly Oxbridge or *victor ludorum*, well, they've got a soft spot for the old place. And they don't like the way you used it as a venue for your weird little games.'

'I'm going now.' She snatched up her handbag and room key.

'Oh, I wouldn't do that,' Maxwell said loudly, fingering the nets again. 'You see, I'm an ex-public schoolboy. Never been known to hit a woman in my life. Remember that immortal line from *The Go Between*? "Always remember it's never a lady's fault." But the Hippos? Well, they're chaps of an altogether different kidney. Wouldn't know a Go-Between from a knuckle sandwich. Three tugs on this curtain and you're history, Ms Meninger.'

She turned to him, mouth open, silenced for the moment. 'That's preposterous,' she said eventually. 'You can't be serious.'

Maxwell shook his head. 'Not a very good John McEnroe,' he felt bound to comment.

'I don't respond to threats,' she snapped.

'Well, that's good,' Maxwell nodded. 'How, I wonder, will you respond to this?'

He pulled a folded scarred photograph from his jacket pocket and held it out to her. Hesitantly at first, she took it. 'Well?' she raised an eyebrow. 'Am I supposed to know who this is?'

'Of course you do,' Maxwell said. 'Do you

remember *Petrocelli*?'

'Who?' Sally looked blank.

'My, my.' The Head of Sixth Form shook his head. 'We are being economical with our age, aren't we? *Petrocelli* was an American cop show of the seventies. Or, to be precise, a lawyer show. Barry Newman played him, a hick attorney building his own house in the middle of Nevada somewhere. Or was it New Mexico?'

'Does this have any purpose?' she sighed.

'Indeed, indeed,' he smiled. 'Well, Petrocelli just happened to have a mind like a razor and his favourite phrase in court when he was getting to the truth and persuading the jury was "let me take you back".'

'Really?'

'Really. So let me take you back, Ms Meninger, to a dim and distant night, Tuesday if memory serves. I'd gone into a local hostelry called the Vine to slake the chalk dust and drown my sorrows with a few colleagues. We were all feeling pretty got at—you know how Ofsted inspections can be, when who should walk in but a couple of those self-same inspectors. They looked to be all over each other in the most adolescent way, but on closer inspection (and you'll excuse the pun) *she* was all over *him*. Does any of this seem familiar?'

'I have to go,' she spun on her heel.

'I know what you did this summer,' he shouted and it stopped her. Then, quieter, 'I

367

went to answer the call of nature and caught these same inspectors at it in the gents—not an edifying spectacle, but then it wasn't supposed to be, was it? No sooner had the female of the pair emerged from the cubicle of shame, than that gentleman there whose photograph I notice you are still holding, entered stage left. Now,' he got to his feet, 'this is where I'll admit to being just a teensy bit hazy, but you said something like "typical" or "fantastic" or something and vanished. I called him Joe Public. Now, I know his name was Craig Edwards. Well, you can't win them all, can you?'

'Look,' she put the photograph down. 'I know Alan and I behaved stupidly. I tried to apologize for that. I even, God help me, offered you money . . .'

'Yes,' Maxwell nodded. 'You also tried to implicate my Headmaster, didn't you?'

'That's rubbish.'

'Oh, he's not my idea of what a Headmaster should be. No fire in his eye, no steel in his stride, no gravel in his voice. But he's a human being, Sally. He doesn't deserve you.'

'James and I . . .'

'You see,' it was his turn to interrupt. 'You didn't let me finish about Iron Man down there. Now, Iron's not as other men—a few numbers short of a gig in some ways, but he doesn't miss much. He saw you and Edwards going at it hammer and tongs in the Vine car park afterwards. He'd fouled up, hadn't he? Got his times wrong or something. You had to rethink the whole thing.'

'Max,' she leaned towards him, licking her lips as though she were about to eat him, then smiling. 'You're talking bollocks.'

'He's dead, Sally,' Maxwell told her.

'What?' she stood bolt upright as though he'd slapped her.

'Craig Edwards, Joe Public, the man you harangued not a fortnight ago, is dead. Murdered.'

Her face had drained of colour. 'You're lying,' she blurted.

'My God,' he looked deep into her eyes. 'You really didn't know, did you?'

She blinked, her lips suddenly parchment-dry, her throat tight in panic. 'Um . . . Hall said there'd been another murder, on the day we left Leighford. But he didn't say who and I didn't make the connection.' She sat down on the edge of the bed. 'What happened?'

Maxwell sat next to her. Instinctively, he fetched her a glass of water from the bathroom. He needed Jacquie more than ever now and not just as the companion of a mile. 'I don't know the details,' he said. 'But it's the same MO as the others. Sally, when I came here this morning, I'd hoped to get the truth out of you. Except,' he lapsed into his Jack Nicholson, 'you couldn't handle the truth.' He eased the glass from the grip of her fingers.

369

'For a while I thought you'd tried to seduce Whiting and he wasn't having any. In a fit of pique you set the fire alarm and killed him. You could have bought the skewer in any High Street store—Skewers 'R' Us and so on—and hidden it in your handbag. True, you were with me when the alarm sounded, but it is possible you got some kid to do that for you or maybe even hapless, unsuspecting Paula Freeling. After that, I didn't see you. I was too busy getting kids to move. You would have had time to double back, do the deed and join us all on the tennis courts before you were missed.'

'For God's sake . . .' she muttered, eyes wild.

'Then there was Paula. Did you know, like Bob Templeton, about the old duck's little habits? Glitzy objects just stuck to her fingers, didn't they? I'm sure she'd be all too ready to conspire with you with a little whistle-blowing threat from you. Had she rung the alarm for you and then realized why you'd asked her? Not to test the school's fire drill efficiency, but as a cloak to kill Whiting? Or had she just got back too soon and caught you checking the scene of the crime? It would have been an easy matter to whisk her out of the Cunliffe that night and stash her somewhere. Now it would have got difficult, though. To find somewhere safe you'd need to have hired a lock-up and that's not easy in a strange town without attracting too much attention. The boys in blue will have been house-to-house. They'd

370

have turned over your stone.'

'That's not what happened.' Sally was shaking her head.

'No,' Maxwell nodded. 'I realize that now. I pride myself on the old body language. Either you deserve an Oscar for Best Actress or you had no idea about Edwards. Since whoever killed him killed the others, you're sort of off the hook, Inspector.'

She sighed and shuddered.

'So what *was* it all about?' he asked.

Nothing.

He made it easy for her. 'Why don't you tell me about your sister?'

She turned to face him, eyes smouldering. 'You know, don't you?'

He nodded. 'Yes, but I'd rather you told me.'

She got up and wandered to the window. The Hippos still dawdled by their van, Wal now stretched out on the low wall that formed the hotel's boundary. 'Pamela and I . . .' she said. It sounded like 'James and I . . .' but this time it had an altogether truer ring, 'by definition go back a long way.'

'She's the elder?' Maxwell checked.

'Elder, brighter, smarter. Daddy's girl who got all the boys.'

'Maybe you tried too hard,' Maxwell suggested.

'Save me your homespun psychology, Maxwell,' she snapped. 'Let's just say Pamela

371

and I didn't get on. Everything she wanted, from dolls to roller skates to university choice to men—dear Pammie got the lot. She even inherited Daddy's money. I mean, can you believe that? The partisan old bastard left her everything. The house, the shares, the lot. Did I resent it? You bet! Did I get mad? Yes. And then I got even. Or tried to.'

'The seduction of Alan,' Maxwell said.

'The irony was she'd only met him because of me. On the Ofsted circuit. It was lust at first sight. Although to this day, I could never understand that—the Vine merely confirmed my suspicions. He was about as well hung as an old tea-towel. Have you ever hated someone, Max? Hated them so much you lived with it, slept with it, couldn't spend a waking moment without thinking of it?'

'I can't say that I have,' he murmured. 'Not like that.'

'You can't imagine what joy it was when Alan and I were working on the same team at Leighford. It was like manna from Heaven. I hatched, in the Baldrick phrase, a cunning plan and contacted photographers. Oh, the first couple were useless. Didn't want to know. But Edwards was quite amenable. I was to take Alan to the Vine—Edwards told me where it was—on the Tuesday and get him into the gents. I'd tease him, get him worked up and have his wicked way with me while Edwards took some compromising photos.

372

The fact that you and your colleagues were there just gave me a captivated audience—so thanks for that. I nearly trod on Armstrong's tongue, I seem to remember. Then with the photos done I'd decide—either blackmail poor, squirming Alan or send the piccies to Pamela or both. It would be a hoot.'

'But it didn't work,' Maxwell said.

'Edwards blew it. I knew Alan would be a walkover, vain, conceited sod that he was. But the photographer was late. Traffic, he said, on the Flyover or somewhere.'

'It happens,' Maxwell nodded.

'That's clearly what your idiot drummer overheard in the car park. I was bloody furious. And after Alan's pathetic behaviour in front of your lot from Leighford, I wasn't sure I could arrange an action replay. I refused to pay Edwards his fee and in fact demanded my deposit back.'

'And your action replay was, in any case, spoiled a little by Whiting's death the next day?'

She turned to face him, nodding. 'Yes,' she said. 'It was. Oh, Max, I'm sorry. I'm sorry I lied to you and to the police. Above all, I'm sorry about James Diamond. He was just a bit of fun once on a weekend conference, you know how they are.'

Maxwell shrugged; perhaps he'd been going to the wrong conferences.

'What are you going to do?' she asked him.

'No, Sally,' he said. 'It's more a matter of what *you're* going to do. You've left a lot of loose ends in Leighford. Go south. Maybe it's time you tied a few of them up.'

*   *   *

Now, Peter Maxwell was already middle-aged when they'd invented mobile phones. He'd been a slip of a thing when the aptly named Alexander Graham Bell had called from one room to another, 'Come here, Mr Watson, I need you.' And truth be told, he'd never been really au fait with the things. For a start, they reeked of built-in obsolescence and backward technology. No sooner had the Great Man mastered one set of incomprehensible symbols, they streamlined/upgraded/outmoded the old one and on with the new, simpler of course, cheaper certainly and even more designed to confuse. But Maxwell had one in his pocket and if there was ever a time to use it, it was now.

Once out of the Wheatsheaf, he was striding across the tarmac, pushing buttons with the best of them. It was ringing. Good sign. He'd triumphed again. He heard her voice as the Hippos hove into view.

'I can't come to the phone right now,' she said. 'But leave a message and I'll get back to you.'

Will you, Jacquie? He wondered as he

waited for the bleep. Will you?

'Jacquie. It's Max. Look, I can't tell you in detail now. It's the sister. Got it? The sister . . . Damn!' He knew the change of sound, for all he hated these things. He looked at the screen. Menu. He'd lost her.

*　　　*　　　*

Jacquie touched base that lunchtime, hurtling through her hallway to grab a sandwich before getting back to the nick. She pressed her answerphone on the way through and was in the kitchen before she heard his voice. 'Jacquie. It's Max. Look, I can't tell you in detail now. It's the sister. Got it? The sister . . .' and it went dead. She stood there for a moment, staring at the machine, willing it somehow to go on with the rest of the message. Nothing.

Whatever emotions churned inside her, she stifled them, the copper kicking in. Think. She replayed his message, as though this time he'd say something more, something else. He didn't. She returned his call, landline to mobile. Nothing. Not even a ring. Just the faceless woman telling her that the subscriber she was calling was not answering. She rang his number at Columbine, punching numbers wildly, feeling the seconds crawl like years.

'War Office,' she heard him say. 'If you have a message for me or the cat, please speak

375

clearly after the Anthony.'

She slammed the phone down. Did he get any messages at all with nonsense like that? Her heart was thumping under her blouse. She switched on the kettle and fumbled in the cupboard for the instant coffee. The sister. She kept repeating it over and over in her head. Fuck communications! Why was it, in the brave new world of super-technology, you might just as well bash the jungle drums?

Jacquie stood there, fingers tapping the smooth work surface, waiting for the watched pot to boil. She felt like crying all over again, hearing his voice one more time. But his voice sounded urgent, needful and she hadn't heard that often. She shook herself free of it, switched off the kettle and grabbed her car keys. She drove to Columbine.

*   *   *

'Hello, Jacquie,' a voice called from beyond the privet.

'Mrs Troubridge,' the girl had her breath in her fist, peering over the leaves. 'Is he home?'

'Why, no, dear,' the old neighbour smiled, pinging off one pink rubber gardening glove. 'It's Wednesday, I believe and he's at school. Always sounds so silly, don't you think? A grown man still being at school. He's at work, I should say.'

'Thank you, Mrs Troubridge, I just left

something . . .' and she was in through his front door, up the stairs past the uncollected mail with its offer of Saga holidays and pension plans, to his lounge and kitchen on the first floor. Nothing. A half-empty bottle of Southern Comfort still graced his coffee table and a set of scruffy exercise books that looked as if the dog had eaten them all and shat them out. Of Metternich and Maxwell there was no sign.

She climbed the stairs to his bedroom two at a time. The bed was unmade, the duvet thrown back and a pair of slippers on the fleece rug. She noticed a book there too, some historical tosh by somebody she'd never heard of. *Vlad the Impaler.* Was Maxwell losing it in his old age? She looked at his pillow for a moment, the dent where his head had been still visible. She'd lain there with him now for nights without number, feeling his kisses warm on her cheek, his gentle hands fondling her breasts and tickling her navel until she shrieked with mock-hysteria. How many times, she wondered, had she lain there as dawn's rays crept over his windowsill, watching the steady, rhythmic rise and fall of his chest, the soft smile on his lips. She glanced up at the open door to his attic. Some people never imagine the man they love dying. They just live in a cloud cuckooland that they never would. But Jacquie was different. She was a policewoman and that made all the difference. And for all he'd always promised her they'd jump off that cliff together, leaping hand-in-hand into that great goodnight at the surging sea's edge, she'd always known he would go first. Logic and all her training told her so. And she always imagined him dead among the soldiers in his attic. She'd come upon him one day when they were both very old. He'd just have put the last one in place in the diorama. She knew who it would be, too, because he'd told her. It would be Edwin Hughes, late private of Her Majesty's Thirteenth Light Dragoons. She could hear Maxwell say it as she climbed the open stairs. 'He was born in Wrexham, North Wales, Woman Policeman, and his horse was killed in the Charge. He died in 1927, the last survivor of the Light Brigade.'

Jacquie popped her head into the attic, shielding her eyes as the sun streamed in through the skylight. The Light Brigade she swore, shifted slightly in their saddles at her approach, scenting an intruder on the breeze. So did Metternich, the black and white bastard, lowering his head and staying upwind of her.

'Tut, tut,' she smiled, tilting her head to one side to look at him, perched on a linen basket as he was. 'I don't think you're really supposed to be up here, are you, Count?'

No woman could get round Metternich, dimples and angel voice though she may have. He'd heard it all before. Anyway, he was a *man's* cat. Nothing odd about Metternich. He extended an elegant dancer's leg and began the serious work of licking his bum. Just because he could.

She was gone, down the stairs at breakneck speed, scribbling a note on the white board in Maxwell's kitchen. *I love you, you old bastard. Where are you?*

'Have you time for a cup of tea, dear?' Mrs Troubridge asked on the path outside. 'I've just put the kettle on . . .'

'Sorry,' Jacquie waved back. 'Haven't the time.'

And the Ka was screeching out of Columbine like a bat out of Hell.

*   *   *

'But he must have said where he was going!' Jacquie exploded in Bernard Ryan's office.

'Can you hear yourself?' Ryan was equally forthright. 'This is Peter Maxwell we're talking about. I'm only the Acting Bloody Headteacher. And, as Max would no doubt be the first to announce, I'm doing it bloody badly. You live with him, for God's sake. He doesn't let his left hand know what his right's doing.'

Silence lay between them. Jacquie had parked illegally outside the school's front doors, much to the chagrin of a delivery man with a large consignment of new chairs. She'd flashed her warrant card at Thingee Two on

379

Reception and had made for the History floor. She'd got a confused wave from Paul Moss and in Maxwell's room, facing thirty-four of Tomorrow's Finest, a weasly-looking man with glasses was posing as a supply teacher.

The Great Man's office was empty, post-it notes stuck at rakish angles all over his desk, the aspidistra in the corner still flying, the film stars of yesteryear looking down at her.

'We don't know,' Helen Maitland had appeared at her elbow, answering Jacquie's question before she'd asked it. 'Better see Bernard.'

So here she was, doing just that.

'When are we going to get our Head back?' the long-suffering Deputy wanted to know.

'Content yourself,' she said in a phrase worthy of Peter Maxwell. 'It's not many people get to take over a school because their Head has confessed to murder.'

'Jesus!' Ryan hissed, eyes wide. 'You mean he did it?'

'No, Mr Ryan,' Jacquie told him. 'I mean he confessed to it. Which, believe me, isn't the same thing at all. Now, let's go over this again, can we, please?'

Ryan sighed. He'd been Head of Leighford High now, man and boy, for forty-eight hours, give or take and he looked like Methuselah. 'Max asked James for a couple of days unpaid leave. Well, I'm not sure he actually *asked* for unpaid leave, but that in effect is what he's got.

But I've no idea, Jacquie, where he was going. If I knew, I'd tell you. He did promise, however, to bring Alan Whiting's killer's head back on a plate.'

Jacquie was already on her way out. 'Well, that'll pep up school dinners, won't it?'

And she understood now how easy it was for Peter Maxwell to loathe the man.

*   *   *

'Miss Freeling?'

The dead woman's sister looked up from her knitting. It was cool here in the otherwise sweltering mid-afternoon sun, and quiet. The world and his wife were on the beach or in the Amusement Arcades on the pier with all the fun of the fair.

'I'm DS Jacquie Carpenter.' She held her warrant card high. 'Could I have a word?'

'Ah, yes. Miss Carpenter. We met at the police station. Has there been any progress?'

'I was hoping you might tell me.' Jacquie sat down in the chintzy chair opposite.

'Shall we have some tea?'

It was like something out of Jane Marple. A dotty old spinster helping the police with their enquiries.

'Why not?' Jacquie said and called the lad over from the bar.

'A pot of tea for two, please,' said Deborah. 'Would you like some cakes, my dear?'

'No, thanks,' Jacquie said. 'I'd like some answers.'

'Oh?'

'Tell me about your sister,' she said. 'Your relationship with her.'

'Relationship?' Deborah resumed her knitting, clacking the needles together with a practiced hand.

'Did you get on?' Jacquie asked.

'Do you have any siblings, Miss Carpenter?' It was Deborah's turn to ask the questions.

'No, I'm an only,' Jacquie said. 'And that's Detective Sergeant, Miss Freeeling.'

'Oh, dear,' Deborah pulled a face. 'How formal. You said a moment ago you hoped I might tell you how it's going. Well, nothing's happening, really. I mean, I understand why Mr Hall wanted me to stay on in the town, but I'm not sure it's working. Since that poor man died in his studio the other day . . .'

'Were you there?'

'I was, as a matter of fact. Soon afterwards.'

'What time would that be?'

'On the Saturday? Ooh, let me see, ten, ten thirty. I'd been wandering about all week, as your Mr Hall asked me to. I will admit I had one or two odd looks, from people who no doubt had seen poor Paula's picture in the paper. When you left me at Leighford High, several teachers there seemed a little, shall we say, confused? But really, it's frightening how unobservant people are, isn't it? As a policewoman, you must have noticed that. If Mr Hall was hoping for someone to leap out on me or scream that I was a ghost, I'm afraid it hasn't happened yet.'

Jacquie leaned back in the armchair, looking the woman in the face, staring down suddenly at the knitting needles, sharp and gleaming, dancing in a blur in her hands. 'No, Miss Freeling,' she said, 'I think you must have misunderstood the situation. Mr Hall asked you to stay in Leighford because he suspects you of murder.'

* * *

Luck like that didn't often come to coppers. And when it did, it was hardly ever to coppers like Geoff Baldock. He couldn't wait for the summons from the DCI's office so he barged straight in.

'Come in, why don't you?' Hall looked up at him, the glare icy, the glasses blank. How *did* he manage to do that? No matter what the lighting or what the time of day, subordinates rarely caught the look in Henry Hall's eyes.

'Sorry, guv.' Confidence had made Baldock jump from 'sir' to 'guv'. This had better be good, Hall thought. 'I just thought you might like to know.' He put the scanned photo set, the one he'd dug up the night before, on the DCI's desk. 'That's Ken Lummis. That's Barbara Payne.'

'Ken and Barbie?' Hall said. 'You're having me on.'

'House to house came up trumps. Mr Lummis is a worried man now. We know these were taken three weeks ago, when Mrs Lummis thought Mr Lummis was away on business. And Mr Lummis knew nothing about the photos.'

'And Miss Payne?'

'Is a neighbour. They've had the hots for each other for months and started an affair in early May. Mr Lummis started denying it, according to house to house, saying it was a stitch up and remember how they doctored the Lee Harvey Oswald photos.'

'Which you didn't?'

'Have a heart, guv,' the lad said. 'I wasn't born.'

'Indeed,' Hall nodded. When policemen started to look younger than you . . .

'Miss Payne was more forthcoming. Said, yes, it was her.

Proceeded to prove it by showing me a mole on her left buttock.'

Hall's eyebrow threatened to reach his hairline. 'You had a policewoman present while all this was going on, I trust?'

'Well, er . . . no, sir . . .'

'Then you'd better pray she doesn't realize the possibilities and blackmail the shit out of you. Where were these taken?'

'Um . . . right here in Leighford, sir. A

B and B in Cherrygin Street.'

'You spoke to Mrs Lummis?'

'House to house did.' Baldock pulled up a chair unbidden. 'And this is the good part. She suspected dear old Ken of being up to no good and bearing in mind he runs a software company, he's worth a bob or two. So she employed a local photographer to follow him.'

'A local photographer called Craig Edwards?' Hall checked.

'Exactly. One night, he got lucky.'

'Right.' Hall sat back in his chair, his hands cradled behind his head. 'So we've confirmation that Edwards took shady photographs. Does that get us any nearer to his killer?'

'Er . . .'

'No, constable, it doesn't. What it actually does is open a whole new can of worms. So thanks for that.' He got up, brushed past his man and bellowed into the outer office, 'Has anybody seen Jacquie Carpenter?'

Chapter Sixteen

'Has anybody seen Jacquie Carpenter?'

Peter Maxwell was standing in Reception at Leighford police station, waiting for an answer. The desk man looked at him through the protected glass.

'Now, why would you want to know that, sir?' he asked. Politeness and correctness went with the job.

'Because she's just won a dream kitchen for two in our The Only Intelligent Policeperson competition. Is she here?'

'If you're going to be flippant, sir . . .' Politeness and correctness and a mastery of repartee.

Peter Maxwell didn't often lose his cool, but when he did, it was worth the wait. 'And if you're going to be a stupid, obstructive wanker, sergeant,' he roared so that the glass partition rattled, 'you may be responsible for the death of a colleague. Now, where is she?'

The desk man blinked. 'You're Peter Maxwell, aren't you?' he asked quietly; the moveable bits in the office behind him had stopped shaking now.

'I am,' Maxwell told him.

'Could you wait a moment, sir?' and the desk man was gone.

All the way down from the Dales, Peter

Maxwell had been trying his mobile again. Useless. His batteries were deader than Queen Anne. Duggsy's had gone missing at his last gig and Wal's had never been the same since it landed in somebody's beer. Iron Man never used mobiles—they damaged your brain cells, he knew that. And the two or three times they'd found a call box unvandalized on the way south and Maxwell had got through, no answer. Just Jacquie saying calmly, 'I can't come to the phone right now . . .'

He'd tried the station, not once, but several times, to be met by the same stonewalling he was getting now.

'Mr Maxwell.' A dark-haired, worried-looking copper popped his head round the door. 'I'm Detective Inspector Bathurst. What seems to be the trouble?'

*   *   *

The diners at the Cunliffe weren't *quite* ready for the cabaret that accompanied their evening meal.

'Hello, Mr M . . .' but loquacious George never finished his sentence. Bathurst and Maxwell hurtled through Reception, batting open the double doors at the end and swerving around waiters, looking this way and that for their quarry. Please God, please God reverberated around both their brains. A table went flying, soup, crockery and cutlery

387

spattered and scattered in all directions. Nothing. They stood there, like a pair of bulls in a china shop, as the silence they'd engendered turned to angry complaints and the flinging down of napkins. People had paid good money for this.

They turned simultaneously back to the foyer, racing for the lounge and the stairs. Then they stopped in their tracks. In the corner, a little alarmed by the noise and ruckus from the next room, sat two women. One was a rather demure spinster, knitting with a feverish speed. The other was Jacquie Carpenter.

'Max?' She was on her feet.

'Jacquie!' he rushed to her, held her close. But she stayed rigid. Cold. 'Thank God you're all right.'

'Why wouldn't I be?' she frowned.

Bathurst looked at Deborah Freeling. 'Blind alley,' he said. 'Miss Freeling, would you excuse us?' and he took Jacquie aside, leading her past George's counter while Maxwell made small talk with the old girl.

'Police.' He flicked a warrant card at George. 'I'm borrowing your office for five minutes.'

'Righto.' George was still a little bewildered from the grand entrance of a few minutes ago, mindlessly polishing glasses as he still was.

'What did you get?' Bathurst asked Jacquie when he'd closed the door.

'Not a lot,' she admitted.

'You've been here for bloody hours,' the DI reminded her.

'Yes, Phil, I'm sorry,' Jacquie said. 'I thought she was worth working on. Softly, softly, you know.'

'Why did you want to re-interview Deborah Freeling in the first place?'

'A tip-off,' Jacquie said.

'Who from?' Bathurst wanted to know.

'I can't say.' Jacquie Carpenter would be loyal to Peter Maxwell to the end.

'Yes, you can, Jacquie and he's not a million miles from us as we speak. What did Deborah Freeling tell you?'

She looked at him. What was Max doing here? What were they both doing here? 'Thank God you're all right,' Max had said. Why? Could there be anything more harmless than the old girl he was chatting to in the lounge out there? For once, Max's famous intuition had let him down. The Great Man had got it wrong.

'Paula Freeling has a record,' she said. 'For shoplifting. Oh. Ofsted didn't know anything about it, of course. She'd deliberately kept that particular bit of achievement out of her CV. She's a klepto, apparently. If it's not nailed down, she'll have it. That's why she had no friends and why her sister was more than a little distant.'

'It also explains the threatening letters,'

389

Bathurst nodded.

'Exactly,' Jacquie concurred. 'Although Deborah pretended not to know why she was receiving them. But as for murder, Phil,' the girl was shaking her head. 'I don't know what M . . . my informant was thinking.'

'Oh, I do,' Bathurst said. 'You only got half the message, that was the problem. Fancy making an arrest tonight?'

*   *   *

Peter Maxwell made his own way home from the Cunliffe. He walked. The Hippos, his Irregulars, had dropped him as near to the nick as any of them dared, given their lifestyles, and he'd eventually been able to explain the whole thing to DI Bathurst. Jacquie had jumped to the wrong conclusion, but it was the only safe one. And she was fine. *They* however, were not. When he'd hugged her, it was like grappling with a tree, hard and unyielding. When she and Bathurst left the hotel, in a hurry, she'd looked at him. Just looked. No smile. No sneer. No sign that until days ago, these two were lovers. And she'd gone.

He wandered along the Front that night as the last signs of day sank below the misty levels of the sea. The drunks weren't out yet and the kids had gone to bed. It was that brief window of peace, when you could still see the sky and

390

the sea and the beauty of it all as it must have been before it had been ruined by man.

He stood on the edge of Leighford Beach and breathed in, watching the sea's frothy ripples curl white in the darkness ahead and he looked out to the sweep of Willow Bay. Armed with the information he'd given Bathurst, the DI would make his arrest tonight and that would be a feather in his cap and hopefully in Jacquie's. But Maxwell felt a shiver along his spine and after the heat of another day, it had turned suddenly cold. This, he knew, as he turned for the long trudge home, wasn't over.

*   *   *

'Could you tell us about your relationship with your late husband, Mrs Whiting?'

'My relationship?' Pamela Whiting was sitting across the desk from DI Bathurst and DS Carpenter. It was the loneliest place in the world. The neon strip lent a cold, harsh light to the room and the blinds were drawn. The furniture was plain, cheap and institutional. Even the tape recorder, its spools whirring silently inside, had seen decidedly better days. 'He was my husband.'

Bathurst rested both elbows on the table. 'You see, Mrs Whiting, when a husband or wife dies in suspicious circumstances, we automatically consider, I'm afraid, the involvement of the spouse.'

391

'I see,' Pamela bridled. She was not at her best. There had been a knock on her hotel door at a little before ten and Jacquie Carpenter had stood there, warrant card in her hand, requesting that she accompany her to the station. Time-honoured words, a time-honoured tradition. But Pamela Whiting had been ready for bed. She had not expected the Spanish Inquisition. 'Are you accusing me of murder?' she asked, her voice brittle, her eyes hard. 'For that, I believe you have to establish means, motive and opportunity. Would you like to try to do that?'

Bathurst leaned back. The woman was clever. She was confident. She was fencing with him. And all he had to go on was the instinct, the gut-reaction of Peter Maxwell. All the way from the station to the Cunliffe, the Head of Sixth Form had been bombarding the Detective Inspector with theories, facts, suppositions, scenarios. And he'd been doing it at high speed as Bathurst's car screamed around Leighford's streets, burning rubber to get to Jacquie who was facing a killer on her own. Except that Jacquie was facing the wrong sister.

'Let's look at motive.' The DI was happy to fence at the moment. 'It's not financial. We know that. Your bank was very helpful in providing the necessary details, Mrs Whiting. You are a reassuringly wealthy woman in your own right. Your husband was insured, but not for a fortune.' He looked at her clothes, her jewellery. 'And I don't think you needed the money.'

'All right,' she said. 'I didn't kill Alan for his money.' She looked at them. 'What, then?'

'There are surprisingly few motives for murder, Mrs Whiting,' Jacquie said. 'Financial gain, lust, jealousy, revenge. We can rule out the first and the second . . .'

'Well, that's something at least,' Pamela said.

'But that still leaves us with the last two. Jealousy and revenge.'

'You'll have to enlighten me further, I'm afraid,' she said. 'It's not making much sense so far.'

'You told us you thought your husband was having an affair,' Bathurst said, her signed interview notes with Hall in front of him.

'It happens.' She dismissed it. 'Men of a certain age . . .'

'. . . Men of a certain age,' Bathurst cut in, 'are seduced by their fiancée's sister. Oh, it's not their fault exactly. Bit of cleavage, lots of "Come hither", plenty of availability. It's all part of a little game you've been playing for years, isn't it?'

Pamela Whiting looked at her watch. 'I think I've been patient long enough,' she said. 'I can't tell you how much I've enjoyed your little fishing expedition . . .' and she was on her feet.

393

'Sit down, Mrs Whiting!' Bathurst roared. For a moment, the woman swayed, hesitating, uncertain what to do. Then she sat, arranging her skirt just so and composing herself. 'I'd like a solicitor present,' she said.

'Do you like films, Mrs Whiting?' Jacquie ignored her. 'Horror films in particular?'

'What?' Pamela was thrown.

Jacquie was in Peter Maxwell country by now, but she had a point to make. *Whatever Happened To Baby Jane?* she said. 'Do you know it?'

'I really don't see . . .'

'It's about two sisters,' Jacquie went on. 'Bette Davis and Joan Crawford. They're old, they're ugly and they hate each other. And in between severe tantrums and serving roast rat with the Sunday lunch, they're trying to bump each other off. Oh, it's in black and white and wonderfully over the top, but you're the living embodiment of it, aren't you? You and your sister.'

Only the ticking clock disturbed the silence.

'My sister?' Pamela said.

'Sally Meninger,' Bathurst blurted. 'We haven't had time to check records yet, Mrs Whiting. The boys back at the station are doing that as we speak. So I can't give you Ms Meninger's maiden name, except that it's the same as yours.'

'What of it?' Pamela snapped. 'So Sally and I are sisters. Where does that get you?'

'It gets us to two little girls,' Bathurst said quietly. Peter Maxwell had coached him well, he realized, on their way to the Cunliffe. 'One clever, the other cleverer; one pretty, the other prettier; one the apple of Daddy's eye, the other not. How many times I wonder did you metaphorically stab her in the back? Drown her in the bath?' And he took a leaf from Jacquie's film book, itself borrowed from Mad Max. 'Drive at her in your car?'

'This is nonsense,' Pamela insisted.

'No, Mrs Whiting,' Jacquie said, shaking her head. 'It's fact. Oh, Sally was the jealous one, eaten up by resentment, waiting for her chance of retribution. You even stole her man, didn't you? Alan. And that gave her her chance. Oh, she didn't deliberately set out to do it, I don't suppose, but when the Ofsted situation at Leighford High presented itself, it all fell into place. She'd seduce him all over again, get proof to you that it had happened, send you photographs of them at it, rub your nose in it, for all the years of you always being in the limelight, always being number one.'

'This is preposterous,' Pamela said. She was on her feet again now, twirling round the room, her hands in the air. 'I'm not listening to any more of it.'

'The point is,' Bathurst looked up at her, 'you've won again, haven't you? I don't suppose Sally would see it that way, but you have. She was planning to wreck your marriage

395

when you had your own plans to do that, permanently and forever. It's a nice little twist she couldn't possibly have expected.'

Pamela Whiting stopped whirling as a thought struck her. She turned back to face the pair, sitting, oh, so smugly, side by side.

'If you think you've established motive,' she said, resting her knuckles on the desk and supporting her weight on her arms, 'that still leaves you with means and opportunity. You seem to forget that I was in Matlock when my husband died. That's one hell of a long barbecue skewer, isn't it?'

'You hired someone,' Jacquie told her. 'Just as Sally hired a photographer to take compromising pictures of her and Alan, you hired a hitman to kill him. Poor bastard was going to get it either way, wasn't he?'

'A hitman?' Pamela scoffed. 'Can you people hear yourselves? This isn't some cheap, trashy Raymond Chandler thriller. People like that don't exist.'

'Oh, but they do, Mrs Whiting,' Bathurst said. 'Killing is a skill, just like any other. No, not like any other, because to do it several times and get away with it, well, that's damned near impossible.'

Pamela slid back her chair and sat down. The cat and mouse game had gone on for long enough. 'It said in the papers—quoting your beloved Chief Inspector, if I remember rightly—that Alan, Paula Freeling and Craig

Edwards were all killed by the same hand.'

'We believe so,' Bathurst nodded.

She leaned back. 'All right,' she said, smiling. 'Let's suppose I go along with your idiocy that I engineered my husband's death. Did I also engineer that of *another* Ofsted inspector and a seaside photographer? And what little psychodrama from my girlhood would you conjure up to explain the slaughter of these particular innocents? Well, I'm waiting.'

*   *   *

Peter Maxwell had reached the rise overlooking the sea by a little after half ten. All the way down from the Dales he'd been wrestling with it and every minute since. Pamela Whiting was behind her husband's death—that much he knew. But she couldn't have done it herself. She wasn't the Boiler Man who had sneaked unobserved into Leighford and set the fire alarm before pinning Whiting to his chair. And although she was in Leighford by the time of the other two deaths, she hadn't popped unnoticed into the Cunliffe and abducted an Ofsted inspector or rung a photographer's doorbell bright and early last Saturday morning. And if it wasn't Pamela Whiting, then . . .

'Mr Maxwell?'

He turned at the sound of his name to see a

white van growling at the grassy kerb next to him.

'Hello, Iron,' he said. 'I was wondering when you'd come calling.'

The drummer switched off his engine and got out of the van. There was a gleaming blade in his hand, long and tapering and he held it out horizontally, pricking the skin of Maxwell's neck.

'Taking a bit of a risk, aren't you?' Maxwell asked. 'Using the Hippos' van? I'd have thought you'd have used your other one, which I assume is plain. Out for a late night barbecue?'

Iron Man shrugged. 'I've been a bit sloppy on this one, Mr Maxwell,' he granted. 'Now, you just walk ahead of me, slowly and level, all right? It's just a *bit* too open up here for my liking.'

Maxwell obliged, taking each step one at a time, knowing that Iron Man's skewer could be through the back of his neck before he could break wind. The breeze from the sea ruffled his hair under the tweed cap and he looked out at that breathtaking view for perhaps the last time. The drummer was taking him steadily downwards, away from the road and into the gorse bushes, darker still against the dark pearl of the night sky.

'Far enough,' Iron Man tapped his man on the shoulder with the skewer.

Slowly, Maxwell turned to face him. 'Before

you use that thing,' he said. 'Can you fill me in a bit? I'm naturally curious, you see, can't help myself. I'd hate to die not knowing why.'

Iron Man looked at him. He was close enough so that if he extended his arm now, he'd kill the Head of Sixth Form. One swift, sudden thrust and the blood would spurt above the ludicrous bow tie as it had from the throat of Alan Whiting.

'You're a clever bastard,' Iron Man said. 'Why don't you tell me?'

'All right,' Maxwell was already counting his blessings. He couldn't imagine the man giving Alan Whiting time to wheedle. And he was desperately playing for time. 'I will. But first, you've got to tell me something, Iron. How did you . . . get into this in the first place? I mean, at school, when you were filling in those endless careers forms, what did you write? Professional murderer?'

'It's a long story,' Iron Man smiled.

'We've got all night,' Maxwell hoped.

'No, we haven't,' the drummer corrected him. Maxwell noticed that his piercings were gone, those obvious metal dangly bits that drew people's attention to him. And his voice was not slurred and his sniff had gone. And he was a killer, just doing his job, as lethal and as focused as Metternich the cat. He'd be out on the night air now, scenting his prey on the wind, facing his luckless rodent as Iron Man faced Maxwell. 'It just happened,' he said darkly. 'I killed my first man when I was eighteen. That was in Bristol—a gang thing. He took the piss out of my drumming at a gig. So I kebabed him with my drum stick down an alley. By the time I was twenty, it was a nice little earner. 'Course, the sticks was a bit of a giveaway, but a skewer . . .' He held it up to the light. 'Untraceable.'

'You were working for Pamela Whiting,' Maxwell said, hoping that while he was still actually talking the drummer wouldn't strike.

'That's right,' Iron said. 'Had a bit of husband trouble. She told me where he'd be— which school, which hotel.'

'That was a hell of a risk,' Maxwell chuckled. 'Killing him at Leighford High like that. I take my hat off to you,' and his hand came up.

'Uh-huh.' The skewer glinted wickedly against Maxwell's throat. He felt the razor point nick the skin again and knew that he was bleeding.

'You . . . got the layout of the place, of course, from Duggsy and Wal. What more natural than three old mates, nattering away nights after a gig, eh? Few bevvies, few joints, few reminiscences of where the fire alarms were and the security cameras, and how they'd no doubt dodged past them all in their day. They're great lads, Duggsy and Wal, but they're not the brightest jewels in the crown, are they? You must have been a *bit*

400

disconcerted though when your target turned up at the Vine?'

'A bit,' Iron conceded. 'That's why I followed him outside, thinking to hit him there, in the pub car park. Instead I find that tart Sally Meninger screaming at the photographer. So I stuck with Plan A.'

'Plan A.' Maxwell's eyes were swivelling frantically. The pair were totally alone. No passing car, no courting couples, *nothing* between him and a sudden, violent death. 'You borrowed a boiler man's suit.'

'Had one already,' Iron told him.

'And . . . what? A baseball cap to hide the ponytail? Whipped out the old piercings so they wouldn't flash on any CCTV camera that might still accidentally catch you? That took some nerve, Iron.'

'That's what it's all about,' the drummer said. 'The risk, the thrill, if you like. It's what they call job fulfilment, ain't it? I couldn't do it just for the money. Whiting was about to get out of the room, you know, for the fire drill. I told him he didn't have to. Pretended I was the school's odd job man and I was on to it. Then I stuck him.'

'Neat. So, tell me, Iron . . . this is rather a personal question, I know, but what do you charge for something like this? A murder, I mean.'

'Got someone you want doing, Mr Maxwell?' Iron chuckled. 'Bit late now, maybe.

401

But no, it's not a personal question—as long, of course, as you keep it our little secret. I'd hate the Chancellor of the Exchequer to find out. Five large, Alan Whiting cost.'

'You killed a man for five hundred pounds?' Maxwell was incredulous.

'Five *thousand*,' the drummer corrected him. 'I don't come cheap.'

'How can you put a price on somebody's life like that?' Maxwell was in the twilight zone.

'That first bloke in the alley I killed for nothing,' Iron reminded him.

'A bit like Paula Freeling and Craig Edwards,' Maxwell said.

'Like I say,' Iron Man clicked his teeth. 'I been a bit sloppy. The one thing you learn in this game, Mr Maxwell, is split-second timing. It's a bit like drumming really. In, out, hit, move. And never, *ever* look back. That's what I did. I turned instinctively to see who'd just opened the door. It was that Freeling woman. I didn't have time to do anything about it just then, so I had to bide my time. Christ knows what she'd tell the police.'

'Nothing,' Maxwell told him. 'Paula Freeling was too traumatized to remember anything. Ironic, wasn't it? You were in the clear.'

'Yeah,' Iron shrugged. 'Ironic. I had to go to her hotel. The Filth were guarding the place and following them everywhere. Still, there's a back way into everywhere, ain't there? That stupid bastard on the front desk didn't notice

402

as I clocked the old girl's room number.'

'Why didn't you kill her there?' Maxwell asked. 'You took a hell of a risk getting her out.'

'I didn't want her screaming the place down and I needed to know what she'd seen, what she'd told Johnny Law. I took her to my garage.'

'And that's where you killed her.'

'Kept her in my bass drum case, Mr Maxwell. You've been sitting on it in the van for the last couple of days.'

'But she couldn't stay there,' Maxwell said.

'The Filth were searching garages, lock-ups, that sort of thing. It would have looked a bit suspicious if I'd refused them a shufty, wouldn't it?'

'Hence the waterworks?'

'I know a bloke who works for them,' the drummer said. 'He told me they was filling in holes, ready to move on. Seemed the ideal choice. Guess he was wrong.'

'Why Edwards?' Maxwell could feel the pressure of the skewer-point growing on his epiglottis. 'Why the photographer?'

'When he turned up for the gig at the Old Mill, I . . . well, I don't mind confessing it to you, Mr Maxwell—I was a bit rattled. I'd seen him in the Vine, in the car park. Had he seen me, prowling around the cars, carrying the pig-sticker here? And I didn't know what you knew either, how far you'd got. Bastard took a

403

photo of us playing, didn't he? I wasn't having that. Couldn't take the chance. I wanted the film.'

'But you couldn't get it that night?'

'No, the wanker had gone by eleven and we was booked till twelve. Can't let 'em down, can you, the kids? How do you do *School's Out* acoustic? You've just got to have drums, know what I mean?'

Maxwell did.

'So I went a-calling bright and early next morning. Took every bit of film he had. Burnt the lot.'

'And killed him.'

'Yeah, that was unfortunate, but I sensed he wasn't going to be reasonable, so, wallop, really. And that was nearly my last loose end, so to speak.'

'Until me.'

'Yeah,' Iron Man chuckled. 'Oh, I've always stayed one step ahead of the Filth, Mr Maxwell. Sure, they've got forensic and all that bollocks coming out of their ears, but deep down, they're Mr Plod, ain't they? Terminally stupid. But you . . . well, you're clever, Mr M. I got to hand it to you. *And* you're stubborn. Like a dog with a fucking bone. You'd have sussed me eventually. That's why the Hippos had to follow you everywhere. Take you around half the fucking country. I had to know what was going down; how close you were.'

'Well, that's nice of you, Iron,' Maxwell said.

His heart was pounding, his throat tight. The old flight or fight adrenalin was whirling through his bloodstream. Except that he was too slow for flight and as for fight . . . well, he'd seen Iron Man in action.

A roar shattered the night and a flash of white light illuminated the scene. Maxwell batted aside the skewer, feeling it lacerate his throat and struggled with the drummer on the ground. From nowhere, Harley Davidsons were hurtling over the ridge of the hill, snarling through the gorse bushes in a spray of soil and gravel.

'Yawning Fucking Hippos!' one of the Bikers yelled, skidding his machine to a halt and hurling himself onto the nearest body. 'I've been waiting for this.'

Maxwell rolled clear to find himself facing Death, the slob whose eyes he'd poked back in the Vine when he'd met Iron Man for the second time. 'You!' the slob hissed, but Maxwell was faster this time. He brought his boot up smartly in between the Biker's legs and the thud brought tears to the man's eyes. Then he caught his hair and pulled savagely, so that Death squealed before stumbling backwards through the gorse.

To his left, Iron Man was kicking and gouging his way clear of three or four of them, his skewer gone, his fists crunching into leather and metal.

'Kill the fucker!' came a screamed order

and a circle of bikes snarled to a standstill, their headlights lighting the weird arena in which Iron Man and Maxwell stood alone. It was like Tony Curtis and Kirk Douglas in Laurence Olivier's fatal circle at the end of *Spartacus*. One by one, the engines were switched off. Death and the Bikers damaged by Iron Man were spitting out teeth, re-arranging their hair, adjusting their leathers. Spanners came out of tool boxes, chains and knives as the circle drew tighter. Instinctively, Maxwell and Iron Man moved back to back, the only sound now the grating of their breath.

'Any ideas, Iron?' the Head of Sixth Form hissed.

'You could always tell them there's a reward on my head,' the drummer told him. 'As long as we're both unmarked, of course. Or all bets are off.'

Then, they both heard it. A sound that to Peter Maxwell was the most welcome in the world. And Iron Man? Well, he had mixed feelings about it. It was the wail of a police siren and the flashing blue lights crested the hill, as the white squad cars screeched to rock at crazy angles in the gorse.

'Fuck. It's the Filth,' and the Bikers revved up, twisting their cow-horn handlebars and kicking away into the night. Not all of them made it as Henry Hall's boys in blue launched into them with assorted rugby-tackles and arm-locks and some interesting moves very

406

definitely not in the police handbook.

It was DI Bathurst who snapped the cuffs on Iron Man's wrist.

'You'll find the skewer somewhere over there,' Maxwell said, only now realizing that the front of his shirt was soaked with blood. 'With a bit of luck, it'll be the one that killed Craig Edwards.'

'You're nicked,' the DI said to the drummer, summoning two uniforms to his side.

'Sorry about all this, Mr Maxwell,' Iron Man said. 'But you know, I'm sort of glad it's turned out like this.' He winked at the Head of Sixth Form. ' 'Till next time, eh?'

'Oh, there won't be a next time,' Bathurst assured him.

'Won't there?' Iron Man asked him. 'Trial is . . . what . . . eighteen months' time at Winchester Crown Court? Know it well.' He winked again at Maxwell. 'There's lots of back ways out of there.' And he was gone, his head ducked down into the black interior of a squad car that purred away into the night.

'Are you all right, Mr Maxwell?' Bathurst was checking that order was being restored to the scene. Three or four Bikers were being rounded up into cars, muttering and grumbling, ready to follow a killer to the station. 'We got a station call about the Bikers' antics. Didn't realize you were in the thick of it.'

'It's nothing that several stitches won't cure.' Maxwell's fingers were sticky with his blood.

'Look, I'm grateful to you for the info on Mrs Whiting, but this . . . You took a hell of a risk. He could have killed you.'

'I wasn't sure it was him,' he croaked, the exhaustion of the last half hour taking its toll and the shock beginning to kick in. 'And I didn't expect him to find me so quickly. Man's like a bloody will o' the wisp.'

And Peter Maxwell never fully understood why Philip Bathurst seemed to wobble up there on that gorse-strewn hillside overlooking the sea and why he became so very small and blurred and so very far away . . .

Chapter Seventeen

He passed the battlefield again the next morning, like Napoleon's grumblers, marching back over the frozen wastes of Borodino. There was no ice, of course and no bodies to speak of. Just crushed and trampled gorse bushes, churned up grass and a lot of tyre tracks. A police pick-up truck was about to tow away the Yawning Hippos' van and two rather sorry-looking rock stars sat disconsolately by the kerb.

' 'Morning, lads,' Maxwell eased the brakes on Surrey and straddled the crossbar.

'Have you heard about Iron, Mr M?' a bewildered Duggsy asked.

'Yes, I have, as a matter of fact.'

'Iron, a hitman.' Wal was shaking his head. 'Sort of shakes your faith in human nature, don't it?'

'It does, William,' Maxwell nodded.

'Defies belief,' Duggsy agreed. 'The real bitch of it, though, is that we're booked to play the Leighford Festival week after next.'

'Well, that's gone, ain't it?' Wal muttered. 'Without a drummer.'

'What about a different drummer?' Maxwell asked.

Duggsy looked up at him. 'Do you know anybody, Mr M? somebody at Leighford maybe?'

'In a manner of speaking,' Maxwell said.

'Who?'

'Peter Maxwell.'

'Fucking A,' Wal murmured.

'I don't want to be personal, Mr M,' Duggsy cut in, 'but . . . you?'

The Great Man leaned forward over the handlebars of Surrey. 'At Cambridge I was known as the Buddy Rich of Jesus College.' He fluttered his hands in the air like a true professional. 'Anyway, one way or another, I owe you guys.'

'OK,' Duggsy nodded slowly. 'We'll give you a try. No promises, mind.'

'Maxwell appears to be wearing a white cravat.' Dierdre Lessing was sorting her papers prior to her day spent sorting papers. She hadn't been known to *teach* for years.

Bernard Ryan, the Sir Mordred to her Morgan le Fay, peered out of the window from her office. 'At least he's here. I don't see anybody's head on a plate.'

'That man could hyperbole for England.' Dierdre always was rather hazy on her nouns and verbs. 'More importantly, Bernard, there's talk in the staffroom that James is back too. You'd think he'd see us first, wouldn't you? There goes your promotion down the Swannee.'

'Can't say I'm sorry,' Ryan said, folding his arms as he watched Maxwell park his bike. 'Dead men's shoes,' he shook his head. 'Don't like 'em, Dierdre.' He could go back to being Deputy Head again—everybody's punchbag. He wouldn't have it any other way.

Peter Maxwell walked into the dining room where the Breakfast Club were just finishing up. Gary Spenser and Tony Weatherall were there as usual, wondering what colour Miss Greenhow's knickers were today. Was it them, or was the old bugger hobbling a bit? Still, he cycled in every day and had to be a million, so it wasn't surprising, was it?

'Pale blue,' he leant over the lads.

They looked askance.

And he tapped the side of his nose, before throwing a wave to Sally Greenhow.

'Hello, Mr Maxwell.'

He half-turned, staring in astonishment. There, beaming at him under her silly white cap, with toast crumbs all over her fingers, stood Sharon. Silent Sharon. Sharon who had never, until now, had the nerve to talk to the man she'd adored from afar for years.

'Hello, Sharon,' he said. 'How are you today?'

And she grinned, bright crimson, and dashed into the kitchen to get on with the next phase of her life. Maxwell let it go. He had just witnessed a miracle.

*   *   *

'I've resigned, Max.' Another miracle at Leighford High sat behind his desk, twiddling his fingers, a white enveloped letter on the empty desk in front of him.

'Is that strictly wise, Headmaster?' the Head of Sixth Form asked.

'Max,' Diamond got to his feet. 'I confessed the day before yesterday to a murder. Well, actually to three. Could I be taken seriously ever again if I stayed on here?'

'Nothing has changed, Headmaster,' Maxwell said.

'What?'

411

'Why did you confess?' Maxwell asked.

'Oh,' Diamond was pacing his office, 'I don't know. You see, I thought Sally had done it. Killed Whiting and the others. I was . . . being stupid, I suppose.'

'Does she mean that much to you?'

Diamond looked at his man. 'No,' he shook his head. 'No, she doesn't. It was a ludicrous gesture. I was just trying to help her out of a jam, that's all. I wasn't thinking rationally.'

'Well,' Maxwell sighed. 'We've all been there.'

'I think the police intend to prosecute me for wasting their time. Hence the resignation. I'm a laughing stock, Max.'

'Surely not, Headmaster,' Maxwell frowned. 'Although it sure beats life imprisonment, doesn't it? Is that your resignation?' He pointed to the envelope.

'Yes. Why?'

Maxwell took it and tore it up in one fluid movement. 'I expect in these days of computers, that you've got this on a disk or a floppy drive or whatever, but if you want my advice, you'll forget all about it.'

'Max,' Diamond stood there blinking. 'What's happened? Have the police . . .'

'I promised Bernard I'd bring him a murderer's head on a plate,' he told him. 'Well, that was a little politically incorrect of me, wasn't it? They just don't make hacksaws like they used to. But if you care to read

412

tomorrow's Dailies, I think you'll be satisfied with the outcome.'

'You've done it, haven't you?' Diamond said. 'You've solved it.'

'With a little help from my friends,' Maxwell smiled.

Diamond reached out suddenly and grasped Maxwell's hand in both of his. The Head of Sixth Form froze. He didn't know the man was capable of emotions like this. 'Thank you, Max,' he said. 'For my job, for my life. Thank you.'

'All in a day's work, Headmaster,' and Maxwell pulled gently away.

'By the way,' Diamond said. 'The neck. Did that have anything to do with . . . ?'

'Oh, this?' Maxwell touched the bandages gingerly. 'No, no. Cut myself shaving.'

*   *   *

'Coffee, Max?'

A slightly chipped mug appeared under Peter Maxwell's nose. He was used to the mug. He was used to the awful coffee. He was even used, chauvinist pig that he was, to Helen Maitland making it for him. What he was not used to, at this time of the morning and in this particular office, was the voice.

He stood up quickly. 'Jacquie?'

She stood by his desk, smiling, the tears streaming down her cheeks. 'They said you'd

413

been hurt,' she said, her words thick, her lips trembling. Her fingers reached out, carefully, so carefully, to touch his neck.

'You should see the other guy,' he smiled.

'I did,' she sniffed, wiping away her tears with the back of her hand. 'He's implicated Pamela Whiting up to her murderous little neck. Chief Inspector Hall would like to see you.'

'Would he now?' Maxwell raised an eyebrow. 'What for, I wonder? To arrest me for helping police with their enquiries or to give me the George Medal? No, don't help me.' He held his hand up. 'I think I know the answer. How are you, Jacquie?'

'I'm fine,' she said.

'Is that why you came?' he asked. 'To give me Henry's summons?'

'No,' she sniffed. 'When you were at mine the other day, I think you left something behind.'

And she held up a key. Her house key; the one that usually lived in his pocket. They fell into each other's arms and he cradled her head, smelling her hair, stroking away the tears that splashed onto his shirt.

'Oh, Max,' Bernard Ryan popped his head round the door. 'Oh, sorry . . .'

'Not now, Bernard,' Maxwell didn't bother to look up and Jacquie didn't bother to move. 'I'm sure whatever it is can wait.'

'Oh, absolutely,' Ryan smarmed, embarrassed

414

as only Deputy Heads can be. 'Absolutely. I just thought you'd like to know.' He was holding a sheet of fax paper in his hand. 'It's just come through, the date of the rescheduled Ofsted inspection.'

WILLENHALL

APL		CCS	9/2 5/11
Cen		Ear	
Mob		Cou	
ALL		Jub	
WH		CHE	
Ald		Bel	
Fin		Fol	
Can		STO	
Til		HCL	